P9-CFM-555

LIKE WE USED TO BE

By the same author

Dear Laura
The Painted Face
The Golden Crucible

The Howarth Family Chronicles:
By Our Beginnings
An Imperfect Joy
The Vivian Inheritance
The Northern Correspondent

A Lasting Spring

Like We Used To Be

Jean Stubbs

St. Martin's Press
New York

THE PEABODY LIBRARY
Columbia City, Indiana

The characters in this novel and their actions are imaginary. Their names and experiences have no relation to those of actual people, living or dead, except by coincidence.

LIKE WE USED TO BE. Copyright © 1989 by Jean Stubbs. All rights reserved. Printed in the United States of America. No part of this book may be used or reproduced in any manner whatsoever without written permission except in the case of brief quotations embodied in critical articles or reviews. For information, address St. Martin's Press, 175 Fifth Avenue, New York, N.Y. 10010.

Library of Congress Cataloging-in-Publication Data

Stubbs, Jean.
  Like we used to be / Jean Stubbs.
      p.   cm.
    ISBN 0-312-03858-5
    I. Title.
  PR6069.T78L55   1990
  823′.914—dc20   89-27133
                                                                          CIP

First published in Great Britain by Macmillan London Limited.

First U.S. Edition

10 9 8 7 6 5 4 3 2 1

To Tess Sacco, editor and friend for twenty-five years, my love and thanks

Acknowledgments

My thanks are due to Georgie Fame, for the title of his 1965 hit-song, *Like We Used To Be*; to Tess Sacco, to Ian Atlee, to the staff of Helston Branch Library for finding relevant books, and to their authors, particularly Brigid McConville for *Sisters*, Edith Horsley for *The 1950s* and Francis Wheen for *The Sixties*. I am indebted to my nephew Jon Higham, illustrator, for first-hand information as to how professional freelance artists survive; to the artists whose works inspired Leila's pictures – Louise Barton for *Beach Scene*, Linda Douglas for *The Watching Eye*, Michael Lacey for *The Cornish Chough* – and to Andrew Wyeth for his notes on working in drybrush. I am especially grateful to my editor, James Hale, for being even more terrific than usual. And, as always, to the man who lives with me and my books.

Leila

1

July 1953

Just as the photographer was ready, an impudent summer breeze blew my sister's long veil up and across her face again. And from the summit of her happiness Zoe laughed aloud while everyone else murmured and smiled. The photographer could not be heard to swear, but I translated the word which his teeth imprinted on his lower lip and winked at my friend Jeremy Purchase, who winked back.

'And once more, ladies and gentlemen!' said the photographer, not entirely resigned to misfortune, since it was a Saturday and he had other engagements.

We composed ourselves. I knew now why Chagall painted his bride flying horizontally in the sky. Transcendent, our bride floated in a cloud of white and silver. Her face, beneath the coronet of wild silk flowers, had become unearthly in its beauty. Not Zoe, but Titania, was in our midst.

As chief bridesmaid, I endeavoured for her sake to be Peaseblossom but felt like Puck in drag. Muslin and meadow flowers were not my garb. Second always to Zoe, I was the younger, plainer, smaller sister.

The breeze freshened, embracing both bride and groom with swirls of fine white net. In another moment the man with the camera would ruin the illusion that our wedding was peerless and of unique importance. Jeremy Purchase, standing apart as befitted an ordinary guest, with his light-brown hair slicked down and his light-green eyes missing nothing, solved the predicament by picking up a large smooth white pebble from the edge of the church path. Walking sturdily across the gravel, with a quick bow to the bride, he anchored her veil at last.

There ensued a little hush. Then my father gave his deep rich guffaw, which was followed by feminine giggles and masculine neighs of amusement. The photographer grinned. We all settled into smiling silence for the final time. And Zoe, Matthew and their court were immobilised for posterity.

Slipping his arm through mine, as family and guests broke up, scattering, chattering, on their way to the cars, my father said, 'That new boyfriend of yours is a bright spark, Leila. I suppose you'll be the next one to go? But give me time to save up. I couldn't afford another wedding like this just yet!'

We fell into step, talking, not needing to look at each other. I was a very modern girl. I called my parents by their first names. Zoe, being old-fashioned, still Mummied and Daddied them.

'I'm not planning to get married at all, Cass, and I wouldn't go in for this sort of thing anyway. I'm not the organdie, lace and roses type.'

'Zoe's enjoying it, though, isn't she?'

'Loving every minute, looking glorious and behaving perfectly, as usual. You might say that it was just her glass of champagne.'

'Then she'd better make the most of it. Matthew will be a while before he earns a champagne income. They say his prospects are good. I suppose they mean that he might become a partner in that firm of solicitors in twenty years' time. What are they called, now?'

'Watson, Lucas and Abercrombie.'

'Good God, what a mouthful! I can see Zoe sacrificing herself while he climbs the ladder. That young man of yours now – what did you say his name was?'

'Jeremy. Jeremy Purchase.'

'I like him,' said my father positively. He snorted with amusement. 'Putting that stone on Zoe's veil to

4

hold it down! Did you see your mother's expression? Well, the veil will clean, no doubt. What does this Jeremy fellow do?'

'Medicine. Very clever. Very ambitious. Wants to do research on tropical diseases. Preferably abroad. Wants to travel. Doesn't want to marry.'

'How do you know that, Miss? Did you ask him to marry you?'

'No. It came out in the course of our first conversation. We met at a students' engagement party. Everyone else was ooh-ing and aah-ing about how marvellous it was. We were alone in thinking that marriage meant bondage.'

Nevertheless, I could sense my father thinking what a good match it would be eventually. He believed in marriage. Good wives were an essential commodity for a man in his position, and he had one. Long and graciously suffering wives were pearls beyond price, and my mother was a positive rope of pearls.

'Oh well, there's plenty of time for both of you. You've got another two years at art school and he'll have longer yet at the university. Besides, you should play the field for a year or so before you settle down. Not like Zoe. Throwing herself overboard for that fellow, just as she got her diploma. She could have found herself an interesting job and had a good time. Travelled, looked round a bit. Earned her own money. Done better for herself . . .'

My mother's voice was belling us back to duty, sorting guests into appropriate groups in the waiting cars.

'Coming, darling!' he cried. And then to me, 'I wish I liked Matthew. What the blazes does Zoe see in him?'

He did not need to ask whether I liked Matthew.

'His boyish charm, I expect. Zo has a strong maternal instinct. Anyway, whatever you and I feel about him, he's what she wants.'

'H'mph. She doesn't want much!'

He switched on his own charm then, holding out both hands and advancing towards my grandmother crying, 'Magda, my darling, you look absolutely wonderful!'

Although she and my father were a generation apart, and

5

their relationship and her years forbade mutual attraction, they recognised the aged nymph and ageing satyr in each other and paid it sly homage. She was short and fat and very Welsh, and I loved her. Once her hair had been a crowning glory. Now she tucked it over a ribbon, and spaced it into a thin grey roll round her head. She had tried to sober up her clothes for the occasion, but in this smart London crowd was as conspicuous as a gipsy fortune-teller and looked like one.

I said with truth, 'I'm madly envious of your Chinese red shawl!'

My mother had been busy calming the billows of Zoe's veil and stowing it into the bridal limousine, while remaining alert to the wants and needs of her guests.

Stepping back, she whispered to my father, 'Cass, dear, we really must take Matthew's parents in our car. Their own seems to have broken down again.'

For Mr Barber had given up cranking his shabby Morris, while Mrs Barber stood helplessly by.

'Ruddy old heap, I'm not surprised . . . '

'*Darling!*' my mother chided under her breath. Then aloud, 'Can you fix Magda up with someone else?'

Something impish in my father made him turn to a grave and scholarly male guest and say, 'You must have heard of my mother-in-law, Magda Lewis? The well-known seascape artist from Cornwall? I wonder if you'd be kind enough to give her a lift to the house?'

So that the man had to reply, 'But of course!' And, 'How very nice to meet you, Mrs Lewis. What a long way you've come for your granddaughter's wedding. But well worth it, eh? Well worth it!'

And to hear Magda say roguishly, '*Miss* Lewis, if you please. I'm not married.'

Whereat he flushed up and compressed his lips, but had to watch my father walk off and leave him stranded, with Magda in piratical mood, jingling her many-coloured beads and bent on mischievous conquest.

My mother, resigned to her own mother's idiosyncrasies, whispered, 'Really, Cass, it's too bad of you. That poor man seems very shy, and probably knows nothing about art. Besides, he's a friend of Matthew's parents.'

To which he replied cheerfully in passing, 'More fool he, on all counts!'

My immediate family inspired totally different emotions in me. My father awoke in me a debonair and careless self, but as I came into the female orbit of my mother and sister I felt the soft and gentle closing down of wings. They were so lovely, caught up for a moment together over the veil, brows knitted in concern because Matthew's parents' friend might disapprove or be afraid of Magda. Then their foreheads smoothed out and they smiled at each other.

That July day in 1953 was a celebration of female rites for both of them. A shy and promising young man, whom they both loved, had been harnessed. Now, if he allowed Zoe to take the reins, he would be trotted nicely and guided subtly, in pleasant ways, to a suitably happy ending. My father and I had our doubts about this, for we sensed an egotist beneath that boyish exterior. Moreover, he was the only child of doting parents who had sacrificed themselves for his future, and it takes a great deal of toughness on both sides to accomplish that.

'I can guess what Matthew's education must have cost them,' my mother remarked shrewdly, when the two families first met. 'I've seen that sort of thing before. A son at university, and margarine on the bread at home.'

'Turning your old brocade curtain into an evening dress?' I said unkindly.

For Marian Barber had been shabbily if pretentiously upholstered.

'We should respect that sort of pride,' my mother said quickly, fairly.

She was always fair.

'I don't like either of them. He's a maundering fool and she's a po-faced old bat,' said my father, who was always beautifully unfair. 'And I just hope you can get that young man of yours out of her clutches, Zo!'

'Oh, but she's so kind and sweet to me, Daddy . . .'

Zoe's soft contralto wail and Helen's wifely frown had quelled further criticism, but I agreed with him. I don't like fat white women with sugary smiles and cold blue eyes. And I had suspected the way in which Mrs Barber held Zoe's hands and patted them, while talking firmly about the importance of Matthew's future and her own life-philosophy of self-denial. Afterwards, Zoe and Matthew had gone to a concert at the new Royal Festival Hall to celebrate their engagement, and we had gladly left the Barbers' cold and comfortless house and returned home.

'Good God,' my father had said, heading for the whisky, 'what a bloody existence that poor girl will lead if she marries him. High thinking and low living. He's the sort of fellow who can never find a taxi, even if he decided to afford one – which is unlikely. I should have forbidden the engagement. She's still underage.'

He poured dry sherry for us both. My mother was silent, thinking.

'If it hadn't been for you, Helen, so keen on the damned fellow . . . '

'They're very much in love,' she answered, endeavouring to smooth future relations, 'and Matthew can hardly be blamed for his parents. He's a nice shy boy, and very clever, and he works hard. We mustn't hurt Zoe by criticising them.'

'Do *you* like them?' he demanded of her.

'No,' she answered, slowly, truthfully. 'I'm afraid I don't. But they've done their utmost for their son, and should be given credit for that.'

My father surveyed her thoughtfully over his whisky.

'What about you, Miss?' he demanded of me.

I laughed and replied, 'I think they're a pair of old meanies!'

My mother took no notice of us. We had always been allies, knowing that the world was full of rogues and fools, whereas Zoe and she believed in a land of milk and honey, carpeted with spring flowers.

She said, sipping sherry, 'So long as Zoe and Matthew go on loving each other and being happy, I don't mind a bit.'

She was intensely serious about love and loving and those she loved. Nothing was ever too much trouble so long as love was served. Her life, her family and her home were founded on love, order and beauty.

'You really are your own worst enemy, Helen,' my father observed genially. 'You and Zoe will be decent to that old hag and she'll take advantage of it . . . '

Her sense of fun awoke, which I believe she connected literally as well as metaphorically with my father, for she went over to him and linked his left arm and smiled up into his face.

'I should be good at that,' she said slyly, 'I've had heaps of practice. You've been taking advantage of me for donkey's years!'

He was not in the least handsome and yet women adored him and he knew how to charm them. He had a humorous heavy-chinned face, like Fernandel the French comedian, but whereas Fernandel was humble about his ugliness my father was arrogant, and made the arrogance acceptable by lacing it with wit.

'Oh, that's quite different. I'm allowed!' he said, smiling down at her.

'Promise me you won't be unkind to those two young people?'

'Not if they intend to do the decent thing – elope to Gretna Green and save me a lot of trouble and expense!'

'*Darling!* Zoe wants a white wedding. And she'll look so *beautiful* . . . '

'Spare me the sentiment. I'm the fool who's going to write out the cheques!'

As ever, the cheques would be generous, for my father gave us nothing but the best and would have been furious if Zoe had eloped. Besides, such a family show gave him the opportunity to compliment present clients and attract future ones, who would see how cleverly he used his talents in the domestic field. For he was an interior designer, whose charity had begun at home.

* * *

Whitegates, our house in Surrey, was his finest advertisement for combining old-fashioned beauty with modern convenience, and he was much in demand in those years of restoration and rebuilding after the war. Clients were captivated first by him, then by his home, and finally by his wife's feminine talents. Men wondered what it must be like to have a woman who seemed to be everything any husband could desire. Women imagined themselves in her place: beloved and cosseted, surrounded by the latest labour-saving devices, perpetually arranging flowers from a subtly landscaped garden. With the flippancy of youth I had dubbed my mother's role 'Helen of Whitegates', and though she lived it truly, and believed in it sincerely, I did despise her a little for playing it.

So I sought my grandmother, who never tried to please people and would be even worse when she had had more to drink. She was already holding her glass at a peculiar angle and her Welsh accent was stronger than usual. I took her arm and led her a little to one side.

But before I could question her she said, 'Lily, love, don't go near the vicar. He's a bottom-pincher.'

'I know!' I said. 'He pinched Julia in the vestry!'

And we both collapsed into giggles.

When she could speak, she went into one of her monologues. 'Zoe's not going to have much of a wedding night. Regular old sober-sides, that Matthew, isn't he? Won't know her head from her heels! And I always say virgin should never marry virgin, they're only asking for trouble. Now that young man of yours . . . ' nodding her head towards Jeremy Purchase, who was standing on his head on the lawn to amuse the younger bridesmaids, 'he's worth a roll in the hay. If I was forty years younger I'd beat you to it!'

'He's a virgin,' I said smiling, 'like me. I happen to know.'

'Not for long,' said Magda, closing one eye meaningfully. 'You can tell what a man is by the way he holds his body and uses his eyes. Such a nice sturdy body. I always liked a quick-moving man. Oh, yes! Do you know, he reminds me a little bit of Walter Liddy, my best lover. He got me

10

by looking, you know, just looking. Yes. Very light eyes, like your Jeremy Purchase. Watch out for men with light eyes, my girl. Good lovers, bad husbands. Make up your mind which you want, and don't confuse the two. One's for pleasure and the other's for durability. Mind you, I never wanted durability. No surprises. You keep on waking up to the same old day. Stops you from flying, you see. Grounds you for good . . . '

My mother would have been sorry to hear her talking like this, but she was busy buttering up a lady journalist, who admired my father's work as an interior designer and was interested in doing a feature on him for her magazine.

'Such a wonderful idea!' we heard my mother say. 'And of course I can show you round the house any day – any other day than this, of course! Oh, but why don't you stay on afterwards and have supper with us? Just to get the feel of the place. All very informal. Just the immediate family, in fact . . . '

'Magda, why in God's name does Helen never let up?' I asked. 'That means we'll have to eat in the dining room instead of putting our feet up in the kitchen!'

'Her standards are too high, you see. Doesn't take after me, I can tell you. It'd be a cheese butty, take it or leave it!' She gauged the situation shrewdly and decided against it. She said to me confidentially, 'Lily, love, I think I'll catch the late afternoon train from Paddington after all, instead of staying the night. They'll be chatting about *Toile de Jouy* curtains, and fitted kitchens, and I shall be tempted to say something *rude* . . . '

'Oh, but I was going to spoil you, Magda. Give you breakfast in bed. New-laid eggs and hot buttered toast, laid out on a tray all proper like, with a linen napkin and a single rose in a glass.'

'Better the meal of herbs,' said Magda philosophically.

'Herbs?' I said drily, knowing her standards of housekeeping. 'Shop bread, and shop jam, tasting of linseed oil!'

'Anyway, you'll probably be off courting that lovely boy tonight,' said Magda unperturbed. 'You'll need to sleep in,

11

after. No time for making breakfasts. How long have you known him?'

'Three months.'

'Long enough,' said Magda enigmatically. Then, narrowing her eyes at the bride and groom, she echoed my father, 'Whatever did she see in *him*, I wonder? I wouldn't even want to *train* him . . . '

The speeches were brief and good. Matthew's best man, reminding everyone that this was one of the longest days of the year, said he couldn't imagine why the bridegroom had chosen it. Wouldn't the longest night have been better? Whereat Oberon adjusted his glasses nervously, and Titania's flowery coronet ducked in a pretty gesture of embarrassment, as everyone laughed. The toasts were drunk, and my mother raised her eyebrows to Magda and me to indicate that we were required to attend the bride in her disrobing.

A little bevy of close female relatives left the marquee for this ritual, Magda whispering to me, 'No better than men watching strippers!'

A willing lamb, my sister stood slim and pale in her camiknickers as her fairy wedding dress was borne away. She seemed more human now. The faces around her were absorbed and rapt, their voices soft and nostalgic. They were remembering their own weddings.

'Just the sort of show we had in the thirties. Helen, I don't know how you did it and perhaps I'd better not ask! But could any of us have imagined that eight years after the war we'd still be coping with food rationing?' said Aunt Edith.

'So nice to have a real wedding. I used to feel sorry for those wartime brides in their utility costumes and gallant little hats,' said Aunt Caroline.

They were my father's sisters, hard-faced, handsome and well married.

'I'm sure the brides were every bit as happy,' said my mother firmly, 'whatever the shortcomings.'

'Oh, surely not, Helen dear? To miss their one great occasion? They must have minded ever so much afterwards. I know I should have.'

12

Magda kept in the background. This was not her sort of conversation. And I stayed silent because I was struggling with three sorts of jealousy. Everyone adored Zoe, as they adored my mother. They were automatically lovable people, whereas I was regarded as an attractive little thing, but a bit too clever and rather odd. Then Helen loved Zoe more than she loved me, and I was speared by the knowledge that she and I would never share a day like this. Finally Zoe, my closest confidante, had replaced and superseded me with Matthew Barber. So I was envious and angry and sorry all at once. My reflection in the glass showed me standing insignificantly apart, a sullen elf.

The twin beds in our shared room reminded the assembled company of my new and involuntary situation.

'You'll have the bedroom all to yourself now, Leila!' said Grannie Cullen kindly, turning to include me in the conversation. 'But how you will miss Zoe!'

It was taken for granted that Zoe would not miss me, being occupied with Matthew.

'Such devoted sisters, I tell my two girls. Look at the Gideon sisters, I say. Never a cross word.'

'You're exaggerating, Edith,' said my mother sensibly. 'They have many a cross word. Particularly as Leila has always tried to usurp the pecking order.'

Everybody laughed, but as Zoe walked towards me, smiling, I was overcome by love. Sibling, other-self, drogue anchor and touchstone, Zoe had entered this world two years and three months before I had. My parents had been careful to stress that I was *her* baby, so that she would not be jealous. But jealousy was not in Zoe's nature, though it figured largely in mine, and she had spent the next nineteen years trying to bring me up properly. We were quite unalike, but we sprang from the same parents, had shared the same background, grimaced at the same family dramas and rejoiced in the same family festivals until she chose to be sacrificed on the altar to Matthew Barber. I resented that betrayal, that preference, most bitterly. Without Zoe I should lack a mirror in which to view myself, a compass with which to guide myself. And though I had fought her

13

throughout our sisterhood for independence and self-rule, the moment it was granted I felt lost.

She smelled delicious as she wound her arms round me, using my childhood nickname, whispering, 'Darling Lulu, my being married won't make any difference to *us*, you know. You must come to see me whenever you want to – and Matthew says so, too.'

Innocent Zoe. Matthew will say anything at the moment. But give him six months, and his response will be different. More worldy-wise than she, I know that much. I know from my father's example that men are not to be trusted, and love creates more problems than it solves. But Zoe, who will be a good wife like our mother, has lightly entrusted this dark, inward-looking man with her entire life and the lives of her future children. And though she says that they will be ages before they start a family, because Matthew mustn't be dragged down with too many responsibilities, Zoe will have children very soon. It is written in her, despite the present resolve to wait.

Zoe, my sister, I'll bet my childhood coral necklace that you produce a baby within the next two years. Why don't *you* know that?

She says, hugging me, trying to comfort me, 'I like your Jeremy Purchase very much. You must both come to supper with us.'

My Jeremy Purchase and I know better than to mortgage our futures with a wedding ring. We nourish a healthy prejudice against bondage, Jeremy Purchase and I. We prefer single freedom. This I cannot explain to Zoe, and would not want to since I should be wasting my time.

So I say, 'I'm glad you like him.' Which is not true, because I don't care one way or the other. And then, 'Take care of yourself, Zo!' Which is meant.

My father has paid for their honeymoon and an air-flight to Paris, otherwise Zoe would probably have ended up with a weekend in Brighton at a boarding house, because the Barber family not only have to live an economical life, they prefer it. Fortunately my father has a fine sense of occasion and will give Zoe the right

14

background for her great event, a place she can enjoy for itself.

Waving and waving as they drive away, I ask Jeremy, 'Do you like him?'

I don't ask whether he likes my sister, because that is not his business and he had better not dare to dislike her. It is Matthew Barber who can be put in the scales and found wanting.

Jeremy answers, 'Not my type. Can we scarper now?'

'After supper,' I say. 'You're invited to supper.'

He has had enough of socialising, but at this stage in our relationship he will be polite and forbearing to please me. Later on, no doubt, he will override such obligations. I expect nothing more of him than I would expect of my father, but I want more, of course, and I suppose I hope for more.

'Now that the dutiful daughter has gone,' I say, making a joke of family obligations, 'I really shall have to help my mother with the supper. But after that, Jem-boy, we can scarper.'

His quick light eyes are already looking past me for another solution, and find a female group agitating over my grandmother, whose stockings are wrinkled round the ankles, whose Chinese red shawl trails dejectedly over one shoulder.

'But you can't go home *now*, Magda! You only arrived *yesterday* . . .'

My mother is doubly concerned, thinking of appearances as well as Magda's health. What conclusions will people draw about an elderly parent, however odd and out of place in this sophisticated company, travelling all the way up from Cornwall one day and going back the next? Was she not made welcome? Did her daughter neglect or offend her?

'It's the *cat*, you see,' said Magda, twisting her coloured beads round her old brown fingers, like a child being scolded. 'He misses me. Goes right off his food.'

'But you'll never catch the train, Magda! It's half-past four already.'

15

'Besides, you'll be exhausted. It is quite unnecessary,' said Aunt Caroline.

Now my father was bearing down upon the group, full of masculine authority. In a moment he would forbid Magda to escape.

'It's not so far from here to Paddington,' Magda was protesting. 'I've got no packing to speak of. And you needn't bother to take me. A taxi will get me there in no time at all.'

'My dear Mrs Lewis! A taxi will cost a fortune from here!'

Once more Jeremy stepped forward to save the occasion.

Saying, 'I'll give you a lift to the station, Mrs Lewis.'

'Oh, would you, love?' she cried, transformed. 'I'll be ready in five minutes if Lily will come and find things for me.'

'Nonsense!' cried my father, who had seen the state of Jeremy's car. 'If you must go, Magda, *I'll* drive you to the station.'

'But surely you're not . . . ?' my mother began, and stopped.

She meant, 'Surely, you're not going to leave me with your journalist to look after, as well as all our guests and the supper?'

'No, I'm going to jilt you for once, Cass,' said Magda roguishly. 'It's a long time since a young man took me for a joy ride. Lily! Come and help me pack.'

A hypocrite, I said to my mother in passing, 'I'd better go with them and see Magda off properly, don't you think? It's the least we can do.'

With which she had to agree.

Her final words to me as we crushed into Jeremy's BSA three-wheeler, whose bonnet was tied down with rope, were, 'But darling, why haven't you changed?'

'No time!' I answered, grinning like a cat.

Actually, I rather liked wearing that Peaseblossom outfit at the wrong time in the wrong place. I clapped my circlet of flowers more firmly on my flying hair and sat up on the top of the seat between Jeremy and Magda. And we all waved our hands at the assembled company. Waved them away with triumph and relief, as we chugged off to endanger ourselves on the summer Saturday roads.

Excitement made my grandmother vivacious, garrulous, but Jeremy behaved beautifully, smiling and listening. At the station he offered her his arm, carried her carpet-bag on to the train, found her a window-seat, and stood back like a gentleman while we made our private farewells.

'You'll come and see me, love, won't you? And if this young man would like a holiday in Cornwall, you must bring him with you. Mind you,' she added, turning to him, 'I don't live at the Ritz, you know. Just a fisherman's cottage. You must take me as you find me!'

'Paint-brush hairs in the butter,' I said demurely.

'Don't be so cheeky! When were they ever?'

'And the bed falls down in the night.'

'Do you want me to ask him by himself, Miss?'

Jeremy was taking charge of the pair of us, restoring us to order.

'Thanks a lot, Mrs Lewis. That's extremely kind of you. Sounds wonderful. I can bring my sleeping-bag.'

She looked at him slyly, sadly. She corrected him mildly, mischievously.

'*Miss* Lewis. I'm not married, you know.'

The whistle blew. The green flag dropped. We stood together on the platform, waiting for the train to move out so that we could send her off with a final flourish, but she had withdrawn from us and the long day. As the carriage window glided past we saw her sitting back in her seat, very small and stout, with her freckled hands folded in her lap and her eyes closed. Unanimated, she looked old.

'She'll wake up as soon as the train crosses the Tamar,' I said. 'Then she says,' and I imitated her, '"Goodbye Devon! Welcome Cornwall!" because she's at home there.'

'What time will she get back to her cottage?'

'Some time before midnight. Then she'll make tea and toast, and feed the cat, take a critical look at her latest painting, and fall into bed about two o'clock.'

'She's quite a girl, isn't she?' said Jeremy, as we walked

17

hand in hand down the platform. 'Did she mean that about not being married?'

'Oh, it's a complicated story. She was married once, but she left her husband and reverted to her maiden name of Lewis. She only says that to shock people.'

'I wasn't shocked. Just interested.'

'It made life very difficult for my mother as a child with only one visible parent, down in Cornwall forty-odd years ago. And with her surname being Richards, and Magda's being Lewis, people thought she was a bastard. Then, when she was four or five years old, Helen was adopted by the Cullens. They were here today. You were introduced but I don't suppose you'd remember. Really sweet people. My mother was given their surname and brought up by them. She looks on them as her proper parents, and Zoe and I call them Grannie and Grandpa. We knew Magda was our grandmother too, but she insisted we call her Magda.'

'Why was your mother adopted? Couldn't Magda afford to keep her?'

'She was desperately poor, yes. But to be quite frank it was the best arrangement all round. The Cullens had no children of their own and they gave my mother the sort of home she wanted. Magda's a bohemian. She shouldn't have had a child at all. There's no hidden drama about it. Everyone is quite amicable.'

He had heard what he wanted to hear, and now moved on to what really interested him.

'Lee, must we go back? Can't we go to the pictures instead and have a snack afterwards?'

'That was why you offered to take Magda to the station, wasn't it?'

'Partly, but not entirely. I like the old girl, and she was desperate to escape.'

'I was glad to escape, too. I expect you guessed. Have you got any change on you? I'll telephone them.'

We were riding on a big wave that year. The Queen had been crowned the previous month, and though royalty seemed out of date I was captured, like so many others, by the notion of its being a second Elizabethan age, a renaissance. And then, on the morning of the Coronation, almost in homage to her future reign, came news that Everest had been conquered at last by a New Zealand bee-keeper called Edmund Hillary and a dignified sherpa by the name of Tensing.

Young and healthy and fortunate, we were among the favoured children of that time, Jeremy Purchase and I. So we rode the big wave with certainty and with tremendous style.

Zoe's marriage had sparked me off, not in her direction but my own. I had always hated her being ahead of me. Such an occasion persuaded me to emulate her. My muslin and meadow flowers brought smiles and sometimes side-comments from the passing crowd. Heedless of these attentions, Jeremy bought us an *Evening Standard* and we found a coffee-bar and studied the entertainments page. Again, shadowing Zoe, who was on her way to Paris, I chose to see *Monsieur Hulot's Holiday* with Jacques Tati. That was not a romantic choice, as it turned out, since he was funny in a vulnerable way. Still, I thought of the evening ahead when we should be alone together. Because we had been discussing love-making, Jeremy Purchase and I, and as marriage was neither wanted nor possible we had no reason to wait. The difficulty was that neither of us had any previous experience.

After the film, eating meat pies at a coffee stall, Jeremy said, 'How about it?' very casually.

And equally casually, I replied, 'So long as I like the surroundings I don't mind. But have you got anything with you?'

'Yes. I've had something with me for weeks.'

'Then how about driving me home right now, and finding a nice private thicket near Whitegates? I shall have to be in by midnight, or they'll throw a fit.'

He asked me if I wanted anything else to eat but my appetite had gone and so had his.

Where is Zoe, my sister? I wonder, as Jeremy makes a bed for me with the car rug. What was it that Magda had said about virgins? A recipe for disaster?

It is not a disaster so much as an anti-climax. Jeremy is quite unable to come to terms with the condom, and he has finished before we have time to begin.

'I'm terribly sorry,' he says miserably.

I hold his head and kiss him and croon to him, but a man has his pride and he pulls away. We sit in our little dell, both puzzled and out of sorts. This was not what we had been led to expect, though the setting is perfect. We are in a midsummer night's dream of our own. The thicket is dark and protective, but round our bed moonlight has paled the wildflowers. Their faint rustle and phantom scent promise us magical bliss.

Being young and in his prime, Jeremy tries again and yet again, with more success. I give up my virginity, though without the savage splendour I had imagined. And now it is past eleven o'clock, so we call it a day. Quite a day. And he drives me slowly home, with a long deep goodnight kiss over the car door to celebrate our changed status, and a promise to meet tomorrow.

The house is quiet, cool and intimate. I hear a double murmur of voices in the kitchen. My parents are still up, alone at last and mulling over the wedding. I stand in the kitchen doorway for a few minutes in my crumpled finery, yawning prodigiously and telling them that Jeremy's car broke down, as it often does, trying to look and sound my former self. Luckily they are too tired to notice. I kiss them both goodnight, and climb the stairs. It is only when I enter the room which has been Zoe's and mine since we were children that I realise she has finally gone.

My mother has turned down one corner of the sheet to welcome me to sleep, but the other bed lies smooth and undisturbed: made for an absent sibling. In our adjoining bathroom, in my bathroom as it now is, I take a long warm reflecting soak and later a long look in the glass.

Mirror, mirror, on the wall, why do I not change at all? Why does Zoe's nose stop delightfully short and mine go on a fraction too long? Why is her smile full and generous, and mine wide and crooked? Why should her hair be dark gold and abundant while mine is pale and fine? Why is her

20

gaze grey and calm and mine treacle-dark and inquisitive? Why should *she* be Titania?

No answer. My reflection gives me a last devilish elfin look as I turn away. I lie down with my back to Zoe's bed.

Last night we were both virgins. Tonight we are deflowered. What a subject for small hours' conversation that would have been, when the two of us were together. Or will Zoe in her new state have new loyalties? In any case, Zoe was never very forthcoming about life's intimacies. It was I who wanted to talk about them and find out what was happening. So I sleep in double disappointment, going back and back until I reach the family account of our first meeting.

There I am in my mother's arms in the private nursing home, a cross pink shrimp. And here is Zoe looking like every dear little girl should, in a new straw bonnet with blue ribbons tied under the chin, and a matching blue cloth coat such as the two Princesses wear. My father sits her carefully down on the bed beside us. She has been told that I am her baby sister, and she must take care of me.

I reflect that it is fortunate our positions are not reversed because I should have refused the responsibility. But Zoe, at two and a quarter, is already a miniature woman and prepared to take me on. Close to sleep now, I see her as she must have been then, gravely pretty, bending over me with a smile. I feel her kiss, placed softly and carefully on my yelling cheek, and her small hands holding my furious fists. I hear her lovely chuckle at my rage with the world.

The past image is superimposed by the present. The bride smiles with faery radiance as she becomes Mrs Matthew Barber. I smell the fragrance and feel the warmth of her afternoon goodbye. She is transfigured by love and towers in dream-stature over Jeremy Purchase, who has failed to transfigure me. And I miss, miss, miss her.

21

2

Almost as soon as they arrived home, the newly-weds came to dinner with us, bearing as a compliment to the occasion and to my father's choice of honeymoon a bottle of rather acid red French wine.

My father said to me afterwards, 'It would be the cheapest he could find!'

We answered the front doorbell as a family, in order to savour the first moment of seeing Mr and Mrs Matthew Barber. Whatever Magda's reservations on the subject of virgins, they had a very young and tender and joyful air, standing together arm in arm in the porch, smilingly conscious of their new dignity and status. And however successful or unsuccessful their joining might have been, joined they certainly were.

They charted each other's faces and movements constantly. Is he happy? Is she happy? Are we happy here? Whenever they were separated, and however temporarily and briefly, they drifted together again as if magnetised. They had developed personal phrases and personal jokes. They smiled upon us from behind a personal fence. Though Zoe was glad to be within the family circle again, she was no longer a member of it, and Matthew wore a proprietorial air as if to remind us that from now on she was on loan to us, but never given. His darkness had been illuminated and he intended to keep the light for himself.

Since they represented a pinnacle of young love my mother was untouched by jealousy or envy, busy finding her place with them, accepting them, asking nothing of them. But my father was more reserved in his manner and approach than usual, assessing these new boundaries, and so was I.

Paris, apparently, had been perfect. The small hotel in Rue de Bac was wonderful. The food was out of this world. And the *directrice* had worn a pink silk peignoir trimmed with lace, even at three in the afternoon. So French! Their room had looked into a central courtyard, in the middle of which grew a great tree. No, neither of them had noticed what sort of a tree. A plane tree, perhaps? said Matthew. Yes, Mat, it must have been a plane tree! said Zoe. And all around them were windows, and lives being lived behind the windows. They breakfasted in bed on coffee and croissants. They bought a picnic lunch in the market and travelled out on buses to the country. At night they walked round Paris, hand in hand no doubt, reading the menus chalked on the blackboards until they found their restaurant of the evening.

'Only ten shillings for a marvellous meal for the two of us. With wine!' said Matthew, nodding his head.

His forelock swung forward, dark and boyish, and he swept it back.

'I can't *tell* you!' Zoe cried, throwing out both hands in delight and despair. 'I couldn't possibly *describe* how beautiful it all was!'

They began to look at the clock around ten, and talk about catching the last train to the city, for Matthew had no car of any description. But my father said that there was plenty of time yet, and he would drive them home. And he opened a bottle of cognac which had been given to him by a grateful client, while my mother went into the kitchen to make more coffee. She and I had been over to their flat in Clapham the previous Friday to make it ready for their return. In consequence she had so many things to give them which she felt they needed that it was almost eleven before they started out. Even then she thought of one last lovely gesture, and ran into the darkened garden and cut the finest of our yellow roses and heaped them in Zoe's arms.

'That's a dozen King's Ransoms you're holding!' my father said, joking.

'Zoe's worth a thousand kings' ransoms!' my mother cried.

My sister stood there, laughing on the verge of crying, with the yellow roses glowing against her dark-blue velvet coat, and Matthew faithfully holding innumerable parcels and staring proudly at her, and I wanted to protect her happiness. Even if Matthew had to be included, I wanted them to stay like this, forever on the brink of something marvellous.

On the doorstep, Zoe said, 'Mat's going back to the office on Monday. So I'll ring you tomorrow, Mummy, and we'll arrange for you to come over to dinner as soon as poss. Not next Saturday, perhaps, because we haven't seen Mat's parents properly yet. Probably the Saturday after.'

'Darling, don't worry about us. We've seen you this evening. We can wait.'

It was Zoe's cross that as she was liked by everybody she had to please them all. She and my mother both wore the same little worried frown as they tiptoed carefully round each other's feelings.

'And, Mummy, you wouldn't feel desperately hurt if I asked Lulu to a sisters' lunch party one day next week, would you?'

'No, of course not. You and I can have lunch in town one day.'

'Oh that would be lovely! Then how about Wednesday, Lulu?'

'Wednesday will be fine.'

'Twelve o'clock. On the dot. We housewives can't be kept waiting!'

My father said confidentially to my mother, kissing her cheek, 'My darling, I need to drop into the office to pick up the Brennan file, ready for tomorrow, but I'll be back as soon as I can. Don't wait up for me.'

My mother's expression did not change, though she took a quick breath through her nose before she smiled and nodded. Perhaps she was wondering, as I was, whether he would visit not the office but his new secretary, as soon as he had driven Zoe and Matthew home.

New places, new departures, are always enthralling. When you contrasted Zoe's flat in Clapham with Whitegates you could not fail to see that she had come down in the world. So had Matthew, of course, but as his parents lived at the end of a terrace in Southfields he had not fallen so far. Yet to see my sister's face you would have thought she lived at Hampton Court.

The house had been a handsome family residence once, but was now down-at-heel and meanly divided into four units, of which the basement flat, whose dark windows peered into a damp area surrounded by railings, must have been the most dismal. But Zoe, running downstairs and flinging open the front door in welcome, was in her blue heaven.

'Oh! Oh! Oh!' she cried, hugging me. 'You can't think how I've missed you, Lulu. Goodness, you're laden like a pack-horse. Just look at that Constance Spry effort! Mummy won't have a rose left!'

'The roses are nothing. Wait until you unpack the basket. I hope you haven't made lunch for us because we could feed the five thousand on this.'

'Let me have it. Heavens, it weighs a ton. Come in, come in!'

There was a pay telephone in the narrow hallway, scratched and battered, with old telephone numbers and messages scribbled on the wall around it. I deciphered a few while Zoe was giving me a thumbnail description of her fellow tenants. It was typical of her, that though she had only been living there for a few days she knew everyone and their histories.

'Mr Connolly has the flat downstairs in the basement. He keeps his bicycle in the hall when he's home from work. He's a bank clerk and an orphan. Terribly young and shy. He only asks me in when Matthew is with me.'

She dropped her voice, nodding towards a large brown door to our right.

'And Mr and Mrs Montrose have that flat, which is the

25

best and biggest in the house, completely self-contained. Anglo-Indians on a pension. Awful snobs, poor things.' Zoe always apologised for people's vices as if they were not responsible for them. 'Bearing the present by living in a glorious past, as Mummy says.'

We climbed the first flight of stairs.

'Miss Babbage is on this floor. She's about forty, and works at an office in Percy Street. Very mouse-like. And straight in front of you, in case you need it, is the loo, and the bathroom is next door. We share them with her.'

We climbed another flight, and she squeezed my arm and gave a chuckle of excitement and pleasure.

'And here we are!' She made a trumpet of her hands and cried, 'Ta-rah!' and flung open the door.

She had done marvels with the few pieces of second-hand furniture and their wedding presents.

'I've moved everything round, and tried for a cottagey effect, with it being under the roof and having dormer windows.'

Our old nursery sofa spread comfortably along the back wall. 'Mummy and I are going to make new covers for that.' The books of her childhood and girlhood stood in an old glass-fronted bookcase of my father's by the fireplace. On the other side, its twin held Matthew's law books. Four windsor chairs tucked their polished seats under a square deal table in the bow-front of the window. She had laid it with a scarlet cloth and pale-green Denby ware. A bowl of nasturtiums looked wonderful and smelled rather nasty in the centre. At least, they smelled nasty to me. I have always loathed capers.

'Zoe! You've utterly transformed it!'

'Of course, it's darker than the other flats, but it is rather sweet, isn't it?'

'Such an interesting shape!'

She smiled upon me, tall and fair and splendid.

'I want you to see everything, because I've had lots of second thoughts.'

So I admired the bedroom full of utility furniture, whose window overlooked a side-alley, and the minute kitchen like a ship's galley which overlooked a neglected garden, and we unpacked the basket and arranged the flowers. But once I had seen Zoe's domain the conversation did not expand, even over lunch. It was our past, the long past or the immediate past, that we discussed, as if we did not know how to cross the river into this new territory which divided me from them, and so we remained on the old bank.

She wanted to know if my father had seen the flat. Had he come with us, when we brought the milk in and tidied round. He had not? Oh, well. She did wonder what he would think of it. She knew how particular he was about conversions. Of course, Matthew and she knew its faults.

I could not imagine what was worrying her. Cass only criticised or advised in a professional capacity and when he knew he could improve something. Mentally, he would cross this place out from the start and be utterly delightful about everything else. I could not say so, and compromised.

'But Zoe, don't you remember that when Helen and Cass were first married and moved into Whitegates it was practically falling down, and they camped in one room for months with a primus stove.'

'Yes, but that was Whitegates, and it always had style even when it was decaying, and they made it their own. I mean, this is only a beginning for Matthew and me. We shan't stay here.'

Then she came out with the truth.

'You see, Matthew is very sensitive about its short-comings. He's very particular about having things nice but he can't afford anything better than this at the moment, and I shouldn't like Daddy to upset him. You know how Daddy can tease. Not meaning to offend anybody, of course.'

An unpleasing light dawned. Matthew had been finding fault with our family.

'Oh, don't worry!' I said reassuringly. 'Cass will arrive well primed and horribly threatened and behave himself beautifully.'

She was relieved then, and said, 'And how is your Jeremy Purchase?'

I felt the need to rival Zoe's new state of womanhood.

'He's – we're – actually, we're lovers!'

For once I had impressed my elder sister. She set down her spoonful of strawberries and stared at me, and touched her lips with a scarlet napkin.

'I haven't told anybody except you,' I said defensively. I wondered how far marital loyalty went. 'And if you don't mind, Zo, I'd rather you didn't tell Matthew. I hope that's all right?'

She picked up her spoon again, thinking, selecting another strawberry. Then she swallowed it and nodded. The nod was curt but satisfactory. We could still have secrets between sisters. She assumed her mantle of elder wisdom.

'I hope you're being careful, Lulu. You don't want a forced wedding, do you?'

'We don't want a wedding at all.' I saw her expression and added quickly, 'He's got to qualify first, and so have I. There's no question of marrying.'

Since Zoe equated love-making with marriage this took more swallowing than the strawberry, but she had inherited our mother's gift for finding something with which she could agree.

'I do see that it's much wiser to wait. Later, perhaps?'

I let that question go. She laid down her spoon again and spoke affectionately.

'I knew you liked each other but I never imagined you were in love.'

I had no idea whether we were in love with each other or not. I found him attractive and was fond of him and we laughed a lot together. Was that love?

'Are you happy with him – you funny obstinate little thing – or do you argue like mad?'

'We both argue like mad. And we're very happy.'

I heard Magda's voice in my head saying, 'Only a pair of *sheep* would be nice all the time!'

Zoe said, very elder sister, very practical again, 'Just what method of birth control are you using?'

'French letters,' I replied sulkily.

'They're not all that safe. And I wouldn't like to leave that side of things to the man, anyway.'

28

This was my mother talking. Zoe had not the experience to know one method from another, nor the reason for adopting it. I attacked them both.

'Why? And why not?'

'It's no use getting fired up, Lulu. You were the one who confided. If you don't want me to talk about it then I won't.'

But she wanted to, very much. And I needed help. I put my palms together in a mock gesture of supplication, our way of apologising without losing face.

'Men,' said Zoe, who had two weeks and four days' knowledge of living with one, 'even the nicest of them, are not always reliable. They're much more – passionate – than we are, and sometimes they think it won't matter this once, and sometimes they're careless about – putting things on. And French letters have been known to burst. Leila! It's not a giggling matter. I'm talking seriously.'

I sketched another gesture of supplication.

'Mummy talked to me about this . . . '

Ah, I thought, now we're getting down to facts.

' . . . and she advised the use of a Dutch cap and a cream. It might seem a bit of a bore using it, at first, but you soon get used to it and the double barrier of spermicidal cream and cap make insemination virtually impossible.'

Someone else was talking through Zoe now.

'Where do I buy these things from?'

'Oh, you can't just buy them. You have to be fitted and shown what to do by an expert. Mummy went with me to a special clinic.' Zoe appeared again from behind the medical jargon. 'I don't quite know what you'll do about that. I was going to be married, you see, and Mummy was with me.'

There was in my sister's tone the sound of hierarchy, and I disliked that.

'I'll manage. Their clients can't all be pure as snow. Where is this clinic?'

'Near us – near you – in Surrey. But Mrs Prothero is in charge there, and everyone will know you've been.'

I was simmering with resentment over my strawberries. 'Then why tell me about it? I don't see the point of giving

29

me information that I can't use. If birth control is that important then there must be clinics all over the place. I can find a clinic where nobody knows me.'

Zoe said lovingly, 'Don't be cross, Lulu. We've got to make sure you don't get pregnant. And you're absolutely right. There'll be heaps of clinics in the London area. I'll bring the telephone directory upstairs and we'll find one for you.'

So we picked one out over our coffee.

3

The clinic was temporarily housed in part of an old building belonging to the local council. It was a comfortless room, with a row of hard chairs round the wall for clients and a dog-eared pile of magazines and comics to distract them while they waited. A tea-chest full of discarded toys stood by to amuse any children while their mothers made sure there would be no more of them. And over us all presided a stout lady with a magisterial air and a hushed voice, whose table and chair were placed where she could keep an eye on everybody.

'Name, please?' Smiling and watching.

'Leila Gideon.' I spelled it for her.

'Mrs or Miss?'

'Miss.'

She glanced automatically at my ringless finger. Her manner altered subtly, but she gave me the benefit of the doubt.

'And when are you expecting to be married, Miss Gideon?'

I compromised.

'We haven't decided on a date yet.'

'But you are engaged?'

I compromised again.

'Not officially.'

Her eyebrows lifted above her horn-rimmed glasses, but the form drew her inexorably on.

'Date of birth?'

'June the seventh, 1934.'

The eyebrows signalled 'Under twenty-one'.

'Your home address and telephone number if any?'

When I said 'Surrey' she laid down her pen.

'We have clinics in Surrey. Surely your family doctor could have recommended one closer to home?'

'I didn't consult my family doctor.'

We looked very hard at each other.

'Have you consulted your mother, or other female relative?'

I was very angry, but remembered that I needed a Dutch cap.

'I consulted my sister.' I amended this. 'My *married* sister.'

She picked up her pen again, only slightly reassured.

'Her name and address?'

I trusted Zoe, but Matthew was an unknown quantity.

I said, far too loudly, 'Why is that necessary?'

The waiting women looked up from their magazines.

She put down her pen and clasped her hands in front of her.

'Miss Gideon, may I speak personally?'

She did not wait for me to say no.

'Evidently you come from a respectable home, and I have a daughter of nineteen like yourself. I should be most distressed if I thought that she was contemplating such a serious step without my knowledge. I really think it would be more satisfactory for all parties if you talked this over with your mother first, and preferably brought her with you.'

I did not know how much power she wielded. Had she, for instance, official permission or encouragement to inform my parents? I could not imagine either of them treating the matter lightly. Helen and Cass believed in chastity for unmarried daughters.

I jumped up, breathless with rage, sounding and probably looking small and shrewish when I needed to be tall and dignified, saying, 'Your job is to stop girls from getting pregnant, not to conduct an inquisition. It's none of your damned business anyway!'

Then I twitched the form ferociously from beneath her clasped hands, so that she could not use the information against me, and marched out.

32

The entire day was a desert. I telephoned Zoe's place, but neither she nor Matthew were in and Mrs Montrose was very annoyed because she had had to climb two flights of stairs. I telephoned Jeremy to warn him that I was still unprotected, for we were meeting that evening to celebrate, but he was out too. Then I missed the train home by one minute, and when I tried to telephone my mother I found I had no small change. The ticket office refused on principle to give me any, and I had to buy a cup of very unpleasant coffee before I could get some. When the telephone rang nobody answered. Finally, Jeremy and I had our first quarrel that evening because he had come ready to celebrate his new freedom, unprepared.

We sat in our usual thicket on the car rug, and berated each other.

'I'm not going back to that clinic again for anybody. I'm sure Zoe is exaggerating about the risk.'

'No, she isn't. I asked Reggie Reardon . . . '

'Don't you dare talk about me to Reggie Reardon. I loathe his guts . . . '

'I spoke in confidence and never mentioned your name! Anyway, he said I was mad to use FL's just by themselves. Besides, it was much more fun without.'

'He would know that, wouldn't he? The Playboy of the Medical School. The Nurses' Delight? More fun for you, maybe. What about me?'

He saw that I was prepared to go to war on the issue, and used his pet name for me.

'Sparky, Sparky! Regard this simply as an exploratory survey. You've drawn a blank at one clinic, but now you know what to expect at another.'

'Another? What other? Do you think I'm going to tout myself all round London, being insulted?'

He returned to battle.

'For God's sake, Leila, why make a drama of it? All you have to do is to go to a different clinic and tell them what they want to hear.'

'You mean, tell lies? You're asking me to lie so that you can have more fun?'

33

THE PEABODY LIBRARY
Columbia City, Indiana

DISCARD

I watched him master himself in order to get what he wanted, and I hated him.

'Look, Leila. Officials of any kind are not interested in people, only in statistics. That interfering old trout had no right to say what she did, but she's probably typical. So stick a ring on your finger and give a false name and address. Who's to know? Don't tell me that they've got time to check up the background of every woman who comes into the clinic.'

I weakened, slightly.

'Suppose they ask me for a marriage certificate?'

'Say you'll bring it in, and scarper quietly. No scenes. Then we'll have to think again. We might have to pay a private doctor in the end. You can always get something if you pay for it. Sad, but bloody true.'

The next clinic was in two classrooms of a disused school, and I did wonder whether these surroundings were a reflection of the official attitude towards birth control. Shabby places for shabby practices, smelling of ink and chalk and dust, overlaid with memories of caning and childish tears. This time there were three rows of hard chairs, a rack spilling over with thumbed comics and last year's magazines, and a respectable matron with a flowing bosom and iron waves of hair sitting behind a desk, filling in forms. Another sizeable lady stood by a worn rocking-horse, prepared to distract children while their mothers were otherwise engaged. And as I walked up to the desk on weak legs, one under-nourished boy was smilingly but forcibly separated from his mother and seated on its back. We spoke through his screams, as he was rocked back and forth, back and forth, by the voluntary helper who kept on saying, 'Aren't we having fun, dear? Aren't we having fun?'

'Name, please, dear?'

I wore a wedding ring I had bought at Woolworth's. I gave a false name, address and birth-date. I said we had no telephone number at present. I fabricated a husband who was at present unemployed, and gave this as the reason for needing protection. I kept my manner humble and grateful and smiled as much as she did. And within a very short time

THE PEARADIY LIBRARY

Colombia City, Ind. and

I was undressing in a cubicle formed entirely of rather dingy white curtains, preparatory to being examined by a junior doctor.

The atmosphere and smell were clinical. Clambering on to the high couch I dislodged the absorbent paper covering and felt the chill touch of red rubber sheeting beneath my buttocks.

The doctor, who was young and jolly, read my record of lies, looked into my face, drew on his rubber gloves which smelled of Dettol, and said, 'So you're an old married lady are you?'

I was terrified that he had somehow found me out, and was wondering how to escape, minus my underwear, when he made his little joke.

'Then you know all about it! Knees up, legs apart!'

The antiseptic nurse pursed her lips into a smile, and I giggled miserably. As he chatted and probed and tried different rubber caps, I knew why girls went into nunneries. I had not even the consolation of thinking that afterwards I should drown the memory of my humiliation in a tempestuous embrace. Our love-making had been a profound disappointment. Four weeks away from virginity I was still waiting for something wonderful to happen.

'There we are!' said the doctor cheerfully. 'Now you can enjoy yourselves without having to worry.'

Antiseptic nurse said, 'But come and practise first!' and swished me back to my cubicle. 'One leg up on the chair. Then put your fingers inside, like this, and hook them round the cap.'

Oh God, I thought, if one more person takes liberties with my insides I will surely kill them.

From the adjoining cubicle came a despairing Irish voice.

'Nurse! Nurse! Is that you next door? Will you not come and see to me?'

The nurse became human, saying, 'I'll have to leave you, dear. I'll be back directly.' She added, in a whisper, 'She's been here ages and can't get the hang of it, but I'm sure a bright little thing like you won't have any trouble.'

On the other side of the curtain, which was bellying fearfully, a litany began.

'Mary, Mother of God, this is what comes of going against the creed. Where's the bloody thing gone to now? Nurse! Nurse! I've lost it. Jesus, Mary and Joseph, it'll be up in me t'roat next.'

I practised removing and inserting my cap without much difficulty, listening.

'Rubbish!' said Nurse, on the other side of the curtain. 'It can't go anywhere except where it's supposed to go, Mrs McNulty. Have you no idea of your anatomy? Good gracious me, you've put it in the wrong way round.'

I began to laugh silently, so as not to hurt the Irish girl's feelings. Then I cried silently, because love-making had been ruined for me.

Jeremy took me to see *Shane* at the local Hippodrome that evening, and I let him hold my hand because I needed all my strength to finish with him once the film was over. While one half of me tried out final speeches the other half envied the people on the screen, whose world was narrow but secure. I wondered how Jean Arthur had managed to keep her family down to one boy in the days of no birth control at all. Was she just lucky or had she, fed up with being messed about, said 'No more hanky-panky!' And would she have been prepared to try again with Alan Ladd, given the opportunity?

Outside the cinema it was beginning to rain. We sat in Jeremy's car with the canvas roof leaking on us, and I stuck my hands in my mackintosh pockets so that he could not hold them, and jerked my face away when his approached.

He drew back as if I had hit him and said quietly, 'What's wrong, Sparky?'

My voice came out abrupt and thick.

'Everything!'

'But you got fixed up?'

'Oh yes, I got fixed up. I could have a night of love with a regiment if I wanted to. The only trouble is that this sort of fuss puts me off the physical side for life.'

He stared at me anxiously, uncertain how to handle the situation. I was not going to help him.

'Oh, come on, Sparks. Let's find a coffee bar and talk it over.'

'No. It's all spoiled. I don't want to see you again. Let's forget it.'

'Look – I know it hasn't been up to much so far but I've borrowed a – I've got a book from – about how to do it properly— '

'You've borrowed a book from whom? Not from Reggie the Rotter?'

'He's been very decent, actually. He said the physical thing didn't come naturally. You had to learn what to do.'

That was the final insult. If he thought I was lying there while he leafed through Reggie's book of instructions he had another think coming.

'Bugger Reggie and his book!' I said, and scrambled out of the car and walked off, collar turned up against the rain.

He jumped out from his side, swearing under his breath, and began to crank up the car. The engine came to life like a consumptive in the terminal stages of illness. I was halfway down the street before it caught me up and crawled along the kerb beside me.

He leaned towards me, crying, 'You'll get wet through, you bloody fool!'

I stopped and confronted him, firing off each word like a bullet.

'Mind – your – own – damned – business!'

He had braked to hear me, and the engine died on him.

'Oh, Christ!' he shouted, hammering the steering wheel with his fists.

I walked on. He flung open the door again, jumped out into the road again. Passing cars honked at him furiously.

Waving the crank handle at them, he yelled, 'And up you too, mate!'

The rain was running down his hair and face. He cursed and cranked the car like a maniac. I wanted to giggle, but giggling was not in my script. This scene was serious. I hurried on as fast as I could. Behind me I was aware of the car repeatedly coughing and dying, of his despairing shouts as he endeavoured to rally it. Then there was as much silence as one man and one car could create in a busy street. I looked back, and saw that he was looking after me. He had given up the struggle and was standing there, letting the situation happen to him. I shrugged to myself. So be it.

But, amazingly, he laid the crank handle on the car's blue bonnet, lifted his head, like a dog about to bay at the moon, and hallooed after me.

'Sha-a-a-a-ane!'

Like the boy in the film.

Transfixed, as I had been at the moment when the boy called, I stopped dead. And again he lifted his head and bayed at his personal moon.

'Sh-a-a-a-ane!'

I stood irresolutely. The call and the intent touched me deeply.

Passing citizens glanced at him and at me, and smiled and hurried on in the rain under their umbrellas. Londoners have seen all of life, many times. They may note it but they will not stop for it. Your private life is safe with them.

At the third piercing cry I gave up my pride and my intention and began to walk slowly towards him. He waited for me, grinning, dripping. And as I drew nearer his smile widened and my steps quickened, until we were together, laughing and hugging each other and wondering why we had quarrelled.

Looking back, I think that was the moment when I started to love Jeremy Purchase, but how was I to know what love meant, when there was so much to know about each other, and personal freedom to be preserved, and the ancient sport of pleasuring to be learned into the bargain?

4

Summer 1954

Outside, the slapping of wind and the pounding of sea. A salty shellfish smell mingles with linseed oil and strong brown brewed tea. Red coals and living flames in a small black grate. Shadows on whitewashed walls, ghostly cobwebs swinging from beam to beam, and an incredible clutter of furniture and art materials softly disguised by the light of two oil lamps. Jeremy and I are visiting Magda in her wild kingdom.

'I was born of poor Welsh parents in the Rhondda Valley in the last century, but I'm not going to tell how old I am . . . '

Jeremy and I sat head to head and hand in hand on Magda's sofa-bed, solemn and listening as evening owls, and he squeezed my fingers when anything amused him, or pressed my foot with his.

'My Dad was a miner who thought the world of education,' said Magda. 'To be educated, you see, was to get out of the pit. But times being what they were then, it was only the sons that were educated, not the daughters – though I was brighter than any of them. Top of the class, I was, and could draw from the moment I held a pencil. I wanted to be a teacher, but there was no money for that sort of luxury. So they sent me up to the big house as a scullery-maid when I was fourteen. There was nothing else for my sort of girl to do in those days, except to get married.

My Dad was fond of me, and sorry too, and he gave me a little box of Rowney's water-colours and a drawing block to sweeten the parting. I was never very good at domestic work, and I scrubbed and drudged without a bit of pleasure, except my day off once a month and my bit of painting.

'I was a little rosy girl, with a good head of nutbrown hair like Leila's mother, hair so long that I could sit on it. And before I was Leila's age I had *two* men courting me. One was Elwyn Richards from our village and the other was the younger son at the big house, David Griffith. My parents didn't know about David, of course, and they were very pleased about Elwyn. He was a lot older than me, and shy with women, but he had a nice steady job as a clerk up at the pithead. I don't remember very much about him, except that he was regarded as a good catch. I wasn't in love with him, that I do know, because I said so to my Mam. And she said that for a woman love came after marriage. Anyway, for me it had come before, and not with Elwyn, and I was pregnant before the end of the year.

'My parents took the news very bad. My Mam cried, and my Dad would have thrashed me but for the child I was carrying. There was no use complaining up at the house, unless I wanted to lose my job right away. So they did the next best thing. They went to Elwyn and told him. He was a decent man in his way, and he offered to marry me. And in desperation I did.

'I was just twenty when Helen was born, and full of life as an egg is of yolk, and I found marriage a dull business. Elwyn was set in his ways, and jealous of the baby, and he liked things kept tidy, and he wanted his food on time and cooked as his Mam cooked it – and she was for ever interfering. I couldn't stand it. Cast your bread upon the waters, the Bible says, and I did.

'One Saturday evening, when he was down at the pub making his half-pint last all night, and I had the week's housekeeping in my purse, I packed a bundle of clothes and my painting materials, wrapped the baby in a shawl and hitched a lift with a friendly lorry-driver who was going to Bristol. And from there I hitched another lift to Exeter,

40

and then to Plymouth, living in lodgings and working in pubs mostly. But I couldn't settle. Someone told me that the far end of Cornwall was very popular with artists. So I crossed the Tamar, and the further down I went the better I liked it. I found work as a housekeeper to a retired gentleman in Penzance. He was a nice old bachelor. Took quite a fancy to the pair of us. And when he died, two or three years after, he left me his money. I was never very good at keeping house, but I always knew how to make a man happy.

'Now if Helen had been his own child Elwyn might well have come after the pair of us, but as it was I daresay he went home to his mother, for I never heard another word from him or about him. I wrote to my parents when I settled in Penzance, and to my brothers and sisters. And later, when I travelled abroad I sent postcards. But nobody ever answered. It was as if we'd both died.'

She broke off, and patted Jeremy roguishly, lightly, on the knee.

'I wish I had a nicer tale to tell you. You look such a nice young man.'

This was to make sure that she had his full attention, and he unwound his foot from round my ankle and smiled upon her.

'When I met Walter Liddy he couldn't earn a crust. Wandered all round the coast, like a gipsy, painting seascapes. Lovely brushwork. Big canvases. Dramatic compositions. *Wreck of the Queen Margaret. Launching the Lifeboat. Storm off Land's End.* That sort of thing. After we parted he became quite a fashionable artist. Funny thing, fashion. Nobody remembers him now, but Lily found him mentioned in a footnote, didn't you, love?

'They say there's one man for every woman, and though I've had some lovely men, he was the one for me. He came to live with me and for a year or two we led a wonderful life. Spent every penny of my money, mind you, but he knew I wanted to be an artist, and he taught me all I know about painting. When the money was gone we lived hand to mouth. I got another job as a barmaid. Sometimes I sold

41

a picture to a summer visitor. But Walter used to get mad if I sold something and he didn't, and then we quarrelled. That was hard on me, because I loved him, you see. But hardest of all on my little daughter, playing by herself and watching and listening.

'I didn't do right by Helen. It was Janet and Robert Cullen who did right by her. English, they were, but lovely people. Very genuine. Well, you saw them at Zoe's wedding. Mad on Cornwall, they were, and are still. Came down for a month every summer, all the way from London in a big white car. Childless couple. Plenty of money in those days. We were living in Newlyn then, and they bought one of Walter's pictures. That was when they met Helen and took a fancy to her. She would be about six at the time, and a pretty little girl. Kept herself neat and nice-spoken. Very lady-like. Took after her father's side. It's funny how people become what they are. The only sort of life she knew was with me, but she was meant for something different.

'The next time they came to see me Walter had left us and I was desperate for money. They saw how things were and they offered to adopt Helen, but promised to keep in touch so that I didn't lose her altogether. Robert Cullen was a good businessman. He asked me where I wanted to live, and I chose St Ives. So he bought me this cottage and made me an allowance, paid every week, for life. I know what he was doing, mind! He was making sure I wouldn't go hungry and that no other man could leave me penniless like Walter did.

'It was hard to part with Helen, and it hurt me to see how willing she was to go to them. But I knew it was no sort of life for the child, and I never could give her the home and education she needed. So I signed the papers.

'Family ties are funny things, you know. I love my daughter, but I never feel easy with her. She frightens me sometimes. Being so good at what I was so bad at. And I know I'm a problem to her. I hope she loves *me* a bit, but I'm not sure. Well, what have I ever done to deserve it . . . ?'

Magda had accepted that Jeremy and I were lovers. Indeed, she expected us to be. For the first time we could be honest about our relationship. For the first time we slept together all night, and every night, on the flowered sofa, which could be pulled out to form a double bed. She kept her own hours and placed no restrictions on us. Cooking and cleaning were done when she felt like it, or we could do it ourselves. Generally speaking, we made our own breakfasts, washed up last night's dishes, left the day to her and returned in the early evening. Her banner was personal freedom and we flourished under it separately and together. Above all else, as far as I was concerned, she loved Jeremy. She was the only member of my family who did. My father liked him in an easy off-hand way. Helen found him amusing and presentable. Zoe accepted him, and Matthew went along with Zoe. But Magda loved him, loved me, loved us together.

We went to her for a fortnight and stayed six weeks. Summer was the highlight of that year and of our affair. Jeremy was a stranger to Cornwall and I became our guide. In his car, which did well for us on the whole, we visited all the places he had heard of and wanted to say he had seen, and then the places I loved and knew. And finally we returned to my childhood pleasures with adult delight. Running barefoot along the beach in the early morning, sandals in hand. Digging and creating, throughout one long hot afternoon, such a castle that other smaller diggers came to marvel. Sauntering along the beach, arms round waists, in the cool of the evening, seeing silent anglers casting their lines for sea harvest. Climbing down steep paths into little sheltered coves of pale gold sand and picnicking. Standing on cliffs watching wild walls of water rush, break, fall back, and mill round the rocks below us. Swimming on a moonlight night. Cycling round the country lanes. Eating ice-cream cornets. Buying fresh-caught fish from the harbour. And making love wherever we could find privacy and a patch of grass or sand.

'Radiant, you look,' said Magda, half-teasing, half-wistful.

The radiance was both physical and emotional, as if sunlight rather than blood coursed through my veins. Inspired and renewed, from day to day, by Jeremy Purchase. 'The look of love!' Magda mocked, smiling. I could not contemplate life without him. He had become as necessary to me as painting: a terrifying notion, since painting was part of me but Jeremy was not. Still, I answered her in the pride of youth, abundant with my riches of the moment.

'It's the first and very best sort of love.'

'The first is the hardest, and the best is always the most expensive.'

I see Magda superimposed upon that summer. We come in late and find her drinking red wine by the red fire, and mulling over the past. She has lunched lightly on a pork pie and pickled onions. The lardy crumbs and spiky smell remain. Accustomed by now to her wayward catering we have taken the precaution of bringing in three portions of cod in batter, chips and soft fat peas. She is miles away, staring into the fire, thinking of Walter Liddy or of those other men she loved when she was young and could sit on her length of nutbrown hair.

Aware of our entrance but still dreaming, she says, 'Late you are, tonight.'

'The car broke down, Magda.'

'Ach, that old car!' she says.

She shakes herself, wakes herself, smelling the vinegar seeping through its hot newspaper parcel.

'Clever you are! If I didn't forget all about supper!'

Jeremy says, as we all eat ravenously off plates on our knees round the fire, 'But what if you forget about supper and the shops are shut, Magda?'

'Oh!' she says scornfully. 'I can always buy a pint and a pie at the pub!'

He stops eating for a moment and looks at her with admiration.

'People fuss too much about comfort, don't they?' he says.

'Comfort, respectability *and* security,' Magda corrects him. 'I never bothered much about any of them!'

Around that hour of the evening, when most people

44

were thinking of going to bed, Magda's friends would drop in. She had a wide range of them, rejecting only the foolish and the dull. Saints, sinners, failures, so long as they were entertaining and lived life as lightly as she did, were welcome at her hearth. The air of freedom is heady. Seeing Magda in her element we felt sustained in our beliefs, restored in ourselves. Let the sheep bunch and breed together in the mild valleys. Let them safely graze. Our world was to be found in thinner air and higher regions, in places often solitary but always holding the promise of adventure.

I see Magda on the day that we had to leave, getting up early, scattered in wits and appearance like an old grey witch who has lost her broomstick. She beckons me apart on the pretext of giving me a chambered nautilus shell.

'Listen to me now, Lily, because this is good advice. Love that boy as well as you can and as long as you please, but don't change your life for him. You're not like Helen and Zoe. You'll never make a career out of a husband. Stick to your canvas and paint, girl. Remember that.'

Jeremy's car, whose exhaust pipe will drop off five miles from Plymouth and whose big end will go at Ilminster, is crammed with our rucksacks and bound by a fresh length of rope. We are ready to depart, and I do believe that she is ready for us to go. We have invaded her citadel with ourselves and our affair. She loves us but does not want us for ever. As in the train at Paddington she has withdrawn from us and looks suddenly old.

The car is cranked to life and continues to throb while Jeremy runs round and jumps into the driving seat. Its noise and smell bring Magda to herself. She makes the final effort and waves in an animated fashion as we chug across the cobbles.

Crying vivaciously, 'Come again in the spring, won't you? Lovely it is, in the spring . . . '

Her advice still holds good. Her shell is still with me, years later. I watch the sunlight making rainbows in its empty house.

5

Autumn 1954

It is a Saturday morning in October. My mother is celebrating the end of food rationing by baking cakes and pastries, and I am sitting at the kitchen table with my drawing pad, making rapid sketches of her as she moves to and fro. In my third year at art school my drawing pad and I are inseparable. My pencil produces a running commentary on life. I sketch on buses and trains, while I am eating at café tables. Indoors or out, night or day, it is all the same to me. I can draw blind. I produce clever squiggles, memoranda of what has just been.

My squiggles are good. I know because my teacher said so. The sad thing is that while I can capture the essence of what I see in that squiggle, it vanishes when I try to translate it into oil-paint, poster-paint, water-colour or pastel. It loses life and wit. As an annotator I am fine. As a maker of ultimate statements I am a total failure.

The first two years at art school are general grounding as we find our way. Quite early I discover that my particular gift is not what I want it to be.

'Perhaps you're not a painter,' says Mr Wiley the painting master, who should know, since he is. 'Have you thought of that?'

I don't want to think of it.

'Oh, but I *must* be a painter. I'm *dying* to be a painter. An old-fashioned classical artist who paints in oils.'

46

Mentally, I go back to my first year, when Cass said I could do what I liked and Helen said surely it was a good idea to aim for a useful goal. Why not become an art teacher, she suggested, or a textile designer? Surely I don't want to starve in an attic, waiting for my talent to be recognised? Rembrandt, she says, died poor.

Mr Wiley brings me back to my approaching third year, when I must specialise.

'What we want is seldom what we need, or what we can do,' he reminds me. 'You're good at line-drawing. If you had topical ideas and were a political animal instead of a funny little thing you could be a cartoonist.'

'But I'm *mad* about colour!' I cried. 'I'm *passionate* about colour.'

'Your sense of colour is good, but colour alone won't make an artist. Add it to the line-drawing, give it your imagination which is both peculiar and extensive, and what do we have? I think you should consider illustration. And remember this, whenever you're tempted to paint some eternal truth and present it to the Royal Academy for viewing, it is the *immediate* that appeals to you. You deal with the here and now. No looking back or looking forward, no philosophising. You capture the moment. That's your strength – and that's your weakness.'

I swallowed my answer and his advice, not wholly convinced.

Inwardly, I thought, he is wrong, Goddammit. Bloody wrong. I'll paint if I like. Paint what I like. Whatever *he* thinks.

Someday.

I am capturing Helen's moments, now food is plentiful once more, and they are abundant with vitality and nourishment. She has a strong face, handsome rather than beautiful. Cinnamon eyes, chestnut hair, a wide white smile. She gives the impression of a sound mind in a sound body. A good nose, a determined chin, a clear intelligent gaze. I have inherited her excellent teeth, for which I am grateful, otherwise I bear no resemblance.

47

When she is entertaining for my father's clients or their friends she dresses with quiet elegance. But in private she prefers slacks, shirts and sweaters. I should like to paint her as she is now, with floury hands and a large white apron. And I know I should fail. Instead I capture the zest with which she rolls pastry; the hint of high priestess in the way she presents the finished product; the sturdy stance as she mulls over a recipe book, frowning slightly, hands on hips.

I am enjoying this morning with her in the kitchen. I am enjoying the kitchen itself, which is large enough to have a huge scrubbed table in the middle, and is fitted with hand-made oak cupboards and shelves. Even its tools are ornaments. Blue and white china, Welsh pottery mugs, a shiny brown china hen sitting over the egg bowl. Helen's rolling pin is made of bottle-green glass. Her pastry-board of a slice of elm. The plants on the window-sill grow for her.

Joy surges from the roots of my childhood. Zoe, the favourite, is absent, so I have my mother all to myself.

She has taught both her daughters to cook. From the moment we could stand on stools by her side we were pressing down heavily on our little mounds of pastry with our miniature wooden pins. My pastry remained grey and lumpy, but Zoe's became lighter and crisper with the years. It was she who was allowed to transport our rations, and Cass's black-market deals, into the realms of puff, flaky, flan and choux.

I like my food too much to starve, but I am a simple cook. On the rare occasions when Helen is out for the day, I roast, grill or fry, and serve up fruit afterwards, alizarin crimson apples, mandarin black or citron green grapes, oranges like suns, pears like sunsets, cadmium yellow bananas. Shape and colour, colour and shape. But with my mother and Zoe food itself is the passion. They read recipe books for fun, interrupting each other to say, 'Oh, this would taste heavenly! Listen!' In consequence, Zoe has become a fully qualified domestic science teacher: a diploma which will be wasted on producing food for Matthew, who has been reared on watery rice pudding and minced beef.

48

There is an interval between fruit pies, and Helen puts the coffee percolator on the gas stove.

'Where can your father have got to?'

We both guess that he is prolonging Saturday morning with his secretary, Mrs Celia Piper. He may take her out to lunch, too, and spend the afternoon with her before coming home laden with expensive autumn flowers for my mother, which she will receive with sincere delight though knowing the reason for them.

'Darling! How beautiful. You shouldn't have!'

'Darling, I've been neglecting you.'

True.

'The flowers are my apology.'

Ah, but an apology does not mean a change of heart. He will ask for pardon and sin again.

I don't know why I regard his vices with amused affection instead of shocked resentment, but I do. My father has style, and that makes his faults acceptable. I suppose it must be something to do with the fact that he is half-French.

Zoe and I have inherited my paternal grandmother's colouring and when my father remarks upon it he never fails to add nostalgically, 'Ah! The French. They make an art of everything, including their women!'

Grandmère died before we were born, but we have a photograph of her in the family album taken in the 1920s. She has narrow treacle-brown eyes and a long nose like me, but is tall and fine-boned like Zoe. Her expression and her short skirt are decidedly provocative. I wonder if she is the one from whom Cass inherits his ongoing need for romance? I wonder if she was unfaithful to her husband in deed as well as thought?

'May I look?' Helen asks, pouring my coffee.

I hand her the sheets of herself and she laughs and shakes her head.

'Clever,' she says, handing them back. 'Very clever. Don't throw them away. You may be able to do something with them. You could make a series of them, called 'The Happy Housewife', and send it up to a women's magazine.'

Helen is a born manager. She likes to encourage other people's careers.

'I'll think about it,' I say amicably, sipping coffee.

Coffee I can manage. Even the smell of tea makes me feel sick.

'Try a cook's taste!' Offering me a less-than-perfect but delicious bun.

'No thanks. I'm not hungry.'

She frowns and says I'm not eating properly. My joy vanishes. The serenity induced by sketching and her company gives way to overwhelming apprehension. Cornwall has given me something to remember it by. My stomach is queasy, and my period is six weeks late.

Jeremy and I walk glumly, hands in duffle-coat pockets, shuffling the autumn leaves before us. I have once more subjected my body to strange hands and eyes, because of him. A friend of Jeremy's, who has just qualified as a midwife, has examined me and pronounced me with child.

I prefer medical terminology. The last fortnight has been demented. At this point to admit that we were going to kill our baby would be the final straw. I should begin screaming and be unable to stop. So I will just say that he and I have agreed to terminate the pregnancy.

Since abortion is a criminal offence Jeremy has been careful and tentative with his enquiries. The friendly midwife retreated from his hint into chilly silence, and pretended not to hear. We have been driven to asking one of the people I most dislike for assistance.

'Reggie says that this chap is sound and fully qualified. None of your backstreet abortionists. He had a bit of bad luck and got struck off the register.'

'What sort of bad luck?'

'An affair with a woman patient.'

'There must be more to it than that.'

Our voices are either subdued or harsh. We speak to each other like enemies.

'The woman got pregnant and he aborted it. The nurse

50

snitched on him. She fancied him herself. In fact they'd had an affair, too.'

'Oh, that was jolly bad luck! One woman got herself pregnant and the other told tales. Poor man! Is there no loyalty in the world?'

'It's no use being sarky, Leila. His morals may be dodgy but he's competent. I'm concerned that the – person – who does it knows what he's doing.'

'How much will it be?'

'A hundred pounds.'

'A hundred pounds?'

My cry is the ultimate in dismay, because neither Jeremy nor I possess a hundred shillings between us.

'I've thought it out. I'll get it from my father. I'll tell him I've got a girl in a jam.'

'You're not going to tell him about me?'

Being no longer in control, I now understand all this wittering about a woman's reputation. I am in a place where I can be stoned by criticism, ruined by word of mouth, turned from a beloved daughter and promising art student into a promiscuous slut with an illegitimate child to prove it.

Jeremy's reply is tetchy.

'Of course I shan't mention you! *You* couldn't be shuffled under the carpet as if you were nobody. He'd be forced to tell my mother and your parents. They might all get together and decide we should be married anyway, and support us until I qualified. That would be the bloody end. No, I've decided to say it's a barmaid from Wapping. He won't approve of it, but he'll understand. Put it down to young blood and no commonsense. Keep it to himself and shell up.'

I am learning a great deal more about men than I care to. My father's love affairs, which he conducts unobtrusively and apparently skilfully, are nosegays of flowers compared to Jeremy and his father and my mythical substitute.

I ask bitterly, 'Does she qualify as nobody because she comes from Wapping, or because she works in a pub?'

He turns on me, then, and in his rage I see the panic and

51

despair which have been my companions since the middle of September.

'Will you for Christ's sake stop picking on me? I know it's harder on you than it is on me but I'm taking responsibility for what happened. I'm doing the best I can.'

We stand still, staring at each other. Do I look as I feel? That I am cold to my bones and too stunned to cry?

He says in quite a different tone, 'Sorry, Sparky. Truly, I'm sorry.'

We hold each other and cry together, and sit under a tree like the babes in the wood, and wish we could both die with the doomed child who is our doom.

The nightmare goes on. This time the setting is a corner table in a Notting Hill coffee bar, dark and intimate. Fruit is the only food I can face or digest. I sip a glass of orange squash.

Jeremy's father, with whom so far I have been on casual and pleasant terms, but never again, has indeed shelled up to obliterate his son's mistake. He did not shell up easily. Jeremy has been castigated for irresponsibility and culpable carelessness which might have ruined his career. The barmaid is not mentioned except as an accessory after the fact.

He says with cheerless humour, 'It was a bit of a joke, actually. He said that at least I'd had the decency to find myself a trollop instead of fooling about with that nice little Leila Gideon.'

It is a mark of the distance lengthening between us that he does not know why this statement flays me. I retreat hastily to the lavatory and bring up the squash. When I come back Jeremy makes matters worse by explaining himself.

'He likes you a lot, Lee. He said you were the sort of girl I ought to marry when I came to settle down.'

The further flaying concentrates my mind wonderfully. I have nothing more to bring up. Now I know exactly what I must do and say, quietly and with emphasis.

'Jeremy Purchase, I wouldn't marry you to please your father if I lived to be a thousand. Fix this thing up. Let me know when and where it will take place. And then leave the rest to me and your disqualified doctor – and hop it.'

'I'm not going to ditch you, Sparks. I want to come with you.'

'But I don't *want* you.'

Emotionally adrift, he seeks to distract me with the sight of land ahoy.

'We'll celebrate when it's all over, Sparks. I'll take you out. Wherever you want to go. We haven't seen *The Seven Samurai* yet. Or *Hobson's Choice*. What about a night at the Palais? Rock around the Clock. Shake, Rattle and Roll. Jitterbug. We'll have fun.'

'We will do nothing afterwards. Ever. I'm not going to see you again.'

Then he seems his very young age, even in the romantic dusk of the coffee bar. He looks at me sideways. The light slides down his hair and on to his cheekbones. We are silent. I watch him mentally trying out ideas and putting them down again. Finally he nods jerkily, pays the bill and drives me home, without saying a word.

The doctor's room overlooks a railway siding, and our conversation is punctuated by the sound of wagons being shunted. If the body is our temple then his temple was deserted long since, and grass grows between the flagged stones. He has left his eyes to look away, his voice to speak without him, and his hands skilfully to destroy. He has a nurse out front, to keep the patient in her place, take the money and give final instructions.

I am helped on to a high couch which creaks with past terrors. Nothing good has ever happened on it. Looking everywhere but at the shining instruments and the kidney dish, waiting to receive, I part my legs. The feeling of being naked in the wilderness is worst. No, worst of all is the helplessness of the child. For there is still a child within me, the first blueprint of a human being, relying on me for nourishment and safe shelter. I have a choice. It has none. The instinct to protect almost overwhelms me. The fact that nobody wants it intensifies my desire to scramble off that table and run. It is my business to fight for it, to cherish it. I wish that I had used the past eight weeks to think instead of panicking. I am being humiliated, assaulted, but a child is being deliberately murdered. As the wagons clash together I shriek with pain and outrage.

'Hush!' says the nurse sharply. 'There's no need to make that much fuss!'

They help me off the table. I am sick and shaking, and I wish Jeremy had come to look after me because I feel incapable of looking after myself. I hold on to the nurse as she helps me to dress. I wonder how I am going to get home. The nurse makes me a cup of tea on an old gas stove in the kitchen next door. A bare-faced alarm clock ticks loudly on the dresser. On the table are the remains of some meal, dirty dishes, a cup of cold coffee, half-empty and slopped in the saucer. They must live here.

Outside, the shunting goes on at intervals. Clatter, clatter, clatter, bang, crash. Clatter, clatter. I wonder, as I sip the tea clumsily and burn my lips, whether she is the nurse who had an affair with the shell next door, betrayed him, and has now resumed her former post and role. Her questions as to where I live and how I shall travel are not prompted by solicitude, but by fear I might be taken ill on the way and traced back here.

'I'll order a taxi for you as far as the tube station,' she says. 'And then take another at the other end. You should walk as little as possible. You've no need to worry. Nothing will happen for twenty-four hours. It's Saturday tomorrow. You can stay in bed. It'll be like a heavy period. If nothing has happened by Monday then ring up and the doctor will help you again.' Help me again. 'Now, if you've finished . . .'

There's another baby to murder, so please get out and leave us to it.

I don't believe my baby has gone. In the taxi on the way to the station I resolve that if it does not abort I will keep it, fight for it, renounce my family, leave my home, and bring it up all by myself. I cannot expect my mother to face the social music and fit us into her showcase life, but Magda might take us in. I picture myself sitting on a pale-gold beach in a Cornish cove. The child lies beside me, kicking his legs, waving his arms, squinting at the sun. I bend over him and feel his breath coming on my cheek, soft and warm and vital. He is abundant with life, busy learning a thousand things as he contemplates me and the world about him.

In a state of euphoria, I realise that I have been put to the test because I had to learn what mattered. Previously, I had thought it was art. Now I set my chosen work aside like an old box of water-colours. The child is everything.

It is three o'clock in the afternoon and we are passing a series of autumnal window-displays in Oxford Street. One of them is of children's wear. On an impulse I stop the taxi-driver and pay him. I can manage a brief shopping excursion and a few yards' walk to the tube. If anything terrible happens then I must take a taxi home. In any case, nothing will happen until tomorrow. No, I remind myself, tomorrow nothing at all will happen, and I shall not ring up on Monday to be helped again.

With some difficulty, for I have taken no interest in children until now, I find the infants' department. There, with the last of my monthly allowance, I buy the most beautiful hand-knitted cream shawl that I can find.

The assistant says, smiling on me, 'If I was expecting a baby this is the shawl I should choose. It was knitted by one of our regular ladies in the Shetland Isles.'

For the first time in weeks I am utterly content. In a state of grace I make my way home, taking care of us both.

'Don't you worry,' I say inwardly. 'I'm on your side, child.'

In order to cover myself for the weekend, which will be momentous, I tell Helen that I have broken up with Jeremy and am feeling a bit down in the mouth, and that my period is due and making me feel rotten. She accepts both explanations with exactly the right amount of sympathy, and I retreat to bed carrying a jug of orange squash and a bottle of aspirins.

* * *

The child tore and ebbed its way out of me the following afternoon. Helen was in the drawing room giving tea and a listening ear to one of Cass's more difficult clients. My father was away in London. Zoe and Matthew had invited his parents to dinner that evening, and were busy shopping and cooking together. And Jeremy had been forbidden to contact me.

A heavy period, the nurse had said. It was a slaughter-house. Sickened, horrified, in grinding pain and hopeless misery, I attempted to staunch, to mop up, to conceal the flood. Life itself was seeping and bubbling forth in liquid and solid form. I tried not to look at it. I crept to the bathroom to find a towel, and was immobilised in an agony of mind and body. There, drawn by the same instinct which had made me buy the shawl, Helen found me, knelt by me, held me, regardless of the fact that the skirt of her afternoon dress was being slowly ruined.

'Oh, my baby,' she said, over and over again. 'Oh, my baby. What have they done to you? Why didn't you tell me?'

Of course, she hushed it all up. To have brought it out in the open would have meant social disgrace, and all sorts of unpleasantness with the police and the law. Helen confided only in our family doctor, and only after making sure that he would act as an old friend and not pursue the matter any further. He examined me grimly but pronounced me to be in no danger. His manner towards me had changed in the space of a telephone call. I was in the worst kind of disgrace. I knew more than a decent girl should. I had transgressed not only against a social code but against life itself.

'I'd like to know who did it,' he said.

'He never gave a name,' I replied mutinously.

'He had an address, presumably?'

But he knew I would not tell him.

My mother said hesitantly, pleadingly, 'I should like this to remain between the three of us, Colin. I don't even want her father to know.'

56

And when he had gone she particularly asked me to say nothing to Zoe.

In her hands, in her power, I asked why not.

She said, 'I have a hunch that she might be pregnant. Just as I sensed that you were – but I couldn't face the fact until this happened. If Zoe is expecting a baby I don't want her to be troubled in any way, either worrying about you or feeling that she must hide her own happiness in case you're upset.'

She asked, of my silence, 'Do you understand, darling? I don't mean to be unkind to you. I know it's going to be hard. But I'm thinking of Zoe.'

Shipwrecked on a shore of my own making, I agreed.

'It was your Jeremy Purchase, of course?' Helen asked.

I nodded. I thought that an unnecessary question, but it was her way of discovering more information.

'Did he pay for the abortion?'

'His father did. He thought I was a barmaid from Wapping. As if a girl didn't matter unless she came from a nice middle-class family. I've finished with the Purchase family for good.'

She was contemplating me, trying out a theory which she could understand. She put it with great delicacy.

'Of course, young people in love play with fire without meaning to. I expect Jeremy lost his head – went too far – for once?'

I saw the trend of this question. To tell her that we had been conducting and controlling an affair, until that treacherous moment when we thought we were safe, would have shocked her profoundly. She needed to be reassured, to be returned to a world she comprehended. Her hour of heroism, of loyal and passionate motherhood, was over. As was mine.

'Yes,' I conceded, telling a half-truth. 'We went too far, for once.'

She nodded, and stroked the hair away from my forehead. Truly, she loved me, and truly she did not know me. Longing to connect, I said, 'I went along with the abortion because I didn't know what else to do. But I wanted to keep

57

that baby. I was working out a way to keep it, by myself.'

She was sitting on the side of the bed, hands clasped in her lap. Her face looked bruised and tired.

'And how did you propose to do that?' she asked gently.

'I thought – I wasn't going to bother you – I thought Magda might have us.'

Helen's face changed.

'My dear child,' she said, with uncharacteristic bitterness. 'Magda has never cared for babies. I should know. I was the only one she ever had.'

And of course I knew that she was right.

Then she returned to her charitable self and spoke kindly, using my childhood nickname, 'You should have told me, Lulu.'

I was very tired, and the end of one of my worlds had come.

'But what could you have done?' I asked her.

'Well, my dear, you could have married Jeremy. There are worse things than having to struggle for a year or two, particularly when you're young. I'm sure the Purchases and ourselves could have come to some arrangement. Neither family is short of money. These accidents happen, you know, and often turn out well.'

'Jeremy thought you'd do that. He didn't want it.'

'Ah!' she said.

She sat, head bent, musing sadly over her capable hands.

'How selfish men are!' she said to herself.

We were very close over the next weeks, as I worked my way towards healing and sanity. I had a week at home, during which she kept me in bed and I was glad to stay there. She even brought in the old screen, which had kept her and us company through the innocent illnesses of childhood, and put it round my bed. I lay for hours, looking at its myriad pictures chosen from illustrated magazines at the turn of the century. Years ago, Janet Cullen had patiently cut out and collected them, pasted them on, varnished them over. It was the colour of clear honey by now. It was the past, safely embedded, untouchable, and immensely comforting. While I lay there Helen covered for me, with my father, with my sister, with everyone. She divided my obvious physical and mental distress between the quarrel with Jeremy and a vague internal female problem. We visited our family doctor together, and he gave me a clean bill of health. Afterwards, she let it be known that the problem was not serious, and would sort itself out in time.

Once, Jeremy rang, and she answered the telephone.

I heard her say, 'I'm sorry, but Leila doesn't want to speak to you, and I don't blame her.' Then she added, 'You have nothing to worry about. The child has been aborted and Leila will recover. But let me say this. You have behaved very badly, Jeremy Purchase,' and put the receiver down.

I had a recurring nightmare. I was being shown round a factory which made dyes. It was a poor dark place, full of ill omen. The manager said, 'This is where we get rid of the waste!' He pulled a lever and a great stream of foaming scarlet dye flowed out from a tunnel below. He said, 'They keep complaining that we're polluting the river!'

For a long time afterwards I would wake up screaming and screaming.

One afternoon, early in December, I came home from the art school to find Helen and Zoe in the kitchen. Zoe was sitting on the table, swinging her legs and smiling most beautifully. As I came in they turned towards me with the same look which told me my time with Helen was at an end. She still loved me, she had tended me without stint, and was now returning to the daughter who most pleased and most resembled her. But first she came over and put her arms round me, to apprise me of what was coming and to comfort me for it.

'Darling, Zoe has some wonderful news for us.'

The light on Zoe's face was the light I had felt within me, as I pictured myself sitting on the beach and felt the child's breath upon my cheek. For once I had been as transfigured as she was.

'Oh, Zo!' I said. 'Oh, Zo!' and burst into tears.

The tears, which Helen interpreted as misery and remorse, were accepted by Zoe as a right and proper tribute. She jumped down from the table – 'Zoe! Be careful!' Helen cried – and cuddled me, crooning, 'Darling Lulu. What a dear little aunt you're going to be!'

'I think we'll all have a sherry to calm us. Even if it is only half-past four in the afternoon!' said Helen, and poured out a tranquilliser for each of us. 'A little mild alcohol won't harm you,' she told Zoe.

Wiping my eyes, sipping a glass of sherry when I felt like drinking a tumblerful of whisky, I could not help saying shakily, 'I thought you said you were going to wait for years.'

'I was getting broody,' she replied, without resentment. 'And I persuaded Matthew. I'm awfully naughty, and awfully lucky. He lets me have all my own way. And now he's as thrilled as I am.'

More steadily, I said, 'Helen had a hunch that you were pregnant.'

'When? You didn't tell me that, Mummy. When did you have a hunch?'

'Three weeks ago,' I answered for her.

She was remembering my trauma, wondering how to buffer the impact of Zoe's exaltation.

'Mummy, you are a witch!' Zoe cried.

I topped up my sherry while they were admiring each other.

'And when's the baby due?' I asked.

'July the fifteenth. If I hold on for three days it might arrive on our second wedding anniversary. They say that first babies are usually late!'

My baby would have been born in June.

'Helen's not the only witch in the family!' I said. 'I've got something for you.'

And I ran upstairs. For the first time since the abortion I ran upstairs. And came down with the shawl, still lovingly

60

wrapped in sheets of tissue paper, and protected by its smart carrier bag, waiting for an acceptable mother to wrap her acceptable baby in.

'It's for you,' I said, though I found it tremendously hard to part with. 'It's your baby's very first present. What about that for witchcraft?'

The shawl, shaken out, was even more beautiful than I remembered.

Zoe's face was my reward.

That, and Helen's voice saying in complete understanding, 'Oh, my dear Lulu. Oh, my dear child.'

6

We suffered one of those family Christmases which cost a great deal of time and effort and turn out to be disappointing and quarrelsome. Edmund and Marian Barber, already staking a heavy claim in the coming baby, wanted the young people to spend Christmas Day with them, but Zoe had grown wiser on close acquaintance and said to us privately that it would be a dismal way of celebrating, and apparently Matthew agreed. So Helen decided that the only way to prevent the Barbers from being upset was to invite everybody to Whitegates.

All the men behaved badly. Mr Barber ate and drank hugely, and then gave a little homily on the evil contrast between Western gluttony and the starving East. My father had previously organised an urgent telephone call for himself and disappeared early in the afternoon. And Matthew, who was fretting about bringing up a baby in a top-floor flat, and wondering where they would keep the Dunkerley pram my parents had bought as a special present, sulked.

The women, with the exception of the Lady Marian who preferred to pour oil on troubled fires, behaved beautifully. My mother spread her wings over the disconsolate company. I remained amicable on the surface and sketched viciously undercover. And Zoe, though frequently assailed from without, was protected within by the comfort of her pregnancy.

Fortunately the elder Barbers never stayed up late enough to see the New Year in, so we had Zoe and

Matthew back by themselves six days later and launched 1955 with champagne, which made up for the Christmas fracas.

A novel was published that year by a French girl called Françoise Sagan. The title was *Bonjour Tristesse*. I like to read books and eat apples at the same time. Most books and most apples are grist to my mill and when they are finished I forget them, but I actually bought a copy of *Bonjour Tristesse* and read it again and again because Sagan knew that love failed and life was empty without it. She became an invisible, a fictional sister to me now that Zoe had disappeared into successful marriage and motherhood.

That was a strange year. Returning to the world slowly and cautiously, a crippled thing, I only remember flashes of it.

I progress step by step.

At the art school two students in my group, at whose engagement party Jeremy and I had met, suddenly break up. Their obvious devotion has earned them the nicknames of Darby and Joan.

Joan is small, prim and bespectacled. Darby towers over her, speechless and protective. They are both very shy and have been grateful to and for each other so far. Then a tall languorous Indian girl from the dress-design department, known behind her back as Delilah, turns glittering kohl-lined eyes upon Darby. He succumbs without a struggle, and now they are walking round the art school arm in arm and cheek to cheek, lit up like a pair of Christmas trees, while Joan cries at unexpected moments helplessly, hopelessly, soundlessly in cloakroom, classroom and canteen.

'Don't think I'm being unsympathetic,' says one of my friends, seeing the rejected one dissolve suddenly over a coffee cup, 'but there's no need to make a public exhibition of yourself like she does. After all, Leila, you and that Purchase boy from the medical school went round together for ages, and you didn't make a fuss when it split up. Of course, you're the proud and silent type, aren't you?'

She looks flustered then, and says, 'What I mean is that you've behaved well and she's being a drip!'

I am both complimented and insulted. Being me I answer the insult.

'Joan didn't choose to break up the friendship,' I reply from a great distance. 'In the Purchase case I did.'

'Oh, I see. I didn't know. I wasn't trying to pry.'

Someone else says quickly, tactfully, 'Old Darby will have to take a back seat while the Paris Fashion Shows are on. Did you know that Delilah sits up all night cutting out and sewing new creations à la Dior? In the last few months we've had the H-line, the A-line, the Y-line, bouffant petticoats, and now she's in a pencil dress. I wish to God someone would tell me what she does with her cast-off clothes!'

I lead the laughter that follows, and inwardly award myself a medal for bravery above and beyond the call of duty. My despair has been construed as proud silence. I have not made a fuss. I have behaved well.

I say, raising my canteen coffee cup. 'Here's to Delilah. May her scissors rust and her painted talons break!'

And I retrogress.

One mad March day, coming out of the National Gallery, I see Jeremy Purchase waiting at a bus stop in Trafalgar Square and am suddenly as stricken and breathless as if someone had punched me deliberately, viciously, in the throat and stomach.

He, on the contrary, looks extremely well, steady and cheerful. He is talking to another student whose back is towards me. His fine brown hair is blowing. Their familiar striped university scarves, undulating in the wind, seem about to entwine like friendly snakes. In answer to some remark he throws back his head and laughs. I remember how his light-green eyes squeeze tight shut while he enjoys a joke.

The summer in Cornwall is back with me, but in reverse. As the maimed are cruelly plagued by phantom limbs, so I am by my phantom lover. Iced water flows through my veins

64

that once were full of sunlight. My arms are empty and my flesh is cold. Once more I tread the mill of regrets, round and sorrowfully round. Once more I am declared bankrupt in the courts of love and for the first time in months I want to run down the steps, calling to him to wait, for I am here and all is forgiven. And have him hold me again, very hard and tight, and be glad beyond all gladness to see me.

I am not in pursuit of sex, God knows. That side of me has so far been switched off like an electric light. What I need is the familiarity and warmth of us, and the privilege of loving and being loved. For life has been sad and drab and old without Jeremy Purchase.

The other student turns round for a moment. I recognise Jeremy's dark star, Reggie Reardon, and all my hopes and defences crumble. I walk quickly away, far away, from them both, and sit in Joey Lyons' white and gold palace a long time drinking coffee before I find the strength to go home.

Helen and I are by ourselves that evening. As usual she is sewing small exquisite clothes for Zoe's baby, stitching good thoughts into the Viyella, biting off the thread with sound white teeth. As usual I am working on a personal folio for the diploma I hope to achieve that summer. For one submission I have decided to illustrate *The Secret Garden*. Mary Lennox comes to life beneath my fingers, a quaint, contrary, spidery child. I grow a garden round her, green and grey and mysterious as another world. I find her and Colin querulously easy to create, but must make an effort with honest Dickon and rosy Martha because they are simple people on whom life smiles, and though I may appreciate them I do not understand them.

Art has been my salvation. Inside it I am as safe and happy as Zoe in her pregnancy, but tonight its magic cannot protect me. After a while I put my head in my hands and cry as if I will never stop.

Instantly, my mother forgets Zoe and her baby and concentrates on me and my grief.

'Let it out, darling. Let it out. I do understand, Lulu. I

65

do. I do. You've been so brave, but you must mourn, you see, before you can be comforted.'

When my sobs cease and my eyes are dry she offers me a small glass of sherry.

'I blame myself,' she says, distressed. 'I should never have sewed the baby clothes in front of you. It was gross. Unthinkable. Unforgivable.'

Dry in more ways than one, I answer her objectively.

'But you couldn't hide the fact that you *are* sewing them. And of course you mustn't. Life can't stand still because I'm in trouble!' I finish my sherry and feel a little better. 'In fact, life doesn't give a damn that I'm in trouble!'

'Darling, don't despair. Things do come right in the end if your attitude is right. Truly. Shall I make us some tea, or coffee, or Horlicks?'

'Horlicks,' I say, because that choice will please her most. It takes us both back to childhood.

While she is out I fill my sherry glass to the brim with Cass's malt whisky and drink it neat. By the time we are sipping Horlicks contentedly together I am back inside myself. Later on, I put aside the illustrations to *The Secret Garden* and draw a series of savage cartoons in which Reggie Reardon figures largely and to his complete disadvantage, and entitle them, *Let's Have Fun!* Then I set the illustrations side by side with the cartoons, wondering, not for the first time, if I am schizophrenic.

I achieve a precarious balance while Zoe blooms.

For once I can understand her emotionally. She has the rapt air, the swollen flower-crowned beauty of Flora in Botticelli's *Primavera*. In those days maternity clothes meant shapeless skirts with an expanding waist-band and a smock to cover the bulge. But Zoe and Helen, witches with their needles, concoct the loveliest costumes which flutter and flow and glow, enhancing rather than concealing her condition. And since the final part of her pregnancy comes in late spring and early summer, I remember my sister during that time as a goddess of fertility, a golden diaphanous presence exuding life and hope.

I remember also that she unwittingly upstaged me on my twenty-first birthday. Everyone who came to my party brought a little something for the baby as well as a present for me. And everyone who wished me well said, ' . . . but isn't Zoe looking *wonderful?*'

All things pass. That's the real mercy.

Zoe's son is born on the twenty-second of July in a long horrendous thirty-six-hour labour which has the Gideons and the Barbers sitting on the edge of a hospital bench in the early hours of the second morning. Afterwards we are allowed to see mother and child, in order of our importance. First of all Matthew, who has taken to approaching fatherhood with great trepidation and needed almost as much attention as Zoe. Then Helen, drained by the demands of them both. And finally me.

Sister tells the two new grandfathers, kindly but briskly, that they must wait until tomorrow afternoon before they can be admitted to Zoe's presence or peep at the baby. My sister has attained the status of royalty. Sister refers to her in the plural.

'We shall be feeling brighter then. We've had a rather rough passage!'

I am delighted to report that the Lady Marian is also banned as being 'One too many, I'm afraid, dear. I know you'll understand.'

The lady does not choose to understand. Her eyes turn a colder shade of blue, and she is seen to toss her white-waved head and jerk her double chin.

Zoe has been washed up, colourless and spent, on some remote shore from which she gazes at me abstractedly with a little frown. She is skilfully propped up with pillows so that she can hold her son in the crook of her right arm. It would be stupid to ask her how she is, so I kiss her cheek and touch the baby's mottled fist, and stand in sympathetic silence, looking down on them both. A damson-blue bruise on the crown of his head is witness to the struggle he has undergone, in an effort to butt his way into the world. My shawl swaddles him to drowning point. Being unused to babies, I had no idea how small they were.

Zoe says in a tired voice from a great distance, 'We're going to call him Simon, and we'd like you to be his godmother.'

I have no idea what to say, since I am not a practising Christian and would make the worst godmother imaginable. Not for the first time I wonder if my sister draws a blind down over my true self, and only addresses that part of me she likes and comprehends.

Prevaricating, I thank her, resolving to bow gracefully out later.

Dredging up her strength Zoe assures me, 'They've all been very kind and good to me here.'

'So they should be,' I reply curtly. 'You've had a bad time.'

I think she is trying to erase any unfortunate impressions I may have had about childbirth.

'But the baby's worth any amount of trouble,' she says. 'Truly.'

I am relieved to see Sister appear, with her 'Time's up!' expression.

As I bend over to kiss Zoe again her eyes fill with tears, and she says, 'You mustn't mind me, Lulu. I'm a bit tired. I'll be brighter tomorrow.'

Sister is taking the baby away as I depart. A nurse is removing the pillows, settling Zoe down again. The show is over. They can rest now.

And life is being merciful to me. Throughout this appalling performance I have never once regretted that I was not on stage. I have been content to watch from the wings. I feel no jealousy of Simon, no envy of Zoe. I feel nothing but anger and pity for their struggles to separate, one from the other, in order to come together as mother and child. And I cannot help thinking that nature should have found a more civilised way of reproducing humanity.

Driving home in the dawn the light is pearl-grey and beautiful, kind to our tired faces.

My mother, drained and fulfilled at once, says, 'I saw quite a look of you in the baby, Cass.'

To which he replies typically, 'The only thing any new baby resembles is strawberry jam!'

She remembers – when does the maternal mind ever forget? – that I may be experiencing a return of trauma. I should, after all, be a mother myself by now if nature had been allowed her way.

She says anxiously, 'Are you all right, Lulu?'

My father answers for me, drily, steadily, 'Good Lord, Nell, haven't you worried enough the last two days? Of course she's all right. She'll be off to a life of her own and a place of her own, doing the work she wants, in a couple of months. Why shouldn't she be all right?'

The early-morning road stretching and winding ahead of us is symbolic of my present state. While my sister is settled in green pastures I have freedom to travel, to stay, to move on, exactly as I please. Anywhere.

'Yes,' I reply, in tune with him and the road. 'You needn't worry about me. I've never been better, Helen.'

7

I left home without entirely leaving its protection. One of
my father's clients, a fragile-looking lady with shrewd grey
eyes, who called herself Constantia Blezard, ran an escort
bureau in central London. And there we went together on
a three-day foray, as soon as I was awarded my diploma,
to gain a foothold in the city. We stayed in a small hotel
in Bloomsbury, which was comfortable and intimate in a
family way, and had an air of faded elegance. Looking
out of my bedroom window on to its back garden, that
late summer morning, seeing the sun slanting through the
trees at the side of the British Museum, I fell in love with
my life all over again.

'Business first,' said my father, buttering his breakfast
toast. 'Pleasure afterwards. Pour me a cup of coffee, will
you, my darling? We're meeting Connie at the bureau for
coffee at eleven, and taking her to lunch at the Ritz – she'll
love that, and so will you, I daresay! – and she will give us
a start.'

He cut up his bacon and popped the first piece into
his mouth. In my mother's absence, taking her place, I
waited to see if he liked it before I spread marmalade on
my toast. In turn, he looked at my plate critically over his
reading glasses.

Out of habit he said, 'Why don't you women eat a
decent breakfast?'

And then continued to plan our campaign.

'I have other people marked down as being possibly
useful to you, now or in the future, but we'll contact

them according to need. If we work hard in the mornings we should manage some sight-seeing in the afternoons, and we can take the evenings off. From experience I suggest that we either find a good restaurant and eat very well or have a snack before a show. You can't do justice to both.'

He disentangled the entertainments page from *The Times*, saying, 'Here you are, my darling. Your choice entirely.'

Had Helen and Zoe and I been by ourselves in London then every night would have been a snack and a show. Art galleries in the afternoons for me. A concert at the Royal Festival Hall and two visits to the theatre. Knowing my father's tastes, I guessed that we should dine extremely well on two of our three evenings, and the other would be devoted to a musical comedy. I pencilled a circle round *The Boy Friend* and put a question mark after it, which turned out to be right.

Appraising me in the lobby, before we set out for Connie's bureau, my father said, 'Did your mother choose that outfit? I thought so. It's the kind of thing Zoe looks good in.'

I stood there pensively in my trim-waisted, full-skirted Horrockses cotton dress. White flowers on a blue ground: crisp and fresh and pretty. I wore short white gloves and white button earrings. She had persuaded me to have my hair set in a bouffant bob. I carried a smart little box-shaped handbag.

His heavy-chinned face was amused. He gave his tremendous smile.

'You're not a pretty English bread-and-butter miss. Too much of my mother in you for that. Too much of an individual. Still, we can't have you in black slacks and a corduroy shirt, or one of your artier concoctions, can we? They wouldn't let you into the Ritz!'

Unperturbed, for he had told me I was unique, I replied, 'I knew it was right for the occasion and wrong for me, but it's no use arguing with Helen.'

'But you look deceptively sweet!' he said, winking, putting one hand on my shoulder, steering me through the swing doors.

71

As I came to know Connie better I suspected that her bureau was a more complex organisation than it seemed, though I never enquired as to its underground activities. Apparently it did well enough to provide Connie with a large house in Sussex, which my father, with the aid of a blank cheque, had brilliantly refashioned in her image. And her wardrobe of furs might have been designed for Lady Docker. I think she modelled herself on Lady Docker. She was always formally well dressed and well groomed. Her hair was tinted baby-gold, and her limousine upholstered in (imitation) zebra skin.

I wondered, with merely passing curiosity, whether she and my father had ever been lovers. If so the flame had guttered out long since, but they still liked each other in a tough, shrewd way. He was charming to her, and she was graciously pleased to help him.

I had taken my portfolio with me but she only glanced through it, saying abstractedly, 'Oh, I can see you're a clever clogs like your father! We must do what we can for you, dear.'

And was glad when I relieved her of it.

'Connie doesn't know anything about art, does she?' I said to my father as we consulted the menu at Scott's restaurant that evening.

'Couldn't tell the difference between a Rembrandt and an advertisement for Ovaltine. But she knows people who can give you work. And as far as you're concerned that's what matters.'

In return for her lunch at the Ritz Connie came up with a soap-manufacturer who wanted a cartoon strip to advertise his products. 'And he's well worth cultivating, dear, because he knows a lot of people in trade who want art work.'

Art work!

She also contacted a very shady gentleman I never met, who owned property in Camden Town which was due to be demolished, and could rent a bedsitting room to me, provided I understood that the accommodation was temporary and I did not make trouble for him with the authorities.

Connie said, 'You needn't bother your head about the demolition order, dear. It's been due for a few years now. Something to do with a tax loss and a row with the council. It'll be standing as long as you need it, and by the time the axe falls you'll be looking for a nice little flat in Chelsea, won't you?' Then she turned to my father and said, 'She'll be all right in that house, Cass. It's full of students. And though the neighbourhood is a bit run-down it's quiet. Besides, Maury knows I'm keeping an eye on her.'

Despite her Christian name and her pledge, that eye was hardly a constant one, and on the rare occasions when I visited the bureau she had to focus for a moment or two before she remembered who I was. But with work to do, somewhere to live, and her token guardianship, my future was established. We rang Helen that evening to report progress, and my father said we had worked so hard that he wanted to give me an extra day in London.

I was not surprised when he disappeared the following afternoon, murmuring about 'other possible contacts', which must have been his not mine for none of them ever materialised. But I was not sorry. For though I adored him and enjoyed his company his absence meant that I could spend hours and hours by myself in the Tate, wandering round humming under my breath, and utterly utterly happy.

A chameleon, I took on the colour of the city. Mine had been almost a rural upbringing, with night separated from day, birds in trees, and pools of silence. But London never slept. At night the sky was still rosy, the sounds of the day muted to a dull roar, and in the distance I could hear the lone hooting of ships on the river. Pigeons roosted in buildings, fed on pavements. Flocks of starlings twittered in the twilight. And great events seemed just around the corner.

One commission and a vague promise of others was not enough.

'Remember,' said my father, 'that the salesman who gets the most commissions is the one who knocks at most doors!'

I heeded his advice. I screwed up my courage and made my own opportunities. First of all I approached the great publishing houses, one by one, asked for an interview, and took along my college folio bulging with illustrations and ideas, round which glowed an aura of star-pupil promise. My reception was universally cordial and equally promising. I was greeted like the answer to a prayer, offered coffee and cigarettes, and from receptionist to secretary to editor it was smiles all the way. Without exception the editors said they loved my work. One of them even took photocopies and said she would be in touch if anything turned up. By the time I was ushered out I felt I had made friends for life, and was wondering how I should manage to keep up with the future flood of commissions.

Then there was a universal silence, which I did not notice for a while because I was busy knocking on other august doors. When I telephoned some weeks later not one of them remembered my name, though they made a charming pretence of finding it that moment on their desk in front of them.

'Leila Gideon? Oh yes, of course. I have a note here. There doesn't seem to be anything at the moment, Miss Gideon, but we'll keep you in mind.'

No one was too high or too low for me to approach. I followed up every connection, however vague. I hung on to the coat-tails, or smocks, of artist friends who were making their way in this new jungle, adopted their suggestions, took their advice and accepted every invitation I was offered. I stood around at cocktail parties hoping for lucrative intro-ductions, or hovered on the fringe of chatting circles, eating too many peanuts because I was so hungry. I carried my folio round with me and left it in the cloakroom, just in case it was needed. It never was. I thought seriously about an agent, but none of them thought about me, and the prospect of paying them anything from ten to thirty per cent on each job put me off anyway. I tackled anyone who might possibly help me, on the slightest pretext. And God help those who gave me the smallest commission, for I never let them go. In short

I made a bloody nuisance of myself, and spent more time trying to find employment than being employed.

Have you ever thought how necessary artists are? Look around your home at the packets and bottles and jars in your food cupboard, children's comics, calendars, newspapers, books and magazines. In the streets are hoardings full of posters, billboards, pub signs. There are postcards on stands and greetings cards in stationery departments. Shops and cafés advertise themselves and their wares. In the cinema foyer you see an illustration of the film, inside you watch cartoons. Someone is paid to draw and paint all those things. That's what I told myself during the first year, as I tramped London in search of work.

The first year is the worst. It is the first year which divides the student from the professional. No one can even begin without talent, but talent is not the only necessary ingredient. Self-belief, stamina and bloody-mindedness are equally important. Parents who help you back on to your feet during a weekend at home are a bonus. And the ability to find and keep a part-time job is essential. I can still pull a fair pint in a bar, if required, or wash up in a restaurant kitchen, or act as waitress in less salubrious places, or deliver the Christmas post. So I learned, as we all do, the hard way, but I did learn.

After the first few months I had some professional work to show, and no longer took my college pieces to interviews.

My first real break was by courtesy of an editor's assistant, who had sat silently by at one interview. Apparently my work spoke to her, and she cleverly married it up with a children's writer whose words had the same effect.

She said, 'I think the Leila Gideon girl could do this new book of Bill's. I really liked her stuff.'

The editor rang our communal telephone, and someone brought me running wildly down the stairs to answer it.

She said, 'Come and see me.'

That afternoon telephone call stands out in my memory as one of the great moments in my life.

So the first little plum fell from the tree into my

waiting hands, and was gradually followed by more and bigger plums. Sometimes they came all together, sometimes singly. Sometimes there were fruitless periods. I suppose it took three or four years before I could reckon to earn my bread, but I found the way at last.

Out of my year at art college only five of us survived as freelance illustrators. I am one of them.

I loved that house in Camden Town, even though only a bit of it was mine. Its tenants were poor and powerless enough to be thankful for an over-priced and under-furnished room anywhere. There were nine of us, all transients in a city of transients. Like me, the other eight possessed little more than their clothes, crockery and what Helen insisted on calling 'linen' even if it meant frayed tea-towels. My room had been a front parlour in the house's palmy days, and the light enchanted me even on the greyest afternoon, coming in through a great bay-window. A framed photograph of Zoe's wedding, a couple of Toulouse-Lautrec posters, a bunch of flowers bought from a pavement stall, and my books and my art materials, made this place home for me.

Cooking and sanitary arrangements were primitive. I had a sink and a gas-ring in one corner, and the use of a very old gas-cooker in the communal kitchen downstairs. We all shared the single bathroom and lavatory. A notice on the wall said 'Please Leave The Bath As Clean As You Found It', and on the windowsill stood a battered container of Vim and a grey slimy cloth to underline this request. Either no one bothered to read it, or else the bath was in such a revolting condition that no amount of cleaning could make any difference. Turquoise–green stains and pits of rust vied with a permanent tub ring imprinted in its grubby white paint. The notice itself was damp and flaking, printed in uneven capitals on a sheet of cardboard. So I spent the whole of one evening creating a new one and making a protective covering with cellophane. I took the old notice down and put mine up, and made a new friend in the process, who thumped on my door while I was heating supper on a gas-ring and making toast.

'Well, hello there!' he cried, smiling down on me from his great height. 'Are you the creator of that serendipitous notice in our ghastly bathroom? You are? Oh, splendid. I've been knocking everyone up asking them. Came to thank you for it.

'And who am I, you might well say? Well, I answer to the name of Montague Brown for long, and Monty for short. I'm a sort of artist too. Freelance shop window-dresser, ever hoping for permanent work and preferably in Knightsbridge, but we take what we can. I did the saucy lingerie window at Marie's Boudoir in the High Street. Have you seen it? Oh, do drop by. I say, can I just take the tiniest peek inside your place? I love to see what people have done with their rooms. Oh, naughty Toulouses! I can tell you're the bohemian type.'

I did not know how to refuse him entrance and felt rather cross, because I had treated myself to Françoise Sagan's new novel, *A Certain Smile*, and was planning to eat my supper with the book propped in front of me, thus nourishing mind and body at once. Come to think of it, Montague Brown had a certain smile. It meant that he knew exactly what he wanted. I stepped back and he came in, treading accidentally on my foot in passing.

He was a long rambling young man who reminded me of Gulliver in Lilliput, or a giant puppet without its master. He seemed too far from his limbs to control them. Size and clumsiness were the first impression. But then I saw that on top of this shambling mountain was a long gentle face and a shock of babyish butter-coloured hair. His eyes were a washed-out blue, his expression mild and melancholy. He would have made a perfect White Knight for Alice. He had a wandering nose and a beautiful mouth, and was looking for someone to take care of him. Much later and much too late, I realised that people had been taking care of him all his life. I happened to be around when he was in need of a new nursemaid.

'Oh, snuff, snuff!' he said, nosing the air like an overgrown Bisto Kid. 'What a heart-rending smell!'

'Tinned spaghetti,' I said drily, and rescued my bread

from Helen's old electric toaster, which was disinclined to give up its contents.

'Not really? You must have done something terribly special to it.'

'Just added a chopped tomato and a sprinkle of grated cheese.'

'There you are, then. I can always tell. I've *hungered* after your cooking on the staircase. You had kippers fried in butter one night. My mouth was watering, positively *watering*. I've bought some sausages and that dried potato stuff, but I don't know what to do with them.'

'You fry the sausages and add water to the potato,' I said tersely, stirring my spaghetti to show him that my supper was ready and I wanted to be left alone.

He looked wistfully at me, and shuffled his enormous feet.

'I wish I knew how,' he said. 'But sausages always go black on me and those sort of potatoes get lumps of powder in them.'

He was not a scrounger, being prepared to contribute his share, but he intended someone else to cook for him. Half an hour later we were sitting in front of my gas-fire, eating spaghetti, sausages and mashed potato on toast.

He said, 'I lost a friend today. We were going to share a flat together, but he sent me a note. Not a very *nice* note, either. He said he couldn't live with perpetual optimism. He used to call me Pangloss Brown, but I took it as a compliment until another friend explained. I didn't know he was being hurtful. You see, Leila – Leila, may I call you Lady Lee? I may? Oh, what heaven! As I was saying, Lady Lee, I believe that life is here for our enjoyment and the Good Lord meant us to be happy. Do you?'

'That depends on whether life deals you a decent hand of cards or not,' I replied, making one of my father's favourite remarks. I followed it with one of my mother's. 'And I don't see how anyone can be happy if they're systematically starved or ill-treated – which applies to millions of people.'

'Oh let's not have the horrors,' said Montague Brown quickly. 'Let me tell you about the art of being happy. Did

78

you know that you could make wonderful things happen by accident?'

'How can they be accidents if you make them happen?' I asked, watching his guileless face in the glow of the gas fire.

'Oh, I can't go into great philosophical *discussions*,' he said plaintively, 'but it does work. It's called serendipity. Isn't that a sweet name?'

He did not wait for me to disappoint him this time, but hurried on.

'Take today for instance. Losing a friend and a flat. I'd had a terrible day. One of those days when you simply want to lie down and *die*. But I kept on thinking lovely positive things. And when I came in this evening I said to myself, "How about a nice long bath with a handful of lavender salts to cheer you up, you poor soul?" I often talk to myself as if I was somebody else. Do you do that? No? You should try it. It's awfully comforting. And when I reached our communal washpot, there was your notice, positively crying out *Friend, friend, friend*! And here we are. Friends. *That's* serendipity.'

He insisted on washing up and managed not to break anything. In fact he could be incredibly deft. I once watched him dressing a window for a summer sale, when he didn't know I was looking. His feet were moving carefully, shrouded in towels, knowing they had to behave themselves, and his hands were performing miracles, pinning dozens of butterflies on to a shimmering azure curtain. Quite a crowd of us collected eventually, fascinated by the contrast between art and artist, but he never noticed: an expert when he was absorbed, but outside the world of windows a social catastrophe.

I christened him Serendipity Brown, and called him Sep for short. He had grown skilful in the art of living on the outskirts of other people's lives and now he clung to mine, cleverly and not too tightly. He did not make the mistake of trying to own me. He guessed when I needed to be by myself or with other people, and would absent himself a while. But he was always there in my background, waiting to come forward. I bossed him about a great deal and enjoyed my power over him. It was some time before I realised that it was he who had power over me, as the weak always do over the strong.

Released from Helen's routine of invitations and appointments and arranged dinner parties, I enjoyed an infinite number of acquaintances, and acquaintances should not be undervalued. I watched and sketched the passing show, for I love shows but I like them to pass. Each day had a surprise in store. I was crowned with youth, ignorance and single blessedness, and I had a father who gave me a modest allowance while I found my way in the world.

Looking back I wonder how I dared, but my faith in myself was absolute, and materially speaking life had not failed me so far. I had never gone hungry, homeless or uncared for. And any rags I owned were artistic, and worn by choice.

Zoe

8

When the war began I, Zoe, was seven, and my sister Leila was five. Ours was a wholly feminine household, like so many thousands of others with the man of the house away, and though my mother was our shield and buckler and we were safe in her, we learned that life was not a safe business. After the London Blitz, though we were only on its outskirts, we had nightmares, my sister and I. Leila dreamed of being trapped in a bombed building. I dreamed that I was walking towards home, and on turning the corner of a familiar street found myself in an unknown place.

At that time we slept in a double bed curled up together like a couple of commas, with Leila's bottom in my stomach, and the fear of one transmitted itself to the other. Hearing us shrieking either 'Let me out! Let me out!' or 'Where am I? Where am I?' and a cry of 'Mummy, mummy, Lulu's/Zo's having a bad dream!' she would hurry into the room bringing reassurance and a nightlight, and settle us down again. As we grew older and the war ended, our fears subsided. The return of my father in 1945, the excitement of rebuilding his business and recreating Whitegates, and the feeling that life was henceforth for us and before us, wiped the shadow away.

Now, many years later, I was living through another bad dream, which took the form of a large and stately woman with fine white hair drawn into a bun on the nape of her neck, a cold handsome face, and clothes which were once expensive and in formal good taste. The name of my

83

day-and-nightmare was Mrs Montrose, who had begun a systematic campaign to get us out of our flat.

At first she attempted to persuade me with what I thought was kindness, waylaying me in the hall as I returned from an afternoon's shopping with Simon.

'Ah, it *is* you, Mrs Barber! I thought I heard you pulling that heavy pram up the steps. I was saying only the other day that you modern young mothers have far too much to do. Of course, living in India with plenty of money and servants, I suppose I was particularly fortunate.'

I felt my legs trembling and leaned on the handle of the pram to steady myself.

'I was saying to Arthur only the other day, poor Mrs Barber has to carry baby and shopping and washing up and down all those stairs, and it can't be good for her health. You really should be in a self-contained ground-floor flat like mine.'

She always said 'mine', not 'ours', though her good-natured, red-faced husband lived with her.

I had got my breath back and agreed with her that this would be far more convenient. In my innocence then, I wondered whether they were leaving and she was giving us an opportunity to ask the landlord before he found another tenant. The rent was thirteen shillings a week more than ours, but it might be managed.

She said, smiling, icily civil, 'Is baby asleep at last? Then why not come in and have a cup of tea with us? My son sends it regularly from Ceylon, you know. You simply cannot buy the same quality in the shops here. Arthur! Mrs Barber is coming to take tea with us, dear!'

I heard him shambling round their little kitchenette, as I skirted several pieces of ponderous carved furniture and sat at the beaten-brass table. I was grateful for the tea, and even more grateful to have it provided. Simon's birth had debilitated me, and despite iron tablets and a glassful of Sanatogen a day I still felt like a soft toy from which the stuffing had been removed. The early delights of living with Matthew in two rooms of our own had dwindled. Simon's needs and demands, Simon's accoutrements, swallowed up space and privacy. Things we had once giggled about, lying in our world of bed together, now menaced us. As soon as I came home from the hospital Matthew had written a letter to Mr Pescod the landlord, which I felt was frank rather than diplomatic, to complain of the leaking roof, rotting window-frames and inadequate plumbing. A month later, having no reply, he fired a second missive into the void. In answer we received a badly typed letter which told us that Mr Pescod was looking into the matter. He had, of course, done nothing since.

Warmed by Ceylon tea, a four-bar electric fire which kept the room at hothouse temperature ('We feel the cold, you see, dear, after India!') and her seeming sympathy, I confided our difficulties. She patted my hand.

'You need a ground-floor flat,' she repeated. 'Leave no stone unturned to find one. It shouldn't be too difficult. There is so much redevelopment going on. Why, only yesterday I saw an advertisement in the *Evening News*. You remember, Arthur, that I said this would just suit Mr and Mrs Barber?'

He roused himself, murmuring, 'Oh yes, my dear, I recollect you did.'

'Then would you like to find it for me, dear?' she reminded him, her smile fixed.

He pulled himself out of his easy chair obediently and shuffled off to hunt through the paper rack.

'Three pounds ten shillings a week. Or was it four guineas?'

The prices appalled me. Worse still, I realised that I had mistaken her intention. She was not moving. She wanted us to move. The raw sensitivity of a nursing mother betrayed me. I pulled out a handkerchief and blew my nose, trying to wipe my eyes at the same time so that she should not notice my tears.

But she said, smoothly, pityingly, 'My dear, I have been a mother myself. I know what you are going through. You have not the strength to sustain yourself. Arthur! A glass of sherry for Mrs Barber.'

I was shaken by sobs as violent as hiccups, tears leaving

snail-tracks down my cheeks, while Arthur stood patiently and kindly by, holding out last night's evening newspaper and a small glass of sweet dark Oloroso. When my grief had subsided Mrs Montrose patted my hand and gave me practical advice.

'I notice that you take baby for a walk after lunch, unless the weather is poor. But the thing to do, my dear, is to go in the morning and buy the first edition of the evening paper. I believe it comes out at twelve o'clock. Mark down any possible flats and telephone at once. That's the only way to find one – unless someone gives you a hint that they're moving themselves. I'll ask around among people I know, and Arthur will also do his bit. Between us, my dear, we'll leave no stone unturned until you're settled more comfortably. And now, dear, I think I hear baby crying, so drink up your sherry, we mustn't keep you . . . '

In our own rooms, feet up on one chair, sitting back in another, feeding Simon and drinking one of my compulsory pints of barley water to help me to make the milk, I looked back on the past hour with astonishment and apprehension. Mrs Montrose had persuaded me to a course of action which I knew Matthew would not countenance. Indeed, we had produced this baby on my pleading and against his better judgement. Having sworn that I could manage in this flat for at least two years, how was I to turn round now and say I could not?

In my present weak state, the thought of being divided between opposing camps frightened me. Anxious to appease both sides I said nothing to Matthew, but went out with Simon the following morning and bought the first edition of the evening paper. Only three of the flats advertised approximated to our financial condition, and even these would be slightly more than we could afford. I telephoned each number. All of them had been taken.

As I hauled the pram up the three front steps Mrs Montrose was watering geraniums in her front window. She set down her little spouted brass jug and opened her door just as I came breathless into the hall.

'Any luck, my dear?' she asked brightly.

A coward, I said, 'Three. But they'd all gone.'

'Keep your pecker up!' she said, smiling. 'You're going about it the right way.'

Once started, she would not let me stop. Like a French concierge she kept an eye on my incomings and outgoings and monitored my progress. Whether she ever tried to find accommodation for us I don't know. Certainly, she never mentioned anything. Knowing I could do nothing without Matthew's approval, and becoming afraid of the manner in which she lay in wait and questioned me, I began to avoid her as best I could. She must have grown suspicious. One evening she made it her business to be in the hall when Matthew came home. I had been collecting nappies from the clothes-line after a wet October day, and walked in from the garden to hear her greet him.

'Oh, Mr Barber. I was just about to climb the stairs with the evening paper for your dear wife. You'll be able to save me the trouble.'

'Very kind of you,' said Matthew vaguely. 'But Zoe usually buys one.'

'Oh yes, the first edition. But this is the third one, and Arthur has found just the flat you're looking for. He marked it for you. There! Look!'

'I know nothing about a flat,' said Matthew. 'We're not thinking of moving.'

He sounded annoyed and puzzled. Her voice rose, brittle and cold as an icicle in the cold dark hall.

'Oh, but I understood you were. Your wife confided in me about your little difficulties with the landlord, and I have been trying to help her. You must understand that your wife is close to breakdown, Mr Barber. She simply cannot manage under her present conditions.'

In the darkness of the downstairs corridor I stood numb and dumb, clutching my basket of damp washing.

Matthew said quite sharply, 'This is the first I've heard of it.'

Her voice was ice and honey, and for the first time I recognised her, not as an interfering neighbour with good intentions, but as an enemy.

'Your wife is a dear sweet girl. She wouldn't want to worry you. But I assure you, and Arthur will bear me out, that we have had that poor girl crying in our sitting room before now, not knowing which way to turn.'

There was a silence. Then Matthew mumbled something about appreciating her kindness, and took the stairs two at a time.

When her door had shut I tiptoed through the hall and followed him.

He was standing there in his old overcoat, dark forelock over one eye, glasses slightly crooked, looking young and lost, but when I came in he turned on me furiously.

'What's all this about looking for a flat? And why tell Mrs Montrose our private business? She says you're ill, that you've been crying in front of her. I felt such a damned fool, standing there, not knowing what she was on about.'

I should have admitted that Mrs Montrose had dragooned me into this situation in a weak moment. But at that period of my life I was not in control of anything, let alone myself. Instead, I tried to persuade him that this was a good idea.

'I just thought that as we hadn't enough space and the landlord won't do repairs, I might look round for something more suitable. At our sort of price, of course. It was to be a surprise.'

'It certainly damned well was! Why do all this behind my back? Why not discuss it with me?'

Trapped by my own weakness I answered him too sharply.

'Because you wouldn't listen! I thought if I could find something reasonable you might think about it.'

'And have you found anything at all for two pounds ten shillings a week, which is what we pay here?'

He had me, and he knew it. He threw the third edition of the *Evening News* down in front of me. Arthur's fountain-pen had scored a cross into the cheap paper. The ink had run into the shape of a spider.

He quoted derisively, '"Ground-floor flat with access to garden. Two rooms, kitchenette and bathroom. Three guineas weekly." That's virtually what we have already – apart from the stairs.'

I recognised the legal tone. He was on to me, harrying me, pinning me down, nosing out the truth.

'We haven't got a bathroom to ourselves!' I cried defensively. 'We'd be self-contained. And three guineas isn't much more.'

'It's thirteen shillings a week more. Could you manage a cut like that in your housekeeping?'

I was silent, because I could not.

'Then why expect me to find it? You know how tight our commitments are.'

I could not please Mrs Montrose, fight him and feed a three-month-old baby. I capitulated.

'All right, then. Let's drop the subject, Mat. We won't discuss moving.'

His pride was hurt, and I had discovered that when Matthew was hurt he hit back as hard as he could.

He shouted, 'I told you from the beginning that it was mad to have a baby in these conditions. But, oh no, you won't listen. You've got the Golden Girl mentality – ask and it shall be given. Were you expecting Daddy to come up with a nice little house as soon as we produced a grandson for him?'

In a turmoil of fear and anger, I cried, 'That's not fair, Matthew. I expected no such thing.'

'Then let me tell you this. If he did I wouldn't take it. He may be used to lording it over you and your mother and sister, but he won't run my life for me. And in future don't tell anyone our business. I won't have it. Is that understood?'

Aroused by our voices and his inner clock, Simon woke up and shrieked with the shocking suddenness of a train whistle.

Matthew clapped both hands over his ears in a manner I recognised as being over-dramatic, and hated.

'And there's that damned kid yelling again. I'm half asleep at work because I can't sleep at night. And when I get home there's no comfort. Just look at the place. Full of kids' stuff and wet nappies. And that old snob in the hall telling me I can't look after my wife properly. Right! That's it! I'm going out.'

'Where to?' I cried, catching at his sleeve as he brushed past me.

He twitched his sleeve away, pale with temper, and did not answer.

Seeking a way to his heart, I made an offering to his stomach.

'Matthew, we've got a treat tonight. I've made you a steak and kidney pie.'

'Have you?' he said. 'I thought you said that we could only afford mince on the housekeeping money?'

'I've been saving up threepenny bits . . . '

He snatched his briefcase and went.

Simon was shrieking in short sharp bursts. It was six o'clock. Feeding time. I picked him up and cried while he sucked nourishment from me.

At half-past seven, burped, topped and tailed, changed and put down he fell asleep. I percolated a pot of coffee, hoping that Matthew would come back, because this was the time we usually ate.

At half-past eight I decided not to cook the steak and kidney pie until tomorrow. I warmed up the coffee and made myself a cheese sandwich.

At half-past nine Simon woke up, demanding his feed early.

'Be firm!' my mother said, when I came home from the hospital. 'If you don't teach a baby that food comes at regular intervals you won't train him properly, and you'll be making a rod for your own back.'

For Leila and I had been reared by the Truby King method. And, as usual, I had conformed beautifully and Leila had brought my mother to the point of nervous breakdown.

'But I would not let her win,' my usually gentle mother said. 'I let her scream. It is essential to form good habits.'

So I sat glancing at my wristwatch every five minutes, hands clenched, waiting and listening. By ten o'clock Simon was hysterical and sucked so ravenously that he brought up the milk whenever he paused, and I was crying again with misery and exhaustion.

At eleven o'clock, when I had mopped us both up and restored us to order, I heard Matthew climbing the stairs. But by that time I had been beaten too badly to acknowledge his entrance, and sat with my back to him, rocking the baby in my arms, staring into the long shining bar of the electric fire.

He said humbly, sweetly, 'Sorry, Zo. Didn't mean to lose my wool.'

Clearing a space on the small table by my nursing chair, he laid down a peace-offering of violets between the bottle of Nurse Harvey's Gripe Water and the roll of cottonwool.

He said, 'Sorry I was rotten about your steak and kidney pie. I think you're bloody wonderful with the pittance I give you. Don't know how you do it.'

I managed to nod, first at the little cold purple flowers and then at him. We seemed to be a long distance from that enchanted July day when he promised to love, honour and cherish me. I tried to be generous.

'Have you had anything to eat?'

'Oh, I dropped in at Mum's place and shared a meal with them.'

That spelled disloyalty to me. He had said wounding things about my father.

He read my expression and absolved his treachery by adding, 'I didn't tell them we'd had a row. I said you were over at Whitegates. They sent their love.'

'What did you have to eat?'

'Some sort of minced meat concoction. It was decent of her to feed me at short notice, but she doesn't cook like you, Zo. Too much water in it!'

His tentative compliment restored me.

'Are you still hungry? Would you like anything now?'

'Yes, I would rather. I'm as hungry as hell. No, don't get up, Zo. I'll cook us something,' he added quickly.

But Matthew, though willing, could only warm up tins

91

of food and make toast. Mentally, I surveyed the contents of the larder and found it wanting, apart from eggs and cheese.

'If you'll put Simon down in his cot I'll grill us a Welsh rarebit each.'

He took the baby from me gently, deftly.

Walking through to the bedroom he said over his shoulder, 'If I had more time I'd help you more, Zoe, but I'm trying to build up a good future for us.'

And so he was. No one could work harder than Matthew, and he never missed an opportunity for advancement.

'I know that, Mat. I do understand.'

We were healing each other. My spirits rose as I found a tomato in the bottom of a paper bag. I added an egg to the cheese mixture, cooked two majestic rarebits, trimmed them with parsley and grilled tomato, and brewed more coffee. I laid two trays with green linen napkins. I found a long slim wine-glass for the violets. My mother had taught Leila and me how to make much with little.

'Ah! The magic touch of Whitegates!' cried Matthew cheerfully, rubbing his hands. 'I like that. Zoe, one day I shall find us a house even bigger and better than Whitegates. One day I'll put a blank cheque in your hands and tell you to buy whatever we need, and nothing but the best.'

As we finished the last mouthful he said, grinning like a naughty schoolboy, 'Mum would never let me eat this sort of thing late at night. She always said it was indigestible. But it's a picnic, isn't it? That's one of the things I like about being married to you, Zo. We have treats, don't we? Even if I do lose my rotten bad-tempered old wool from time to time.'

I leaned forward and kissed him on the mouth, and I could feel his lips smiling beneath mine.

'You taste indigestibly delicious!' I said.

'So do you.'

Lying in bed afterwards, holding each other and thinking, we talked about the possibility of another flat, and Matthew said he should be getting fifty pounds a year more next October, and then we could move.

As I came carefully down the last flight of stairs, arms full
of Simon and his pram bedding, Mrs Montrose opened her
door and put a finger to her lips. Though I had been quiet
enough I tiptoed down the final three stairs, and whispered
my query.

'Is anything wrong, Mrs Montrose?'

'It's Arthur, dear. He's just taking a little nap. He's
had a broken night.'

I was afraid of her. My heartbeat quickened. I knew
what was coming and pretended not to understand.

'Oh, poor Mr Montrose. I am sorry. What's wrong?'

She smiled in chill disbelief, saying, 'I should have
thought you need not ask. Surely you didn't get much
sleep yourselves, did you?'

I looked at the serene and sleeping face of my son.

'It was only the once,' I said humbly. 'Just between
two and three o'clock. He was all right when I'd fed him.'

'Dear little fellow,' said Mrs Montrose unfeelingly. 'You
see, my dear, you young people can take that sort of thing
in your stride, but we old things must have our rest. Once
Arthur was awake he couldn't get back. And then he
disturbed me, and my health, as you know, is not good.'

'I'm terribly sorry. I really am. I do my best to keep
Simon quiet at night.'

'But he cries during the day, too. He cries such a
great deal. I wonder, have you taken the advice of a
more experienced person?'

Furious, helpless, I tried to placate her and defend myself.

'Yes, I have. I've asked the clinic, my doctor, my
mother. I've tried all sorts of remedies. The clinic says
that it's infant colic. It's only while his tummy's settling
down. But he's much better than he used to be.' I
remembered the stern rulings of Truby King. 'And it
isn't good for babies to be picked up every time they
cry.' Her expression forced me to add, 'Of course, I
didn't realise you could hear him from the top of the
house.'

'Oh yes. The sound carries. Quite piercing at times. And

93

poor Miss Babbage is directly underneath you. Though of course she would never complain.'

I apologised again, trying to muffle the sound of the pram being eased out of the front door.

As I negotiated the top step she said brightly, 'Never mind, my dear, you'll soon find a more convenient place. How's the flat-hunt going?'

I slipped and almost fell. When I had regained control of my feet and the wheels I looked back and she was standing in the doorway unconcerned, waiting for an answer.

I said, 'I'm afraid we've had to give up that idea. We simply can't afford to move for another year. But next year we shall be looking round again.'

Her brightness disappeared. She went inside without speaking.

I gave Simon his bath in the mornings, and we were at the slippery stage, reaching round for a clean towel, when I heard a knock at the door and a conspiratorial voice announced itself as being 'Only Mr Coombes, dear. Calling on be'alf of the landlord.'

Simon was coming out of his three-monthly colic stage and the Sanatogen was having a beneficial effect on me. The tone made me smile.

I called out cheerfully, 'Are you a family man, Only Mr Coombes? If so, please walk in. If not I must warn you that I have a naked baby in my lap!'

The voice, husky and confidential, assured me that Mr Coombes had fathered three of his own, and his daughter was expecting her first any day now.

A bowler hat appeared, followed by a lugubrious face and a long drooping moustache. As I indicated a chair he sat down opposite and removed the hat, leaving a damp red line across his forehead where it had lodged. He made clucking noises to amuse Simon, who ignored him, and cleared his throat.

'I won't be a minute,' I mumbled, safety pin in mouth.

'Take your time, dear. Take your time.'

Taking his own time, he put on a pair of metal-rimmed

spectacles, brought out a small black cloth notebook and studied it.

I made a neat turkish parcel of my son's lower regions, tied up the back bows of his Chilprufe gown, threaded his arms through his cardigan sleeves, brushed his hair into a quiff, and sat him up dressed, smart and proud.

'Now, Mr Coombes,' I said, at peace with the world, 'what can I do for you?'

He repeated confidentially, 'I've come on be'alf of the landlord, Mrs Barber.'

'Oh, is it about the leaks in the roof, or the plumbing?' I asked hopefully.

His voice was pained and hushed.

'Not exactly, Mrs Barber. No, I wouldn't say that exactly. But it is a complaint. Well, one or two complaints actually.'

I patted Simon's back absently, and said, 'Oh yes?'

'Number One Complaint. I'm sorry to say that it's come to Mr Pescod's notice that you keep the hinfant's pram in the 'all. I'm afraid that's not allowed.'

If he had emptied Simon's wash bowl over my head I could not have been more surprised or shocked.

'But where else can we keep it?' I asked. I thought of the bank clerk in the basement. 'And what about Mr Connolly's bicycle? Has anyone complained about that?'

'Oh, the landlord agreed to the bicycle when Mr Connolly first come here. But when you and Mr Barber come here there was no talk of a pram in the 'all.'

'But we had no baby when we first came here.'

He consulted his notebook again and continued as if I had not spoken. 'Number Two Complaint. The baby's washing. Drying nappies in the bathroom and hanging them in the garden. Which is all communal property.'

I reflected that Mrs Montrose must have coerced poor Miss Babbage into agreement, for the bathroom was shared between us.

'There is a clothes-line in both the bathroom and the garden which no one else uses. I thought it was all right to use them myself.'

Mr Coombes shook his finger at me.

'No 'ogging the clothes lines!' he said, and consulted the notebook again.

'Number Three Complaint. The baby crying. Keeps the other tenants awake. And con-stant commo-tion,' he read these two words so carefully that I guessed they were a quotation from the complainant, 'on the staircase and in the 'all, owing to the baby and the washing and the pram being taken in and out.' He quoted again, bending over the words to get them right, 'And con-stant dis-tur-bance by day and by night.'

Simon had fallen asleep, arms outflung, a picture of peace and plenty.

'Is he disturbing anyone at this moment?' I asked sarcastically.

Mr Coombes glanced over the top of his spectacles and said reproachfully, 'Nothink personal in this, dear. I'm just doing my job.' And returned to it with, 'The landlord 'as considered these Complaints, and 'is opinion is that a top-floor flat is hun-suitable for the re-quire-ments of a married couple with a young baby. The rent being paid monthly, 'e suggests you look round for something more con-ven-ient, and give a month's notice of same as soon as possible. Meanwhile, Mrs Barber, 'e suggests you put the pram in the garden shed, stop 'ogging of the clothes-lines, and keep the baby quiet.'

He returned the notebook to his pocket, the metal-rimmed spectacles to their case, and the bowler hat to his head.

The small world I called our home had become a hostile place.

'He's throwing us out?' I cried, aghast.

'Not at all, dear. Mr Pescod is a 'umane gentleman, and hunderstands as it might take two or three months. But 'e wants you to start looking round now.' He slipped into landlord jargon. 'And hif you fail to comply then further steps must and will be taken.'

'It's only a month until Christmas. We're very unlikely to find something in mid-winter, aren't we?'

Mr Coombes stood to his full height, which was not great.

He spoke in sorrow rather than anger, 'Like I said, dear. Nothink personal. But we 'ave to look after our tenants. And the others 'ave been 'ere longer, and are not likely to go helsewhere.'

'It was Mrs Montrose who wrote that letter of complaint, wasn't it?'

'I'm not at liberty to say, Mrs Barber. I'll let myself out.'

When I had finished crying I wrapped myself and Simon up warm, and crept downstairs in my stockinged feet. The weather was not in a friendly mood but I preferred to be buffeted by wind rather than worries. Holding my breath I sidled the pram down the steps and put on my shoes. But she was not waiting, though she might have been watching from behind the long lace curtains. For the time being, she had shot her bolt.

Matthew took the situation personally, as a blow to his pride and a reflection on his ability to provide for us. He forbade me to tell my parents that we had been given notice, and would not tell his own.

'This is our problem and we deal with it by ourselves,' he said. 'Of course, there's no harm in telling them that we're looking for a larger flat. But make it sound as if it's our choice. No more crying and confiding, Zoe. I won't have my business broadcast all over the place.'

I made the mistake of arguing with him.

'But why shouldn't we tell our family and friends how urgent it is? Surely, we need all the help and sympathy and moral support we can get? After all, it's not our fault that we've been given notice.'

'It leaves a bad impression. Makes us sound incompetent, undesirable. Makes us sound like penniless squatters.'

'Honestly, Mat, I cannot agree with you.'

His temper was quick to rise.

'I don't give a tinker's cuss whether you agree or disagree. Just do as I say. If I've learned nothing else in my profession I've learned that appearances do matter, and that it's absolutely necessary to stay in control of a situation. The last thing I want or need is pity for the mess I'm in.'

I dared say, 'Not pity. Sympathy. And the mess that *both* of us are in, if you don't mind. Or have you forgotten that I'm in this too?'

Matthew in happier circumstances gave the impression of being a shy young man. Under stress he paled into a demon.

He shouted, 'If you're in a mess then it's your own damned fault. The baby was not my choice. All I wanted to do was to get on with my work.'

I loved him even though I was angry with him, but at that moment I heard hatred in his voice when he spoke about Simon and me, and I was appalled.

When I could speak I said, 'Let's not quarrel, Mat. If we're not going to confide in anyone then we've only got each other.'

'Yes, I'm sorry,' he replied curtly, as if the apology were a matter of expediency. 'We must have a plan of campaign. We must work together on this.'

But of course he had an exacting job to do, so the task of finding new accommodation fell mostly to me. I planned my daily routine round flat-hunting, and now I had Matthew driving me instead of Mrs Montrose.

Keeping the pram in the shed meant a long trip down the side-alley and up the garden path. That grey coach-built Dunkerley had been my pride and joy. Now, like me, it bowed to the inevitable. With the approach of winter the coachwork became spotted with mould, the inside was so clammy that I was afraid of Simon catching cold, and the metal parts started to rust.

Banned from bathroom and garden, the baby washing filled our flat twenty-four hours a day. Whichever way I turned there were obstacles. Simon's infant colic had gone and he was sleeping better at night. But after a brief interval he began to cut his teeth, and we started all over again. Desperate to find a solution, and to get away from a place I had once loved and now dreaded, I went out morning and afternoon, following up every lead and contacting anyone who might help.

If I had to find a single image for that crisis in my life it would be of me walking the friendless London streets in winter, pushing Simon's pram, afraid to go back to the flat.

9

1956

That January was the coldest for nearly sixty years. The electric fire made little impression on the living room and the bedroom was a refrigerator. The only reasonable place was the kitchenette. I would light the gas oven and warm myself in front of it. Simon cried whenever I changed him, and his little fists were mottled with cold. Now the weather was a more terrifying enemy than my environment. I made two hot-water bottles for the pram and forced myself out on the daily flat-hunt. Unable to sit anywhere outside, or to afford the heat of a café, I hurried back as soon as I could.

Every event conspired against us. Christmas, instead of a family celebration, had become a family battleground of Barbers versus Gideons. This year it was to be the Barbers' festival, if such a word could be used in connection with my parents-in-law. By this time Marian had realised that my mother's hospitality would always far outdistance her own in art and loving kindness, and her resentment came out in the form of spiked apologies.

'Of course, I know we can't provide worldly luxuries like your dear clever Mummy, but Edmund and I always say that it's the *spirit* of Christmas that counts. And, my dear,' taking one of my hands in both of hers, which used to touch me and now annoyed and disturbed me, 'and *love*. All the luxuries in the world can't cover a lack of *love*. Can they?'

And I, who used to think that my father was inclined to cynicism, would conjure up his worldly face and worldly words and worldly goods as an antidote to such artificial sweetness.

So Matthew and Simon and I returned to our martyrdom as comfortless as before, and weary with the effort of pretending to enjoy ourselves. New Year should have been a Whitegates celebration, and to this I looked forward so much that I crossed off days on the calendar like a child. Then my mother went down with influenza, and we were warned off. Like a child I cried from utter disappointment.

Matthew, standing behind me in the kitchenette, nursing the baby while I wiped my eyes and nose and made tea for us, said miserably, 'We've got to get out of here, but I don't know how. You see, Zo, this flat was a snip. Oh, it has its drawbacks but there's nothing on the market now to touch it for price. If we're honest with ourselves we must admit that the sort of family accommodation we need will be in the region of four guineas a week. Old Abercrombie at the office says we should buy, not rent. Houses are the best investment. But I told him we had no capital, nothing to invest.'

He hesitated, finding his way through this particular thicket. 'Zo, I lost my wool about the idea of your father helping out, but who else do we know? I mean if it's a matter of my bloody personal pride then I shall just have to swallow it. Zo, do you think your father could put up a deposit? Lend us a few hundred, on a proper financial basis.'

As I didn't answer straightaway, remembering how hurtful he had been, he said quickly, 'I could pay him back in a few years. He'd get his interest meanwhile. And it would give us the start we needed. Get us over that initial hurdle.'

As I remained silent he said accusingly, 'You don't like the idea?'

I said, 'Not very much. No. But as you say, who else could do it?'

He looked more hopeful. This time I hesitated before I spoke.

'There's just one thing, Mat. Would you let *me* ask him, via Mummy?'

Now his face cleared. He pushed back his lock of hair, pushed up his glasses, smiled on me.

He said, 'I was going to say, actually, that you should make the suggestion, and via Helen. Women are so much better at these things than men.' Then he jigged Simon up and down and nuzzled his neck, singing, 'Bye Baby Bunting, Daddy's gone a-hunting!'

Until the baby chuckled with delight and struck him on the nose with a wandering fist.

Then Matthew looked up at me, laughing, and said, 'You know how disappointed you were about missing our holiday at Whitegates? Well, as soon as Helen's better why don't you take Simon down and spend a week there by yourselves? You could bring up the subject quite naturally then. They're bound to ask how the flat-hunt is going.'

I nodded. My pleasure at the prospect of a holiday was somewhat marred by the underlying purpose. He watched my face and nursed the baby, warning me, reassuring me.

'But don't throw a wobbly on them, Zo. Play the situation down a bit. No dramatics. We want practical help. Not pity. And you needn't worry about me. I can manage here on my own. Just ring me in the evenings to report progress. I can always join you at the weekend if everything goes according to plan.'

I wished that he could have spoken of my father as I knew him: as a generous rather than a rich man. And I was sorry that we seemed to be plotting against him rather than coming out into the open and asking for assistance.

Leila was waiting for us on the platform, watching the carriages rumble past. Simon and I were in the last one, owing to Matthew getting us to the station late, and I watched her head turn from right to left and back again like a Wimbledon tennis fan. She was wearing a cherry pink trouser suit with big brass buttons, over which was slung a black wool cloak. Her hair flew in long pale wisps from beneath an orange tam o'shanter. A mustard-yellow scarf and mittens completed the outfit.

I whispered into Simon's soft cheek, 'That artistic vision on the platform is your one and only aunt!'

She saw us. A shriek brought everybody, and seemingly the train as well, to a halt. Waving wildly she began to run towards us, calling out our private business to the world.

'Zo! Zo! We've got *the* pram for Simon. Our own original sit-up-and-beg pram. Every bit of twenty-three years old and you'd never know. Mummy got it back from the last borrower and had it refurbished . . . '

She was level with the carriage now, obstructing a chivalrous city gentleman who was trying to let us out and take our baggage.

' . . . in navy-blue to match the coachwork . . . '

'Lulu! Darling! If you'll just let this gentleman – *Thank you so much. So very kind* – Lulu! Will you please stand back?'

'Oops! Sorry!'

She disarmed the man with a wide crooked smile, and stood politely aside, while he brought us safely to the platform. As he departed, lifting his hat, she came forward, grinning, stood on tiptoe and hugged us both.

'Hello, you!' she said to Simon, as from one child to another.

Then on to her news again like a dog to its bone.

'The old navy-blue pram, Zo! I thought it had died years ago. But there it is looking terribly Royal Family, waiting in the hall. Daddy pretends to make a fuss about it, but actually he's thrilled to bits. We all are. It'll be so lovely to have you both to ourselves for once.'

She registered the gaffe in passing, but let it go by with a little smile which was half pleasure and half embarrassment. I knew she was not fond of Matthew. My mother thought she was jealous of him, but it went deeper than that. Well, I had learned much in the past two and a half years. Making do with in-law relationships was part of marriage. So I let the remark go by me, too. Besides I was longing to throw off my responsibilities, to be a beloved daughter at home again.

Leila was chattering on.

'As soon as Helen told me you were coming I invited me and a friend down for a few days. We're both out of work after Christmas.'

Settling into Helen's little car, I said, 'Who's the friend?'

'Oh, a fellow lodger called Serendipity Brown. You'll adore him. No need to look coy and hopeful, Zo. It isn't *lerv*. Tell me, why do crooners pronounce love as *lerv*. I've often wondered. No, Sep's not interested in women, except as friends. But he's fallen respectfully in love with Helen and is dancing attendance on her this moment. I couldn't tear him away. Whether I'll ever get him home again depends on the strength of kick Cass administers to his backside.'

She shot away from the kerb with more dash than skill. My father had taught us both to drive, but neither of us possessed cars, so we were always out of practice.

'You're looking a bit pensive,' she remarked to the road ahead. 'No luck with the flat-hunting?'

I was pleased to see her but dismayed at the way she had transformed a personal homecoming into a general party. I had been thinking of quiet private hours with my mother, talks full of wisdom, silences full of understanding, sleep full of healing, and a gradual building up of energy and self-confidence until the moment was right to ask that important question.

'Not so far,' I admitted. 'The winter is a bad time.'

'Cass was saying that the sort of flat you needed would be the best part of five pounds a week, and why spend that much money in rent when you could get a good mortgage instead.'

Unwittingly, she had dashed me again.

'We haven't the capital for a deposit,' I said, so discouragingly that she was silent until I made another remark. 'Do tell me about yourself and this Septimus Brown.'

She brightened up again.

'Actually, my name for him is Serendipity, Zo. Sep for short. Oh well, never mind. Helen calls him Septimus too.

And he answers just the same. He's simply a great baby who attaches himself to any available apron strings or – in my case – smock hems. I look after him, and in his way he looks after me. End of story.'

It seemed unsatisfactory to me, unfinished, futureless, like all her male friendships. She took no man seriously, and chose men who would not or could not take her seriously either. I set it down to the Jeremy Purchase affair, which my mother said had been traumatic.

Lulled by the atmosphere, Simon's eyes were closing, his hands unfolding.

'And how's the work going?' I asked.

She lit up then.

'Oh, I finished such a lovely commission just before Christmas. Illustrating a children's book. It's called *The Fly-Away Balloon*. It'll be published in the autumn. I'll give you a copy. It'll do for Simon when he grows up a bit. Written by a man who might be a retired admiral. You know the type. Bluff. Distinguished. Public school. In his fifties. But the gentleman's imagination is none of those things. He writes quite weird and wonderful tales with a magic element. We clicked immediately. They're the best thing I've done since my diploma work. Makes a change from the hack stuff. I wish he'd write another.'

Her eyes lost their glitter. She brooded.

'How unusual that a retired admiral should write children's books,' I said absently, more to myself than to her.

Then she sparked up and at me.

'I didn't say he *was* an admiral, just that he looked the type. Actually he runs an antique shop with his wife, and writes in his spare time.'

'Oh, he's married, then?'

For I had been wondering if.

'Yes, he's joined in awful wedlock,' said Leila scathingly. 'They're stuck with each other. Glued together by habit and possessions.'

'Oh!' I said, comprehending that the man was right but the situation was not.

105

'And don't go oh-ing me in that understanding way. It's his problem, not mine. *I* don't want to marry him, and I don't want his possessions either.'

I could not make up my mind whether she had begun an affair or was hovering on the brink of one. Either way it was an emotional dead end.

'And there's no other man around at the moment?'

'There are plenty of men around at any moment but they're not round me – apart from Sep. Oh, look!' as we turned in at the familiar white gates, narrowly missing one post. 'There he is – the useless heap!'

A smile touched her mouth which I recognised. Proud, possessive, irritated. The smile of a mother whose child is a poor thing, but her own.

An animated lamp-post was shambling towards us, waving its arms.

'Darlings!' Septimus cried. 'Mama sent me forth as a humble baggage-carrier. She didn't trust me with the coffee tray. Not after last night – wasn't that too awful, my dear, and weren't they sweet about the sugar basin! And she showed me how to cut out biscuits while you were gone, and we baked them. My first culinary triumph. We've tried one apiece, and they taste wonderful.'

'I forgot to tell you,' said Leila in an aside. 'He calls Helen Mama.' Then she nipped out of the car and said sharply but affectionately, 'Be quiet, you great ape. You'll wake the baby up. Come and meet my big sister. Best manners, mind!'

He wiped his hands on his trousers before offering one of them. His clasp was warm and surprisingly gentle for such a large young man.

He tried my name over to himself, radiating admiration, 'Zoe. Zoe. Zoe.' Then burst out, 'Oh, but you're a veritable earth goddess, like your Mama. And how very clever of her to call you Zoe. Did you know that Zoe meant life? That's a most serendipitous name.'

He turned to Leila, who was standing hands on hips, looking cynical, and said with childlike sincerity, 'I find your sister a truly beautiful person.'

'I thought you would,' she replied drily. 'So does everybody else. Now say something nice about her baby.'

He eyed Simon from a respectful distance, clasped his hands together beseechingly, and said to me, 'He looks an exceptionally fine specimen, Zoe darling, but please don't ask me to hold him. I'm absolutely *terrified* of babies. You see, they're so *small*.'

'Isn't Sep a perfect love?' said Leila, grinning unkindly. 'Doesn't he make you want to shelter him from the wicked world?'

I shared the feeling but would not join with her in teasing him. Divining this, he gave me a look of gratitude.

Then cried, 'But why are we standing in the cold? Let us bear the lady and her goodly son into the family mansion forthwith!'

And with an air of devotion he picked up two large suitcases and a folding pram as if they were weightless, and followed us into the house.

My mother said to me, after dinner, when Simon was asleep in our old nursery, and everyone was fed and wined and mellow, 'Daddy would like a private word with you in his study.'

The study was my father's chosen family council room, from which he issued edicts and listened to petitions. It was never included in a client's itinerary. Only our discussions over the years stirred its tranquillity. Here my sister and I had been received after the war to bring him up to date on our achievements, hopes and talents. Here Leila had brought her art folder to speak for her, and I had produced my domestic science reports and – Mummy's inspiration – his favourite chocolate cake. Here Matthew and I had come hand in hand, on a winter evening such as this, to ask permission to be engaged.

There were provisos, of course, in all these meetings. There were warnings and ifs and buts and whys and hows and wherefores, but I could never remember my father being angry with me or forcing me to a decision or denying me a wish outright. So I went in puzzled, but without trepidation, and found him drawing curtains to close out the night.

'Ah, Zoe!' he said, turning round and smiling as though I were a lovely surprise. 'Come and sit by the fire, my darling. Wonderful to have you home.'

He stood in front of the hearth and clasped his hands behind his back. His ugly–attractive face was genial. His mood was gentle. Treats then, were in store.

He came at once to the point, saying, 'We've been having a family confab. Putting two and two together and making five as usual. You've not said much about it, but we feel you've been having a bad time lately. Flat-hunting. We must do something about that.'

The opportunity I had planned to grasp was being freely given.

'It's a pity, in one way, that Matthew didn't come with you,' said my father judiciously, 'and then the three of us could have discussed this together.'

Knowing what he did not know, that my husband had put me out front to ask a favour, I felt again that it was a shabby business to plot for help instead of confiding and asking outright.

'Still, this is intended to benefit you most, Zoe, so perhaps it's better that you and I should talk it over first. Do you mind if I smoke?'

This was mere courtesy. He always smoked in his own study, and the ritual of selecting, smelling, shaking, listening to and finally lighting a cigar from the box of Havanas was all part of an interview with my father.

When he and cigar were at one he continued.

'I know of a property in Kent which would suit you, not just as a temporary measure but for the conceivable future. It's going cheap because it needs a thorough conversion. I'd be prepared to buy it for you, and gradually do it up.'

I heard Matthew shouting, 'You've got the Golden Girl mentality – ask and it shall be given. Were you expecting Daddy to come up with a nice little house as soon as we produced a grandson for him?'

My father translated my expression and said, 'I'm not

dispensing charity. The house would be an investment for me. The value of property always increases. And Matthew can pay me the rent you're paying at the moment for that heap in Clapham. He'll have other expenses, living so far from London. A season ticket to buy for one thing. That should soothe his pride. And the house will be worth his while in another way. It's a fine property, a good address, for a young solicitor on his way up the ladder.'

I looked down at my feet, half-pleased and half-ashamed.

'I have a personal reason for doing this, too,' he continued. 'I want to make sure that you and your children will have a roof over your heads, whatever happens to me – or to Matthew.' As I looked up quickly he said, 'I'm not being gloomy, Zoe, simply practical. Young men can die young. I'm certain that he'll live to a ripe old age, and so shall I. Meanwhile the property will remain in my custody until my death, and then be willed to you as your inheritance of my estate.'

I saw order, beauty and security for me and my children. I also saw a perpetual crown of thorns drawing beads of blood from my husband's brow.

To show my father how truly I appreciated and loved him, and truthfully to gain a few moments while I wondered what to say, I got up and hugged him.

Then I began, 'Daddy, although it's a wonderful idea . . . '

He chuckled to himself, as if he had been expecting this reaction, and said, 'Matthew wouldn't like his father-in-law to be his landlord?'

'It's not exactly that. But he has his own views about the sort of house he eventually wants to buy us.'

'I doubt he would quarrel with my choice of this one. Or do you mean he doesn't want a landlord who's an interior designer?'

'Something like that.'

'I shan't interfere with interior decoration. That's your business. You tell me what you want and I'll go along with it, though reserving the right to remark upon it if I think it's absolutely appalling! But anything in the way of structural alteration must be discussed with me, obviously.'

I patted his back, and laid my face against his shoulder. He smelled of Old Spice and cigars and good living. I wondered whether Matthew would refuse his offer. I suspected he would try to alter it in some way to suit himself and his pride. I also sensed that my father intended to have his own way.

I said the only thing I could say.

'Daddy, thank you very very much. As far as I'm concerned that's marvellous. But I must speak to Matthew first.'

'Of course,' he said easily, amicably, and kissed the top of my head. 'Of course you must, my darling. Ask him to join us for the weekend and we'll drive out and take a look at it. That'll make his mind up.'

I was aware, as with my sister, of an undercurrent of disapproval with regard to Matthew, and I was sorry. Still I clung to my father, prolonging the sense of childish dependence.

'Daddy! What does the house look like? What is it called?'

He was smiling into the top of my head. Whether his offer was accepted or rejected, he had won this round on points. Once again he was the benevolent ruler of my life, and I recognised the peculiar magic of that bond. He even teased me with an old childhood quiz game, holding me away from him, smiling, delighted with himself and my reaction.

'I'll tell you the name. You must guess what it looks like. The Old Rectory.'

'The Old Rectory? Oh, Daddy, what a perfect duck! Oh, Daddy!'

He laughed because I was so excited. His hearth-stance and the proposal were over. Time for relaxation. He sat down, patting the broad leather arm of the chair to indicate that I should sit by him. He drew on his cigar with deep enjoyment. He held up one hand before I could begin.

'No marks for saying it's in a village near a church-yard!'

I stared into the distance, trying to picture the house.

'No. That's fair enough. Now – let – me – see. "Old

110

Rectory" suggests a more convenient new rectory. Am I right?' He nodded. 'How new?'

'Nineteen-thirties and purely functional.'

'Has the Old Rectory been empty since then?'

'No, it's been used as a sort of way-station for evacuees and refugees. At the moment it's acting as a general dogsbody for community projects and meetings.'

'So it hasn't been a family home since the last rector left? And you say that it needs modernising? In that case I'd guess that it's large, cold and inconvenient. Has cellars as well as attics. One primitive bathroom upstairs and one equally primitive outside loo. Stone sinks and lots of stairs.'

He nodded, smiling.

I dared say, 'No electricity?'

He shook his head, and replied, 'There *is* electricity, but it's been there from the year dot. The whole place needs rewiring.'

'It's going to cost you a bomb to do it up!' I said, and giggled from a light heart, and squeezed his hand.

'That's my business, Missie! Now tell me why I like it! What century is it?'

I knew his preferences and answered with confidence.

'Eighteenth.'

'Early or late?'

I was about to say 'Late', but read his face.

'It *can't* be Queen Anne?'

He laughed and patted my cheek and asked why not.

'*Not* Queen Anne? Beautifully symmetrical? Bow-fronted sash windows either side of a porch? A fan-light over the front door? A gracious little flight of steps down to a gravel path?'

'All of that, plus a multitude of cracked panes and all the basement windows boarded up.'

'A lawn at the front with rose-beds? A kitchen garden at the back?'

'And ivy on the walls, which will have to come out. Trees obscuring light, which will have to be pruned back. The flower beds gone to seed and not a square inch of glass in the garden frames.'

'But Daddy! A Queen Anne rectory going for a song!'

He pointed his cigar at me.

'Remember this, my girl. In the business world you get what you pay for – if you're lucky. There are good reasons for every bargain, and most of them are waiting to be found out. Besides, we're not talking about a grand establishment or a national monument. Even when we've re-created it, it will be no more than a modest, pleasant country house. And it's forty miles from London, and inconveniently situated. You'll need some sort of transport to drive Matthew to and from the station and do your shopping. Nell and I are putting our heads together about that. We thought we might spring a small second-hand car as your joint Christmas and birthday presents for 1956. But this sort of housing venture takes time, money, energy, a lot of physical hard work and several years to come to fruition. Young Simon will be going to preparatory school before you can charge an entrance fee to see the Old Rectory in its glory.'

I felt as though my spirit had separated from my body and one part of me stood aside, watching the other marvel. For though a miracle had happened the miracle was fate that had long since been written. I was as sure of my home in the Old Rectory as I had been sure of my husband in Matthew. While my spirit floated from room to room and out into the summer garden my father was still talking practicalities.

'We'll reckon to start you off with the minimum of conveniences. A kitchen and bathroom fitted and a couple of rooms cleaned up so that you have somewhere to sleep and live. I shall rely on you two to do the decorating – no doubt you'll get help from inside and outside the family as well! I'll have the place rewired and the roof done sometime during the first year. The rest can be taken at a steady pace, a room at a time. I don't know why in God's name I'm doing this!' he cried, mocking himself. 'I tell you frankly that only a fool or an adventurer would take it on. Well, I was always a bit of both!'

I heard my voice, quick and high with excitement, saying, 'Daddy, I don't care what it costs – in terms of my effort, I mean, not your money! – we must get the house absolutely right. I'll study the period. I'll go round auctions and find things. I'll do anything to make it as beautiful as it must have been once.'

'There speaks my daughter!' he said, patting my hand. 'That's my girl!'

Then he called over his shoulder. 'You needn't crouch at the keyhole any longer, you lot. Come on in!'

And there were my mother and sister and the shambling Septimus, as delighted and garrulous as myself, bearing with them a bottle of Moët et Chandon. The contrast between past misery and present promise was too great. I plunged from exaltation to abject confession.

'Daddy, Mummy, I haven't told you. Matthew wanted to keep it secret, so promise you'll never say anything to him. He feels so badly about it. As if it's his fault. And of course it isn't. He does his very best for Simon and me. But we're not just moving because of inconvenience. We're being hounded out.'

I poured out words and tears indiscriminately.

'That terrible Mrs Montrose complained to the landlord and he sent a man round with a list of complaints. And I've done nothing but push the pram all over London looking for somewhere else to live, and I didn't know where we could go or what would become of us. And they made me keep the pram in a shed and it's going rusty. And I've had bad dreams. And Matthew and I did nothing but quarrel. And the flat was freezing cold. And the baby cried and cried. It's been a nightmare. I've never felt so frightened and so lonely in the whole of my life. It's the worst thing that's ever happened to me. And though I know that everything's going to be all right, and though it's awfully silly of me, I simply can't stop crying!'

My mother and sister hugged me, making incoherent noises of sympathy. My father lent me a clean white handkerchief and popped the champagne open. I came round in peace and dried my eyes. Then we raised our glasses to the Old Rectory.

Daddy had a client to see that evening, so the rest of us drifted into the sitting room after he had gone out and put more logs on the fire and settled down. And while Leila sketched, and Septimus sat enraptured in front of the television set, Mummy talked to me quietly and wisely.

'You mustn't feel hurt or angry with Matthew, darling. It's hard for a young man to find that he can't protect and provide for his wife as he'd like to, and I can quite understand why he didn't want any of us to know. And then, strictly between us, it's very difficult for him to have a father-in-law like Cass, who doesn't realise how dominating he can be. And men *will* compete with each other for power . . . '

Her voice was soft but my sister's ears were sharp.

' . . . and for the most beautiful women,' said Leila clearly, drily. 'And women compete with each other to marry the most powerful men, who then imprison them in a house and encumber them with children and possessions. And women then become servants to their husbands and homes and possessions. And so the world goes round. Why any of them bother I shall never know!'

There was a short pause.

My mother whispered, 'Don't take any notice of Lulu, darling. I think she's going through a bad patch. From what I can gather – the wrong sort of man again.' Aloud she said, 'I know that Matthew will love the Old Rectory, and of course it's the opportunity of a lifetime. Cass won't be able to make this sort of gesture as he approaches retirement . . . '

Leila did not look in our direction, but her smile was wider and more crooked than ever.

Only Septimus, absorbed and unhearing, said, 'I wish we could afford a television, Lady Lee. I could watch it all day. I think it's perfectly *riveting* . . . '

'In which case we're better without it,' said Leila briskly. 'Our time is money, remember. We have to work – not watch!'

'Of course, I don't want to sound as though the matter were settled,' my mother said, catching herself up, reproving herself. 'Naturally, we must wait for Matthew's reaction, and abide by his decision. Cass and I don't want you to feel that we're taking charge of your lives.'

114

But mentally I had burned Matthew's boats behind me. His approval had been forgotten. And he must follow the Gideon wake.

As we had been unhappy now we were happy. Dealing with Matthew's pride, and moving house from London to Kent in the April of 1956, were both accomplished with great skill and tact. I saw my parents in a different light, as partners in a mature marriage. They put forward their proposals delicately, and effaced themselves while Matthew made up his mind. When he decided in favour of the Old Rectory they were careful not to seem too pleased or relieved. And all subsequent consultations were held in Leila's absence, since her hostility could cause an imbalance, and Matthew had detested poor Sep on sight.

There were bad times. We had nearly three more months to live through in the Clapham flat, and the glory of any vision can fade a little when you begin to count its cost. Removal expenses, Matthew's season ticket and the upkeep of our future car, small and economical though it would be, seemed insuperable obstacles to overcome. Until the autumn, when Matthew was given his rise in salary, we should be poorer than we had ever been, so that the added income would save us rather than enrich us. Often I lay awake, feeling as trapped and frightened in this new situation as I had in the old one, wondering how on earth we should walk such a slender and perilous financial tightrope. Sometimes Matthew said bitter things.

'Of course, I know why your father's *really* doing this. He's cutting me down to size and taking you over at the same time.'

Then I would put aside my own fears to assuage his.

But our new life held so much hope that the 3 a.m. terrors gradually faded. My father and his solicitors, latterday musketeers – quite unlike Matthew's dear old Watson, Lucas and Abercrombie – slashed right and left at property red tape. The Old Rectory was in our hands by the end of February. By the end of March workmen had scraped off accumulated layers of green and brown paint and replastered the walls of kitchen and bathroom. Plumbers, installing a large white second-hand Aga in the kitchen and a new ivory suite in the bathroom, found such monstrous inadequacies that they shook their heads and prophesied doom. As if to prove them right, we then had a very sharp frost and the pipes burst.

My father, philosophical in the midst of chaos, recast his plans.

'Good thing it didn't bring any ceilings down! Ah, well. Plumbing first. Roof later. We can patch it up for a couple of hundred, to see it through. Rewiring is essential. Better get that done next. Central heating is a long way down the list, my girl. The kitchen will be warm. Otherwise you'll have to manage with coal fires and oil stoves. I'm going into the red over this elegant old heap!'

A new regime emerged, whereby Matthew and I spent most weekends at Whitegates, leaving Simon with my mother while we decorated our future bedroom and living room at the Old Rectory. My father, approving my choice, provided all materials. In return we painted and papered with meticulous care, partly because I wanted everything to be beautiful, partly because Matthew was a perfectionist in anything he chose to do, and mostly because my father was a benevolent tyrant. Already he tended to adopt the role of overseer and to treat us like workmen. Noticing my husband's involuntary frown I had a word with Mummy, and after that she kept my father away when we were there.

By ourselves, working in contented silence for most of the time, Matthew and I grew together again. He became the young man with whom I had fallen in love four years ago. His earnestness as he worked touched me deeply. Whatever task he undertook absorbed him wholly. When he had finished something he would come down from the ladder, stand back, put his head to one side to judge what he had done, push up his glasses, sweep back his forelock, and smile first to himself and then at me in quiet satisfaction. Often I would stop painting just to watch and marvel at his return to happiness. Sometimes he would look up when I was looking. Sometimes I would catch him looking at me.

116

We drove ourselves hard and made a picnic when we had finished. The house was cold, but the new pipes were lagged, and the patched roof kept out the rain. A new oil stove, literally and metaphorically a house-warming present from Aunt Caroline, heated the area where we worked. We brewed tea on a primus stove, opened flasks of hot soup, and ate the sandwiches my mother had made for us. When we drove home to Whitegates, in the Ford Prefect we had named Minnie, Simon would be asleep, my mother cooking dinner and my father opening a bottle of wine, waiting to hear of the latest progress.

Matthew and I began to make love again, for the crisis had affected even that part of our lives. And I, released from breast-feeding, given space from constant mothering, found my baby delectable once more. Many little tokens materialised of the good life to come. My mother and aunts and the Cullen grandparents ransacked their attics for furniture and elderly brocade curtains which would do until we could afford something better. Magda sent us a painting of the sea-front at St Ives. Leila planned murals for Simon's bedroom, laid them before us all for approval, and volunteered to do a complete job of redecoration according to our present standards. She said it would be Simon's first birthday present from herself and Sep. They would come down as soon as the weather was reasonable, and have the room ready by July.

I could see that Matthew was unwilling to bear with their company, though their offer meant that we could have our bedroom to ourselves and were saved the work entailed in decorating Simon's nursery.

He said airily, 'That's frightfully nice of you both, and of course it would be wonderful, but we aren't equipped for weekend visitors yet. Haven't even a spare camp-bed or blanket as far as I know. Couldn't put you up, you see.'

Leila said, with that derisive smile of hers, eyebrows raised, 'Oh, we're not asking ourselves down for a weekend. We were thinking of coming for the day, some time in the week when you're at work. You don't even have to give us supper for our song,' she added, and the smile turned into a Cheshire Cat grin. 'Particularly if it's a Tuesday. Because Sep and I wouldn't miss listening to the Goon Show for anything, and I believe you don't care for it! No, fret not, Matthew. We shall work like busy bees all day and depart at six precisely.'

We both protested spontaneously at this, and Matthew looked guilty, as well he might. But apparently Leila meant what she said, and sadly it was also the best solution.

So my husband said heartily, 'Well, thanks a lot. Jolly decent of you both. And I must say, Leila, that the designs look very . . . ' He hesitated over the right adjective, and finally said, ' . . . jolly.'

Afterwards my father said privately, coldly to me, 'I think that Matthew could have offered to pay their fares. He's getting enough done for *him*! He should remember that they're no better off than he is, and they give up the chance of a day's work and pay every time they come down to the Old Rectory.'

I had been so concerned about my husband's grudging hospitality that I had forgotten more practical details.

Angry with Matthew and myself, I said stiffly, 'He didn't think.'

'But he should have done,' said my father.

I was now annoyed with him for picking on Matthew.

'I meant that it didn't occur to him at that precise moment, but of course he would have reimbursed them when they came down.'

'He won't be there when they come down. They've arranged to work in his absence – and I can't think that's an accident, either!'

There was an embarrassed pause.

Then my father added, 'And that's what Matthew prefers, isn't it? Well, he needn't worry. I'll see they aren't out of pocket for trying to help him.'

And walked away.

The pin still pricks, and yet, looking back, I can best recall that time in my life as a moment of trans-figuration.

* * *

One June evening, when the moon was high, Matthew and I met head to head over the last waxed floorboard in the sitting room. Laughing, polishing cloths in hand, we stood up to admire the result of two months' cruel hard labour, which had simplified itself into pale walls, pale ceiling and dark-gold boards.

Matthew switched out the light, and through the uncurtained windows shone the magic lantern of the moon. Floor, walls and ceiling became screens reflecting the play of shadow trees. He put his arm round my waist and his cheek against mine and we became one with the empty room we had created. There was no need of words, nor had we any desire to break a perfect silence.

Leila

10

My father had a very healthy attitude towards money. He didn't let it frighten or impress him. He regarded it as a servant, whom you treated well and from whom you expected and got good service. So far the relationship had worked. But on the Old Rectory he spread himself financially thin.

His monthly allowance to me paid for my rent in Camden Town. Otherwise, I earned enough to keep myself from want, and my uncertain income was eked out by the open hospitality of Whitegates and unbirthday presents when my parents visited me. They arrived laden with food parcels, as if I were a refugee, took me out to a substantial lunch, and did some judicious shopping before they left.

My mother's gifts were accompanied by a placatory smile.

'Lulu, you mustn't mind, but I noticed that you had only one saucepan and this set was on offer.'

My father's presents were bestowed with an unapologetic grin.

'This is to replace that perfectly bloody and potentially dangerous electric kettle of yours!'

Sep, hovering worshipfully in the background, buying Helen a bunch of small shy flowers from a pavement stall, said, 'I think your parents are wonderful. As soon as I told Mama that I was a Barnardo's boy she understood me immediately. Because however kind and good they are – and of course they *were*! – it simply isn't the same as having your own family. But now I feel one of the Gideons.'

Cass, sizing up Sep and his relationship to me, treated him with good-natured indifference.

'How's that poofter of yours?' he would ask irreverently, when I telephoned.

Whereas Helen always said warmly, 'Now don't forget to bring dear Septimus down with you. We're so fond of him.'

Zoe and Matthew and Simon moved into the Old Rectory on Saturday, 28 April, begged a month's grace to sort themselves out, and then invited us all to Sunday lunch and tea.

'So that we can admire what's done, and survey what has to be done!' said Cass sardonically to us. 'And you two mugs are in the front line to decorate Simon's bedroom, remember? Gauleiter Barber hath spoken.'

'Darling, I do think you misjudge Matthew,' said Helen, packing a basket full of Fortnum's delicacies for Zoe. 'He's not like us, you know. He finds it difficult to express his feelings, and because he's had something of a deprived childhood – and Septimus will bear me out in this, I am sure . . .'

'Oh dear me, yes,' Sep murmured smugly.

' . . . he tries to make up for it in other ways. He's not yet sure of himself and consequently much too anxious to make a good impression. Now, we know that Leila and Septimus don't mind sleeping-bags and camp-beds, but Matthew feels he must have proper guest rooms before he invites anybody to stay. It's fussy, perhaps, but there's nothing inhospitable about that.'

Cass turned to us, grinning.

'Then why don't you decorate a couple of spare rooms as well? That would put the Indian armlock on him!'

'Darling,' said my mother reproachfully, and touched his cheek, 'I know you're joking, but others might think you were criticising Matthew.'

'I'm being damned serious!' said my father, very seriously indeed. 'And if by *others* you mean Leila and Septimus they don't think much of him either!'

Yet even divided families enjoy their moments of completion. We experienced one as my father's Daimler swept grandly up the drive, and Zoe and Matthew ran out, waving.

'We heard the car!' Zoe cried.

They were young and radiant and excited, as on their wedding day, as on their return from honeymoon. And they could not have given us a warmer welcome. Even Sep, holding out a nervous hand to Matthew, had it firmly shaken. Helen and I were kissed and hugged by both of them.

'Simon's asleep in his pram in the orchard,' said Zoe casually, linking my mother's arm. 'So we can all have coffee in peace without the little beast.'

'Darling! How lovely that sounds!' my mother replied, understanding how much pride of possession lay beneath the deprecation.

But my father said, settling in the most comfortable chair, 'What orchard is that, Zoe? Half a dozen barren apple-trees and a run-down grass patch? It needs bull-dozing and paving over.'

Helen had no need to tell us that he didn't mean it. We knew by the grin of pleasure on his ugly face. And this pleasure deepened as he watched Zoe presiding over her new domain, making little of the things she loved most.

'Sorry to dash in and out like this, but I must keep an eye on the Aga. I never would have believed it, but an Aga is just like another person. Rather a temperamental one. I call her Agatha. She's utterly trustworthy with stews, but if I don't give her my undivided attention with Yorkshire pudding she'll either burn it or flatten it . . .

'Yes, the view from the bedroom window is pure picture-postcard. Such a dear little village and church. So long as you don't mind the clock striking every quarter-hour through the night! And there's no lying in on a Sunday morning. They ring a full peal of bells to haul people out of bed! . . .

'To think that I never appreciated the anonymity of living in London. The villagers positively take you over here. I've already enrolled in the WI and when the vicar's wife heard I had a domestic science diploma she said, "My dear! You're going to be such an asset"! And heaps of people are willing to baby-sit for us. Heavens! I shan't have a minute to myself!'

In the same situation I should have been screaming to get out, but Zoe thrived on being needed.

'All this and fresh air too!' said my father, guessing my thoughts and winking at me wickedly.

But I was glad, we were all glad, to see her in full bloom again, and Matthew was very attentive, and surprisingly good with Simon. I wondered, uncharitably, if it was the feeling of power over a human being which drew him to babies. But for once he was at peace with himself and lost his dark hawk-like appearance. The day was warm and fine. We had tea in the garden. The memory is so vivid that I return to it sometimes to refresh myself.

Sep is sitting cross-legged on the lawn, making a daisy-chain for the baby, who crawls towards him purposefully. My mother's face is half-hidden by her straw hat. She lies back in a deckchair which is striped amber and peppermint. Zoe, making some soft exclamation about the Aga, unobtrusively leaves her own deckchair, striped azure and carmine, and hurries into the house.

Matthew and my father sit in basket-chairs on the lawn, listening to cricket scores on the portable radio. This is the only interest they have in common.

My mother, unmindful of Zoe's departure, says drowsily to her, 'Of course, I don't want to overwhelm you with visitors, but Grannie and Grandpa Cullen are longing to see the Old Rectory, and the aunts would love to come.' In fairness, she adds, 'And Magda will, too, I suppose, but it's so difficult to pin her down. She refused to attend Simon's christening because she said she was a pagan. Such nonsense. No one would have bothered, anyway. The truth of the matter is that she prefers to pop out of the blue, whenever the mood happens to take her. Which is not at all convenient.'

I am sketching Sep and Simon. As the baby rips the

126

daisy-chain apart and sinks six teeth joyfully into his hand, Sep shouts pitifully for assistance. I capture the moment, and scribble underneath:

'Why don't you pick on someone your own size?'

Helen rouses herself and hastens to rescue Sep, who is allowing Simon to maul him without offering the slightest resistance.

'Naughty, naughty Simon!' Helen coos, scooping up her grandson. 'Mustn't bite kind Uncle Septimus!'

'I have totally misjudged Agatha. The cakes are perfect!' Zoe cries from the threshold.

Helen saunters towards her daughter, clasping the baby, saying, 'Darling, you had no summer holiday last year. Wouldn't it be nice to introduce Simon to Cornwall this year? Remember all the lovely times we've had there, even during the war? And the sea air would be so good for him, and Magda hasn't set eyes on him yet. We could rent a farmhouse . . . '

Oblivious of us, Matthew shouts, 'Run, man! Run, for God's sake! . . . '

'The bloody fool's glued to the crease!' my father replies crisply.

Now my mother and sister, bearing the baby like a trophy, come over and smile on us.

'The vicar wants Matthew to join the local cricket team,' says Zoe proudly. 'Matthew thinks he will, next year. I shall be helping with the cricket teas, of course. You must all come down and watch one of the home matches!'

'That would be lovely, darling,' says Helen, blissful in her daughter's bliss.

Sep, safe from marauding milk teeth, collapses on the grass beside me, murmuring, 'This is serendipity absolute. Lady Lee, I never want to wake up from this dream. Tell me, are we really going to come down here once a week, and see the gorgeous Zoe in her prime, and decorate that little cannibal's bedroom?'

Dream is the right word.

I have always been a realist. I never indulge, as Helen

and Zoe and Sep do, in the feeling that the good time has finally come. The good time, like the bad time, comes and goes and is never for ever. So I do not encourage him, but answer drily, 'Make the most of it, Sep!' Then, screwing up Shelley and ruining the rhythm, 'If spring comes can winter be far behind?'

The dream continues. Despite Helen's protests, my father gives me a motor-scooter for my birthday in June. He says it will be cheaper in the long run than paying our fares down to Kent, and besides I can racket round London on it. This is what my mother is afraid of, but very gamely she acquiesces and buys me one of the latest vinyl leather-type scooter coats and a helmet. In which, as Sep truthfully says, I look like a space elf.

'But a piss-elegant space elf, love.'

Piss-elegant is his latest and most favourite description. Out of respect for Helen's sense of decorum I ask him not to use it in front of her.

'My dear,' says Sep, appalled at the thought, 'I wouldn't let so much as the tiniest "damn" escape in front of Mama!'

People say that you never know when you are happy. That's rubbish. I always know when I'm happy. I was happy in Camden Town with Sep that summer. Weekly, we roared down to Kent on the motor-scooter, to be treated like royalty by Zoe. Hard-working royalty, mind. We rocked and rolled with abandon in the local palais. We must have queued for a seat in the gods at most of the London theatres. I went by myself to see *The Chalk Garden* and *Long Day's Journey into Night*, because Sep said they were not conducive to serendipity. But, like my father, he loved musicals and that was the year for them. *Oklahoma! Carousel. The King and I. Guys and Dolls*. We strained our eyes in the cheapest cinema seats. We loved *Rebel Without a Cause*, and Sep pinned a photograph of James Dean on the wall over his divan. We saw *The Dam Busters* twice. We sang *Around the World in 80 Days* until we told each other to shut up. Sep had nightmares after *Moby Dick*, but made enquiries about emigrating to Australia after *A Town*

128

Like Alice. We shared out invitations, casual and formal. We shared meals and shopping. The only thing we didn't share was a bed, which cut out a lot of complications. We were, as Sep told all our friends and acquaintances, *celibrate.*

'Do you use that word incorrectly on purpose, Sep?' I asked.

'I didn't at first, Lady Lee, but I do now. It's my party opener. Begging a laugh, dear. Just begging a laugh.'

His birthday was in August, and Helen made him a kingly cake and threw a family party, to which we all brought piss-elegant presents. Drip-dry shirts were the rage. Cass presented him with three. Zoe had knitted a Scandinavian sweater in cream and granite-grey. I had bought a nineteenth-century scarlet army jacket for ten shillings in the Caledonian Market, short of only three brass buttons, which Helen almost matched. She sewed them on for me, too. Sep gave a short speech about the unique serendipity of the occasion. He wiped his eyes on a red and white spotted handkerchief before blowing out twenty-six candles, and said that though he was now over the hill he intended to grow old gracefully. I was glad we were staying the night at Whitegates. I should have worried about his ability to hold on to me as we roared home through the London evening traffic.

In September we rode down to Cornwall in stages, with rucksacks on our backs, to meet Magda and hear the truthful side of the Gideon–Barber holiday saga, which had taken place six weeks earlier. This time, though we shared my grandmother's living room, I slept on the sofa bed and Sep had a mattress on the floor. He was bizarre enough to delight Magda. They got on a treat, and I loved showing off Cornwall. We rode up to Tintagel and down to St Michael's Mount, and visited the most famous standing stones, and Sep adored all of it.

'So magical, my dear. I hadn't *lived* before I saw this county! Why don't you and I leave the Smoke behind us, and rent a studio in St Ives?'

'Because we couldn't earn a living away from darling dirty old London!'

129

'Why are you so *practical*, always?'

I was not always practical. Now and then I suffered a silent moment, remembering the days of summer love and Jeremy Purchase, and the child who was begotten but never brought to fruition.

Magda, busy with the present, did not allow the past to encumber her.

'Zoe reminds me so much of Helen. Those two beauties only see what they want to. That Matthew was as black as thunder the day they came here. But to hear them talk you would have thought he was the life and soul of the party. He doesn't approve of me, you know, and I don't give tuppence for him, but at least I was pleasant. Cass drove Helen down on the Saturday, and went back again on the Monday. I can guess what *he* was up to, the fortnight she was down here! The baby is nice, as babies go. I'm not *much* for babies. I like them better when they get older.'

'That baby bit me deliberately. Several times,' said Sep, brooding over his evening wine.

'Ach, that old baby! Did he, now?' said Magda soothingly. 'Well, you should have bitten him back, boy!'

She continued, 'After the Matthew had paid his duty visit I didn't see him again. But Zoe and Helen and the baby came two or three times.'

'Zoe's happy with Matthew, though, isn't she?' I asked.

I needed her to be happy. Her unique beauty of flesh and spirit had been squandered to no purpose, otherwise.

'As I said, my girl, Zoe sees what she wants to see. When she wakes up, or when he finds a better place to go to, there'll be a different story. That's why Cass has bought her a house.'

And she nodded her head several times and looked cunning.

Halcyon days. I wrung the last drop of joy from every one of them. Why is it that I know I must save crusts against future hunger? Others throw them to the birds, and remind themselves that there is a special providence in the fall of the sparrow. But is either providence or the sparrow going to feed *them* when the famine comes?

130

At the drear end of the year, when dead leaves were slippery underfoot, every tenant of the house in Camden Town received a month's notice to quit. The council had won its protracted battle with our absentee landlord, and though we might postpone our sentence by appeal and petition we were condemned to leave.

We called a meeting, and I have seldom seen a more unlikely bunch of people in one room. Not calculated, as Cass would say, to impress the City Fathers. I knew we stood no chance as a group, so I left Sep behind and visited Constantia Blezard in her escort bureau, to ask for advice.

She had not seen me since the previous Christmas, when my father and I delivered a bottle of champagne. Failing to recognise me, as usual, she assumed I was looking for work.

'Sorry, dear. No use. You're not tall enough. I'm surprised Bettina gave you an appointment.'

Loud and clear, I reminded her.

'It's me, Connie! Leila Gideon. Cass Gideon's daughter.'

She stared again at the card and then at me, patted her bright gold hair, and said, 'Oh yes, of course, dear. How's things?'

Unperturbed, she switched from her business to her social manner, swayed over to a corner cupboard and brought out a bottle of Irish whisky, a syphon of soda water and two tumblers. She found ice-cubes in a minute refrigerator on the side-table.

'Now, Leda,' she said, giving me a smile and a drink of equally generous proportions, 'what can I do for you?'

I put her in the picture. She was sympathetic but unhelpful.

'He's in Persia at the moment, dear,' she said of my landlord. 'And of course I did warn you that the let wouldn't be permanent. But my ear's to the ground, as you might say. Write down your name, address and telephone number. I'll let you know if I hear of anything.'

I wrote it down without hope, feeling that I was more likely to receive news of an escort than a flat. She asked

131

about my father, and my commissions. The conversation languished, though her crimson leather smile remained. I finished my drink, thanked her, and wove back to Camden Town on the motor-scooter.

Sep was in my room, wearing a frilly apron which Helen had given me, and studying a recipe from a book majestically named, *International Gourmet Dishes*. He looked dazed, whether from our bad news, culinary apprehension, or the glass of gin he was replenishing, I didn't know.

'Jesus Christ, Sep!' I said. 'Don't strain yourself. Scrambled eggs will do.'

'That's a relief,' he replied, shutting the book. 'I bought this for a song in the summer sales and felt I had to use it. But I came all over faint at the thought of boning out a pheasant.'

'We haven't got a pheasant. Have we?'

'Nor anything else they describe, my dear. Even the mushrooms have special names. Just shows you how the other half live.'

'I should give that book to Zoe, if I were you. Even if she can't afford the ingredients she'll love reading it. You might pour me a gin, too. Seeing that my father gave us the bottle.'

'Sorry, love. I'm all of a flutter. Have you any nice news?'

'No. The landlord's done a bunk, and Connie can only make sorry noises. I think we'd better find ourselves a couple of packing cases and a bottle of meths, ready to sleep underneath the arches.'

Sep said seriously, 'If you'd ever come that close to being homeless, love, you wouldn't joke about it.'

'They haven't got rid of us yet,' I said, swaggering with gin. 'We can make a hell of a nuisance of ourselves. Write to the newspapers. Stage a public demonstration. Barricade ourselves in.'

Sep flopped on to my divan like a discarded puppet.

'I can't fight. I never could. They must do what they like with me.'

I was disgusted with him. I also suffered a twinge of foreboding. For I must either desert him or battle for both of us. So far the friendship had been a mutual delight. Now it looked as if it could become my responsibility.

11

Temporarily at least, Cass had lost his air of insouciance. He looked older and a little greyer, faced with the second housing problem in a year. He fed the study fire with two more logs and dusted his hands thoughtfully.

He said, 'It's going to be Zoe's trouble all over again. Your salary hasn't risen but the rents have. Connie's right, of course. We knew it was a temporary measure. But at the same time I was hoping it would last longer than this.' Absently, automatically, he asked, 'Do you mind if I smoke?'

He selected a cigar, smelled it, listened to it, cut and lit it.

'I must do what I can, but it can't be what I hoped. Zoe's skimmed the cream, and will go on skimming it for some years. Every time I go there something vital needs doing. The Old Rectory is not a short-term investment.'

'Oh, don't bother about me,' I said lightly. 'I can look after myself. I just thought you ought to know.'

He took the cigar from his lips and looked down at me, amazed.

He said emphatically, 'My dear girl, of course I shall bother about you! You're my daughter. Besides, Zoe has a husband to give her moral support and protection, but you have no man – apart from me.'

Then he returned to his cigar and got down to business.

'Keep looking for rented accommodation by all means, but if I can persuade my bank manager to extend my overdraft I might think of buying you something which would be adequate for the time being. I'm thinking in terms of a flat in an unfashionable area with a short lease. That would give us both a breathing space. Then I could fix you up properly later on.'

His concern threw me off balance. In thanking him I called him 'Daddy' for the first time in years. He was tactful enough not to remark upon it but his tone became noticeably softer.

'Don't thank me yet, Lee. You'll have to do the leg-work. Or wheel-work. And it's the worst time of year. As soon as you find anything suitable let me know at once. Here or at the office. Celia always knows where to find me.'

I'll bet she does! I thought. Celia Piper had lasted longer as a secretary and mistress than anyone I could remember. Perhaps my father was getting older.

Sustained by his cigar, he brought a writing pad from his desk and sat with it on his knees, jotting down the points I should look for.

'The other thing we might consider', he said, thinking aloud, 'is to buy a *house* on a short lease, and let the rooms that you don't need as bedsitters. Many a fortune has been made with poorer beginnings! The rents will be used to meet payments on the loan and essential repairs. Do you think you could tear yourself away from the drawing-board once a week or month, and collect the rents for me? Can you be practical about it?'

I thought of the homeless Sep safely tucked under my wing and said, 'Yes, of course I can. You can rely on me absolutely.'

'Meanwhile, if you're evicted before we find a suitable place, you can always live at home while we sort something out.'

After lunch, the weather being cold and fine, Helen and Cass and I went for a walk and then had an old-fashioned Sunday afternoon tea in the sitting room, toasting muffins on the fire.

When we were agreeably buttered inside and out, I said, 'Might we talk about Sep for a minute? I expect you know that although he's very sweet he's totally unworldly. If we're thrown out, and I have to come here for a while,

135

would you mind if Sep came with me? He's not a sponger. He'll make himself useful, as I shall. And we'll pay our way. But I can't just leave him to fend for himself. He's not awfully good at it.'

My mother said at once, 'Of course he must come. Dear Septimus.'

But my father said, 'No, I'm afraid he can't, Nell!'

They looked at each other: she with an enquiring frown, he half-sorry but resolute. He spoke to me directly.

'I should strongly advise you to cut your losses where that young man is concerned, Lee. He managed before he met you and he'll manage when you've gone. Friendships have their time, like everything else. Perhaps it's time to part and let him stand on his own feet – or someone else's!'

We were quiet for a few moments. I had not given up hope of changing his mind, with my mother's help, but I moved on to the next question.

'If a house turns up, instead of a flat, would you object to my letting one of the bedsitters to Sep?'

'I shouldn't forbid you to do so, because this must be your house and your life. But I should strongly advise against it, for two reasons. If he can't pay the rent then you and I will be the losers.'

'Oh, but he will, Daddy. Truly. He's very reliable in that way.'

'Daddy' again. I must be entering a second childhood.

'And the second reason', my father continued, as if I had not interrupted him, 'is that he's a homosexual. Hear me out!' As my mother and I made sounds of shock and protest. 'I am not concerned with homosexuality as a moral question. I don't give a damn about anyone's sexual proclivities. What any man or woman does is their own affair. And I think it's a bloody stupid law which says that love between man and man is wrong, but not between woman and woman . . . '

'Cass! I really think this is quite unnecessary!' said Helen, distressed in case my spotless mind should be sullied.

' . . . but the fact remains that the male homosexual act is illegal.'

My mother and I were silent now.

'Suppose Septimus finds a boyfriend and brings him back to your place for the night or the weekend. If you condone it then you could be heading for trouble. If the vice-squad decide to spring-clean London it could be pretty unpleasant for you.'

I said angrily, sturdily, 'That sounds far-fetched to me. There are thousands of homosexuals in London. They can't track them all down and imprison them.'

My father said, 'It is still worth your consideration.'

We were all silent for a minute or two.

Then he said, 'You seem to have become involved with this Septimus fellow in a way I don't understand.'

My mother now sat up very straight to deliver her judgement.

'But I do understand it,' she said. 'Septimus needs someone to look after him, and Lulu needs someone to look after. And they truly care for each other. Not in a romantic way. In a brotherly–sisterly way.'

My father said to me, 'Surely to God, Lee, if you want to look after anyone, you can find a man who is a man, not a half-baked woman?'

'Cass, that's very unkind,' said Helen, almost in anger. 'That poor boy has a great many problems.'

He spoke objectively, unruffled.

'Which he heaps on to the shoulders of anyone who's prepared to carry them – and him. He's a regular Old Man of the Sea. And I'd rather my daughter was interested in a man who could look after her and provide some fun and companionship.'

'But I don't want to be looked after. And, to be fair, Sep's fun. And very companionable,' I said contrarily.

Yet I knew exactly what he meant. My sensible head agreed with him. My idiot heart wouldn't let go.

'It's time you found someone like that chap you brought to Zoe's wedding,' said my father. 'That medical student who anchored her veil with a stone.'

And he tilted his head back and laughed quietly in recollection.

I knew Helen was watching me covertly, probably bleeding for me, and I hate being watched and bled over.

'Oh, you mean Jeremy Purchase?' I said cheerfully. 'I'm sure I can do better than *him*!'

'I should think so indeed,' said Helen with a perceptible quiver in her voice. 'He behaved very badly to poor Lulu, if you remember.'

This was a reminder to my father that he had been tactless, if not cruel. But he only knew his wife's version of our quarrel. So he shrugged his shoulders. He had no more to say. He had made his point. The conversation was ended as far as he was concerned.

Still, my mother must try to improve on his decision.

'Putting aside the question of whether or not it would be wise to rent a room to Septimus, I really don't understand why we can't have the poor boy here just for a little while, just until he and Lulu find somewhere to live.'

'Then I'll tell you,' he said, friendly but immoveable. 'We have no idea how long that little while might be. When the Old Rectory came up I had money to spare. Now I'm borrowing, and there's a limit to how much I can borrow, which again limits what I can buy. If it's a house then – judging from Leila's reaction – Septimus will have fallen on his feet yet again. If it's a flat then he's got to find somewhere for himself, and as he has no transport Leila will be responsible for ferrying him to and fro. Meanwhile, she could move and leave him behind, and we can hardly turn him out then. He could be with us for months, even years. Why should he move at all if we make him comfortable here?'

'Cass, I think you misjudge the boy. As Leila says, he's not a sponger.'

'No. I agree there. He's a nice enough lad. But he's a leaner. Now I have nothing against that, provided he is not leaning on *me*. Have I made myself quite clear to both of you?'

Defeated on this point, we said he had.

12

1957

My house. My house. My house.

I, Gipsy Leila, who have so far lived from day to day and from hand to mouth, ever ready to move on, am a landlady and property owner. I have settled down, as they say. My caravan has come to rest near King's Cross station. My horses have been put out to grass. Trains and traffic vie with each other to produce the most noise for the longest space of time. The air smells and tastes like old soot. But a passionate feeling of pride and possession fills me as I turn the corner of a London street and see my long thin blackened sandwich of a home. And I love every minute I am there. Now who would have thought it?

Only Cass says ruefully, 'This is chucking capital down the drain! Any rent I'm paid will be swallowed in repairs. And we'll be back to where we started by the end of 1967. Only a ten-year lease to boot!'

Ten years? A lifetime! In ten years' time, if I live that long, I shall be thirty-three. In ten years' time I shall be old.

The Garret, as my family has christened No. 18, will do very nicely for now. The house will accommodate three tenants on its three floors, but is as yet unconverted. Each floor has a large oblong room with one window facing the street and the other looking out on to fire escapes and chimneys at the back. The kitchen, hall and telephone are on the ground floor, the bathroom on the first floor, and a box-room on the top floor. I shall take the top floor for myself since it has more space and light and privacy.

My father says dubiously, 'But this is the most inconvenient choice of the lot. You'll be perched upstairs like an eagle on its eyrie. And every time you want to cook a meal or have a bath or make a 'phone call, you'll be trailing up and down flights of stairs.'

'But I'm used to that kind of sharing. And I can fit up my gas-ring and the electric kettle.'

'Do as you please,' says my father, not particularly pleased himself, 'but, convenience apart, you should be on the ground-floor, Leila, observing the comings and goings of your tenants like a good concierge. Up at the top you won't know what the hell's going on.'

'But that's exactly what I want,' I say emphatically. 'I should be too available on the ground floor. The whole world would be knocking at the door, and popping in asking for things, when I wanted to work in peace.'

He does not tell me I shall be sorry for that decision later. Nor, if I am sorry for it, will he remind me that he said so. My father lets me make up my own mind and go my own way.

He does say regretfully, forced to trim his financial sails for once, 'I'm sorry to treat one daughter less generously than another, Lee, but I'm afraid major renovations are out for the time being. You'll have to cope with the place as it is.'

'You mean I can't have an Aga and an ivory bathroom suite?' I say, grinning. 'I'll never forgive you!'

He puts his arm round my shoulders and hugs me close to him.

'I promise I'll make it up to you as soon as I can. I'll pay for any decorating materials you use. And I will treat you to a cleaning woman to scrub that damned dirty, tatty place from top to bottom before you move in.'

The interval between homes had not been too long. Throughout the winter I obstructed the authorities, and

140

was voted Leader of the Camden Town house committee. Behind me Sep tagged along, vociferous with loyalty and admiration, though if it had come to real trouble I think he would have chickened out even on me. In the end I found the Garret and both our housing problems were solved. Regretfully, I left the other tenants to fight on or drop off, as they pleased, and took my remaining responsibility with me.

'I shall respect your wishes,' my father said, when I entered Sep's name on an official rent book, 'but in my opinion, this is not a sensible choice.'

'It's the only thing my conscience will allow me to do. And I know that he'll pay me on the nail.'

My father said, 'The rent is the least part of this bargain. And I see that he's chosen the first floor, which means that *neither* of you knows what's going on downstairs! Still, you must make your own mistakes.'

I registered his misgivings but they did not change my mind.

'You need another tenant,' he continued. 'But let's take our time about that. It won't hurt to look around for a month or two. Although, legally, you can give your tenants notice because the accommodation is partly furnished, they can – as you have recently proved! – make a bloody nuisance of themselves before they actually pack their bags and depart. So be sure you find someone reliable. A middle-aged woman in a steady job would be ideal. No use wrinkling your nose like that. Those bohemian friends of yours may be fun but they'll leave you to pick up the bill. You would do well to remember that this house is your business as well as your home, Miss.'

Zoe, as elder sister, had taken first pick of the hand-me-downs. All that was left for me in the family attics needed, as my father remarked, either mending or burning. I did not care. I hunted second-hand shops and markets for basic furniture. Carpets and curtains, so called, had come with the house. When the curtains did not survive Helen's washing machine I bought remnants and seconds of bright cotton and she made others. I threw the carpets out, stained

141

the floorboards black and bought pale-gold mats of woven straw.

The whole place needed redecorating. I am not a perfectionist, except in my craft. As long as the general effect is good I am quite prepared to scrape the worst bubbles off the woodwork and slap on a fifth coat of gloss. In any case, my colour schemes are always dramatic enough to attract the eyes away from the defects.

So Sep and I enriched the hallway and stairwell from top to bottom of the house with blueberry emulsion, and painted the banisters and rails stark white. My front door was the succulent pink of a cantaloupe melon. My back door tooth-aching yellow. In the rooms we were to occupy I kept three of the walls pale and papered the fourth exotically. I coloured ceilings and woodwork vividly. The kitchen was tangerine, the bathroom cerulean blue. Sep favoured Thames green and I did miracles with varying mixtures of Munsell red and white. The results were fast and fantastic.

'You'll have to do it all over again next year!' Cass remarked, shaking his head over our sloppy workmanship.

'As far as I'm concerned,' I said, 'it looks great today. And who knows what's going to happen next year? I'll be a different person who wants different colours.'

He shrugged and left me to my own devices.

I had two house-warming parties. Helen gave me the first at Whitegates, which attracted useful presents from friends and family. It was a pleasant, decorous affair at which Zoe stole my thunder as usual.

Aunt Caroline, who had been observing her covertly over a glass of sweet sherry, said coyly, 'What a bloom dear Zoe has!'

And Aunt Edith, putting her head on one side like an enquiring bird and following her cue, said, 'Zoe, dear, you're not by any chance . . . are you?'

Grannie and Grandpa Cullen looked alert and interested. Matthew nursed Simon and kept his head down. And Zoe confessed with a lovely blush.

'Actually, yes. But only just, Aunt Caro. It was confirmed this afternoon!'

My mother's face was pleased and guilty. So she had been informed.

A feminine chorus asked when the happy event was to take place. Exquisitely embarrassed, Zoe admitted to November.

My father's eyebrows were eloquent. He moved closer to me and spoke quietly, drily.

'I can't understand why she's in such a hurry to have these babies, and November is rotten timing! She'll be facing the worst months of the winter with an infant as well as a toddler, and Helen will be coaxing me to put in central heating now instead of next year.'

I answered as lightly as I could, 'Funny thing! I thought this was supposed to be *my* celebration.'

We were the lone dissenters. Forgetting they were here to wish me well, my relatives spontaneously toasted Zoe's coming event. She must have read our faces and came over to us as soon as she could, flushed with apology.

'Lulu, Daddy, I meant to tell you the news myself. But the aunts are so quick.'

I could not help saying rather acerbically, 'Yes, Cass and I were knocked all of a heap — but apparently Helen wasn't.'

'Oh, you know what a witch Mummy is. I didn't tell her. She guessed the moment I arrived,' Zoe replied self-consciously.

Still we felt left out. Our inability to respond to her news as she wished puzzled her. She cast small conversational olive branches before us.

'Daddy, you'll be thrilled when you see the garden. All those bulbs I planted in the autumn are flowering beautifully. And, Lulu, there'll be the same age difference between the new baby and Simon as there was between us.'

My father nodded briefly and walked away on a pretext. My sister waited for me to say something joyful and complimentary, but I could not. She still capped everything I had or did, and I was tired of being second best.

My own house-warming, a week later, was a crazy personal occasion to which my family were not invited on principle. As it turned out I was doubly relieved that they didn't come.

Sep and I, launching the house on very limited means, had decided to invite our closest London friends to a bottle party which was to begin at nine o'clock. This made sure that everyone had eaten beforehand and would bring a little something to supplement the drinks. Our own catering would run to a dozen bottles of red Portuguese wine from the off-licence round the corner (who would also lend us wine glasses), and substantial quantities of French bread, garlic sausage, cheese and pickles. I bought paper plates and cups, plastic cutlery and a bargain pack of one hundred paper serviettes. I also designed and executed amusing invitations, which included directions to the house from King's Cross station.

'There'll be about twenty of us altogether,' I said, licking stamps.

'Those who invite twenty should expect forty!' Sep warned me.

'Twenty, more or less, then! Now, you'll be in charge of the wine and I'll be in charge of the food. And we both do the coffee afterwards. Okay?'

The party lit up hesitantly, travelled a long fuse, and then went off with a bang.

Everyone who had been invited dutifully brought a bottle, and Sep stacked them underneath and to either side of the drinks table in alcoholic abundance. The food went in the first hour, leaving a wrinkled paper tablecloth full of smears and crumbs. Then came a second contingent, being friends of invited friends, who arrived around eleven o'clock with further supplies. By midnight, as Sep had prophesied, more than forty people had spread through the Garret, jitterbugging in the empty rooms on the ground floor, talking and cuddling all the way up the stairs, and migrating to my bedroom at the top of the house for greater privacy.

At first it was heady to be entertaining so many, so successfully. Fun to talk to old friends and make new ones. But whereas the drink diminished, the number of guests continued to increase.

News of parties, in those days, attracted a flock of strange birds who made an evening profession of joining other people's celebrations. They came from every class of society. Some were freeloaders who left when they had had enough, and moved on to the next event. Some were predators, watching for easy prey and small valuables. Some were alcoholics and derelicts, floating on whatever tide would carry them. Some smoked pot. A few were on hard drugs. Mingling unobtrusively with them might be a pusher looking for new clients.

In the small hours of the morning I realised that the number of bodies had become uncountable, the Victorian walls of the Garret were heaving in and out with people and noise, the telephone was shrill with neighbours' complaints, the air had turned to smoke, and the atmosphere had changed for the worse.

I had seen similar crowds before. I knew this happened, but I had not expected it to happen to me. I also knew that the only sensible thing to do was to leave before the trouble started. This is what our personal friends were doing, thanking us effusively and slipping away fast. Unluckily, I had no choice but to stay and deal with the situation. I made a megaphone of cardboard and walked from floor to floor, shouting through it.

'Sorry folks, but we're getting complaints about the noise! Can you tone it down a bit, please?'

The glazed faces of total strangers stared at me, puzzled, hostile. Some laughed, and walked or stumbled away. Some asked me who the hell I thought I was. I said it was my party. They told me to enjoy it and shut up, and turned their backs. The feeling of being out of control was weird and frightening. I went to find Sep, though I knew he was both helpless and hopeless.

He was leaning against the drinks table, smiling vacuously and listening to a dapper young man who wore a parma violet suit with a frilled shirt-front. He looked like a large untidy rabbit transfixed by a small elegant stoat. One drunken girl was lying on the floor trying to set fire to the new curtains with a box of matches.

'For God's sake, Sep, look what she's doing!' I shouted from the other end of the room. 'Stop her!'

He glanced in my direction, uncomprehending, and returned to his fascinator.

I dropped the megaphone, pushed my way downstairs to the kitchen, armed myself with a water-spray and shoved my way back up again.

'I see you've got your gun, Annie!' said a rich dark voice.

On the landing window-seat sat a self-contained man in full and immaculate evening dress, smoking a cigarette and drinking out of a flask. He was handsome in an old-fashioned sort of way. I judged him to be in his forties. Certainly he was far older than the rest of us.

He held the flask towards me, saying, 'Don't touch the plonk here. It'll ruin your guts. This is decent whisky. Have some?'

'No, thanks,' I said, very dignified at the insult to our hospitality. 'I have an arsonist to tackle.'

He was not in the least drunk, relaxed and detached, swinging one patent-leather shoe, watching everyone else make fools or nuisances of themselves.

'An arsonist?'

'She's trying to set fire to the curtains. I'm putting a stop to that!'

'I see. That's very sporting of you.'

I realised he was unaware that I was his hostess, and took my fear and frustration out on him. He became the scapegoat for all these invaders.

'This isn't a question of sport. It's a matter of survival. They're my damned curtains. This is my damned house. And I don't know who the hell *you* are, but I damned well didn't invite you!'

He eased himself off the window-seat, stepped carefully over a courting couple, and said, 'Let me see if I can help.'

In what had been his living room, Sep was leaning towards the young man with the frilled shirt-front, still listening in humble adoration. The girl had fallen asleep on the floor, still holding her box of matches. The noise here had reached such a pitch that my friendly stranger and I cupped our hands over our mouths and bawled at each other like sailors in a storm.

He shouted, 'Someone will call the police soon!'

'Well, I can't stop them!' I shouted. 'I wish I could.'

'Cautions. Fines. Prison. Scandal. Furious neighbours!'

I was frantic at the thought of my future here being blighted before it began.

'But what can I *do*!'

He put his lips to my ear and his moustache tickled me. For the first time in months I felt a little tingle of physical pleasure.

'Ring the police yourself. Now. Tell them you'd invited a few friends but the party has got out of control. Tell them you're frightened. Ask them to help. Otherwise you might find yourself up on a drugs charge. That group over there is pretty high on marijuana, and three kids are giving themselves shots of something stronger in your bathroom.'

As I nodded and began to fight my way out he caught my arm and applied his lips to my ear again.

'Don't use your own 'phone. Ring them from outside. Better not let your guests know you're grassing on them. There are some peculiar people here.'

'Right!' I said.

Still he held my arm and I felt the smile on his lips as he spoke.

'And put that water-spray down before you go!'

I had concocted a dress for the occasion in cat's-eyes green chiffon. Fifteen shillings at a jumble sale. It had once been a lady's evening gown, with slim shoulder straps, a bodice that fitted right down to the hips and a long flared skirt. I had scissored the hem into triangular points, cutting it up to the knees at the front and touching the ankles at the back. I had wound an old silver lamé scarf of Helen's into a turban and bought green and silver bangles and earrings at an Indian shop. I wore silver high-heeled sandals. That night I was not only the cat's eyes but its whiskers as well.

Imagine me, therefore, not lounging in languid grace, smoking a cigarette in a long holder, bestowing wit and hospitality, but scudding down a dark London street at three in the morning, bangles jangling, one hand holding up the tail of my skirt, the other clutching my purse, trying to find a telephone box. As I run the silver turban snakes slowly loose and becomes a scarf again. Snatching it off, turning the corner, I spot a police car and flag it down with a cry of relief.

These laconic men must have seen so much that nothing could surprise them. Even in my state of hysteria I knew what a mad creature I must look and sound. But they acted kindly, blandly, courteously.

'How many people would you say there were, Miss?'

'Oh, there must be a hundred at least!' I cried.

'Anyone hurt?'

'I don't know. There are bodies all over the place!'

Calmly they reported back on the radio, asked for reinforcements, and ushered me into the squad car.

Within minutes, sirens screaming, tyres squealing, four police cars, two police vans and an ambulance converged on the Garret from front and back. Alerted too late, those members of my party who could still stand were shrieking, falling and fighting down the stairs and the fire-escape to meet them.

There was no need to break down my cantaloupe front door. It stood wide open, and across its threshold lay a young man sound asleep with his arms crossed over his breast, crusader-fashion. He was trodden on several times before somebody moved him.

'Like rabbits into a sack!' said one policeman, popping his prisoners home.

I had forgotten Sep until I saw his butter-coloured thatch bobbing distractedly above the heads of the crowd.

'Not him!' I cried. 'He's my lodger. He's done nothing wrong.'

'That's all right, Miss. We'll sort the sheep from the goats down at the station.'

They searched the house from top to bottom, finding people under beds and in cupboards sound asleep. Within a quarter of an hour it was empty and silent, and I locked up and went with them to give a full statement.

They questioned me so minutely and cleverly that I swore by the nine gods I would never give a wild party again, and always pay for my bus ticket even when the conductor forgot to ask for the fare. Smiling, they gave me absolution, and I came out at that hour of the morning when London streets are being washed and swept, dustbins emptied, and only early workers are abroad. Home once more, I clacked slowly across the tiled hall in my silver high heels, trailing my silver scarf, and headed for the kitchen to brew a pot of strong brown tea. I was pouring the third cup when the telephone rang.

A rich dark voice said, 'This is your fellow plotter speaking. Name of Colin Macintosh. We met but didn't introduce ourselves.'

My ear and stomach tingled in recollection.

'I'm Leila Gideon. I'm glad you rang. Thank you again.'

'How did it go?'

'Very well, I suppose. I'm not used to police raids. I'm afraid my friend Sep was jailed too. I didn't think about consequences when I dashed off to tell the police. Anyway, they pronounced me unwise but innocent, and cautioned me to be careful about the company I kept in the future.'

'Good. I scarpered, of course.'

'Of course you did,' I said. 'By the way, who brought *you* to our party?'

'No one. I saw something was happening, and dropped in for half an hour out of sheer curiosity.'

I could think of nothing else to say, so thanked him again, hopefully.

He said, 'The place must look like Hiroshima after the bomb. Much damage?'

'I don't think so. It's more mess than damage. I shall have to spend today cleaning up.'

'All by yourself?'

'Yes. As I said, my friend Sep is in jail.'

'Would you like me to come round and help?'

I smiled into the telephone and made a face.

'That would be very kind. Yes, if you really want to.'

'Now?'

'If you like.'

'Have you had breakfast?'

'No. Just a pot of tea.'

'So have I. Why don't you make a large pot of coffee for the pair of us? I like mine strong. And I'll bring breakfast with me.'

He must have gone home, shaved, showered and changed into a cream polo-necked sweater, a brown suede jacket and cavalry twill trousers. Definitely not one of my crowd. But he understood the importance of good food and liked cooking it: waving me cheerfully out of the kitchen while he fried Ayrshire bacon, farm eggs, butcher-made pork sausages and ripe tomatoes.

I took a shower and brushed my hair, and wished that it grew thick and heavy like molten gold as Zoe's did, instead of ash-pale and wispy. My party costume looked tawdry by light of day. I put on clean underwear and searched through my wardrobe, which my father called Leila's Rag-Bag, for more suitable clothes. I stayed with the green and silver earrings and bangles from last night, and added cherry-pink slacks and a lemon jersey.

When I emerged in my daytime finery he was keeping the breakfasts hot under the grill, and buttering big feathery muffins.

'All right?' he asked, smiling.

The question concerned more than my state of mind and body and the banquet he had prepared. My grin nearly met behind my tingling ears.

'All *right*!' I replied with conviction.

But first things came first. Lust could wait. We pitched into the food.

13

I had been celibrate, as Sep put it, for over a year, and the reasons for this were many, though only one or two were important.

Married women like Zoe and Helen, who have a regular love-maker at hand, and whose only lack is variety, believe that single women like me have a regular supply of lovers, and probably imagine a world of eroticism which would make the Whore of Babylon blench.

Being neither a prostitute nor a nymphomaniac, I have always found that the problem of leading what is called 'an irregular life' is indeed its irregularity. Lovers do not drop like apples from the tree of Eden, and between one lover and the next lie gaps of time filled with heartbreak (Jeremy Purchase), disillusionment (Bill Musgrove), occasional hopes (unfounded) and frequent doubts as to one's physical attractions and sexual ability.

The trauma of abortion had left me numb for so long that I wondered if I should ever want a man again. Bill Musgrove, my literary collaborator with whom I had produced *The Fly-Away Balloon*, put that right, because I did want him and for a little while I even thought I loved him. We were together on a creative level, acting as each other's mirror self, and that is a heady situation to be in. As I read what he wrote the illustrations were born effortlessly and with certainty. When he saw them he said, 'But that's it exactly!' And sometimes, looking through my other work, he would say, 'Ah, that gives me an idea!'

He wrote under a pseudonym, as some writers do.

In his case I have since wondered whether that was a way of separating his creative Dr Jekyll from his dark and secret Mr Hyde. I do know that if we had kept the two of them strictly apart we should have been dear and close friends yet. Even now, I have only to read one of his children's books to experience a feeling of kinship which is close to love. But I was physically hungry at the time and so was he.

Throughout the winter of 1956 I had pursued an affair which never got off the ground. Bill's upbringing had conditioned his attitude towards what he called 'a bit of fun'. His physical expectations of a wife were quite different from those of a mistress. He expected Mrs Musgrove to behave like a lady and endure all. I wondered sometimes whether he apologised to her before and after the act. I gathered she did not enjoy it, but apparently that did not surprise him. Nor, after we had been to bed a few times, did it surprise me. My experience, though limited so far to the virile but puppyish tumblings with Jeremy Purchase, told me that there was more to sex than a man saying, 'Hah!', sinking into me like a set of teeth into a particularly succulent lamb chop, worrying me for a few minutes, and then rolling off saying, 'That was wonderful, darling!'

For him, no doubt.

After a month of this I suggested that I needed warming up beforehand, which gave him the idea that I was frigid. When I protested furiously that I was not, and instanced several escapades with Jeremy – without mentioning his name – he changed his mind and decided I was a naughty girl who really wanted to warm *him* up instead.

'What would you like to do?' he asked. 'Don't be afraid to tell me. I'm not a stuffed shirt, you know.'

As I failed to come up with any suggestions he made a few which I found as disturbing as the gleam in his eyes. He would have done well to seek out a professional prostitute who really knew her job. They could have dressed up in black rubber suits, chastised each other with horse whips, squeezed grape juice on to their bare bosoms and acted out his home-made scenarios of rape and torture with gusto. But again his upbringing blocked him. A gentleman didn't pay for his pleasures. So he was condemned to live with an unawakened wife, occasional (probably disgusted) mistresses, blue films, strip shows, erotic magazines and books in brown-paper covers.

'Of course, it's only in fun,' he would say, after I had fallen foul of some fresh little notion. 'You bring this out in me!' he would add, finding an excuse for his specialised tastes. 'It's because you're such a naughty little girl!'

As I became more and more reluctant to participate he laid the blame on me.

'You know, you *are* frigid. You might as well admit it. It's nothing to be ashamed of. I've known an awful lot of frigid girls.'

He had probably driven them to it.

'I think you should consult a doctor,' he said.

The idea overcame him.

'I say, suppose we pretend that I'm the doctor and you tell me your little difficulties.'

The gleam was in his eyes again. He looked moist and eager.

'You could make things up,' he said, stroking my arm. 'All sorts of naughty things. It doesn't have to be the truth.'

But it did have to be the truth. Spring was calling me and instead of the great god Pan I had this nasty old lecher stepping out of his trousers, already agog and aloft with his own imagination. Enough was enough.

'I don't mind if you use rude words,' he said, encouraging me. 'Normally I don't like to hear a lady swear, but I don't mind if you say "fuck".'

I was still dressed. No doors were locked. I was free to go. Free to find somebody else.

I said, 'How about – fuck off!'

And departed, rather quickly, for good.

But he left me full of fear about my ability to make love, and about the mystery of men. Pre-Musgrove I thought they were all straightforward stallions. Post-Musgrove I wondered what sexual fantasies might slide and glide forth at night into private rooms. Like Jeremy he had damaged me, but in another way.

So though I desired Colin Macintosh I was also afraid of finding him out. While he, unafraid of me, was busy finding out as much as he could.

He was a very attractive man, but what I liked best about him was his air of self-knowledge and self-possession. I would not have to take care of him nor pick him up when he fell and carry him.

'You aren't married, I take it?' he said, looking at the ringless fourth finger on my left hand. 'But you mentioned a friend.'

'Oh, that's my lodger, Sep, on the first floor. We *are* friends, but that's all.'

'I see. And where is friend Sep at the moment?'

'In a prison cell with the rest of them, I suppose.'

'Poor old Sep,' he said carelessly.

We had finished eating and drinking. The morning was well awake.

'Are *you* married?' I asked.

'I'm married in the sense that I took certain vows many years ago. We chose to separate rather than be divorced. It's now a very satisfactory relationship. We're better friends than we ever were lovers.'

'I can understand that,' I said, thinking of Bill Musgrove.

'I have a service flat up in London. She lives in Sussex with the children.'

'And that's the way you like it?' I asked drily.

He raised his eyebrows.

'Not only like it, that's the way I mean to keep it. Permanently.'

The warning was like strolling too close to a fence and seeing a notice saying that it was electrified. In my pride and anger I spoke frankly.

'That's fine by me. Because I prefer to be responsible just for myself.'

His wink of amusement and respect soothed me. I giggled.

154

'My father used to call me "The Thorn without a Rose"!' I said.

He said, grinning, 'Why use the past tense? Nothing seems to have changed.'

I laughed outright.

He sat at his ease, watching me and smiling.

He said, 'I promise you that I really have come here to help you clean the place up, but shall we do that afterwards?'

Whereas I have never seen my mother unclothed, and Zoe was always a one for clutching something to herself modestly, I never mind being naked. You know that dream some people have of finding themselves without clothes, walking down a main street full of staring people, and feeling deeply ashamed? Well, I once dreamed that I was naked in a busy street and I felt absolutely natural.

I like naked men if they have beautiful bodies. Jeremy was young and beautiful, like a silver fish. I don't know why silver or a fish, but that is what he was. And Colin Macintosh, in his maturity, had a hard, trim body with a beauty all its own.

But naked flesh can be less terrifying than the naked soul. Fears flocked in upon me as he put his arms round me for the first time, and I held him off.

'What's wrong?' he asked, and stopped to give me time.

How could I tell him? Dark angels counselling evil deeds. Trains shunting while life was extinguished. A slaughter-house. My child's shawl wrapping my sister's baby. An ageing man mentally whipping himself into a state of desire.

I said, 'You're going to find me awfully dull. The Kama Sutra made me giggle.'

He said, 'I've never read it. Why don't you stop worrying, lie back and enjoy yourself?'

So I did.

He was a selfish man for whom Colin Macintosh came first and last. He was a devious and designing man. It was some

155

weeks before I discovered that he did not come to my party by chance. He worked for the police in a drug squad, and had trailed a pusher to the Garret. I would have spent a night in the cells, too, if I hadn't shoved my way upstairs holding a water-spray, and caught his attention and his fancy. He was brutally frank.

'Let's get one thing straight before we begin. The only thing I'm married to is my work. As long as we're both enjoying ourselves, that's fine. The moment you fall in love with me, Lili Marlene, you'll be underneath the lamplight on your tod! So try to resist my ageing charms, will you?'

But that is beside the point. He healed and reassured me. He kept our relationship light and friendly, so that I look back upon it without remembering a single quarrel. Above all else he taught me that sex was fun. For that I was, am, and ever shall be truly grateful.

We were plying mops and dusters, filling wastepaper baskets and stacking empty bottles by the dustbin, when Sep came home with his new companion. My words of explanation and apology died within me as I realised that he had suddenly and quite completely transferred his allegiance.

'Darling Lady Lee, I've brought Freddie Finch back with me for a spot of food. He's been so sweet. Oh, *what* an experience! The cells, my dear, were beyond everything. And we were *searched*. Searched, my dear, within an inch of our chastity, by the boys in blue. A regular little fascist one of them was. Positively *enjoying* it, wasn't he, Freddie? Then they told us to be good and let us go. Makes you wonder what those poor Jews suffered under Hitler, doesn't it? But through it all Freddie was so *stalwart*, and such a *friend*! He turned an absolute nightmare into the most serendipitous occasion.'

While he rambled on, the stalwart friend and I exchanged wide white smiles and sidelong glances of pure dislike. He was gipsy-dark, with a fetching little face, and dapper despite his misadventures at the police station. His frilled shirt was still perky, his parma violet suit neat, his shoes and his hair still shone. Sep, on the contrary, looked like a plundered haystack.

I introduced Colin and said he had been at the party and had come back to help. Freddie summed up our new relationship with a knowing glint, but Sep was too far gone to understand.

'Oh, isn't that *kind* of him?' he said. 'When we're fed and watered we'll lend a hand too, won't we, Freddie?'

The stalwart friend murmured something which might have been a yea or a nay, and bared his little sharp white teeth in a predatory smile which reminded me of a shark. From then on 'Sharky' was my private name for Freddie Finch. He probably had a nasty one for me too, and he had already begun to wipe out my claims on Sep by rechristening him 'Monty'.

'*Monty* dear, I wonder, could I possibly beg a bath?'

Breathless with love and pride, Sep beseeched me.

'Of course he can, can't he, Lady Lee? Is there lots of hot water?'

'Gallons!' I said through my teeth. 'I've switched the immersion heater on. And we've cleaned the bathroom up. Please leave it as you find it.'

'Your wonderful notice at Camden Town!' Sep murmured fondly. 'You'll have to design us a new one. And does it matter if I borrow an egg or two and a rasher of bacon? I'll pay you back on Monday.'

'Borrow away! And we've cleaned the kitchen, too. So ditto, ditto.'

'Promise! Scout's honour!' said Sep, holding up one enormous hand. He giggled, 'Those naughty scout-masters!' he said. Then, 'We'll see you later.'

My father's warning gave me a momentary twinge. I glanced quickly at Colin, looking for signs of disapproval, but he remained urbane.

He said, watching them go down the stairs arm in arm, 'I don't think they'll be back, somehow.'

He looked amused but I felt curiously chagrined.

I said briefly, 'Then I shan't help Sep to clean up his flat!'

And yet there was no reason to be jealous. The landlady

had her lover. Why should the lodger not have his? Still I stood, arms folded, until Colin rattled the handle of his mop against the bucket to call me back to duty.

'Forget them!' he advised. 'They've already forgotten us.'

And he was quite right. We heard them plunging about and giggling in the bathroom, and chatting long and amicably in the kitchen. Then they departed to Sep's room and locked the door, and we saw no more of them.

When Colin and I had restored my top-floor flat he took me out for a snack. We spent the afternoon walking round London, which is beautifully quiet and peaceful on Sundays, and on a fine Sunday in mid-spring is most glorious. We talked, and fed the ducks in the park, saw *The Bridge over the River Kwai* in the evening and ate late in a Greek restaurant in Charlotte Street, making pigs of ourselves from taramasalata to fresh figs. At midnight he hailed a taxi, dropped me off at the Garret and said he would ring me during the week.

Warm and weary with love and wine I let myself in, and mounted the stairs as if they led to heaven. On the landing of the first floor I heard the subdued and loving double murmur of voices. So Freddie was staying the night. Well, so long as nobody else minded, I could afford to be charitable. Onwards and upwards I went, counting my blessings. Once more in the land of the living and loving. Once more part of a couple. Once more able to say 'we'.

I had a commission to deliver the following morning, costumes to research at the Victoria and Albert, and an interview in the afternoon. So I was out and about until five o'clock. I rather hoped that Freddie might have gone when I returned, and then Sep and I could cook our suppers in the communal kitchen and natter together about our changed states. We had new loves to enjoy separately, and a new home to enjoy together. I was prepared to accept the little wretch with good grace, and to listen to Sep's amorous ravings without looking bored. In that frame of mind, forgetting that one's own plans are seldom the same as other people's, I left the shopping until later and returned home.

158

They must have been there all day. They did not hear me let myself in, and when I entered the kitchen they turned round in astonishment, and stared at me resentfully. To feel an intruder in one's own home is an appalling experience, and the memory of our party was still raw.

Sep, who had good reason to feel guilty, said, 'Oh, hello there, Lady Lee. We've just brewed a pot of the liquor that cheers but does not inebriate. Do come and join us.'

I heard my tongue flicker forth.

'Too kind of you to invite me!'

Sep blundered into explanations and apologies which I waved away, while Freddie watched and smiled, shark-fashion. Slightly ashamed, I accepted a mug of tea and offered my cigarettes round, feeling I had been acid without cause. After all, I knew what Sep really meant. He accepted a cigarette sheepishly. Sharky took one as by right.

'How did the appointment go, Lady Lee?' Sep asked humbly.

'Quite well. It was a one-off illustration to a magazine story. They seemed to like it so I might be given the chance to do others.'

Sharky was smiling to himself and looking down at the tip of his cigarette.

Sep said pleadingly to him, 'This is an exceptionally talented lady, Freddie.'

He drawled, 'So you tell me!' in such a way that it could have been a compliment or an insult, and I chose to take it as the latter.

I said coolly, 'And what is your particular talent, Freddie?'

'Life is my talent,' he said, and tilted his pretty head and blew a perfect smoke-ring to my newly painted ceiling.

'Do you mean you don't work?' I asked sarcastically.

'Not at the moment.'

'But he's exceptionally talented, Lady Lee,' said Sep, agonised, looking from one to the other of us. 'He's a dancer. He's been in all the best shows. Haven't you, Freddie?'

Sharky declined to enlarge on this statement, but nodded negligently.

159

Yes, I could picture him as a dancer. The neat body and graceful movements. The little pointed feline face. And certain attitudes he struck.

'Oh well, here's hoping you find another show soon!' I said, raising my mug.

He did not answer, turning his shoulder ever so slightly to exclude me, and asked Sep, 'What are we doing this evening, Monty?'

Sep asked me out of habit, 'What are *you* doing, Lady Lee?'

'I shall be working at home,' I said briefly. 'I'll get myself something on a tray.'

I remembered that there was nothing to eat in the house. Normally Sep and I would have concocted a list together and bobbed off with a basket. This was no longer appropriate, and I had no intention of cooking for them or eating with them. Nor, it was evident, did they want me to do so. I finished my tea and rinsed the mug under the tap, a visitor in my own kitchen.

I said, 'I have some shopping to do!'

And walked the anonymous evening streets with a sore heart.

Freddie had come to stay. Sep was too transparent to cover up for him, but he did try and I did want to believe him.

At the end of the first week he told me that Freddie was looking round for a new flat, and hinted that he wouldn't mind roughing it in the ground-floor room, which was as yet unfurnished and undecorated. I was able to evade that trap by saying that my father had his own plans and had forbidden me to let it for the moment.

At the end of the second week Sep said he hoped I would not mind if Freddie stayed a little longer, because he was between lodgings.

At the end of the month Sep explained that Freddie had been let down once more, but there was a new prospect in mind.

Meanwhile he paid the rent with feverish punctuality,

160

and even offered me ten shillings a week extra to cover Freddie's use of the kitchen and bathroom.

No, I said, that would be all right, so long as his residence was only a temporary measure. He *was* leaving, wasn't he?

'Oh yes,' said Sep, looking hunted. 'He's just staying with me while he finds somewhere else.'

A new love will always displace and often despatch an old friend. I was aware from experience that I must not cling to the past and feel hurt, but walk on and forget. Unfortunately this was not possible in Sep's case because he was dependent on me for a home. In fact my responsibility had been doubled. I now had to reckon with Sharky.

Spring turned to summer. When Sep asked if I could possibly supply him with another cupboard, because Freddie had nowhere to hang his clothes, I knew that my father had been right, but by then I didn't know what the hell to do about it.

14

From start to finish of our affair Colin Macintosh called the tune, directed the entertainments, and paid the piper. He was far more experienced, more authoritative and more sophisticated than me, and I had a lot to learn about maintaining my independence, but I am still amazed that I allowed him to take me over without so much as a protesting squeak.

The first matter to be sorted out was the question of our meetings. His hours were mostly irregular and full of surprises, therefore I had to be as far as possible in a state of readiness, and to accept that a date might be cancelled. Despite financial commitments to his family in Sussex, and a service flat in St James's Street, his salary must have been large enough to enable him to indulge his tastes and pleasures, or perhaps he had a private income as well. Whatever the reason, I enjoyed a higher standard of living with him than with any other lover before or since. We dined at smart little restaurants which were fashionable at the time, sat in the front stalls at the most popular shows, and from our Centre Court seats watched Althea Gibson win Wimbledon that year.

On my part I was expected to behave with decorum and dress suitably for these occasions. My clothes, ready-made or home-made, came under heavy fire.

'No, love. We're dining at Rules, not hopping at the art school ball!' he would say in our early days, sending me back to change.

I had been a humble patron of Mary Quant's Bazaar

since it had opened in Chelsea two years previously, and she and I were on the same wave-length. He allowed one of her speedwell blue sheaths with a primrose cummerbund for casual occasions, but said that my green baize jacket reminded him of the stuff used on the doors of servants' inner halls, and my raincoat looked as if it had been made from the oil-cloth spread on truck drivers' café tables. When I told him they had indeed been created from these materials, he banned them for good, and gradually replenished my wardrobe at his expense with clothes which I could never have afforded.

As a gesture to their elegance, I had my hair cut and styled like Doris Day, which then needed to be put in curlers every night and became a thorough nuisance until I grew it again later. Why he was interested in me I shall never know. Grace Kelly was his ideal. How could I compare with a cool blonde film star who had recently become the Princess of Monaco?

We lived in a delightful limbo, and this may well have been a major attraction for me. I like men to complement my life rather than share it.

He had many acquaintances but no close friends. I never met any of his colleagues and he told me from the beginning that he never talked about his job. I was not allowed to ring him at work, indeed I did not know where he worked. He did give me the telephone number of his flat, but he had one of those answering machines which held me at bay on most occasions. From a mature standpoint I suspect his work was far more important and secret than he led me to believe.

He was generous with money but niggardly on loving kindness. I had to be undemanding, in tip-top condition and ready for fun. If I had a period or felt ill or tired he stayed away until I was back to normal. All this I accepted because he was my companion and lover of the moment, and it was interesting and in some ways convenient to be one sort of person by myself and another with him.

Also he distracted me from my worries about Sharky. While I enjoyed myself with Colin I forgot my second burden, though in his absence I suffered moments of total panic as I saw the little fiend establishing himself still more firmly in Sep's affections and in my house.

Sep's link with Whitegates had been broken. I would never have invited Sharky there, and he knew it. Since he would not allow Sep to go with me, and leave him behind, the visits ceased. Helen missed 'our poor dear Septimus' and was genuinely sorry for his absence, but the real sufferer was Sep because he loved my mother and had played the role of being her son at home.

So now I went alone.

My mother and sister, recognising the signs of a new man in my life, made discreet enquiries as to whether I wanted to introduce him. When I said cheerfully that Colin was a confirmed bachelor and would desert me at the first signs of family interest, they had that look on their faces which boded a little chat. So I was not surprised when my father suggested a stroll round the garden one summer evening at Whitegates.

He began amiably, 'We're somewhat concerned about you, Missie.'

'Oh dear! Is it a lecture?' I asked in a tone bright enough to warn him off.

'No, no. Let's say a friendly enquiry as to how matters stand.'

I folded my arms in a gesture of self-protection. He slid his hands casually into the pockets of his country squire's jacket, and jingled keys and small change. We sauntered on, admiring Helen's herbaceous border, the rustling trees and benign sky, looking anywhere rather than at each other.

Cass continued, 'I have no intention of playing the heavy father, but I am assuming that an attractive and independent young woman like yourself, living alone in London, has at last come to grips with the facts of life.'

I did not contradict him.

After a short pause he said, 'This Colin Macintosh, whom you don't wish to bring home, he's not keeping you, is he?'

'Certainly not!' I replied emphatically.

'But he gives you expensive personal presents?' eyeing my dress.

'Is there any reason why he shouldn't?' I asked defensively.

'Only that it advertises the relationship rather publicly,' said my father, light and dry as a fino sherry. 'So, if he's not keeping you but he buys your clothes and takes you out and about, would it be fair to say that your present status is that of a working mistress?'

I glanced at him quickly, stung, but his expression told me nothing. I answered reluctantly.

'I suppose you could describe it as that.'

'And this affair is unlikely to develop into anything more permanent?'

'It's absolutely certain not to!' I hurried to add, 'And I don't want it to, either.'

'But supposing you got into some sort of jam – loss of income, poor health, property damaged – and I'm not around, would this man of yours help you out?'

'I don't expect so. No, I'm sure not.'

'In fact, you still have no one to look after you?'

'I don't need looking after. I can look after myself.'

'But none of us can do that all the time!' And as I remained silent and sullen, he said coldly, 'Then I can only hope that you have sufficient commonsense to know what you're doing, and that you don't get hurt.'

I answered quick and sharp.

'You're looking at marriage from a man's point of view. Once endowed with a man's worldly goods, a woman is on duty for life. Does Matthew, in your opinion, look after Zoe? Isn't it really the other way about?'

His face changed. He recognised the implications and swerved aside.

'Oh, let's leave old Matthew out of it. Neither of us likes him.'

The leaves of the sycamore tree cast long-toothed shadows on the grass, reminding me of Sharky.

I said patiently, 'Colin Macintosh and I are harming

165

nobody, not even ourselves. This is a fun friendship. We don't discuss problems.'

'A fun friendship?' said my father, frowning. 'What a vacuous expression! Good God! To hear a daughter of mine talking about a fun friendship!'

'You're not going moral on me, are you, Cass?' I asked pointedly.

He shrugged. He took the hint.

'But you *are* my daughter,' he said, explaining himself to himself, 'and I want the best for you. I want a man to commit himself to you, make a proper life with you, take care of you. Fun friendship indeed!'

I was touched, but not converted.

'Yes, I *am* your daughter,' I said. 'And I like my life the way it is. The reason you can't see my point of view is because I'm female. I'm pretty sure that if you were faced with the choice of being an interior designer or somebody else's housekeeper you'd feel the way I do.'

He sighed. He shook his head. He shrugged. We strolled thoughtfully through the pleached walk.

In a different tone, he said, 'And there's another thing. I'm not at all happy about the situation with old Septimus. Does that boyfriend of his pay you anything towards the rent, or is he living on you as well as putting you in a damned awkward situation?'

On the subject of living my own life I could fight until I fell. On the subject of Sharky my sword-arm lost its vigour.

'Sep did offer. But as Freddie was only a temporary house-guest I didn't think it necessary.'

My father was now on his own ground.

'Temporary house-guest? The damned fellow's been there ever since you moved in. Hasn't he got a job?'

'Not yet. He's between jobs. He's a dancer.'

'In my opinion he's a professional hanger-on, but it's your business. I know you're fond of Septimus. Do you like this other fellow too?'

I shook my head.

'Then why don't you give him a specified date by which he must be out?'

I felt hollow and afraid. The leaf shadows menaced my feet.

'I just can't do things like that,' I said.

'Then use this Colin Macintosh of yours. He's in the police force. Couldn't you ask him to have a quiet word with the fellow? Suggest that it would be wise for him to leave?'

'No, I can't!' I said, desperate. 'Sep adores him and won't be parted from him.'

'Then give the pair of them notice.'

Adrift, I said, 'I can't. I know it's silly but Sep's trying to be responsible for him. I don't worry about Freddie Finch. He's a born survivor. But I do worry in case Sep ends up sleeping on a park bench because of him.'

'It's your decision,' he said, displeased. 'But I have a suggestion to make, which I should be glad for you to consider. Do you remember Miss Babbage?'

I sought among his acquaintances and friends.

'Should I do?' I asked.

'She had a flat in that Clapham house where Zoe lived.'

'Oh yes?'

'It doesn't matter whether you remember her or not. She's one of those women who are ultimately forgettable anyway, poor devil. It appears that Zoe has kept in touch with her. Had her down at the Old Rectory for the day. Brought her here to meet your mother. And so on. You know Helen and Zoe. They collect lame ducks. Apparently, the lease has run out on the Clapham property and Miss Babbage and the rest of them have to move.'

I said sulkily, 'I suppose she would like my ground-floor room, which incidentally is neither decorated nor furnished as yet?'

He was smiling at my annoyance.

'I'll decorate and furnish it for you, if you'll have her.'

I thought about it. He was planting a concierge in my premises, and both of us would owe him our home and allegiance, but I could hardly refuse.

Aiming at the real reason, I said, 'You don't trust me to run my own house.'

He said, 'You've done very well, apart from your choice of tenants. I admire your loyalty, Lulu, but you let your heart rule your head and that's no good for business. Miss Babbage will be reliable, helpful and grateful.'

'All right,' I said grudgingly. 'But she mustn't expect me to strike up a lifelong friendship with her and have cosy chats. And I won't have Helen or Zoe popping in to make sure she's happy, and keeping tabs on me. If that happens, Cass, I promise you that I shall walk out and leave you and the Garret and its tenants to do their own thing.'

He made a scissor movement with his hands to cut my anger. He was frowning.

'No, no, no! I'm not setting spies on you. Miss Babbage expects nothing from anyone, and will be only too anxious to please, poor creature. My reason for having her is to prevent any more friends of Septimus from imposing on you. She'll be both protection and ballast.'

'You make me sound like Bill Musgrove's book about *The Fly-Away Balloon.*'

He laughed then, and caught my arm and pulled me to him.

'But you *are* a balloon!' he said. 'A highly entertaining but utterly dotty little balloon, bobbing about and floating off on the slightest pretext. And I love you very much. That's why I fear for you. And I do understand about your freedom and independence, Lee, but you're not a son, you're a daughter, and I can't help wishing you were happily and safely married.'

We hugged each other hard and I spoke into the tweed of his squire's jacket.

'I love you very much, too.'

As we walked arm in arm back to the house I saw Helen and Zoe looking out for us from the drawing-room window, trying to interpret how things had gone.

'You're absolutely right, of course,' I said naughtily, 'I really must try to find a thoroughly generous, easygoing, lovable husband – like Matthew, for instance!'

* * *

The affair with Colin died suddenly at the end of summer. In the only note he ever wrote to me, he said, 'Leila, Something has turned up which will keep me abroad for several months. Have fun. Thanks for everything. Best of luck. Colin.'

With him went some of my self-esteem, the distraction which had prevented me from facing up to the situation with Freddie, and the masculine protection which Colin had unconsciously afforded me.

While he was around Sharky had kept a low profile. We only saw the little beast in passing, when he would wave a pleasant hand or say something civil about the weather or the news. We never had to wait long for the bathroom or kitchen to be free, and usually he absented himself until he was sure we had finished washing or cooking. As a professional house-guest he knew how to behave and he made sure that happy-go-lucky Sep toed the line with him.

But as soon as Freddie realised that Colin had gone his behaviour changed. He had a genius for inflicting pinprick annoyances, and they accumulated.

He made a point of lingering in the bath at the most inconvenient times. If I managed to get there before him he knocked on the door, saying, 'Frightfully sorry, dear, but I have an appointment to keep and I must be at my best. Do you mind hurrying up the weeniest bit?' The kitchen, as on that first day, was no longer my own. He took up cooking in earnest, and to be fair he showed talent, but a cluttered gas-stove and a sink full of unwashed saucepans is not helpful at six o'clock in the evening. Then he began to pilfer my food.

I had no public telephone in the house, so I had instituted an honesty box on the hall table, into which other people put the price of their calls. When I received a telephone bill twice as large as usual, and found only a few shillings in the box, I finally lost my temper with Freddie. Confronted, he moved from one lie to another, trying them out for conviction.

He said that he had personally put a couple of pound notes there only last week. A thief must have broken in and stolen them. He said that he never used the house telephone anyway. He always went down to the kiosk on the corner. Finally, he put the blame entirely on Miss Babbage. One night, he said, improvising frantically, he was coming downstairs and heard her putting a call through to Australia.

When, with shrewish logic, I confounded all his arguments he threw a tantrum as terrifying as it was foolish. He stamped and screamed and shook his fists like a demented child. I pushed him out of my room and shut the door.

From the other side of it he battered the panels and shrieked, 'I shall tell Monty about you, you bitch! You're just jealous because you've been ditched by your fancy man!'

I sat in front of my drawing-board for a long time, shaking with reaction.

My relations with my gangling child had grown progressively more distant over the past months. Now they reached their lowest ebb. Sep was incapable of quarrelling, but when I tackled him privately and reported my side of the interview he flushed up like a girl and made a gallant attempt to defend his lover.

'You should realise that Freddie's enormously sensitive, Lady Lee. I know he tells teensy-weensy little fibs, and when he's frightened he says any foolish thing that comes into his head. But he told me that you positively attacked him. Didn't give him a chance to explain.'

'I don't have to give him a chance. He takes everything he wants. Look at the size of that 'phone bill.'

'He's been trying to get work, you see,' said Sep pitifully. 'He has to ring round the agencies every day, just in case something turns up.'

'Well, it costs more than five shillings and sixpence to call every theatrical agency every day for three months, and that's what I found in the honesty box. He's living here on the pair of us anyway. I refuse to pay six pounds extra for his telephone expenses. He can either cough up or get out.'

'Then I'll pay them,' said Sep, defeated.

He insisted on turning out his pockets and his wallet there and then, and stalked back to his lover practically penniless. Obviously Sharky had other plans for the money because I could hear him shrieking, and poor Sep protesting, far into the night. I took the six pounds, for it was mine by right, and I was prepared to keep up an amiable front for the sake of peace. But Sharky, now certain that my affection for Sep would protect them both, waged open war on me behind his lover's back.

He would bounce into the kitchen crying, 'And what is the Lady of the House doing with the sugar basin? Counting the lumps to make sure I haven't stolen any? It'll be tea-bags next, instead of tea!'

After a week of this, and his pilfering, I cooked mostly in my own room and kept my food upstairs, which soon attracted mice.

He bought a tablet of soap and a soap-dish and left it in the bathroom, flagged with a note which read 'Take your naughty hands off me! I belong to Freddie!' But he used all my bath essence and squeezed my tube of toothpaste flat. So I kept everything in a toilet bag, and carried it to and fro like a house-guest.

Nor would he let me retreat in peace. Nowadays, whenever he used the telephone and knew I was at home he brought the honesty box upstairs, stood outside my door, knocked to attract my attention, and shook it noisily, saying, 'I've paid for my call. Listen to the pennies talking. Clink, clink, clink!'

Caught in a trap of my own making, I bore all this until Miss Babbage knocked at my door one evening to have 'Just a private word, Leila!'

Actually, she was incapable of having one word with anybody. A conversation with Miss Babbage was like standing on the side-lines watching a show-jumper perform. She cantered round the fences first, full of thanks and apology.

'Not a complaint, Leila dear. Heaven forbid. No one could be luckier or happier than I am since your sweet sister befriended me, and your kind mother sent fruit and flowers when I was ill, and you and your dear father offered me this lovely room . . . '

'Come in, Ruth,' I said, devastated to realise that I was glad of any company.

I made us a cup of coffee while she began a long run up to the first fence.

'I don't want you to think I'm prejudiced, because they can't help it, can they? It's the way they were born, I suppose. And so many of them are highly talented. One has only to think of poor Oscar Wilde . . . '

I thought, I must have sunk very low to be grateful for this. Fortunately I was not expected to answer, only to listen. By the time she had sipped the coffee and praised me for it, she was ready for the high wall.

'It's not Mr Brown – such a pleasant young man. A hint of sadness about him, I feel. Wouldn't you agree? Yes, I should have thought so. A hint of sadness. Life hasn't been easy for him. I can always tell. Anyway, it isn't Mr Brown, who always helps me in with my shopping, it's Mr Finch.'

She bore her long virginity with fortitude, but must apologise for it.

'I suppose an unmarried woman like myself shouldn't know about such things, let alone speak about them. Not very nice things, either. But this is your house, and I'm sure your kind father would be shocked if he realised. As indeed you would be, Leila dear. Which is why I'm telling you. Not that I want to accuse anyone without cause. Heaven forbid. But I am afraid that Mr Finch is not Playing the Game.'

A highly ambiguous statement, I thought.

'In what way?' I asked delicately, as she struggled to formulate his misdeeds.

'I don't know, of course. I'm only assuming. I may well be wrong. Having had no experience myself. In which case do correct me. But I hope I am a woman of the world. I had assumed that Mr Finch and Mr Brown were, in a manner of speaking, *married*.'

I was so demoralised that even this did not amuse me.

'Yes,' I said, just as delicately, lest she shy at the

172

final jump. 'You could put it that way. They have formed a partnership.'

'A partnership. Yes. Yes, that's the word. A partnership.'

I drank my coffee while she steadied herself for take-off.

She said abruptly. 'You don't know what goes on downstairs. Up here alone at the top of the house . . . '

Oh, my father, my father. I needed a concierge. And now, by God, I've got one.

' . . . I wouldn't have known myself, because that Mr Finch is a clever little monkey. He chooses his times and he's very discreet. But my nerves aren't all that they should be. I suffer from migraine, and I have little problems of a female nature. But I've been with my employer for over twenty years, and when I'm ill he sends me home. He says I'm indispensable to him. I hope so, I'm sure. Such a gentleman in every way . . . '

Here she swerved away and took a couple of side fences before returning. She had no need to tell me that she worshipped her employer, who was happily married with grown children. I gathered that from the way she spoke of him. But she did draw up a calendar of events, chartered by her migraines and monthly periods ('I know I can mention this, woman to woman!') and a cold which she happened to have caught in mid-October.

' . . . feeling better by lunch-time, so I was pottering quietly round when I heard Mr Finch let himself and another man in. And again it wasn't the same person because Mr Finch was making the same remarks he made last time, about keeping quiet and not being seen, and the man said, "Which way, Freddie?" Then, about an hour later, I heard them creeping downstairs, and I looked out of my window from behind the net curtains. And sure enough it was another stranger.

'Unfaithful to Sep,' I said, and poured us both another cup of coffee.

'Oh, worse, much worse than that,' said Miss Babbage, leaping the high wall effortlessly. 'He takes money from them. I've heard him settling up in the hall.'

I drew a deep breath and let out a long quiet sigh for my hapless child.

'There's a name for that sort of thing,' said Miss Babbage solemnly.

'Male prostitution,' I said. 'Thank you for telling me. I shall ask him to leave.'

Miss Babbage now scuttled for shelter.

'Of course, I realise that you'll have to tell him what you know, but I hope you won't mention my part in this. To tell you the truth, I'm a little afraid of him.'

To tell another truth, so was I, and more than a little.

But I said, 'Don't worry, Ruth, I won't involve you. I'll make it sound as though I found out by myself.' After a short pause, I added, 'I shan't be able to say anything about the money, of course, because I couldn't have known that.'

Miss Babbage finished her coffee, and thanked me two or three times. She looked round for some excuse to delay, and found it on my drawing-board.

In a fallow period between commissions, with work completed, money received, and Colin-time over, I had sat for hours recreating in pen and wash a bird's-eye view of Zoe's village fête in minute detail. Finished, it stayed with me still. I told myself I was waiting for the right moment to give it to my sister, to make sure that it was fully appreciated. But in truth I had fallen in love with my own creation and was reluctant to part with it.

Miss Babbage, unexpectedly illuminated, spoke in half-finished sentences.

'Oh, what a beautiful. Oh, I know where this is! My goodness, yes. Oh, look at the people. They're all different. I've met the vicar, you know. And his wife. Oh, look at the cottages and shops, and the church. The greengrocer's display. The butcher's window. The school. The little stalls on the playing field. Look! There's a coconut shy! Oh, Leila, it reminds me – only it's so much more so! – of my doll's house when I was a little girl. Everything so real, but in miniature. Oh, the hours and hours of loving work. What patience. What talent.'

She clapped her hands together in delight, and for the first time I saw the young and simple girl inside her who still hoped that life would be wonderful.

'How lucky you are to be able to create other worlds than this sorry one,' she said frankly.

Glorying in her praise, no longer bored and critical, I stood beside her and smiled on my *Village Fête*.

I said, 'I'd like you to keep it a secret from the family, if you would. It's going to be a surprise for Zoe.'

'Oh, of course. I shan't breathe a word. How honoured I am to have seen it. And how lucky Zoe is to have such a talented and generous sister, and to be given such a unique present.'

I registered that moment as the first time in our lives, to my knowledge, that Zoe had been congratulated on me.

'If it was mine,' Miss Babbage chattered, on her way out, excited, exalted, 'I should wake up every morning and look at it before I looked at anything else. And I should find something new in it every day. It's that sort of picture. Have you thought of sending it to the Royal Academy for exhibition . . . ?'

I closed the door behind her feeling enriched, and ashamed, and looked at my painting with renewed hope. For this had evolved from pure fancy and personal inclination, was aimed at no market and burdened with no deadline. This was me, doing what I liked, and the result had instantly impressed a member of the viewing public – such was the grand title I gave Ruth Babbage on the spur of that moment. Furthermore, this member had suggested that a far wider public awaited me.

I pondered, head on one side, both my work and her suggestion. My ambition to be an artist like my grandmother continued to lurk slyly behind the need to earn a living. I could not discount my painting master's judgement of my ability, but on optimistic days I still believed I could confound it. Now I endeavoured to be my own critic.

Did *Village Fête* seize a harmony between numerous rapports, as Cézanne had said a picture should? I thought it did. Would Sickert have said my figures were related to one another and to their setting? Yes, I was sure of it. Could I walk about in the picture? No doubt of that. Was something exciting happening? Yes, it was – in a modest rustic way. And most certainly it told a story, in fact several stories, which had been the public's demand ever since painter set oil to canvas.

Then doubts set in. Had it fulfilled Whistler's criterion of singing a tune? Perhaps. But, if so, the tune was light and airy and had been sung many times before. Lastly, and most important of all, had I, according to Sickert on Whistler, evolved something new which justified me or my existence? I hesitated. *Village Fête* was utterly delightful, undoubtedly skilful, and very stylish. It was a part of me, certainly, springing as it did from love of my sister and sympathy with her own loves. But it did not express the whole of me.

'No,' I said aloud to the absent Ruth Babbage, 'I shan't be sending it to the Royal Academy for exhibition – but I've a good mind to try it out elsewhere, and see what the general reaction is!'

From that moment Ruth Babbage attached herself to me as well as my home. She was too timid and too sensitive to intrude, but she thanked me for being me in many little ways. The monthly rent was always accompanied by a bunch of inexpensive flowers. She was by nature a home-bird who baked for the week at the weekend. A humble knock would announce the arrival of two buttered scones, a piece of sponge cake or a slice of fruit pie, waiting on a covered plate outside my door while the baker scuttled downstairs.

'Never disturb the Artist at Work, Leila! That's what I say to myself. Goodness knows how many creations have been destroyed by thoughtless visitors. Just think of what we lost when the Man from Porlock interrupted Samuel Taylor Coleridge. Though, of course, one doesn't like to think that the poem was written as a result of drug-addiction . . .'

In turn, I made an effort to be sociable, and instituted

a glass of sherry on rent day, which she drank with great enjoyment and many protests. When Bill Musgrove's book was reprinted that year I gave her one of my complimentary copies, and signed it at her request.

'To Ruth, with love from Leila.'

She clasped it to her flat chest and crossed her arms over it, crusader-fashion, while she thanked me. The Holy Grail had nothing on *The Fly-Away Balloon*.

15

I had delivered Sharky's ultimatum spontaneously, bravely, sincerely, to Ruth Babbage. To deliver it to Sharky was quite another matter. He was a survivor at all costs and at other people's expense. He would spare me nothing in order to keep his present lodging. I feared consequences I could not even guess.

I thought of turning the problem over to my father, but knew he would insist on both of them leaving, and I could not sacrifice Sep. I hesitated to ask Colin for advice or assistance, lest he think I was chasing him. When I resolved this with my conscience and finally rang his flat a stranger answered, and said he was still away. So I spent my nights lying awake and rehearsing what Zoe and I called 'Be Gone!' speeches, and spent my days avoiding the opportunity to say them. At the end of a week's indecision, having reached desperation point, I leaned on a straw and confided in Sep.

The scenes that followered were traumatic. Sep broke down in my living room and actually sobbed with grief. I poured him a glass of wine and lent him a handkerchief, stricken but resolute. He sounded, as Magda would say, like a fourpenny book.

'Oh, Lady Lee, Lady Lee!' Sep moaned. 'I was afraid of this. He's such a capricious little thing. Such a flirt. But I thought he'd settled down. And now you tell me there are others. Oh, Lady Lee, what shall I do?'

My courage was coming back as he leaned on me once more. I could defend others better than I could defend myself.

'You tell him to get out, right now. I'll come with you, if you like. In any case, I'll back you up.'

'But where can he go, Lady Lee? Where?'

'He can sponge on his new friends,' I said briskly.

Sounding like my father, I laid out Sep's line of action with Freddie. With which he agreed abjectly, only spoiling the effect by saying as he stood hangdog on the landing, 'But all I want, Lady Lee, is to bring my boy back to the fold.'

Then he heard Freddie come in and shambled downstairs to confront him with his infidelity.

The row that followed lasted for a very long time. I should have known it would not go my way. Much later, Sep blundered upstairs again, wet-eyed but shining, to tell me they were fully reconciled, and Freddie had promised to behave.

'The poor love was trying to earn a crust the only way he knew how!' Sep explained. 'His pride's been hurt, you know, having to live on me. But I told him I didn't mind. I loved providing for us.'

'Then why didn't he give you the money he earned?' I asked nastily.

'I didn't think to ask,' Sep replied, confused, 'but he must have had his reasons, Lady Lee. Whatever his little faults, he's a loving boy, you know.'

'Christ Almighty, Sep, there's no saving you!' I said savagely.

I had muffed my chance and was now saddled with the role of informer. When Sharky himself was sent up to apologise, crying coyly, 'Darling Lady Lee, naughty Freddie wants to kiss and be friends!' I knew we were in for a real squall.

In contrast to Sep's damp and dishevelled appearance, Sharky looked as chic and dapper as ever. His lilac tie was three shades darker than his lilac shirt. They had both cost a lot of money, and so had his new grey suit. He smelled deliciously of Arpège, a perfume I recognised because it was Helen's favourite.

Once inside my room, with the door closed, he leaned against it, and spoke softly to me alone.

179

He said, 'My, my! What big eyes and ears you have, Grandmother! Well, I'm willing to let bygones be bygones, but before you set your teeth into me again just think of that saucy twist to the Thurber tale. This Little Red Riding Hood can shoot too, when she's really pushed, and don't you forget it.'

I told Ruth Babbage frankly and fully what had happened, swore her to secrecy in case she told my father, and entered on another period of indecision, during which my imagination plunged to unsuspected depths.

I had my three doors fitted with Yale locks. I stretched threads of cotton across the thresholds of living room, kitchenette and bedroom, so that I should know at once if they had been entered. I listed the contents of my food cupboard. I hid all my work, particularly *Village Fête*, lest Sharky burgle my room and wreak his spite on it. He would always know the subtlest way to hurt an enemy. Outside or inside my home, I lived in a state of constant apprehension. And though Sharky was making no trouble for the moment, he reigned supreme.

Zoe's daughter was born easily and quickly that November, arriving so soon after the village midwife that the good woman said, 'My word, this one's in a hurry!' as she brought Caroline into the world.

I was making breakfast when my mother telephoned to say that labour had begun. I had scarcely sat down at the drawing-board, thinking good thoughts for Zoe, when Helen rang again to say I had an eight-pound four-ounce niece and mother and child were doing well.

'And Caroline is such a pretty baby!' Helen cried, fulfilled. 'Just as fair as Simon is dark. And Simon is here, sitting on my knee, aren't you darling? Such a handsome big brother. And he wants to talk to his Auntie Lulu.'

Simon's voice crooned into my ear with breathy intimacy.

He said, 'Hell-o-o-o?' invitingly. Then firmly and sweetly, 'Bye-bye.'

Goodness and mercy shone into my winter world once

180

more. I forgot to hide my work and lock up my door. I pulled on my white high-heeled Russian boots, cloaked myself in scarlet, donned my black Garbo hat, and clattered gleefully down the stairs and out into the foggy morning to send a bouquet to Zoe. I was extravagant at Interflora. I bought an exquisitely smocked dress in New Bond Street for Caroline, and a bright red wooden London bus at Hamley's for Simon. All of which left me with enough money to buy myself a cup of coffee before I went home.

Striding jauntily down Carnaby Street, one of the passing show, I bumped straight into Jeremy Purchase.

He had caught hold of my arms to steady me, and for a moment we stood quite still together, silent with shock and pleasure. His eyes were a subtler green than I remembered, flecked with hazel round the pupil, the irises darkly ringed. They seemed ready to smile, but wary as if waiting for permission. My own must have answered them kindly. He gave a great grin and hugged me so hard that my ribs nearly met in the middle.

'Sparky, for Christ's sake. Sparky!'

The passing show flowed round and by us, taking no more than cursory notice. He held me at arm's length and shook his head in delighted disbelief. Then his expression changed. I recognised that stubborn hopeful look which admitted that he was about to take one hell of a chance, and would be furious if he failed.

He said imperiously, gaily, 'Whatever you're doing, forget it. We must celebrate. Spend the day together. Talk ourselves hoarse. What do you say?'

Though awash with joy, I thought it wise not to be swept entirely under. I was in sufficient trouble already.

I said, grinning back at him, 'Did you have to break my bloody ribs?'

He threw back his head and laughed in his old way, eyes tight shut. Then took my arm and began to lead me back towards Regent Street.

'We'll find a taxi. Lunch first. How about Stone's Chop-house?'

181

He had grown older and richer, had grown up into the world and its ways. Four years ago he would have offered me a sandwich in a coffee bar.

I placed the palms of my hands on his beautiful sturdy chest to stop him.

I said, 'Wait a minute, Jeremy. Look, it's too long a tale to tell this minute, but I need to keep an eye on my house. Why don't we buy a picnic lunch and take it home with us?'

He was momentarily dashed. Then revived again.

'All right. If you prefer that. Where are you living?'

I was garrulous with delight.

'At the back of King's Cross station. It's my own property. Jeremy, I'm a landlady with tenants – actually, that's the problem! – but I'll tell you all about it while we're shopping. Otherwise, I'm a self-employed commercial artist, making out pretty well and paying my own way – though I must admit that I can't afford to go Dutch with you today because I'm temporarily broke. Zoe produced her second baby this morning – yes, the *second*! A daughter, Caroline. She already has a two-year-old son called Simon – and I've blued the week's housekeeping on them! I tell you, simply *everything* is happening at once! Oh, there's a wonderful delicatessen near me, where we can buy German garlic sausage and rye bread and wicked cakes, and an off-licence which sells marvellous beer.'

He burst out laughing again.

'Sparky, you never change!' he said. 'Let's alter that order to smoked salmon and champagne – and wicked cakes!'

So off we went, arm in arm, and I poured out my confession as if he had been a priest, instead of my erstwhile love and father of my unborn child.

The tide, as tides do, had turned again. And the gods were with me.

Coming in, laden with shopping, we found Sharky and an unknown friend in the hall using the telephone. They had heard the key in the lock, but been unable to react quickly enough.

With a fixed smile in my direction, Sharky said into the mouthpiece, 'Must go now, my dear. See you later!' and put down the receiver.

The friend, who was much older and richer, dressed in City clothes and carrying a rolled umbrella, looked extremely worried.

He cleared his throat and said too loudly, 'Well, Freddie, best of luck and all that. Nice to have bumped into you again, old sport. Sorry I can't stay. See you around.'

And was obviously relieved when Jeremy held the door open to let him out.

Sharky spoke to me, but his eyes were all for Jeremy. He took a shilling from a little purse shaped like a Dorothy bag, and dropped it ostentatiously into the honesty box.

'That was an important business call, Lady Lee. Nigel has theatre connections and he's given me such a good reference. Actually, I'm just on my way to an audition, so wish me luck, dear.'

Jeremy put his warm square hand in mine and gently squeezed a message of encouragement.

I said crisply, confidently, in my old style, 'You're a lying hound, Freddie, and you can go right upstairs and pack. You're leaving now. And for good.'

He made a curious, sinewy movement, a cross between a wriggle and a curtsey, and pouted for Jeremy's benefit.

'Oh, we're not going through the same boring old hoop again, are we, dear?' he said, half-jeering, half-cajoling. 'If I get this job I promise to be a good boy and pay you a little something towards the rent.'

Jeremy said softly and clearly, 'Upstairs. At the double. And pack.'

Sharky gave him a sultry look and lowered his eyelashes. It was evident that the situation excited him and he found Jeremy immensely attractive. I could tell from his expression that it was almost worth losing everything to be dominated in this fashion. He reminded me of a girl I had known whose husband used to beat her up. I acted as counsellor and friend until I realised that she invited the beatings and enjoyed the pain he inflicted. I had

found that relationship pretty sickening. I found this one
obscene.

'Upstairs and pack!' Jeremy repeated more loudly.

'This very minute?' Freddie asked, dipping and bridling.

'Yes. And be quick about it!' said Jeremy.

'Oh, isn't he masterful?' said Freddie to me, envying,
admiring.

Sulky, silky, he preceded Jeremy up the stairs, swaying
his neat little bottom, one hand trailing suggestively along
the banister rail. He led us into Sep's bedroom and opened
his wardrobe. The single suitcase he had brought with him
was obviously inadequate to hold these later acquisitions.

'Wherever shall I pack all this?' he mused, one finger
on his rosy lips.

'I don't know, and I don't particularly care,' said
Jeremy easily, sitting on the bed and folding his arms.
'You can put it in carrier bags or stick it in the dustbin,
so long as it doesn't stay here. And if you're not ready in
five minutes I shall take very great pleasure in throwing you
and your sharp little suits down the stairs and out on to the
pavement.'

'The idea!' said Sharky to himself, entranced.

Then, like a lamb, he began to pack.

So I took possession of my house again, and Jeremy
and I ate and drank in the communal kitchen, finished
the champagne, and were still there, talking and laughing,
when Sep drifted home at six o'clock.

It was typical of Freddie that he had left no note.
He would always move on and leave his host unthanked.

His only message was oral, an afterthought, spoken over
his shoulder as he was leaving, eyes lingering on Jeremy.

'Tell Monty I'll see him around!'

As I embroidered this statement for Sep's benefit, I
opened a bottle of wine to soften the blow.

Sep received the news with pale resignation and without
reproach. He shook hands absently with Jeremy and smiled
his foolish lovely smile.

We invited him to join us, but he wanted to be alone.

So I assembled a plateful of delicacies left over from our luxury lunch, and a glass of red wine, and he shambled off to grieve in solitary state.

I was too relieved, too high in spirits with the joy of the day, to take more than a passing concern in his response. I meant to have a long loving helpful talk with him later, but talk and time were all for Jeremy and the opportunity was lost.

From then on we rarely saw him. His room became a temporary perch for sleeping, and he was out from morning to night, probably looking for the little brute. At the end of the month he left the Garret for good, with his few possessions in a rucksack and his rent paid up to date. He left a note for me, who had supported and harboured and suffered through him.

'Sorry things didn't work out in the end, Lady Lee. We had some good times together. Take care and God bless. Love, Sep.'

But to my mother, who had simply dispensed her usual hospitality, he wrote a heartfelt letter.

'Dearest Mama, for Mama you will always be to me. I want you to know that I'll never forget the wonderful days I spent at Whitegates, which was my first real home. Pure serendipity. And I'm sorry I haven't seen you the last few months but things have been difficult. Wherever I am I shall always remember you, and feel a part of the family. My love to you and Zoe, and kind respects to your husband. Say a little prayer for me sometimes. I shall need it. Your devoted Septimus.'

I still catch myself hoping to find him, one serendipitous day. That is, if he is still alive. I glance sideways, at places where serendipity does not exist. Vagrants queuing outside night shelters. Drug-addicts waiting outside Boots in Piccadilly for their prescriptions. Down-and-outs in newspapers, huddled in cardboard boxes, sleeping rough on park benches and in doorways. Meths drinkers, drinking, stinking, dying, underneath the arches. I search the anonymous changing faces of London crowds, and hope, and do not hope. For Sep was never a survivor.

* * *

A winter interior. Winter light. We lie together, fingers loosely clasped after the frenzy of love-making, and look up at my bedroom ceiling on which I have painted a fantasy forest.

'You could get lost in there,' says Jeremy lazily.

I muse on his face as a sailor's wife must muse when her husband is home from the sea. I am learning him all over again.

This once delightful and vulnerable boy has become a man of authority. The promise of physical power was always there, in his sturdy stance, in the tilt of his head, the set of his lips, the way he moved. Now it is manifest. His skin is tougher, his muscles harder, his body scent stronger, less sweet, more salt. We bring the experience of other lovers, other mistresses, as trophies to this present.

His ideas have undergone a similar process. I catch up on news of his career to date. He did well in his finals, but not well enough to be offered research work in tropical diseases, though he keeps up his studies in his spare time. His lust for travel has been temporarily assuaged by serving as a ship's doctor. At present he is passionately convinced that the true doctor is a general practitioner, and is about to set up a combined practice with three other enthusiastic young men, in Blackheath. But they are all married and housed, and he must find a flat.

At the moment he is staying at the Garret, and occupying Sep's bedsitter. His presence is unofficial, because my father has forbidden me to get another tenant as yet, and talks about conversion. Ruth Babbage has been sworn to delicious secrecy and the present situation suits everyone very well.

In fact I would say that life was almost perfect. Just occasionally I find myself catching or swallowing a yawn because Jeremy is a great self-debater, and at times I feel more like a public meeting than a companion. There were hints of this in his earlier youth, for he was always a keen medical student, and like so many idealists he favoured left-wing politics and dreamed of saving the world. Now he

186

is dedicated, through medicine, to the service of mankind, and too much of this can become tedious listening for a non-medical, non-political realist who is absorbed in life and art.

He is tough and forthright, too. He knows exactly what he wants and where he is going. He marches straight forward, and probably over and through as well. I should not like Jeremy Purchase to be my enemy. I love him to be my friend and lover.

As the room darkens we leave my bed and dress before Miss Babbage comes home. We are always thoughtful for this maiden lady, who has been in a state of delectable shock since Sharky was banished and Jeremy arrived. She has fallen in love with Jem, of course, and blushes when she meets him in the hall. I am afraid that she is being mentally unfaithful to her employer. With Mr Carmichael she has enjoyed a marriage in the head, but Jeremy is her new lover. She indulges her appetite for him by popping arch little questions to me about our relationship. To jest about the love we have for each other's company, the lateness of our nights on the town or indoors, to hint at future wedded bliss, is her own bliss.

In a light and careless fashion we are fond of Ruth Babbage. For her sake, we keep up a respectable front. We do more than that. I show her my work as it flowers forth, and Jeremy flirts with her subtly and advises her medically. She has grown pink and skittish in the past months on our affair.

And what of our two conservative families? We lead lives apart from theirs and tell them only what we want them to know. I doubt whether Jeremy has mentioned my resurrection to the Purchases at all. I only mentioned him to my family the other weekend out of sheer necessity.

During the spring of 1958, out of the goodness of his heart and the faith of his bank manager, my father had the Garret converted into three self-contained flatlets. We occupants no longer share the family-sized kitchen and bathroom but enjoy a kitchenette and bathroomette apiece. Each of us has our own telephone and a personal front door fitted with a Yale lock. Only the staircase and hallway remain common ground, and I am responsible for keeping them spick and span.

My solitary grumble is that I must carry two keys, one to enter the house and the other to enter my flat. In fear of losing or forgetting one or both of them, and being locked out, I leave duplicate keys in a hollow brick by the front door. My father says I have thus nullified all his attempts to make the place burglar-proof.

'By the way, I don't intend to raise Miss Babbage's rent,' he says, 'but I shall certainly charge full market price for that first-floor flat.'

He and Helen and I drive down to visit Zoe on Easter Sunday, to admire her garden full of daffodils and primroses, and the Old Rectory which grows grander every year. We shall romp with Simon, croon over Caroline, and put up with Matthew who is, as my father says, the original pain in the bum.

I am longing to tell the Barbers my own house-news, but must first bend a deferential knee to the beauty and dignity of Zoe's new dining room.

Once this is done I strike an attitude like a trumpeter and say, '*Tah-rah*! The last builder has left the Garret, and I am the landlady of three self-contained flats!'

Simon laughs so much that he makes the rest of us laugh too.

'This is my best audience!' I say, and kiss the top of his silky black head.

Zoe, adopting the tones of a dove, croons, 'So you'll be finding a new tenant for poor Septimus's flat?'

Helen also becomes dove-like, echoing the coo with, 'Poor Septimus. I wonder whatever has become of him?'

My father dismisses such sentiments with a huff and a puff and blows their dove-cote down.

'Lee's well rid of him.'

Then turns to me, to avoid their reproachful looks,

and says, 'Have you advertised the flat yet, by the way?'

I draw a deep breath and bring out the news at a quick trot.

'I didn't need to. I let it by word of mouth. I have a tenant, as of this week. A young doctor from abroad.'

'A young doctor?' Zoe murmurs hopefully, and Helen says, 'From abroad?'

'Yes. He was a ship's doctor, but now he's working as a partner in a general practice in Blackheath.'

The questions come thick and fast, and more and more they come.

'Is he single? Is he British?'

A pause. 'Is he coloured, darling? Because . . . '

The reason trails away because they are liberal-minded people. But that possibility has been worrying them ever since I brought a West Indian rock musician called Zak Blueberry home for the weekend. Although he was a friend, not a lover, his visit was not a success from anyone's point of view.

I say, 'He's single. He's British. He's white.'

'Do you like him? You must bring him down to Whitegates/the Old Rectory one weekend,' say Helen and Zoe together. 'What's his name?'

I am about to ruin their Sunday.

'We like each other very much, and you've already met him. It's Jeremy Purchase.'

Helen looks at me as if I were no longer a child of hers. Zoe is sorry too, and sensing a deeper darker undercurrent of feeling between my mother and me, is uncertain what line to take.

My father says very seriously, 'I thought, after the last fiasco, we had agreed that business and sentiment don't mix? There's no hope for you, Lee!'

And to show me that I have disappointed him, he puts his arm round Zoe's fair shoulders and walks her over to the kitchen window.

Turning his back on me, he says, 'What about knocking an archway in the garden wall, Zoe, setting a wrought-iron

189

gate there, and growing a white-flowered creeper up and over it. Then you'll be able to look right out across the meadow, and on to the hills beyond . . . '

That was the year when my life and London began to swing. The year when Mary Quant opened a second Quant's Bazaar in Knightsbridge, and broke all the rules with her opening fashion show, and every smart girl who could afford it had a Vidal Sassoon haircut. The year when afternoon gowns died and the fashionable dressed either 'up to six' or 'after six'. The year when it was chic for the young to wear blue jeans, but even chic-er to team them with an expensive silk shirt or handmade leather boots. The year when I saw a slim dark girl wearing a leaf-green suit, whose skirt stopped just above her knees. She walked on to the platform at Charing Cross tube station, and I swear that every man turned round to look at her legs, and every woman registered some degree of shock.

It was also the year that the CND was formed, and four thousand protesters, including Jeremy Purchase and me, marched from London to Aldermaston, carrying banners which demanded 'Ban the Bomb!' As usual, Jeremy went as himself, but I made a costume out of black cloth and painted a silver skeleton on it and wore metal bracelets and anklets which looked like chains and rattled like dry bones.

Zoe

16

We knew, of course, that the Jeremy Purchase affair would never last, though we could hardly say that to Leila. So I was not a bit surprised when Mummy telephoned later the same evening, and talked for so long about my sister that Matthew grew impatient, and came into the hall and stood by me, whispering, 'When are we having supper? Is she going on all night?'

So I said, 'Mummy, I must go now. Mat's making tea and a-little-something-on-toast noises. Why don't you pop down for lunch on Thursday and we'll have a good old natter?'

Immediately she moved into her wifely gear, crying, 'Heavens above! It's nine o'clock. Darling, I hadn't realised. This new business with Leila has been going round and round in my head since she told us at lunch-time. I simply didn't think. Yes, I'll come on Thursday. There are some things which can't be said over the 'phone.' Then her tone changed and she spoke teasingly, affectionately, as usual, 'Off you go, and feed the brute!'

'What on earth was all that about?' Matthew asked.

He sounded annoyed, so I made light of the conversation.

'Oh, Mummy's just having a little fret about Leila renting her flat to Jeremy Purchase.'

'Who's he?'

'Darling! He was the joker who anchored my wedding veil with a stone to stop the wind from blowing it about. On our wedding day! You must remember *that*!'

'Don't remember a thing,' said Matthew offhandedly,

'except for standing round like a spare part, and wishing your parents had spent their money on something more sensible.'

I skirted that criticism.

'Darling, you're teasing me! Surely you remember Jeremy. He was Leila's first serious boyfriend. They came to dinner at our Clapham flat half a dozen times.'

Matthew stuck his hands in his pockets and walked round the kitchen, whistling softly under his breath and frowning to himself. I cut four thick slices of Hovis and set them in the wire toaster on the Aga. I began to scramble eggs and watch the toast at the same time, talking as if nothing was the matter.

'They went out together for a couple of years. We all thought they'd be engaged. Then it broke up. Mummy told me he'd behaved very badly. I know Leila was quite ill for a while and took months to get over it . . . '

Matthew stopped at the kitchen window and said, back turned on me, 'Your family has been talking at me most of the day and your mother has been on the telephone most of the evening. I really don't want to hear an account of Leila's past tribulations as well.'

Something had upset him. The only way to deal with Matthew in this mood was to agree with him and then divert his attention.

I said, 'We *are* a set of chatterboxes, I know! Darling, we're practically ready. Could you find us knives and forks?'

He jerked the dresser-drawer open. Banged it shut. Dropped each piece of cutlery deliberately and noisily into its place.

Pretending not to notice, I served up our supper, which we ate in silence: mine apprehensive, his glowering. I made coffee, set a bowl of fruit on the table, and put out the rest of the Simnel cake. He was longing for me to ask him if anything was wrong, but by this time I knew better than to fall into that trap. Still, there was no dodging Matthew if he wanted to quarrel. He picked on my silence instead.

He said, 'You seem unusually preoccupied. I suppose

you're dreaming about that archway your father proposes to make in our garden wall?'

So that was the trouble. I did not dare look at him. I knew he would be colourless with temper, lips compressed.

I said lightly, 'I'd forgotten all about it, to be frank. Daddy throws out ideas like a firework display. Most of them come to nothing. I don't take any notice of him.'

He burst out, 'You don't take any notice of me either, and nor does he. I know your father owns this place but he needn't make the fact quite so bloody obvious. I might just as well not exist.'

We had been over this rough ground many times before.

I said as steadily as I could, 'Matthew, let's not make an issue of this. If you don't want an archway of course we won't have one.'

He thumped his fist on the table, which made me jump, and shouted, 'Trust you not to see the wood for the bloody trees. It's not simply the archway. It's everything to do with this house and our marriage. Most parents allow their children to grow up and leave home for good, but you don't want to, and your father won't let you.'

I said shakily, 'I'm not discussing this again, Matthew,' and took my coffee into the living room, away from him.

My mother passed on all her magazines, because I had to watch every penny and could not afford to buy them. So the contents of my bamboo paper-rack, like the Old Rectory, gave a false impression of prosperity. Appearances, Matthew used to say, were important. It seemed to me that they had taken the place of reality. I picked up a copy of *House and Garden* and leafed slowly through it without seeing anything. I was listening to Matthew's movements, gauging the extent of his anger. Depending on the depth of feeling aroused, he could follow me in with a sheepish apology, sulk for hours, or slam out for the rest of the evening. This time he evidently meant to continue the quarrel from a distance. He had chosen to clear the table and wash up, all of which was accomplished loudly and clumsily with a great deal of grumbling and muttering.

I picked up *Country Life* and turned the pages over

195

faster. There were a few things I would like to say to Matthew about parents who didn't let their children grow up and leave home for good. His mother kept account of my family's visits. She rang him twice a week to check up, and since he was an only child she reckoned that each Gideon visit equalled one for the Barbers. So in exchange for my pleasure in this Sunday and the coming Thursday, I should have to endure and entertain both of his parents twice.

They were incapable of enjoyment, either at first or second hand. My father-in-law was greedy, self-righteous and silent, except when his wife demanded that he chime agreement with her. He watched her all the time, waiting for his cue. My mother-in-law's ruling emotion was jealousy, and if she could find no excuse for exercising it she invented one. I was on duty all the time she was with us.

Keeping her on an even keel, praising and propitiating her.

How nice you always look. I love your hair like that. The vicar's wife was so pleased to meet you, the last time you were here.

Coaxing or tricking the children into gratifying her.

Simon, if you take Tank Engine Thomas *over to Grannie I know she'll read it to you. And if Caroline sits on Grannie's knee she can listen too, even if she doesn't know what it means.*

Taking care not to cook too well.

You put me to shame, Zoe dear, with your wonderful cooking. But isn't roast chicken just a teeny-weeny bit extravagant?

Or too little.

Could I have just the thinnest possible slice of bread and butter, dear? That cheese soufflé was very light. Greedy old us, we're used to eating quite a hearty meal in the evenings.

Disclaiming my own family's generosity.

No, that cotton bedspread is years old. Mummy practically apologised for passing it on to me!

Fielding the swipes.

I think that Leila's just taking her time about getting married. She's really absorbed in art, you know.

Yes, Daddy does work hard and he is away from home a great deal. But Mummy has always understood that. She isn't a lonely sort of person. She has so many interests.

Propping up the shoulder chips.

I've always thought your house was very well situated. Not in the city but near to it. You have all the advantages, that way.

Could you give me your recipe for rissoles? Matthew's always on about them.

Oh, age doesn't matter. You have such good bones.

That dress is ten years old? Well, I never would have believed it. Of course, C & A are wonderful, aren't they?

And after they had gone I hoped that Matthew would not turn to me for physical comfort and relief, cuddling me frantically, making love too quickly, wanting to talk afterwards. I hoped he would just shut up and go to sleep. Because I had done too much for him already, and his parents made me behave like a hypocrite and I hated him for them.

I picked up *Good Housekeeping*. Faster and faster I turned the pages, and more and more furious I became.

The disgruntled sounds had died away. He was probably sitting there, nursing his wrongs. I jumped up and marched in to confront him with his own family's misdeeds. For once, he should hear my point of view.

The kitchen was empty and immaculate. He had tidied and washed up and gone out. Disquieted, I sat down in my domestic kingdom and reflected on its beauty. Family tastes and family offerings were everywhere evident. My father had given me the black oak Welsh dresser as a birthday present. My mother's unbirthday presents, from patchwork cushions to a varied assortment of Victorian blue and white plates, were legion. My sister had rummaged through the Caledonian Market for the French china pots, labelled 'Fleurs Orangers' and 'Cons: De Roses', and the pottery cat which looked like a child's drawing in three dimensions. A brown stone jug full of wild flowers, a wickerwork dish enfolding a clutch of new-laid eggs, were my contribution.

The hands of the kitchen clock, which had once kept time in a country schoolroom, moved towards eleven. Matthew was evidently taking one of his long late brooding strolls. In tune, if not in sympathy, I walked my house like a stranger watching Zoe Barber's life.

197

The mother looked in at the nursery, sat her small lolling son on his pot, changed her baby daughter, tucked them both up and sent them back to sleep with a kiss and a murmur. The wife turned down the heavy cotton bedspread, whose opulence covered a very old red satin eiderdown and unbleached cotton sheets. The housekeeper soaked nappies in a bucket, sorted the Monday wash into piles ready for morning, put out clean clothes and clean towels, laid the breakfast table, ready for another similar day to begin.

But where was I? And who was I? And had I ever existed? Because this house was not a home, it was a stage on which I played many roles. And only the setting was beautiful, for behind the scenes the actress was perpetually short of money and her manager could be a bully.

My father always brought wine with him, but we had drunk that at lunch-time. I wished we had not finished it all. I should have liked a glass, something to smooth the jagged edges of the day. For I had been apprehensive before my family came and while they were here, in case any of them upset Matthew. So all day the actress had been on duty, smiling and accepting compliments on her performance, taut as a drawn wire.

'You need a drink!' I said aloud to myself, and was immensely comforted to hear that somebody understood and cared about me.

One of the domestic luxuries with which Mummy supplied me was cooking sherry. I reached the bottle down from the shelf and half-filled a tea-cup. It tasted sweet and thick but the effect was magical. I sat at the table watching the stage-set recede and the truth emerge.

I said, as in a revelation, 'I'm not happy any more, and none of this is real.'

Then I went upstairs to bed to avoid Matthew's home-coming.

I was still awake when I heard him come into the room just after midnight, but pretended to be fast asleep until he fell asleep himself. And I lay awake for a long time after that, listening to the grandfather clock (our sixth-anniversary present from my parents) strike the early-morning hours in the hall downstairs.

At breakfast Matthew was silent, and though ostensibly together we managed to avoid each other for most of the day: he playing cricket and me helping to prepare a cricket tea while all the cricketers' children amused each other. On Tuesday and Wednesday he stayed late at the office. On the Thursday that my mother came he walked in unheralded, unexpected, two hours early, and in one of his most charming moods.

Simon shrieked, 'Daddy! Daddy! Look what Grandma's brought me!'

And assaulted him with a small wooden mallet and peg-board. Caroline banged her spoon on the tray of her high chair in greeting. And Mummy put up her face for his kiss.

'Why, Matthew dear, what a lovely surprise!' she said.

She spoke with genuine pleasure, for she was fond of him and could usually bring out the best in him, unlike Daddy and Leila.

He said gallantly, 'Well, I knew you were here, Helen, and I skipped work on purpose so that I shouldn't miss you!'

He leaned forward with both hands behind his back, and kissed me very nicely and warmly. Then, with a magician's flourish, he produced a bunch of the miniature roses sold on London pavement stalls, and a bottle of Beaujolais, saying, 'Flowers for you, Zoe! And wine for dinner.'

He had been cool and distant since the row on Sunday, and I had been avoiding a new quarrel or a continuation of the old one, so I was delighted by the largesse. I echoed my mother.

'Darling, how lovely! What a surprise! But how did you get here? I didn't know there was a train at this time. Have you walked all the way from the station?'

'No. A client was driving down to Tunbridge Wells, and gave me a lift. Dropped me off at the village green. I've

199

decided that I take life too seriously and don't see enough of my family. I'm turning over a new leaf.'

This astonishing proclamation silenced me for the moment. But Mummy answered him spontaneously, wistfully.

'How I wish Cass would turn over a new leaf! I've been taking second place to interior designing since we married. It's not easy being the wife of a talented man.' Loyally, she added, 'Though always rewarding, of course.'

We ate a nursery tea together contentedly in the kitchen, and the last of my reservations about Matthew vanished as he helped me with the children. He was particularly sweet with Caroline, cutting her bread and jam into bite-sized pieces and wiping her mouth and hands afterwards. He answered all Simon's questions, which was a feat in itself. He made sure that I drank two cups of tea without being interrupted. He chatted to Mummy about her garden and ours, though gardening did not interest him. He did his best in every way he could to make amends. He even offered to drive her to the station, but I asked him to babysit instead.

I wanted to do a little late shopping for the evening meal. Macaroni cheese, I felt, was inadequate under the circumstances. We could have that tomorrow. A mixed grill from our local butcher would go well with the wine. And a bargain dress-length would have to wait.

Reading my thoughts, Mummy said on the platform, 'Men aren't always easy to live with. They have such different aims and values from women. But these are the very differences that marriage demands in order to strike a balance. I remind myself of that whenever I'm feeling hard done by.'

She said, musing, 'I think that's Lulu's problem. She's so aware of possible traumas that she's afraid to commit herself. And I'm sorry, because marriage can be the most wonderful thing in the world, but you have to work at it and you can't be happy all the time. Lulu wants to enjoy love without paying for it, and that's not possible.'

200

We kissed each other in perfect peace. She had made my day right.

I said, 'Give my special love to Daddy. And, Mummy, will you tell him that I think it's a marvellous idea, but can you persuade him not to knock an archway in the garden wall *this* year?'

She lifted one gloved hand and both eyebrows in acknowledgement and understanding. She bent her head and rummaged in her handbag.

'I almost forgot,' she said, who never to my knowledge forgot anything, 'I meant to give the children a shilling each. Do what you think best with it, darling. Ice-cream or money-boxes. I don't mind. And, Zoe . . . no, don't push my hand away! I want to do this! . . . Zoe, Matthew brought in a bottle of wine as a treat. Here's a pound to buy something special for supper, to go with it.'

Glad to confide in her, I said, 'We had such an *awful* row the other night.'

Smiling, she answered, 'I guessed that. Repentance was writ large all over Matthew's countenance!' And as the train came into the station she said, 'You'll have lots more quarrels and reconciliations. It's all part of being married. Just make sure that you keep the fabric in good repair. And don't believe that a quarrel means the end of the world, Zoe. Never believe that. There's always another day.'

Then I knew that cooking sherry truth was only the truth of the moment, whereas Matthew and I had a lifetime in which to make everything right.

Wined, dined and expansive, my husband said, 'I had a particular reason for wanting to celebrate this evening. Zoe, how would you feel if I said I wanted to leave Watson, Lucas and Abercrombie?'

I had thought the purpose of the evening was to make up a quarrel with me, not celebrate something for him, and I was slow to reply. Fortunately, he put this down to surprise and began to explain.

'I know it's a secure job with a sound company, but the

salary isn't princely and the prospect of a partnership is a hell of a way off. I could slave for the next twenty years, and for what? To fill old Abercrombie's shoes, and bumble along in the same old fashion? I want more than that. I want challenges, responsibility, real power, real status. I'm no better than a glorified clerk at the moment.'

Someone had been talking to him. He was riding high on their assessment.

I said cautiously, 'What were you thinking of doing instead?'

'Working for a new, go-ahead business firm.'

'You've had an offer?'

He smiled into his wine, swirled his glass, drank up with a flourish, and said, 'Yes, I have. A good one. I shall give old Abercrombie plenty of notice. The business is new. I don't start until September.'

So my advice was not being asked. He had made the decision without me.

'Heavens above!' I said faintly.

He was still too absorbed in his own triumph to notice that my reaction lacked spontaneity. Late but willing, I sprang to meet the occasion, reminding myself that I should be delighted with and for him.

I said, 'I'm absolutely bowled over, darling. I never thought, never suspected. What are we waiting for? Let's pour out another two glasses and drink to it!'

He looked young, bemused, vulnerable. He took off his spectacles and polished them and put them down on the table.

He said humbly, 'And another thing. I was thinking I might try wearing contact lenses. I look such a dismal old owl in these specs. What do you think, Zo?'

I did not say that contact lenses were very expensive. I was more perturbed by his sudden interest in his appearance than the expense.

'I always thought they made you look intellectual. But why not have a change if you feel like it?'

He smiled at me as he poured the wine.

'I must smarten up a bit, too,' he said. He turned the

202

joke against himself. 'What's the use of saying appearances matter when I slop round in cheap shirts and old-fashioned suits?'

'Oh, does this new job demand a new image?' I asked tartly.

I sounded like Leila, and softened the question.

'Do tell me about it, Mat.'

'You're going to laugh when I do tell you.'

He was so eager and flustered and anxious for approval that I felt a surge of loving sympathy.

'Make me laugh then,' I said, smiling. 'Drink your wine, and make me laugh.'

'It's a cosmetics business. You'll be given free samples, I don't doubt! The directors are Americans, man and wife. Howard Weingarten and Trudy Olsen. He's putting up the capital but it's her baby and she's running it . . . '

I should have been entertained, hearing her speak through him, but was not.

' . . . She's a human dynamo. Been a Jill-of-all-trades. Done everything. Travelled everywhere. She intends to pay Howard back as soon as she can, so that she'll own Trudy Olsen's outright . . . '

'Oh, she's naming it after herself, is she?' I asked, rather sourly.

He answered defensively.

'Actually, that was her grandmother's name. And quite a few big cosmetic firms are named after their owners.' He added, as if I didn't know, 'Helena Rubinstein and Elizabeth Arden are real people.'

I was annoyed as well as amused. The only previous conversation Matthew had ever had about cosmetics was to tell me that his mother didn't approve of them. Now he was busy selling them to me.

'Trudy's starting in a modest way at first. She's a third-generation American of Swedish stock. Her grandmother used to make creams and lotions from natural products like herbs and honey. Trudy has the recipes. Of course, the lipsticks and eyeshadow and things like that will be modern. But the general image is natural and simple and reasonably priced. She's aiming for the young and single market. That's where the money lies these days, believe it or not!'

'And what exactly will *you* be doing?' I asked drily, sounding more and more like Leila.

Matthew did not notice my tone. In the grip of enthusiasm he tended to overlook other people's reactions.

'I shall be in at the beginning. I'm going to be able to do all the things I ever wanted. This is no dozy old firm of solicitors, this is an adventure. Howard thinks the world of Trudy and he's prepared to back her to the hilt. The sky's the limit.'

He became aware that I had spoken and answered cheerfully.

'My job? I shall be a professional dogsbody! No, seriously, I shall take care of the legal side and keep an eye on things for Trudy. Howard says that she's a whizz at ideas but needs someone else to work out the details. So I shall also be organising things – but then I'm good at organising. They're giving me two hundred a year more than I get now, just for a start, and there'll be all sorts of perks. A decent car, for one thing. So you can have your old jalopy for yourself. Apparently, Trudy's been looking round for a lootenant – as she calls it! – for nearly a year. She dropped into the office with a little problem a few months ago, and I handled it for her. Then we started talking about this and that, and finally she asked me back to their flat for drinks, to meet Howard. And they both seemed to think I would fit the bill.'

He gave a bemused laugh.

'You didn't tell me about all this,' I said, feeling thoroughly left out.

'Tell you?' he said absently. 'There was nothing to tell.'

'Have the Olsens any children?' I asked cautiously, trying to form a picture of this extraordinary pair.

'No. Oh no. Trudy's not the maternal type. Besides, Howard's in his sixties. It's a second or third marriage for both of them.'

'And what age is she?'

He was at a loss, as always when I asked him to describe people or clothes or colours, or to recount a conversation.

'I don't know. A lot older than you. I suppose she'll be in her early forties.'

'Very glamorous?'

He looked puzzled.

'I suppose she's smart.'

Sensing at last that I was not quite as thrilled as he was, he endeavoured to bring me into the picture.

'And you'll be involved too, Zo. There'll be a certain amount of entertaining to do. Not the big stuff, of course. Trudy and Howard will take care of that. But we shall play a necessary and valuable part. People down for the weekend. That sort of thing. I told them you were a marvellous cook and a very beautiful girl. I told them you would be a great asset.'

The tribute warmed me. I reached across the table to squeeze his hand.

He added thoughtfully, 'And the Old Rectory will be a great asset, too.'

I wondered how it was that in the moments we were supposed to be closest I felt furthest apart.

Less warmly, I said, 'You told Mummy that you would be turning over a new leaf. Spending more time with us. Not taking life so seriously. But won't a job like this demand even more of you?'

He said vaguely, 'Oh, but this will be fun, so I shan't be such a grouch. And there'll be more money for us and far better prospects. And on the whole I shall arrange my own timetable.'

He chuckled in recollection.

'Trudy said that she believed in playing hard as well as working hard, and if I didn't take time off to enjoy myself it was my own goddam fault!'

This was so opposite to his mother's philosophy that I said, 'But what will your parents think about this? Mr Abercrombie was a friend of your father.'

He shrugged and frowned.

205

'I hope they'll understand and approve, naturally.'

But if they did not, then – his tone indicated – bad luck!

'It's not their sort of scene,' I suggested.

'No, I suppose not. But then they think of me as more of a stick-in-the-mud than I really am.'

He brooded for a while over this.

Then he said, 'I've been looking for a way out of the rut I'm in without knowing how to find it. Given an opportunity like this I'm not going to throw it away!'

There was another pause.

'Do the Weingartens want you to put any money into the business?' I asked carefully.

'No. Not a penny.'

I pondered the advisability of asking my next question, but had to ask it for all our sakes.

'It's not just a flash in the pan, is it, Mat? I mean, they're not just rich people amusing themselves with a new idea?'

He looked black then, and I was sorry and afraid.

He said, 'Do you think I'm such a fool that I haven't checked them out? I've been keeping this idea quiet for weeks while I made sure everything was all right. Trudy isn't a social butterfly playing a game. She's a hard-headed and ambitious businesswoman. As I told you, her first concern is to repay Howard so that she can call the firm her own. You might find it difficult to understand a woman like that. A lot of people would. She's as tough as a man. She's a power-house.'

She sounded awful, but if this was what made Matthew happy then I must accept her and the job.

'Yes, of course,' I said quickly. 'I'm sorry. I should have known.'

He kept his eyes lowered. I had spoiled his triumph. I got up and hugged and kissed him until he began to smile grudgingly and respond. Then I looked into his brown myopic eyes, which were so vulnerable without the sternness of his spectacles, and said the only thing I could think of to restore his former humour.

'When are you going to make that appointment with the optician?'

Leila

17

Whitsun 1960

The Whit weekend of 1960 was the hottest for a century, and as Jeremy was busy saving the world in one way or another, Matthew was in Paris on business, and Helen and Cass were having an early holiday in Greece, I took a chance and dropped in on Zoe.

My circumstances had improved in the last two years. The day of the moped was over and gone, and a nippy little black Ford Popular bore me across London and had even ventured across France to Spain. Though my income was never steady I now earned enough to keep myself in modest comfort.

The difference in Zoe and Matthew's life was more dramatic still. His new job had 'grieved' the Barbers, and so released Zoe from some of her duties as a daughter-in-law. They were not the only victims of Matthew's career. Family loyalties took a back seat, and our trips down to the Old Rectory had been curtailed. He and Helen still liked each other, and most weeks she bobbed down to Kent to spend a day with her daughter, and Zoe and I kept in touch as usual. But the Gideons were only invited together if Matthew was away, and should a meeting between him and my father be necessary or unavoidable he invariably blocked Cass's schemes for improving the house. Either he intended to do it himself, or it could not be done yet, or he was thinking of something along the same lines. Both

Zoe and Helen endeavoured to cover up the real reason, but Cass was no fool and knew he was being kept at arm's length.

He said, 'Now that the damned place has been rewired, replumbed, and made warm and dry, I'm not wanted. Well, that's no more than I expected from Gauleiter Barber. But my friend Ben Shanklady is a better solicitor than he'll ever be, and I've made sure that the Old Rectory belongs to Zoe and her children after her, and he won't get a brick or a farthing out if it!'

I said pertly, 'Farthings will cease to be currency at the end of this year.'

'Then he'll get even less,' said my father, having the final word.

But the fact remained that work on the Old Rectory had stopped completely since Matthew had been given his new job. And the work involved both of them to a surprising degree at first. As well as her usual duties, Zoe was kept busy entertaining possible, probable or future clients, for visits which seemed to be part bait and part business. They were all foreigners, being sold a piece of English Country Life, being assured that Trudy Olsen cosmetics would have the same wholesome and refreshing effect as a weekend at the Old Rectory. As my father said, high living, low thinking, and Trudy Olsen ruled.

We had only met Trudy and Howard Weingarten once, and that was enough for both parties. The lady glittered too much for my liking. He was very rich and rather sweet, but completely under her thumb.

Apart from our banishment as a family unit, about which Zoe was obviously troubled, she seemed to be doing well. She had twice figured in glossy magazines, due to her husband and her father still struggling for supremacy. Once as Cass's daughter to advertise his skill at converting the Old Rectory, and once as Matthew's decorative wife in an article which was really a long advertisement for Trudy Olsen cosmetics. She had more freedom nowadays, since Simon had just begun school, and Caroline was in a local kindergarten. So when I walked into her much-photographed kitchen at eleven o'clock that Bank Holiday morning, I was amazed to find her somewhat the worse for alcohol.

Like all young wives and mothers who endeavour to stay with or ahead of the domestic rat-race, my sister had no time for herself. When she was not playing hostess or posing for the camera, her daily beauty routine consisted of washing her face, twisting up and anchoring her long gold hair, stepping into a pair of slacks and pulling on a shirt or sweater.

One heavy molten lock now swung free of its imprisoning hairpin. She stared at it as if it belonged to someone else, and cobbled it up again. Her gingham blouse and cotton slacks were clean but unironed, and the sandals slopping on her feet must have come from a jumble sale. Yet Zoe, tipsy and dishevelled, was still lovely. And apart from her slurred speech and glazed blue eyes she still fulfilled the Victorian feminine ideal of home and beauty.

Pointing her tea-cup at me, my sister said, "Sthe only person I wanted to see!' And casting her eyes upward added humbly, 'Thank you, God!'

Flattered but wary, I entered, saying, 'I had a free day, unexpectedly. Tried to 'phone you, but the operator said the line was out of order. So I took a chance and packed a picnic basket.'

'Telephone is *not* out of order,' said Zoe, drawing herself up to her full and most dignified height. 'Took the bloody thing off-the-hook and left-it-off.'

Drinking *and* swearing, I thought.

'Siddown!' she said, and sat down herself, rather suddenly.

'Where are the children?' I asked, listening to the unnatural quiet.

'Ev'rybody's out,' said Zoe, bemused. 'Es-sept me. Matthew's in Paris. Children spending day with my-friend-Penny because I had her two last week. So I thought what-the-hell.' She added inconsequentially, 'And here you are!'

I took a kitchen chair and slid my wicker basket down beside me. I had come for a sociable visit and apparently walked into a crisis. My offerings could wait.

211

'Are you boozing alone or may I join you?' I asked.

Zoe said belligerently, 'Wha' makes you think I'm boozing?' And saved me from concocting a tactful reply by adding in a more peaceable tone, ''Sonly cooking sherry. Mummy gives me a bottle now'n then. Want some?'

'I don't think so,' I said. 'It usually tastes of treacle.'

Zoe said sternly, focusing on me, 'You know what you and Daddy are? You're s-wine nobs. That's what you are.' She thought for a while and corrected this statement. 'W-wine s-snobs.' She surprised herself with a sorry scrap of truth. 'And so would I be, 'f I could afford it. This tastes awful.'

I lifted a mildly snobbish bottle of wine from the basket and set it on the table in front of her.

I said amicably, 'If we're going to drink this early in the day, let's have some decent stuff.'

Zoe sat for a moment or two, looking puzzled, and then pressed her hands down on her knees and rose slowly, like an old woman. She made the journey to her corner cupboard and found two wine-glasses.

I filled them, saying, 'Anything wrong?'

'Wrong?' she cried, belligerent again. 'What should be wrong? I'm h-healthy. I'm h-happily married. Two beau'ful children. Lovely home. Lots-a-friends. S'ccessful husband. Ev'rything. Any woman. Poss'bly want.'

Her wine-glass slopped as she lifted it, and she gave it a reproachful stare as if it had made a fool of her.

''Sjust that I work very hard,' she explained. 'Now'n again need a day off. Having a day off. That's all.'

'You mean you've got pissed on cooking sherry before?'

'Shouldn't say "pissed". "Sloshed" is nicer. I'm not sloshed. I'm re-laxed.'

'All right, then. Have you relaxed on cooking sherry before?'

She nodded and said, 'Now'n again. Can't use drinks cupboard. Matthew notish-notishes ev'rything. He'd see if the whisky or gin went down. But he doesn't notish the cooking sherry. Only trouble is – it runs out. And I need it f'making trifle. But this bloody morning. Thought I'd finish the bottle.'

212

I put my head in my hands and laughed and laughed. I could not help it. She was so dolorously funny. Then I wiped my eyes and apologised, and sipped my wine. She gave me an uncertain smile.

'Do you want to tell me what's wrong?' I asked. 'Or shall we just have a private party and forget it?'

She waved her hand to and fro and shook her head.

'F'get it!' said Zoe.

'Have you had any breakfast, Zo?'

She shook her head again.

I unpacked my basket and made her a garlic sausage sandwich with dill pickle. She ate it slowly, ruminating. She held out her glass for more wine.

'Have you told Helen about these relaxing sprees?' I asked.

Again the head-shake.

'Why not? I thought that you and she were great buddies on the home and marriage front.'

Zoe said, 'She'd worry about me. Don't want to worry Mummy.'

'Mummies are there to be worried,' I said acidly. 'It's all part of their job.'

Either she could not understand my irony or she chose to ignore it. Instead she stood up, rather unsteadily, and spread out her arms to introduce the kitchen to me in a new light.

'See all this!' cried Zoe, inspired. ''Sa dream. 'Snothing but a bloody dream.'

I managed her as carefully as a cargo of cut-glass.

'And what's wrong with that?' I asked breezily. 'I dream all the time. I make my living by dreaming on paper.'

'Yes,' said Zoe sadly. 'But you choosed – you made a choose . . . '

She looked sadder than ever as the words escaped her meaning.

'I made a choice? I chose that dream?'

She said, as if I had given the universe an answer, 'You *chose* it.'

'Seven years ago *you* chose *this*,' I reminded her. 'Love, honour and obey. Remember? To have and to hold from this day forth. For the procreation of children. With thy body I thee worship. Until death us do part.' I could not help adding, 'I baulk at most of that, but it's the life-sentence which finishes me!'

Even stripped to the bone, down on her luck, and needing all the comfort anyone could give, Zoe was full of charity and forbearance.

'Oh, but I meant it,' she breathed. 'Ev-er-y word. But . . . ' She sought clarity. 'Takes two,' said Zoe. 'Takes two to do that.'

I was not surprised. Blasted Matthew was at the bottom of her drinking.

Zoe said, putting one graceful hand to her head, 'Think I need coffee. Black.'

'Yes. I think you need coffee black, too. Sit down, Zo.'

It was a good thing I had thought to bring fresh ground coffee with me. There was only a bottle of Camp Coffee in the cupboard.

'You don't *drink* this stuff, do you?' I asked.

'When I'm by myself,' answered Zoe, an automaton. ''Scheaper. We're not made of money, you know. Ev'ry penny counts. Matthew has a pos-position to keep up. All the best for the guess – guesses – people who come here . . . '

'Guests?'

'Yes. Guesses. All the bess for the guess. But family stand back.'

I nodded my head to myself. I had heard the Lady Marian holding forth in similar vein, some years ago.

Zoe proceeded to give me a short lecture on economics. 'Lunch: sispence a head. That's me and the kids. Supper: shilling a head. That's me and Matthew. Friends come f'dinner. Costs two pounds. Grow all garden produce. Do own housework. But no-bod-y knows! Beaufiful cloves – cloze . . . '

'Clothes?'

'Beaufiful clo'se for going out. Lousy old clo'se for staying home. And that's the way it goes, Lulu.'

I made a pot of good, honest, strong, black coffee and gave her a cup.

'So you're worried about money?'

She nodded, and then shook her head.

'You're worried about money and something else as well?'

She drank reflectively and said with enormous dignity, 'Tell you. Presently. But. Promise. Never tell Mummy. Mummy mustn't know.'

I spat on my finger and drew it across my throat.

Zoe said tenderly, 'Good ol' Lulu. Can be trusted.'

She looked up at me beseechingly, and said, 'Know you don't like Matthew, but could you give me a 'pinion on him, with-out prej-prejudice?'

'I'll try. What do you want to know?'

'Would you say he was a 'ttractive man?'

I conjured up Matthew the last time I had been unfortunate enough to meet him, and contemplated the portrait objectively.

I said, 'As a matter of fact he is, you know. He's improved in the last couple of years. I suppose he always had nice features, though I noticed his horn-rimmed specs more than anything else, and that flopping love-lock of hair. But now he's wearing contact lenses and well-cut suits, and brushes his hair back, he looks rather like Gregory Peck.'

Zoe's nod sank lower and lower.

'Fraid of that,' she said.

'Why?' I asked jokingly. 'Is he being unfaithful to you with Boadicea?'

Zoe's head jerked up and she said, 'Who's Boadicea?'

'It's Cass's nickname for his chromium-plated lady boss.'

Her head slowly sank again.

'Oh, you mean Trudy?' She puzzled over this for a full minute and then said petulantly, 'Why should he be in love with *her*? She's years and years older than he is. B'sides, she employs him and she's married already. What funny things you say, Lulu!'

I said, 'This conversation is like digging a ditch with a teaspoon! What exactly *is* bothering you, then, Zo?'

She twined her fingers together and meditated on them.

Even cooking sherry could not shield her from embarrassment.

She said, 'I can't es-plain. But I don't think he loves me any more. And he said this job meant we'd spend more time together, and have more money. But we don't and we haven't. And he says, can't I talk about something else apart from kids and food prices. But that's my life. And he goes to places like Paris. Without me. Mummy said she'd look after Si and Caro while I went with him. But he said no, business only and anyway he couldn't afford it. And I thought, if he looks so handsome and finds me so dull he might fall in love with a young French girl in a short skirt. And I don't know how to stop him.'

I said, with all the authority I could summon, 'Zoe! You are talking absolute nonsense. Now let me tuck you up in bed before you fall into your coffee cup.'

Mention of bed roused her instantly.

'Can't!' she cried, almost in horror. 'Washing to do. House to clean.'

'I'll do everything necessary and look after the children when they come home. I'll even stay the night if you want me to.'

She quietened down again, thinking.

'Oh, would you, Lulu? That would be nice!' Then, immediately suspicious, 'Why? How can you? What about Jem-Jem-Jememy?'

'He's busy playing Jesus Christ, healing the sick. He'll never miss me.'

'He hasn't lef' you again, has he?' she enquired piteously.

'He didn't leave me the first time. I left him.'

'Oh, that's all right then,' she said with evident relief.

She nodded her head up and down saying, 'Ac-shally, Lulu, it's lasted a lot longer than we all thought it would. Two whole years.'

'Only another thirty-eight to go and we'll be our old Dutches,' I said, more to amuse myself than my sister, who was in deadly earnest. 'Come on, Zoe, get on your feet like a good girl and let me help you upstairs.'

She levered herself up obediently, both hands on my

shoulders, saying fondly, 'But you are happy, both of you, aren't you?'

'Delirious.'

When I had helped her into bed and watched her fall asleep, I went downstairs to tackle her chores. I used the inadequate second-hand washing machine with its miniature rubber rollers, and hung the Barbers' shabby clothes and hard towels and mended sheets on the line in the back garden. Bare sufficiency was the keynote of her larder and of Helen's old refrigerator, which burbled and hiccupped in the corner. Helen's old Hoover was out of action and I trundled a bald little carpet-sweeper all over the house, and plied a dustpan and brush. Even the dusters were long past being good dusters. Halfway through my housework, I went shopping in the car to find one of those places that sells everything and stays open on Bank Holidays, and came back loaded with supplies of every kind. The only thing I did not buy was another bottle of cooking sherry.

Then, shamelessly, when the Old Rectory was beautiful again, I uncovered the deeper secrets of her existence, seeking and finding evidence on shelves and in drawers and wardrobes.

Truly, as my sister had said, 'Bess for guess but family stand back.'

Appearances in this household were paramount. In reality her magazine-style domestic life was a terrible sham.

At four o'clock I took a foaming glass of Alka-seltzers to Zoe, and followed it with tea and biscuits. She sat up and held her head, crestfallen.

She said, 'I can't think what came over me. I must have been depressed.'

'The truth came over you, Zo. Don't let it slide away unnoticed.'

'Cooking-sherry truth!' she said, and gave a shamed little laugh.

'I've been having a look at the Old Rectory truth in the last few hours. Doesn't Matthew give you enough housekeeping money?'

She began to excuse, to explain. I cut across both loyal efforts.

'You mean that he has to have his contact lenses and his smart suits and live it up in the business world, while you sit at home with a cheese butty – and cooking sherry when you can get it!'

'Only while he's making his way up the ladder.'

'Zoe, he's already there! He's Trudy's right-hand man and the company's solicitor. He can't go anywhere else but out. If his salary doesn't allow for that standard of living then he must lower it or ask for an expense account. I thought he was Boadicea's protégé?'

'He is. She thinks very highly of Matthew. But you know how proud he is. He can't bear to be taking all the time. He has to give. He has to put up a show.'

'I never noticed him giving much to anybody!' I said, with good reason.

'I don't know how you can say that!' said Zoe.

And her tone cried 'To arms! To arms!'

She said stoutly, 'Matthew's very generous indeed!'

She sought for proof and found none.

She added lamely, 'Anyway, he's as generous as he can be – with so many commitments.'

'But he's not being generous with the right people, of whom you are first and foremost. Look, Zo, I've washed your tatty old knickers . . . '

She clapped one hand to her mouth and said, 'Did you remember to hang them sideways on the line so that the worn part didn't show?'

'It isn't something I was born to do,' I said, 'but yes. I thought it best not to advertise your poverty.'

She dropped her hand then, and smoothed the bedcover thoughtfully.

'And a' plucked the sheets,' I said irreverently, 'and a's nose was as sharp as a pen! And what are those sheets made of, for God's sake? Solidified gruel?'

'Unbleached cotton,' said Zoe defensively. 'It's very hard-wearing.'

'It would be. Personally, I'd want it to wear out very

218

quickly. And I suppose all your lovely salmon pink and primrose yellow wedding present linen is on the guest beds? No, don't bother to answer that question. I know it is. I've looked.'

She bent her head and smoothed the sheet again and sipped her tea.

'Why won't you tell Mummy?' I said, slipping into the childhood name. 'She and Matthew have always got on well together. She could have a little word with him. You know that if I said anything to him we'd have a blazing row – something we've managed to avoid so far. He needs pulling up and pulling back, Zo. Reminding. He's gone off at a tangent somewhere. Mummy could do it.'

Zoe shook her head, near tears.

'Promise me!' she begged. 'Promise you'll never tell Mummy!'

I shrugged, and the gesture reminded me of my father when he had given up trying to help me.

'I won't say a thing. But, Zo, if you value yourself at all – bring him to heel, for God's sake, before he sets his heel on you.'

We were silent for a while after that.

Then I said, 'I'll take care of the children when they come home with this Penny-person. Who is she?'

And Zoe came back gratefully to her common task, and gave me a potted biography of Penny which ended up, 'You'll simply love her!'

Of course, I didn't. I found her exceedingly dull. But I was very civil and smiling and offered her a drink from Matthew's drinks cupboard, with added zest at the thought of diminishing his supplies.

She refused the offer with a puzzled smile. Like Zoe, she did not expect luxuries. She had long brown hair which needed brushing, and she wore the mother's uniform: old slacks and a faded shirt. But she had heard about my wayward existence, and questioned me eagerly about my life and work. My name was known to her on the covers of her children's books. I lived in a different world which she had invested with false glamour.

219

I agreed that I was very lucky to earn a living doing what I liked, but had to correct the impression that I spent my life at smart cocktail parties hobnobbing with the rich and famous. I said I spent much of my time working at home most of the day and sometimes into the night, with only the radio for company. I assured her that all was not cakes and ale in the world of art, and that the majority of artists were hard working, hard done-by and frequently hard up. My flippancy misled her into thinking I was being modest.

'I don't believe a word of it!' she said, laughing.

She told me she had been a secretary in the City before she married Eric, and though her marriage cup overflowed with milk and honey she missed the fun and company at the office.

' . . . but I tell myself I can't have everything . . . '

As I smiled and nodded and listened, and answered the thousand questions put by Simon and Caroline, who clutched my hands and jumped up and down with delight at my presence, a series of cartoons entitled *The Happy Housewife* clicked on and off in my head like lantern slides. Helen had supplied the original idea. Common parlance and sour truth provided the theme.

' . . . happily married with a lovely husband and two beautiful children . . . '

Unshaven monster shouting, 'Keep those bloody kids from under my feet!'

' . . . and we have the dearest little cottage in the village, which Eric is converting . . . '

Tumbledown shack full of woodworm and dry-rot. Husband sitting in deckchair reading Sunday newspaper while HH turns the cement-mixer.

' . . . but the people here are so friendly . . . '

The vicar's wife and four old toadies drinking tea in the kitchen while HH tries to keep the children quiet and cook the evening meal.

' . . . and Zoe is wonderful to me. I don't know what I'd do without Zoe. I think she's the most wonderful person I've ever met.'

220

For once I did not mind Zoe being exalted above me. I had seen the skull beneath my sister's skin, and though I could not love her any more than I did I liked her a great deal better. I said goodbye to garrulous Penny as soon as I decently could.

How women cling to the chains that bind them, I thought, watching her wander hand in hand with her children down the garden path to oblivion. And Zoe's every bit as bad! But though I knew the price which was being exacted from my sister, her value had not depreciated.

I was touched to see how glad Simon and Caroline were that I had come. The quick and easy food I had bought was a banquet to them.

'Gosh, Aunt Lulu! Fish fingers *and* sausage rolls!'

'And *hamburglers*!' said Caroline.

'And Neapolitan ice-cream and shop cakes,' I said.

'But which shall we *choose*?'

'Why not have everything? With chips and baked beans!' I said wickedly.

I did not ask them what was usual or permissible for high tea. I cooked what they wanted and watched them eat it with deep dark pleasure. Zoe, on my orders, was taking a long soak in a hot bath preparatory to our spending a lazy evening together. I poured myself a mug of tea, and sketched the children while they stuffed themselves.

When my sister trailed in, softly smiling, exquisitely restored, I said dreamily, 'Your babies are delicious and I'd like to eat them right up.'

Simon and Caroline paused, spoons in air, flattered, apprehensive.

'Oh, yes,' she answered, also dreaming. 'I often felt like that when they were infants. Just to sink my teeth into their velvety little arms and cheeks! Though of course,' she chided herself, waking up at once to reassure her small and startled offspring, 'Mummy never would! She's only joking!'

We had put the children to bed and read them two stories each. We had dined royally on pork chops and salad, raspberries from the garden and cream from the

221

nearby farm. We had changed into kimonos so old that they aroused childhood memories. The one Zoe lent me had belonged to Helen during the war. My sister was always a hoarder. We had washed each other's hair, as we did when we were girls, and now sat with towels round our shoulders letting it dry. I had waited for the right moment in which to crown the day, and it had surely come.

I said, 'I brought something else with me today, apart from the picnic basket. It's a special unbirthday present for you, Zo!'

Whereupon I produced *Village Fête* with a flourish, from its hiding-place behind the sofa: finished and framed.

Her squeaks of amazement and delight, her paean of praise, were balm to my soul. Like Ruth Babbage, she was stunned by the detail. She pored over every figure and place, and finally came to my signature and the date.

'Leila Gideon, 1957.'

'I meant you to have it long before this,' I said, 'but first of all I liked it too much to part with it, and then it's been exhibited here and there. With some success,' I added, as modestly as I could.

Her head jerked up.

'Could you have sold it?'

'Yes, but it wasn't for sale. I wanted you to have it.'

She looked at me for fully a minute, humbly wondering.

Then she said, 'I love you very much, Lulu. And if ever the house burns down this is the first thing I shall grab!'

She wanted to cry a bit and sentimentalise, but I didn't think there was any need of that. So we compromised with a long hard hug and a kiss on each cheek, and propped the picture on a side-table where we could both see it, while we combed our hair.

The day, though so late, was still breathless with heat. We talked and yawned and would not go to bed, for tomorrow morning I must leave and Zoe's humdrum life would trundle on again, and at the moment a magical tranquillity prevailed. Time had stopped her clock for us, even put it back to oblige us. The telephone did not ring with any of our interrupters: Helen, Matthew,

Jeremy. Neighbours did not call. No one wanted us, but us.

And when we had exhausted every topic of conversation and remembrance, Zoe wrinkled her forehead in a way which meant she must question me about something that concerned her and would probably annoy me. She approached the subject pleasantly, casually.

Saying, 'And what about you and Jeremy Purchase, Lulu?'

I answered in the same way.

'We suit each other very well. He lives his life and I live mine. We share our bed and company. What more can you ask?'

Evidently a great deal more, judging from her expression.

She said, 'But being in love is only a beginning. You obviously love each other. So why deny yourselves the richness and satisfaction of family life?'

Such as being perennially short of money, wondering whether your husband had fallen out of love with you and was chasing French girls in short skirts, and seeking oblivion in cooking sherry, O Happy Housewife?

These new lantern slides clicked on and off my mental screen. And then dissolved into the supreme crisis Jeremy and I had suffered that morning.

Jeremy had said, 'The reason I'm moving out is not because I don't love you but because I feel responsible for my patients. Based at King's Cross, with a practice in Blackheath, trying to keep reasonable hours in order to get back here, I'm only playing at being a doctor. It's bloody ridiculous. I shouldn't have to bother about time or place. Alan lives over the surgery. Bill and Dennis live a few streets away. They're on the spot when they're needed. Their wives are part of the job.'

I said, attempting to spread marmalade on toast I could not eat, 'Are you proposing to me in a peculiar sort of way, Jem?'

'And that's another thing,' he said. 'You simply cannot be serious.'

'I'm bloody serious!' I shouted, and slapped the toast,

223

marmalade side down, on my French-style red-and-white-check tablecloth. 'I've marched with your CND people until my feet were two big blisters. I've yawned at Blackheath socialist meetings. I've spent whole evenings with your medical friends and listened to you all grinding on about ganglions and other things I didn't understand. I've gone to football matches, even though I can't distinguish between footer, soccer and rugger. In fact, I've tried to participate in every earnest, worthwhile and/or bloody boring project which interested you. Of course I'm bloody serious!'

'This is my way of life you're knocking!' he shouted back. 'My work, my beliefs and my tastes. All the things that are important to me.'

'So I don't count as anything important?'

'Of course you're important. In fact, I was going to suggest that we think seriously about pooling our resources. If you sold this place – after all, it's no palace, and it's on a very short lease – we could put our capital together and buy something much better for the two of us. A decent house in a nice place. Freehold. Something worth having.'

His criticisms of the Garret stung me.

I said very drily, 'And where might this future palace be? Blackheath?'

'Well, yes. Or around there. We'll muck in together at first. Split our living expenses down the middle. If that doesn't work out then we can divide the house into two separate flats. Isn't that fair?'

'You *are* asking me to marry you.'

He hesitated, and in that pause I knew that he wanted to have the freedom we enjoyed now, plus the convenience of being near his work.

'We could marry if you really wanted to, I suppose,' he said reluctantly.

'Oh, you will keep sweeping me off my feet! How can I resist?' I said sarcastically. 'No, Jeremy, don't look worried. I don't want marriage at all.'

'Well then,' he said, relieved, 'what's the fuss about?'

'Nor do I want all the responsibilities of marriage and the disadvantages of living in sin – in short, being pitied, blamed or possibly ostracised by excessively respectable neighbours. That would be very wearing.'

'Rubbish. Who pities or blames you now?'

'Nobody. Because I'm wise enough to live where respectability doesn't matter. "She's an artist," they say, "and this is London. Anything goes." Besides, while we're talking about work, what about my work?'

'Surely that's no problem? You can paint and draw anywhere.'

'Thank you for telling me how simple it all is. Pack drawing-board, will travel. Have you considered that I need a fair amount of light and peace and quiet? That my various employers are in London, not Blackheath. And finally that I can't spend my day, as Alan's wife does, in answering the telephone and dealing with people, but must be left strictly alone. Would any of them understand that?'

He brushed this aside, literally as if waving away a fly.

'Leila! I simply can't divide my attention between you and the practice as I have been doing.'

'I don't see why not. So far, the practice has come first and last, and I'm tucked into the spare time it leaves you.'

'But if we lived at Blackheath we should have more time for ourselves.'

'No. I don't think so. You would have more time for your patients. And I should lose my house, my friends and my way of life. Look at it this way, Jeremy. If you're working late (as usual) and I feel a bit lonely, I only have to step into the street, and all of London's out there. Or I can call up one of my many interesting acquaintances and while away an hour over a bottle of wine. Even if I'm broke I can sit in a Joey Lyons and have a cup of coffee and sketch the world going by. At Blackheath I should be socially isolated, and out of touch with everything that makes me tick. The whole idea depresses me like hell.'

'You talk as if you were going to the North Pole! Meg

225

and Fran and Julie manage to live their lives out there and to enjoy themselves.'

'Your partners' wives? I have nothing in common with them.'

'And don't sound so superior. They're university graduates. Highly intelligent women.'

'And don't for Christ's sake sound so superior yourself. That's your criterion of excellence, isn't it? Going to university, voting Labour, and talking about medicine, the bomb, the Third World and the first division.'

The light drained away from Jeremy. He was no longer my boy but a square-built preacher in his late twenties. He spoke coldly and with authority.

'Rather more useful, I should have thought, than sitting on the floor with a crowd of peculiar people, talking about nothing in particular.'

'How do you know what we talk about? You don't stay to listen. I *have* made an effort to understand your life, and tried to participate. You've never shown the slightest interest or had an atom of respect for mine.'

He said more softly, in honest apology, 'I never could pretend, Sparky. You know I've got a blind eye and a deaf ear as far as the arts are concerned. And what use is art in a world full of atomic weapons and poverty?'

I said sadly, 'That's the trouble, you see, Jem. I think the arts are the saving graces of a world rotten with power and politics. We haven't got much in common apart from loving each other, have we?'

We were silent for a while. He conceded a point.

'I shall only be *living* in Blackheath, Sparky. I haven't got another girl, and I don't want anyone but you. There's no reason why we shouldn't go on as we have done, and see how things work out.'

I tried to formulate my fears.

'But while you live here you have to come home some time. In Blackheath I just know that you'll flop after a day's work and I shall never see you.'

Also, I could lose him to some girl who was prepared to mould her life round his, as his partners' wives did. Meg

(Chemistry), Fran (Modern History) and Julie (Economics) had considered their careers well lost for home and children. That price was too high for me.

He said, sounding as tired as I had pictured him, 'Well, let's give it a try.'

The next silence pressed me to capitulate.

But I answered forlornly, 'All right. We'll see how it works out.'

I knew how it would work out, given time and disappointment. It would not work out so much as wear out, but I could make no other choice.

'And how can you deny yourself children?' Zoe was saying in dovelike tones. 'You're so marvellous with children, Lulu. Look how my two adore you.'

I could not evade her questions any longer.

I said as stoically as possible, 'Jeremy's leaving the Garret at the end of this month and moving to a flat in Blackheath to be near the practice. We haven't quarrelled or anything. We shall still see each other, of course.'

Though sympathetic, Zoe was quick to pin me down.

'Didn't he ask you to go with him?'

'Yes, Zoe, he did. He was even prepared to marry me, at a pinch. But I couldn't do either. So I refused.'

I had expected her to say, as my father had done, 'There's no hope for you, Lulu!' but my sister always saw more than the immediate situation.

She said, 'And so you packed a basket full of good things and came here to find comfort. Instead of which you cleaned the house, looked after the children and comforted me instead? Oh, my darling Lulu. I can't forgive myself.'

I said truthfully, 'I was glad to help. It took my mind off my own problems.'

I was glad I had brought in another bottle of wine. Otherwise I should have been driven to stealing Matthew's whisky or taking a secret tipple of Zoe's cooking sherry. But my sister was wafting far away on her old sweet wings of hope. She hugged and kissed me and crooned over me.

Saying, 'Never mind, my darling. The next time we

meet we shall have wonderful news for each other. I just know it.'

Her face shone with restored belief.

Torn between amusement and despair, I said, 'Oh, Zo! There's no hope for you! No hope at all! But just in case you're right – let's drink to that!'

18

October 1961

As Cass grew out of the rogue-male years and entered his fifties, he seemed to settle for one steady affair rather than a series of new adventures. I expect he found them too wearing, physically and emotionally. And his secretary, Mrs Celia Piper, had fulfilled the role of the other woman for so long that she could be regarded by now as an irregular member of the family.

When we first met her she was a pretty widow in her late thirties with a son at public school. Her husband's death had left her poor, but the school waived fees, her parents paid for her to take a course in Pitman's shorthand and speed typing, and my father gave Celia her first job. She had sold her house by then and bought a two-bedroomed flat in Putney.

Let me say that business came first with Cass and pleasure was a delightful consequence. He would never have employed an inefficient secretary, however attractive and hard up. But Celia was efficient and conscientious and so became an asset to him in every way.

Back in 1952, still stunned by widowhood, she wore little black dresses with round white collars and cuffs, kept her head down and spoke in a subdued voice. But by the time Zoe and Matthew were married the mourning had turned to lilac and Celia blossomed into a chestnut-haired lady with a subtle smile. I knew, when my mother stopped referring to her as 'poor Celia', no longer urged her to come for tea on Sundays, and discouraged us from visiting her at Putney, that Cass had conquered once more.

Celia Piper's son grew up and away, did well, and remained devoted to her. She filled his absence with hobbies and home-making. Her flat was pleasing, light and comfortable. Her window-boxes flowered abundantly. For a fortnight in the summer she took a Cook's tour with an old schoolfriend who was also widowed. They did a different country each year. In the autumn she enrolled in a new evening class, and was an established member of a Bach choral society. Though naturally unacknowledged, her affair with my father had stabilised and could be regarded by all but the respectable as a good second marriage. Women have led worse lives.

You might have thought that Celia Piper and I had something in common, even though I was twenty years younger. Unlike my mother and sister we were career women who enjoyed our work, earned our own money, and were not subject to the whims of a husband. But Celia did not care for me and my mad clothes and unorthodox ideas. She was always pleasant when we met, but I recognised that her glances and silences were at variance with her smiles.

No, it was Helen and Zoe she admired. They led the sort of life she had been used to, and still wanted. Country houses and country magazines. The smell of home-baked bread mingling with the scent of roses. A man providing worldly goods, life insurance and social stability. Celia had cooed gratefully in my mother's dove-cote for a few months until my father took her under his eagle's wing. She looked on Zoe as the daughter she might have had. I think she missed those old-fashioned Sunday teas at Whitegates and the little intimate chats with Helen. And, being a good woman, her conscience must have given her hell.

She reminded me in some ways of Ruth Babbage, who was still playing concierge in my ground-floor flat, though nowadays there was nothing to watch for. The Garret had become a houseful of self-supporting spinsters without men.

Jeremy's flat was occupied by a middle-aged lady archivist called Beatrice, and his visits were becoming rarer and rarer. Sometimes I drove over to spend a day with him in Blackheath, desperation and desire and love of him forcing me to give us another try. But his friends were not my friends. His life had no time to spare for me once news and love-making were exchanged, and I would drive Garret-wards again, feeling sadder and more separate than ever. In fact I had just returned from some such fruitless visit late one autumn evening when the telephone rang, and I did not recognise the hoarse and urgent voice which asked if it could speak to Leila Gideon.

'Leila Gideon speaking.'

'Oh, Leila. This is Celia. Celia Piper.'

There was a long pause, into which I murmured something sociable and utterly pointless.

She said rather shakily, 'I need to speak to you in absolute confidence, Leila. Can you be heard from the hall?'

I did not dislike her as she disliked me, so I answered with some camaraderie.

'You're behind the times, Celia! I have my own telephone in my own flat now. Cass made us all self-contained three years ago.'

She said, as if to a forgetful part of herself, 'Oh, yes, of course. How silly of me. Cass converted *your* house, too.'

Her slight resentful stress on the word caused images of Whitegates, the Garret and the Old Rectory (that beautiful Queen Anne sponger) to rise before me, and for the first time I was appalled at the thought of one ageing man endeavouring to keep three houses good-looking and in good repair.

She said in a rush, 'Leila, I know we've had very little to do with each other, so it seems unfair to turn to you, to ask you for help, but you were closest to Cass, and I can't think of anyone else . . . '

I was closest to Cass? Meaning, I *used* to be close to Cass?

Celia hurried on, trying to sound casual and friendly, and failing.

'I don't know if you realised that he and I . . . and even though you're such a modern young woman . . . but there was never any threat to the marriage.'

She ran out of breath and ideas temporarily. Then began again.

'Still, he was your father. What I meant to say was . . . I just wondered, Leila, if you ever knew that he and I were . . .'

I connected the hour, the urgency and the half-confession. I cut her short, cut through to the appalling truth.

'He's dead, isn't he, Celia?'

She made a curious sound, between a sob and a hiccup.

'He was visiting you and he died, didn't he?'

She began to cry desperately, saying, 'Leila, it's asking too much, but I don't know what to do. I don't know who else to turn to. Can you come over to my flat? Yes, I think he's dead, but I'm not sure. I can't believe it.'

'How long ago?'

'I don't know. Not long. Ten – fifteen minutes. Leila, I don't know what to do and nobody must know. Can you come over now?'

I pulled the telephone pad and pencil towards me. My lips were so numb that I had to frame each word separately.

'Give me your address and tell me how to get there. I've forgotten where it is.'

The theatre and cinema crowds had gone home long since, but the prostitutes and nightbirds were out in abundance as I drove across the city and down into the suburbs. I felt as if I had split into two people: Leila Gideon and Cass's daughter. Leila was busy registering traffic and time and place, standing back from the crisis, driving more carefully than usual, while Lulu was saying to herself over and over again. 'He's not dead. He can't be dead. My Daddy's not dead.'

But her Daddy was.

Celia took me into her bedroom, which looked too chintzy to contain such a staggering event, and gestured towards

232

her lover. He had taken off his coat and was sitting in his shirt-sleeves in an armchair near the bed. One foot was bare. One hand held a burgundy sock.

I walked over, pulling off my gloves and stuffing them into my pocket, and stared at the corpse.

He must have gone in an instant. The astonishment was still on his face, and his ugliness stood forth now, unrelieved by charm or humour. And I saw him for the first time as old and worn and powerless.

Judging from his appearance and hers they must have been preparing to go to bed. Celia was just behind me, wearing a pretty quilted nylon house-coat, sprigged with blue flowers. Her cheeks were shining with tears and some fragrant face cream. I could hear her catching her breath, trying not to cry. Both hands were over her mouth, as if she were holding her face together.

She said, 'He isn't, is he?'

Only hope and terror could have deluded her.

I heard myself say, with a hint of reproach, 'You could have closed his eyes.'

I closed them myself and stood back, hands folded in front of me, head bent, as I had seen mourners do. But I was not imitating them consciously. I was stunned with awe and grief and shock, and the stance followed.

Celia began to sob and wring her hands and take short turns about the room saying, 'What am I going to do? I don't know what to do. What shall I do?'

I knew that wherever my father was there would be a bottle of whisky within range. I took Celia's arm and led her out of the bedroom and into the sitting room and poured a stiff glass for each of us.

'Drink that!' I said, and gulped a reviving mouthful.

Then we both sat down as if we had been clubbed, and Celia cried in earnest.

'Leila, he mustn't be found here. For his sake and the sake of your family . . . ' she added miserably, honestly, ' . . . and, yes, for my sake too. It will do none of us any good for this to come out. Cass is – Cass was – quite a well-known figure in his world. If the gossip columnists got

233

hold of this they'd regard it as fair game. And think of the pain that would cause Helen . . . '

I drank again, but more slowly and deliberately, and said, 'What are you suggesting, Celia?'

'I don't know!' she cried vehemently.

She wore the same expression as Helen and Zoe when they refused to acknowledge the unpleasantness of a situation, but wanted someone to do something about it.

'I don't know. I can't believe this is happening. But he can't be found with me. He mustn't be found here. I couldn't face Helen or my son or anyone else if he were. I might as well be dead myself.'

She kneaded her handkerchief and sipped her whisky and cried again.

I thought incredulously, She's asking me to hide the situation somehow, to take responsibility for his death. And she's threatening that if I don't then Helen and Zoe and she will be disgraced.

I thought angrily, What breath-taking cheek to place her problem on me whom she doesn't like, and of whom she doesn't approve.

I thought indignantly, She's asking me to act against my principles. Because whatever I do I'm prepared to say I do it, not pretend that it's something else or that it doesn't exist. And when things go wrong I don't squeal for help, I manage by myself and pay whatever price is asked for the privilege of making my own choice.

Then I thought more charitably, This doesn't matter one way or the other to me or my father, but it matters a hell of a lot to the three of them. And he's protected them all these years. So what am I going to do about it?

With the courage bestowed by alcohol, I said, 'Did he come by car?'

She nodded and swallowed before she answered.

'Yes. He always left it in the public car park, across the road and up the street, so as not to draw attention to my flat.'

Shock and fear had rendered her unable to think clearly,

or beyond the immediate moment. She looked up at me, pleading.

'Leila, couldn't we take him to his car, and then it will look as though he died sitting there?'

The same emotions had clarified my thought processes remarkably. I heard my voice answer her drily, logically.

'Celia, he's a fair-sized man who can't help us to move him, and neither of us could be described as Amazons. I doubt if we're physically capable of getting him over a road and up a street and into a public car park. But even if we could, it would take us so long and look so suspicious that someone would be bound to stop us and ask questions.'

I did not say, 'And then we'll be front-page news, never mind the gossip columns!'

'Besides,' I said, 'Helen isn't a fool. If he were found dead in a Putney car park it would be obvious he was visiting you. We need him to be a long way from here, and preferably with someone that Helen wouldn't worry about. Like me.'

We journeyed on mentally together, without paying full attention to each other. We had a destination in common, but our rails ran side by side and could not meet.

Celia said, 'It's unforgivable to drag you into this, Leila, but I didn't know where else to turn. And though it isn't right to have an affair with a married man I don't want you to think that I was ever casual or callous about it. I'm not the type to enjoy an intrigue. If my husband had lived I should never have looked at anyone else. But I really loved Cass. I did love him, and he was so good to me. And, believe me, the idea of cheating Helen really hurt me. She was so kind to me in the early days. I never stopped loving and respecting her . . . '

Then she ran out of steam and began to cry again.

I said, 'If you lived anywhere but the ground floor we'd be in real trouble. I can't imagine us negotiating the stairs, but if I drive his car round to the front, and park it with the passenger seat facing the pavement, we should be able to get him inside with the minimum of trouble and effort. It's late at night. If anyone sees us doing it they'll probably think he's drunk. If anyone asks us we shall have to say he's ill.'

'I couldn't believe it. He was joking not long before he died. He'd taken off his jacket and hung it on the chair, and unlaced his shoes, and he was beginning to take off his socks while he told me about Mrs Foreman, who wants cupids on her bedroom ceiling. And he stopped and lifted his head suddenly and stared past me, as if someone had just come into the room, and then he died . . .'

'Where are his car-keys? In his jacket-pocket?'

She nodded, keeping her head down, kneading and smoothing her wet handkerchief.

I avoided looking at the corpse, sitting sock in hand, as I found the keys. I longed for another glass of the whisky which had most marvellously steadied my nerves, but a second might fuddle my head and I needed every wit I possessed. I went back into the living room and parted the curtains.

It was one of those misty, moist October nights without a moon. Fog blurred the outlines of trees and buildings. On the wall of the house opposite a white cat sat with its tail folded across its front paws like a muff. In this quiet street the tenants were all abed, the pavements deserted and not too well lit.

I thought aloud, looking at the rows of vehicles parked there for the night, 'But what shall I do with my own car? I could be down in Surrey for ages with Mummy, sorting everything out.'

Celia did not listen, too busy explaining what had been. And I looked at the white cat and the leafless branches of the trees and the dark houses beyond, and wished I was at peace with them instead of facing a problem as bizarre as this one.

I cut into my fellow conspirator's saga.

'Can I use your telephone, Celia? Don't worry. It's someone we can trust.'

He was not only in but in bed. He answered sleepily, good-humouredly, and my heart and spirits lifted as I heard his voice. I would have given a great deal to ask him to take on me and my present responsibilities, but that was not possible.

I said crisply, 'Jeremy, it's Leila. I'm in a jam. I need information and advice.'

He was on the alert in an instant. He wasted no time in sympathy, which could come later, but did attempt to dissuade me, saying that this was a wild idea which could land me in a lot of trouble. When he realised that my mind was made up, his questions and answers were crisp and to the point. He advised me above and beyond the Hippocratic oath, and finished with a warning.

' . . . just remember that you never rang me, Sparky. I don't want to be struck off the medical register for aiding and abetting!' Yet he added with true affection, 'But let me know what happens, won't you? And the best of luck, you crazy nut!'

My father, master of deception, had imparted his Machiavellian wisdom to me over the years.

Don't tell a lie unless it's absolutely necessary, but if you must lie then make it a big one, tell it well, and stick to it.

A good liar must have a very good memory.

Think your story through from beginning to end so that every detail fits.

I put my hand on Celia's shoulder and shook her gently. There was no fight in her. I was reminded of poor Sep. I spoke firmly.

'Celia, where did my father come from and what time?'

She consulted her handkerchief.

'From the Foremans. In Essex. He got here about eleven o'clock. Helen thought he was staying the night with them. And so did I. I didn't expect him. I was going to bed when he arrived.'

'What food did he have? Had he eaten already, or did he eat with you?'

'He'd had dinner there. A four-course dinner. He said Mrs Foreman overdid everything, including the food. He had a whisky here. Just whisky.'

237

'Did he say anything about not feeling well?'

She and the handkerchief worked their way round this one.

'He said, "If I'd stayed the night that woman would have killed me, either with another idea for decorating her bedroom or with a four-course breakfast. I'm not young enough to live at this pace, C. I don't feel too good. I need a whisky to settle my stomach. And a long night's sleep." I told him that two Alka-seltzers would be more sensible, but you know what Cass was like. He always preferred a drink to a remedy. So I poured his whisky and made myself a pot of tea and we sat talking for about half an hour. Then he topped up his glass and took it into the bedroom, and sat in the chair and began to undress, but he was very slow . . . and then it happened . . . '

I looked at the chatty little brass carriage-clock ticktocking away on her writing desk. He had been dead for almost an hour.

In my head the two men I loved best were advising me.

Jeremy said, 'As he's fully dressed in a warm room you needn't worry about *rigor mortis* for quite a while, and they can't place the moment of death with absolute accuracy. Just keep your account reasonable but vague. You didn't realise he was dead. You thought he was asleep. That should cover the situation. But don't waste time. You've no time to waste.'

My father said, 'Look at every possibility and tie up the loose ends.'

So I sat a little longer, weaving my tale of deception while Celia wove her tale of woe. Then I cut her short.

'Now listen to me, Celia. I'm going to tell Helen that Cass called in to see me, on his way home from Essex. He told me what he told you, about the Foremans, and asked for a whisky to buck him up, but it made him feel more tired. I wanted him to stay with me for the night but he would go home . . . '

That will please Mummy! *He wanted to come home at all costs.*

' . . . so I said that in that case I would drive him down to Surrey. He got worse on the way and died and I took him to

238

the nearest hospital. You know nothing about it, Celia. Now or ever. Tomorrow morning – this morning – round about ten o'clock, or whatever time he would be considered late in the office, you must telephone Whitegates to ask Helen where he is. Have you got that?'

She nodded.

'I shall most probably be manning – or womaning – the telephone. I shall tell you that Cass died with me on the way home. But whether you speak to me or to anyone else you must make the same straightforward enquiry as if you know nothing. Whatever we agree to do now we must do forever. We must always act and speak and think as if he died with me in the car. Always.'

I felt a sudden revulsion with her and the situation.

I said, 'And after the funeral, you and I will forget the whole thing.'

I meant that we should not see each other again, and she knew that. She nodded, dumbly, robbed of her lover and his death and her self-respect.

'Now just in case one of your neighbours does see us, the story remains the same, except that my father was taken ill on the way and we called in and dragged you out of bed for Alka-seltzers. He recovered enough to go bolshie on us and demand another whisky, and then had to be helped into the car. This particular story is only for an emergency which I fervently pray will never arise, and we'll have to keep cool and play it by ear.

'And when I've gone you're on your own, Celia, I'm afraid. You must get through the rest of the night as best you can. No confiding in anyone else, or you'll sink the pair of us.'

She nodded again, more sadly this time, comprehending.

I said, 'There's something I need you to do for me. I'll drive my own car into the car park and give you the keys. I'm writing the licence number down on this business card. My address is on the front. Destroy the card afterwards, just to make sure. Tomorrow morning – this morning – very early, I want you to drive my car to my house, leave it in the street, and post the keys through the letter-box. Ruth Babbage will pick them up, and keep them for me. She's done that before. I sometimes lend the car to a friend.

'I shall probably have one hell of a fine from the traffic warden, but never mind. I'll sort that out later.

'Neither Ruth nor Beatrice – that's my other tenant – leave the house before a quarter to nine. So if you get there before seven they won't even be up. I don't want either of them to connect *you* with my car. Are you with me?'

Again she nodded, but more briskly. The fact that she had something to do in a few hours' time helped her. She was waking up.

'And now,' I said, thinking of the man in the bedroom, whose sock and shoes must be put on again, whose arms must be threaded into the sleeves of his jacket, whose overcoat and hat must be donned, and whose body must be transported between us, 'let's tackle the real problem.'

My hands are shaking as I turn the ignition key. The steering wheel feels clammy, and sweat is trickling steadily down the middle of my back. Celia and I have, foot by dragging foot, moved a dead weight a distance of some thirty yards which felt like thirty miles. No one is about. Curtains shroud the windows. The last bedroom light has been switched off. The mist thickens. Only the white cat still sits upon his wall, musing, and keeps his paws warm with the thick white muff of his tail.

I see Celia's sprigged nylon house-coat move safely indoors. It is just past one o'clock in the morning. Cass and I are on our own. The Daimler, which I have never been allowed to drive, feels too big for me. I am sweating now at the thought of negotiating its majestic black bulk safely between the lines of parked cars and round the corner into the open road. The engine does not spit and shriek into life but purrs and growls. The car responds faster and more powerfully, is quicker to the touch than anything I have driven before. I have the feeling that it is driving me.

Our hearse moves sedately along the Reigate road, and beside me my silent passenger slouches in the passenger

240

seat, hat over his eyes. As we glide through the night of early morning I begin a long soliloquy to explain the situation to both of us. I am calm itself, at the centre of the storm. I shall be his shield and buckler. I have taken his death upon me and no one shall part us.

At Carshalton hospital, though I long for oblivion I refuse a sedative until I have telephoned my sister. Because Helen must not be woken at this hour, alone and unprepared in Whitegates, and be told that her husband is dead and their life together is over. Whereas Zoe is young and strong and Helen's favourite, and will know how best to break the news. And whatever Matthew's failings he is likely to rise to this occasion, for his greatest rival is dead, and now he has his wife and possibly his mother-in-law all to himself.

Zoe

19

Leila's telephone call woke us up in the early hours of a cold October morning, and Matthew was marvellous. He comforted me, made tea for us both, and when my burst of grief had abated he rang the hospital back for details. He was told that my sister was sleeping, and the Daimler was in the visitors' car park, safely locked up. He used the power of his profession and of his gender to elicit off-the-cuff information about my father's death, which appeared to be the result of a heart attack, though they would not know this until an autopsy had been performed later in the day.

My husband put down the receiver looking gravely competent.

'There'll be a coroner's inquest because of the circumstances in which he died, Zo,' he said. 'And Helen will need a man in the family to deal with everything. That seems to point to me. So we'd better take the kids to Whitegates and stay with her until the funeral is over. Trudy will give me time off to be with you and make all the arrangements.'

He had taken upon himself the business appertaining to sudden death, jotting down memos as he spoke.

'The best thing we can do at the moment is to send you ahead, by yourself, to break the news to Helen personally. I'll follow with the children later on. What's the name and address of that cleaning woman in the village who comes in to help when we have weekend guests? I shall need her to stand by.'

Then he gave me a hug and said, 'Let's get a few hours'

sleep. Then I'll cook breakfast while you pack. We're going to need it.'

The amount of organisation and energy required to support and comfort the bereaved, provide a sombre festival for the mourners and bury the dead is vast. Our undertakers undertook a great deal, but the long days and longer nights and the care of two young children were borne by Matthew and me.

I arrived at Whitegates at nine o'clock that morning to find that Celia Piper had just telephoned to ask where Daddy was, and rung off again abruptly when my mother told her that he was staying the night with clients. Her evident anxiety and perplexity had communicated itself to my mother, who was still sitting by the telephone when I rang the front-door bell.

She was wearing a blue cotton kimono decorated with sprays of white plum blossom, which my father had brought her from Japan years ago, and had been about to indulge in a solitary luxury. Her breakfast was laid on a tray, ready to carry back to bed, with the *Daily Telegraph* folded beside it. She had set the tray down on the hall table when Celia rang, and being unable to decide what to do afterwards, had left it there while she sat and pondered on the call. And when she saw me standing unexpectedly on the doorstep she began to cry, because she knew that some fearful event had taken place.

I can't remember how I told her, but we both wept in a wild lost way, for him and ourselves and each other.

She kept on saying, 'But why did Celia Piper ring? Not for information. She knows more about his business engagements than I do! She must have guessed that something was wrong, but how could that be?'

My father's secretary was devoted to him, but I had never believed – as Leila did – that she was his mistress, so I was not prejudiced against her. But she had evidently upset Mummy and was in a fairly hysterical state herself. When I rang her back she started to sob before I had finished explaining the circumstances, and said she would never forgive herself, and asked if she could help in any way. Should she come over? Would Helen consent to see her?

My mother, sitting like a stone image, shook a stony head.

I replied that Mummy was not seeing anyone at the moment but thanked her for the thought and sympathy.

Everything was happening at once, as it usually does in a crisis. Mrs McGann, my mother's domestic help, arrived soon after, and cried with us when we told her the news. And just as we were all feeling calmer and drinking the tea she had made for us Matthew turned up with the children, and I had to deal with them instead of looking after Mummy. Finally, without a word of warning from either herself or the hospital, Leila drove up in my father's car and burst out her extraordinary tale.

Grief affects people in different ways. My sister was tearful and talkative at first, and then white and sharp and silent and withdrawn. But Mummy lost her air of bemusement and turning angrily on Leila, who had borne the brunt of my father's death, said she was dissatisfied with the explanation.

Leila was sitting bolt upright, unfolding and smoothing out and then balling a wet handkerchief. Under pressure, she dabbed her mouth with it and answered as if it were a lesson learned under duress.

'All Daddy wanted to do was to come home. I tried to bring him home. He was ill. I was trying to help him.'

My mother no longer resembled a nutbrown earth goddess but the palest and most shrewish of the furies.

'Then why didn't you telephone me and tell me what was happening? Why assume such a responsibility without consulting me or anyone else?'

Matthew took charge of the situation. He sat beside Mummy and held her hands in his and spoke to her very gently and kindly.

'You're shocked and grieved, Helen, and so is Leila. Why don't you go upstairs to your room and rest?'

She allowed her hands to stay in his. She allowed him to offer comfort. But she would not be side-tracked.

'It seems very strange to me,' she persisted, staring at Leila as if she were an unwanted visitor. 'It seems so strange that you took all the decisions and he allowed you to do so. I can't even imagine him consenting to your driving the Daimler. He must have felt so ill as to be quite unlike his usual self. And if so, then why didn't you call your doctor or take him to one of the big London hospitals? If you'd consulted a responsible professional person, instead of taking things in your own hands, his life could probably have been saved.'

I broke in, then, saying, 'Mummy, that's terribly unfair to Lulu. We can't possibly know that.'

She rode across my interruption.

'And then there's that Celia Piper ringing up at breakfast time and asking where Daddy is. As if she didn't know. Perhaps you *did* consult somebody! Did you ring *her* up? You independent women are all alike. You think you know everything and know it best. Did you or Daddy telephone her and tell her he was ill? Did you ask *her* advice?'

Something incredibly ugly was tumbling out, which we must not allow.

I said, 'Mummy! You're talking nonsense and hurting Leila. Now stop it!'

My mother sat up like a Daniel come to judgement and said, 'Well, I do know one thing. I've had enough of all this subterfuge. I refuse to speak to Celia Piper, either now or ever again, and I forbid you to invite her to the funeral.'

Then we three women all began to talk at once, caught up on a wheel of contradictory emotions, going round and round, accusing, explaining, defending, until Matthew interrupted and took charge of the situation.

'My dear Helen, the best thing for you at the moment is rest and quiet. Now I want you to let Zoe take you to your room. I suggest that we contact your doctor, who will probably recommend a mild sedative. And then I'll get in touch with the aunts and anyone else you feel should be told personally. Perhaps you could give me names and numbers?'

Soothed by his tone of authority, temporarily diverted by having something to do, Mummy found her telephone book, handed it over to him, and walked slowly and meekly ahead of me up the stairs.

Within minutes Matthew had persuaded Mrs McGann to look after the children in the kitchen. Soon after that I heard Leila come up and quietly close the door of our former bedroom behind her. The family doctor arrived half an hour later and ministered to both patients.

I sat with Mummy until she fell asleep, and then looked in on Leila, who had remained obstinately awake, waiting for me. With her long wispy hair and white triangle of a face, she resembled a waif more than ever. She put out one hand, without speaking, and I sat on the side of the bed and clasped it in both of mine.

I said, 'Mummy doesn't mean what she said, Lulu. It's the shock. She knows you did everything you could for Daddy.'

Half-drugged, she seemed to be thinking this over.

Then she gave a dry sad chuckle and said, 'More than you'll ever know, Zoe. More than you'll ever know.'

And closed her eyes.

By lunch-time the aunts had arrived on the scene, supposedly to help but actually needing care and attention, since they had adored Daddy too. I settled them down in the sitting room and went to the kitchen to make coffee and sandwiches.

In the hall, Matthew, who had spent most of his time on the telephone, making and answering calls, put down the receiver and spoke to me. His tone was efficient but kindly.

'I've asked Mrs McGann to come in morning and afternoon, every day until the funeral's over. With all this going on, there's no way we can look after the children as well. Oh, and by the way, your father's secretary rang again and wanted to speak to Leila – which I thought was rather odd. I told her that Leila was badly shocked and under sedation at the moment, but would call back when she could.'

249

He sat nursing his knee and pondering.

He said, 'Actually, I agree with Helen. There's something very odd about this business of your father's death, and I can't quite figure it out.'

Then he made two appalling statements.

First, 'I wonder if he died in Celia Piper's bed, and she's trying to cover things up for your mother's sake?'

And as I exclaimed in anger and disbelief, he answered almost in amusement, 'My dear girl, don't tell me that you didn't know about Celia and your father! I thought everyone did. Of course she was his mistress!'

Then I had my second grief-burst of the day and he was as sweet as only Matthew could be. He put his arms round me and comforted me and said he was sorry, and I mustn't mind, and that he loved me because I was so good and thought no ill of anyone. Only, he added, being a solicitor he saw the other side of human nature, and believe him it wasn't a pretty sight. But please to forgive him.

Which of course I did.

The inquest was a formality, discreetly and sympathetically conducted, and the coroner was particularly kind to Leila. She had refused our suggestions as to the correct way to dress for such an occasion, and arrived in something long, black and ragged-looking, wearing no make-up, with a Garbo hat pulled down over one eye and her hair hanging limply round her face.

Matthew whispered that she looked exactly like a Bisto kid deprived of its gravy, and though it was unkind and I was angry with him for saying it, the description was so accurate as to shut me up.

Fortunately, her waif-like appearance was in her favour. She gave the impression of being young and lost and stoical in the face of misfortune. The coroner was paternal and sorry for her. The cause of my father's death was heart failure. The verdict was accidental death.

Leila, so often the cause of dissension in the family, was no trouble to us in this case. I wish I could say the same of my mother, who became our major problem. Her obsession with my father's secretary reached such proportions that Matthew actually took Celia Piper out for a drink, to explain why she could not be invited to the funeral. He did not, of course, give her the real reason. He said that in view of the numbers we should have to invite if we made it a public occasion, we had decided to keep it strictly to members of the family. But he told me afterwards that she had understood the real reason and accepted her exclusion gracefully, if very sadly.

'She's a woman of the world in her quiet way. Rather admirable. Naturally,' he added, 'I don't condone her conduct, which must have caused poor Helen years of grief. But Celia Piper is a remarkable person.'

'She seems to have impressed you, at any rate!' I said, too sharply.

The truth about my father's affair had thoroughly disturbed me. I think, to be honest, I hated my naivety more than his deception. Therefore I was disinclined to be charitable about his mistress.

Matthew looked at me long and quietly, as if assessing how much more truth I could take.

He said, 'And I was right. He did die at her flat. That sister of yours never ceases to amaze me! You'll never believe what happened . . .'

And he proceeded to tell me, partly horrified and partly astonished.

It was a cold day, but not as cold as I felt then. I thought of Leila taking my father's death upon herself, I saw her lying numbly in bed, holding out her hand to me and saying 'More than you'll ever know, Zoe.' Shouldering the responsibility. Not telling me. Keeping faith.

And I hated my husband for seeing my sister as some sort of freak.

Side by side in body, and far apart in spirit, he and I stood in the sober autumn garden at Whitegates. Our breath smoked up and out on the morning air.

I said, 'Surely to God, Matthew, you're going to keep that quiet?'

He came out with one of Trudy's expressions.

251

'You can bet your bottom dollar I am! I only told you because I felt you ought to know. And I'm jolly glad that Leila got away with it.'

'You mean that Celia Piper got away with it, I think?' I said coldly. 'It was Celia Piper's problem. Leila took the risks.'

'Well, whatever happened,' said Matthew lamely, 'the end result saved everyone a lot of fuss.'

He added, 'In any case, Celia made me promise to keep quiet about it, because Leila had sworn her to secrecy. So don't tell Leila we know.'

I laughed aloud then and said, 'Oh, that's really rich. Protecting the treacherous. And how did the admirable Celia come to confide in you?'

He gave his new smile, which had evolved over the past few years along with his contact lenses and well-cut suits and his business–social life.

He said, 'I'm a solicitor as well as someone who was close to Cass, and she badly needed to talk about him and his death to a person she could trust. I satisfied her on both counts. And I must admit that I felt some sympathy for her, too. She's been through the mill in more ways than one. It isn't an easy world for a single woman of her age.'

Some depth of intimacy had been achieved between my father's secretary and my husband which I disliked, despised, and feared.

I said, 'The person I feel admiration and sympathy for is Leila. But then, you never give her credit for anything. That was a heroic thing to do, and none of her business anyway. And she's said nothing to me, even though I'm her sister and we've always confided in each other. But then, Leila is honourable. If *she* gives her word she keeps it. In my opinion Celia would have done better to keep her mouth shut, instead of tattling to her boss's son-in-law at the first opportunity!'

My tone was savage, but he did not seem to be offended. He took my arm and began to walk me to the house. He was tranquil in his possession of my family's secrets, in

252

his position as temporary head of that family, and in his present power over us.

My mother's suspicions remained uncorroborated, though she confided long and bitterly in me about my father's unfaithfulness, and we cried our eyes red. But as Leila continued to stick to her story, and Celia Piper was permanently banished, Mummy gradually came to accept what she had been told, at least outwardly. Inwardly, perhaps, it was another matter. But then, I reflected, that had been the way of her married life, to know of infidelities without acknowledging them openly.

After the funeral we prepared to leave Whitegates in the care of Mrs McGann and take Mummy back to the Old Rectory with us for a few weeks, while Leila returned to the Garret and presumably her former single life. In the brief time she and I had together, Leila told me that Jeremy Purchase was selling his share of the practice at Blackheath and going to India as a medical worker. Her tone was laconic, and she answered my questions with wry honesty.

Yes, Jeremy had suggested that they married and went off to see the world. There would be marvellous things for her to sketch. It would be an experience, an education and a unique opportunity for her as well as for him.

'But you didn't want to?' I asked, knowing the answer.

No, for a number of reasons. Mainly she refused to exchange her work and financial independence for sketching in India. Then she objected to the idea of marrying him in order to be acceptable to the medical expedition. Finally, she feared that she would not be allowed to stand on the side-lines while everyone else was being useful, and would probably end up rolling bandages and scrubbing latrines.

'Because, like most men, he tells me as much as he wants me to know. And then he's genuinely surprised and sorry when the reality doesn't quite match the intention. But by then it's too late, and hard lines on me if I don't like it! Just remember this, Zo. If I'd gone to Blackheath I'd have been stuck there, by now, as the owner of half a house.'

So she had had to make a decision. Not an easy one. Maybe not the right one. But right for the moment.

'And after all,' she said, giving me a crooked smile from under that ridiculous Garbo hat, 'the moment is what matters.'

She said, 'I shan't see him off, or anything like that. I can't bear dramatic partings. I think I'll clear up my outstanding work and go down to Cornwall to see Magda. It'll do me good. Do her good, too. She was right not to come to the funeral. It was bloody depressing. Not a bit like Cass.'

She did not confide the circumstances of my father's death, and I respected her too much to ask, or to say that the wretched Celia Piper had broken her promise. So our parting was incomplete and yet more deeply affectionate than usual. Mummy was still being cool and distant with her, and Matthew had gone back to work again, so I saw her off on the train alone.

She looked so lost, peering over the carriage window, that I said involuntarily, 'Feel free to come and see us at the Old Rectory any time, Lulu. I'm always there, and you're always welcome.'

She nodded and compressed her lips. For a moment I thought she was going to cry. But as the train began to pull out of the station she pinned a great smile on her face, pulled the hat down rakishly over one eye, and waved like the light of heart until she was no more than a gesture disappearing round the bend.

20

Looking back, I see Daddy's death as the turning point in our marriage. At first I thought it was a turn for the better and believed that I understood why. Matthew had found my father an insuperable problem. That problem removed he was given room to flower, and apart from the Celia Piper episode he and I had worked and thought as one in those turbulent days after Daddy's death.

Afterwards, it was he who suggested that we take Mummy home with us for as long as she wanted to stay. He also gave me a rise in the housekeeping, and suggested that I employed my occasional help regularly, asking her to do housework two mornings a week. I supposed that he must have taken note of Mrs McGann and my mother's domestic arrangements. Matthew was like that. A situation could exist for years without registering, then suddenly he would see it, think, 'That's a good idea!' and adopt it forthwith.

In all kinds of ways, during that demanding time, he showed how much he appreciated me. His kisses of greeting and farewell became warm instead of perfunctory, and were accompanied by a hug. He managed to get home at a reasonable time while Mummy was staying with us, and as she urged her services upon us as a resident baby-sitter we did the rounds of the cinemas. Just for once, when Leila rang up and said, 'Have you seen *A Taste of Honey*?' I was able to say nonchalantly that I had. And I caught up on *Saturday Night and Sunday Morning*, which she had raved about the year before. To be truthful, I was out of tune with both of them. Homosexuality, illegitimate babies, adultery and abortion might fascinate Leila but they saddened me, and Mummy agreed.

'We all know these things happen,' she said, 'but we don't want them flaunted before us, labelled as entertainment.'

And when I met Matthew up in London for the evening, and he had booked seats for *Beyond the Fringe*, I scored a point over my gadabout sister.

I rang her before we drove home, saying. 'We've laughed ourselves silly! So funny, and so witty. And Peter Cook is a *beautiful* young man! You really must see it, Lulu!'

Lovely, for once, to feel part of the mainstream, instead of being stuck in a backwater. Lovely to be a Town Mouse instead of a Country Mouse.

Yes, we seemed to have turned over that new leaf at last. At weekends Matthew played with the children, instead of asking me to keep them quiet and shutting himself up with his papers. Our love life, always the first casualty in any domestic crisis, bloomed again. And there was no doubt about it, he loved having Mummy around and she brought out the best in him. With her he became the young man I had fallen in love with, nearly ten years ago: talkative, hopeful, confiding, boyish. I was pleased, but also faintly galled.

One evening, when she was in bed and I was toasting a late-night snack in the kitchen, I said mockingly, 'I believe you prefer older women!'

He flushed up and frowned.

'I was being funny,' I said untruthfully. 'I'm glad you and Mummy get on so well together. You're the only man I know who likes his mother-in-law.'

His flush subsided. His frown smoothed out.

He said, mocking himself, 'She's the sort of mother I've always wanted.'

'Well, I'm blessed!'

'Oh, you are!' he said, serious, laughing. 'You really are, Zo!'

We said nothing more for a few moments. I was wondering about his own mother, and evidently so was he.

256

He said, 'You don't particularly like my parents, do you, Zo?'

This time I told the truth, but cautiously.

'Not really. No.'

He scratched his cheek thoughtfully.

'I shall always be grateful to them for the sacrifices they made,' he said. 'And I suppose I love them. In a way. But mother, in particular, can be very demanding. Unlike Helen, who fits in so beautifully that one hardly knows she's here.'

Their visits were not as frequent nowadays but the Lady Marian, as Leila called her, would certainly demand a holiday at the Old Rectory simply because poor Mummy had stayed with us. Cautiously, I mentioned their possible expectations of a week's or a fortnight's holiday.

But Matthew said, 'Oh, no. A day is long enough, and it's not so very far for them to travel. Tell them we're busy entertaining people if they happen to ask. And, Zo, I think we should put them off for Christmas this year. I know it's their turn, but in the present circumstances I feel we ought to have Helen and Leila.'

So I cancelled the Barbers and invited the Gideons gladly, and the halcyon period continued until my mother returned to Whitegates, when we began to realise how my father's death would impinge upon our lives.

He was not one of those people who die intestate. Indeed, he had reviewed his will annually and made adjustments whenever he felt the circumstances warranted them, intending to provide for his womenfolk with foresight and care. There were various small bequests to people like Celia Piper, for instance, who was to be given a year's salary, in thanks for her secretarial services.

But he had always said to us, 'I'll make sure, when I kick the bucket, that each of you three will have her own home and her own money. Then you can thumb your noses at the world!'

Looking back, I realise that if any of us had had the commonsense to sit down and work out a few sums, we would have known that we were all living beyond his means, but we had taken his financial wizardry for granted. And he must have intended to live far longer and die much richer because when the will was read we discovered that his original wishes could not be met. Our liberal provider had taken one chance too many, and the future had foreclosed on him.

My mother had Whitegates, which must obviously be sold. Leila could look forward to a few more years in the Garret before the lease ran out, and must thereafter rely on herself. There was enough ready money to keep Mummy going for a while, and Leila and I had a thousand pounds apiece left in trust for emergency use only. Financially, I was more secure than either of them, except that – in death as in life! – my husband was nursing a grievance against my father.

I suppose the terms of the will were provocative to such a man as Matthew: jealous of his status and unsure of his authority. For the Old Rectory, in good repair and condition, had become my sole property, thus bypassing my husband completely. It was unfortunate, too, that Daddy had made a little joke about it in the codicil, saying that his bequest to Matthew was the rent he would no longer pay.

I knew there would be trouble ahead when I saw my husband pondering this final quip silently, brows drawn together, but he waited patiently until we were by ourselves again before he gave voice to his discontent.

He chose his old battleground of the kitchen at suppertime. Then he said that he objected to my father's evident distrust of him. That he, Matthew, had always done his best by me and the children. That he had put as much work and time into the Old Rectory as I had. And that it was a shabby thing, in his opinion, to make a man a lodger in his own home.

Our latest honeymoon was evidently over. Matthew's display of affection must have arisen from the belief that he would benefit by the will, and was feeling kindly towards me as co-owner of a fine property. As he grumbled on I remembered other occasions when I had mistaken

258

self-interest for love of me and been similarly disillusioned.

Eventually, my silence brought him to a halt.

'Still,' he said grudgingly, 'it's not your fault, Zo.'

I did not answer. I wanted to hear what he would say
next, for he had evidently been brooding on the situation.
He glanced at me, and gave a shamed and boyish grin as
though an idea had just struck him.

'No, it's not your fault. So why am I going on like
this?' he said reprovingly.

Still I waited, while he thought again. He spoke casually,
but his intention was deliberate and obvious enough.

'The remedy lies in your hands, Zo. All you have to
do is to put the house in both our names, and then it
will belong to both of us.'

He warmed to this subject over the coldness of my silence.

'The Old Rectory will be *ours* then. We shall be sharing
it as we share everything else.'

Sharing, from Matthew's point of view, seemed to be
a one-sided business. I reflected that he had squashed the
idea of our having a joint bank account, or of running two
separate accounts. He said it would be simpler if he dealt
with all the bills and handed out my housekeeping in cash
once a week. Since working for Trudy Olsen he had become
vague about his salary, putting down his higher standard of
living to an expense account. I did not know, in fact, how
much my husband earned.

Perhaps he had tried to bully or cajole me once too
often. Perhaps I was still angry because he admired Celia
Piper, who had confided in him at Leila's expense. Or
perhaps it was a sweet satisfaction which ran through
my veins when I realised that Queen Anne, as I called
the Old Rectory, belonged to me, that I was no longer
wholly dependent on my husband, that he was in this
part of our life dependent on me. My father had given
me a measure of protection and a means of defence
which I had lacked before. I knew that Mummy, in
my place, would have bowed to Matthew's wishes and
soothed his masculine pride, but all my instincts forbade

me to relinquish a tactical and psychological advantage.

I heard myself, as I might have heard Leila, speak coolly and factually.

'Oh, I don't know. Surely it seems fair that if you provide the income I should provide the house. Wouldn't you call that sharing?'

He sat upright and gave me a look of astonished anger.

He said, 'Have you any idea how impossible my position is?'

I said obstinately, 'Your position is unchanged. As long as we live here together this is our home.'

He cried, incensed, 'You've been given this house for doing sweet damn-all. I work for every penny I earn, and work damned hard, as well you know.'

Still I pursued my argument, remaining logical, even slightly detached.

'But I work just as hard as you do, and have fewer pleasures, and don't get paid at all. What are you worried about? I'm no more likely to ask you to quit the premises than you are to refuse me housekeeping money. We depend on each other. Nothing alters the fact that we're husband and wife and this is our home.'

But that picture of our life was growing further and further away from the truth, and he had most wretchedly disappointed and disillusioned me yet again. My emotions surged forth.

I said in quite a different voice, hurried, choked, 'And I know you resented my father but I loved him dearly. I loved him more than I ever realised. And this is what *he* wanted and nothing can make me change it!'

Then I opened the floodgates because he was dead, and cried without restraint, head in hands, sitting at the kitchen table.

Matthew shoved back his chair and got up, saying huffily, 'If that's the way you feel then we'd better drop the matter for the time being. Later on, I don't doubt that you'll come round to my point of view.'

260

No, I thought. Sobbing, hiccupping. No, I shan't. And no, I won't.

He wandered off into the sitting room to watch *Face to Face* on the television, and presently called to me to come and join him because this was a really good interview, and John Freeman knew how to get the marrow out of the bone all right. Which was his way of apologising.

He was inclined to be sulky for the next few days, and we went through one of our silent phases, but that had happened before when I had nothing to fall back on. Now I was able to think, 'You're all right, Zoe. Whatever happens you've still got Queen Anne!'

Christmas, coming soon afterwards, was a dismal affair. Leila accepted our invitation with evident reluctance and arrived on Christmas Eve, laden with gifts but looking ill and white and tense. She should have been handled with care, but Matthew had to make one of his edged jokes about the CND, pretending that she had been the person who had painted 'BAN THE BOMB' across Stonehenge in yellow letters four feet high, the previous March. She took him seriously and lost her temper. Then they had an argument at the dinner-table about the pros and cons of public protest, which Matthew instigated and won. At the end of a charged evening Leila slung her suitcase back in the car, despite all our protests, and drove off to spend Christmas alone at the Garret.

Mummy and I were dreadfully upset, but the children still had a wonderful time on Christmas Day and some of their joy and excitement rubbed off onto us, though once they had gone to bed the festivities evaporated. In the evening Leila telephoned, sounding slightly sloshed, and apologised for making a scene. I answered her in both roles.

Honest Zoe said, 'It wasn't your fault, Lulu. Mat can be very provocative.'

The loyal Mrs Barber added, 'He doesn't mean to be, of course. It's his legal mind. You should have ignored him, Lulu.'

She said humbly, 'Well, anyway, I'm sorry, Zo. But I'm

better by myself. Daddy's with me in spirit. I'm playing all his favourite records. Can you hear Ella Fitzgerald belting out *Manhattan* in the background? The music helps me to remember him as he was. I'd say that the two of us were having a sentimental binge.'

I said, 'I wish he'd pay a visit here. It's rather dull at the moment!'

She said in a small lost voice, like a child, 'Zo, do you miss Daddy dreadfully? I do. I miss him like an ache in the stomach. Zo, wasn't he a wonderful person? I mean, in spite of the Celia Pipers and Co., wasn't he a great man?'

I felt the blessed relief of tears running down my cheeks. I tried to keep my voice sounding normal while I wiped them away with the back of my hand.

'Yes,' I said. 'Yes, he was. And I miss him. And I think about him. I think about him all the time.'

The one who must miss and think about him most, drawn to the telephone by maternal instinct, had come softly to my side and put one arm round me, and laid her wet cheek against my wet cheek. I gave a gasp and a sob, and heard an answering gasp at the other end of the line.

I said, 'Now you've made us all cry, blast you! Lulu, here's Mummy. Wanting a Christmas word.'

I stayed in the cradle of my mother's arm, listening to her pouring oil and honey on my sister's wounds.

When she put the receiver down she wiped her own eyes and said in what Lulu and I called her let's-be-bright-and-cheerful voice, 'That's all right, then. I was just worried in case she hadn't any food in the house. Poor little thing, all on her own. But apparently Ruth and Beatrice had cooked an enormous Christmas dinner for themselves. Turkey and crackers and everything. And they insisted on her joining them. I'm glad about that. She's sitting by herself now, but she's quite happy, and she spoke so beautifully about Daddy.' Then she said sadly, 'I can't bear family quarrels. And at Christmas, of all times.'

It was her first hint of reproach.

Her second came when she said with quiet dignity, 'Darling, perhaps *you'd* say good-night to Matthew for me?

262

I'm going to bed now. It's been a long day. And bless you, darling, and thank you for all the trouble you've taken to give us a good Christmas. The food was beautiful and the children were a joy – and so are you, always.'

I returned to the sitting room where the villain of the piece was sipping a glass of Drambuie and staring critically at our rented black and white television.

He said, 'Of course, this would look far better in colour, but we can't afford it.'

Once, I would have felt apprehensive about his expression and the remark. Now I ignored both. I had had enough trouble for one Christmas and would not allow him to make more.

He knew I was holding back, that something in me was different, and he resented that too. Mummy went home earlier than she had planned and we entered 1962 alone, and in a state of armed truce.

Winter is always the testing time for houses, particularly old and demanding properties such as mine. In February, Queen Anne had a fit of temperament in her roof and rainwater leaked into the ceilings of two bedrooms.

Matthew said briefly over breakfast, exuding quiet satisfaction, 'You're the owner. It's up to you to sort it out.'

'I'll do that,' I answered, just as briefly.

Our eyes met and measured each other, and looked away again.

'By the by,' said Matthew, 'I shan't be here next weekend when my parents are coming. Trudy needs me with her in Switzerland. So you'll have to cope on your own, I'm afraid.'

'I'll make a mental note of that,' I said hardily.

Actually I made several mental notes.

When I had driven the children to school I marched back into the house, my house, in a mood Leila would have applauded and my mother deplored.

I collected all the bills accumulated during the renovations of the past six years, made myself a mug of fresh ground coffee, took it to the telephone and settled down with a notepad and biro to sort out Queen Anne and my position as a property-owner.

First of all I rang my father's solicitor, who had also been his friend and acted as his executor. Delightfully named Mr Shanklady, he was the senior partner in an old family firm, and though he was the same age as my father they were as different as two men could be. Perhaps their differences cemented them. He was keeping a kindly watch over Mummy's and Leila's properties, but had assumed that Matthew would look after mine. So I felt a little self-conscious in asking his advice about paying for repairs. In fact, I made up a story to cover my husband's deficiencies and explain why I was about to ask a lot of questions: exaggerating the length of his stay in Switzerland, and the possible extent of the repairs, and making up an emergency which had left us temporarily short of ready money.

But Mr Shanklady was so courteous as not to notice the lack of Matthew, and cut across my long-winded saga with a soothing, 'Of co-o-o-ourse, Mrs Barber!' before I had half-finished. He was very understanding about Queen Anne's sins, saying he had an old property of his own, and found it both pain and privilege. Then he got briskly down to business, said that this certainly counted as an emergency and he would make the necessary sum available to me. He added cautiously that my thousand pounds was not a fortune, and suggested that if I ever needed a larger amount of money I should approach my bank manager and ask for a mortgage on the value of the property.

I was busy with my questions and my pencil, and he explained everything very patiently and clearly. I realised that I should need my own bank account, but must have some money to start it. I made a note of that, too. And when I had at last finished picking his brains, and thanked him for his kindness, he said it had been a very great pleasure, and that he would be glad to advise me at any time.

Greatly heartened, I wrote out a short list of my future workmen, selected those necessary to cope with the roof, and enlisted their help.

Business done, I turned to my domestic arrangements and rang Mummy, who was sounding brave rather than happy. And finally I telephoned Matthew's mother and told her, pleasantly but without regret, that I was afraid we should have to cancel the coming weekend because he would be away on business.

The Lady Marian came back fighting.

'Oh, but we mustn't let Matthew disappoint us all,' she said winningly. 'Edmund and I can come just the same. I have the teeniest-weeniest bone to pick with you, my dear – only a teeny-weeny one because we love you so much! But I do think you're far too indulgent with Matthew about this peculiar job of his. In fact, I've been meaning to have a little chat for some time. So really it's quite a good thing that he's away! Yes, Edmund and I will come over to cheer you up. And then we can see Matthew when he comes home. That will be another little treat for us.'

Two holidays instead of one.

'We're very much on our own these days, you know,' she said reproachfully.

I was not surprised.

My new self said lightly, ignoring the pinpricks and the reproach, 'Then we must have a specially nice time later on. But I'm afraid I've already made plans for this weekend because I was so sure that you'd prefer a visit when Matthew was there. And as soon as Mummy heard that he would be away she invited us over to Whitegates. She's invited my sister, too. But we'll fix something up with you as soon as he gets back. Now, how are you both . . . ?'

I didn't tell him what I had done. If he could have a life of his own then so could I. Nor did I tell the children until the last minute, reserving the news as a splendid surprise. And it was wonderful to go home to Whitegates and talk to Mummy and Lulu, without worrying about Matthew and trying to keep him content.

He returned from Switzerland in an affectionate, penitent mood, and brought us all presents. I was pleased and relieved, but not as spontaneously as in the past. Part of me now suspected these happy interludes, and could not wholly enjoy them because I knew that they would end at the first whiff of trouble or disappointment, and might even conceal another purpose.

I had purposes of my own. While he was away I had dealt with more than Queen Anne's repairs. Grannie and Grandpa Cullen and the aunts always gave me money for Christmas, which I usually kept in the house to dribble away on small domestic emergencies. But this year I gathered it all together, chose my own bank and opened an account.

When Matthew returned the deed was done, but he accepted it with surprising equanimity. And during this latest harmonious period I persuaded him to pay my housekeeping money by cheque once a month. It did not cost him anything, and it gave some financial leeway.

Nineteen-sixty-two was a strange year. A crucial year. As it unfolded, and Matthew realised that my new regime was not a whim, he changed his tactics and began to isolate me, not openly or suddenly, but covertly, gradually and always with good reasons. He withdrew from his few village activities, pleading the unexpected nature of his work. He began to withdraw from our friends. On more than one occasion he rang up with apologies just before a dinner-party, and left me to cope alone. On others I had to go out alone, bearing further apologies. I now hesitated about offering or accepting personal invitations. After a while his business entertaining dwindled to such an extent that I ventured to ask him why.

He said offhandedly, 'Oh, there's no point in dragging people all the way down to Kent. It's easier to give them a meal in town. Besides, it meant a lot of hard work for you.'

I felt disquieted.

I said cautiously, 'But Trudy did tell me that a business-man's wife is his best ally on the social front. I know that everyone loved coming down here. And though it was hard work I enjoyed the entertaining.'

He shrugged and returned to his *Daily Telegraph*.

I said, trying to make a joke of it, 'Does this mean

that no one ever comes here again? In which case, do I get invited to dinner in town with them occasionally?'

He looked up irritably and answered shortly, 'I expect so. I don't know. It depends what happens.'

That summer, at the last minute, he cancelled his own holiday and sent me and the children off to Cornwall by ourselves for a month. When we returned he had evidently missed us, and we basked in an Indian summer of our own for a little while. Then the silent hostilities began again.

One evening he did not even bother to telephone. He simply did not come home and I was left waiting, with the first oxtail stew of the autumn keeping warm in the simmering oven. Finally I took it out, to save for the following evening, and made myself a bacon sandwich because I was no longer hungry.

Some time after midnight he tiptoed into the bedroom. Half-awake in the moonlight, I watched him from under half-closed eyelids and gauged his state of temper. Could I ask for an explanation? Would it be wiser to pretend to sleep?

But he was in a mood of sweet contentment, whistling softly under his breath, moving quietly, considerately, careful not to disturb me. He felt in his pockets and I heard loose change chink softly as he laid it down on the dressing-table. The mirror reflected his face, absorbed and relaxed, faintly radiant in the half-light of the room. He looked supremely happy. Something nice had happened to him, and once more I was drawn hopefully towards reconciliation.

I chose to forget about the lack of a telephone call, sat up in bed and made a joke of his lateness.

'Don't tell me! Trudy's putting a beauty parlour on the moon, and she sent you ahead to find a good site!'

He started slightly, turned towards me, smiled, and said slowly, 'I thought you were asleep. It's awfully late, I'm afraid.'

'That doesn't matter. Have you enjoyed yourself?'

'Yes,' he said, musing. 'Yes, I have.'

I hugged my knees.

267

'Tell me all about it,' I said.

He continued to look at me as if I were a stranger towards whom he bore no ill will. He continued to smile to himself.

Then he turned his back on me, saying quite pleasantly but quite deliberately, 'It's none of your business.'

I lay awake long after he had fallen deeply and peacefully asleep.

Leila

21

1961–1962

As soon as I walked into my flat after my father's death, I knew that the Garret would never be quite the same again. I had not realised just how much an attitude of mind affects one's surroundings. I had lived lightly in my house, taking his protection for granted. But in dying he had left me solely responsible for it.

I walked from end to end of my long living room, which looked from one window at the house-fronts opposite, and from the other end at the house-backs. Dank November had crept stealthily upon us. The few spare city-bred trees were leafless. The sky was putty-coloured. The pavements a dirty doleful grey. I was a strange sad person mourning in a sad strange place.

Ruth Babbage was in mourning, too. She had darted out of her own flat to greet and console me downstairs only a few moments ago, but could not speak, so pressed my hands between hers and shook her head. Metaphorically speaking, she had collected other women's men all her life. Jeremy had been her phantom lover while he was mine in flesh. Now she grieved for the loss of my father, who had been a quasi-husband to her.

There was a pile of post waiting for me on the kitchen table, which Ruth had kindly arranged in order of dates. I stood there in my hat and cloak, looking though it. I picked up a telephone bill and an electricity bill, and put them to one side. I opened various letters, which ranged from party invitations to sympathetic notes. Finally I turned over a thick brown package which I recognised as coming from the firm who had published *The Fly-Away Balloon.* My faithful concierge had taped a neat note to its front.

> This will be from the lady editor who happened to telephone while I was in your flat – which I cannot help feeling was *Meant*! I took the liberty of telling her your sad news and said you would be home soon, and that I was taking care of things while you were away. This parcel arrived yesterday and I collected it from the Post Office. I do hope it will cheer you up, dear. I'm downstairs if you want anything at all. Otherwise I shall leave you alone.
> Love and God Bless – We know He does, don't we?
> Ruth.

The editor's letter said that they had just accepted an unusual and delightful book for children of the 7–10 age group, part-story and part-natural history, which they thought I might like to illustrate. She enclosed a copy of the manuscript for me to read. It was called *Night-walks of the White Cat.*

Immediately I was back in Putney, looking out from Celia's sitting room at the curtained windows of the houses opposite, where one or two bedroom lights still glowed. It was still autumn, but this time the fog had gone and a moon shone between the trees, whose branches and twigs were as intricate as lace. And on a garden wall sat the white cat, with his tail furled round his paws.

There was a bird higher up on one bough of the tree. I had forgotten about the bird. And the cat was looking at the bird, although the bird was much too far away and much too wide-awake to allow a cat to jump up to his perch and capture him. Peering through the shrubbery, peeping over a fence, and ghostly in the farthest corner of the garden were the heads of other felines, but the White Cat sat lordly above the rest, and stared at me with amber eyes.

I opened the manuscript and stood there reading.

Further pictures began to form, becoming clearer and clearer, demanding to be made manifest. I threw off my hat and cloak and slung them on a chair. I percolated a pot of coffee for myself, opened a fresh packet of cigarettes, and sat at my work-table. The daily round and common task could wait until later. I began to draw.

And as I created, loving the act of creation, I realised that something new was being set down here, between mind and hand. I was looking at familiar things in an unfamiliar light. The commonplace became extraordinary. Alice-like I had been magically moved on to another square of the chess-board. And the old desire to paint for myself alone, and the old hope and belief that I could, flooded back.

There was a solitary quality about those sketches, a knowledge of the harshness of life and the inevitability of death, which gave them edge. And I saw my White Cat. I saw him very clearly. A big, beautiful, magnificent king of a cat, who walked by night.

Rooms store memories, emotions. This room in which I lived and worked was emulsioned from floor to ceiling in white, flushed with a tablespoon of Munsell red to take away the starkness. I craved light not purity, and only the furnishings provided a drama of many colours. On sunny days it was as cool and delicious as an ice-cream. On dark days it was tinged with warmth. It held my deepest misery and my greatest contentment. When I went out I left it as a sailor leaves harbour, ready for the adventure of a voyage. When I returned it was with a sailor's gratitude to be safe ashore.

I had envied Zoe much in our time together, but I never envied her the Old Rectory and her greater share of my father's professional interest and financial investment. Her house enslaved her, made demands upon her as great and constant as those of her husband and children. Zoe could not saunter down a London street one Saturday morning, buy a sound but shabby deal cupboard from a passing rag-and-bone-man for ten shillings and tip him another half-crown to haul it up to the top floor. Zoe could not

273

spend the afternoon scrubbing it, the evening painting it citron-yellow outside and bowling-green green inside, and decide where to squeeze it in the kitchenette. Any cupboard Zoe needed would require previous consultation, first with Matthew and then with my father. Once they had all agreed as to size, style and suitability, she would spend weeks hunting round auctions for exactly the right thing, and then restore it bit by painstaking bit until it came up to Queen Anne standard. But I was free to make a mistake or enjoy a triumph, unquestioned, uncriticised and unhindered. Zoe's real advantage lay in the fact that the Old Rectory was hers for life, and the Garret was mine for only a while.

For the first time, as I bathed, and heated up a tin of soup, and finally dropped into bed at three in the morning, I thought about the future. As long as my father lived I had not thought about housing myself. Now I was fatherless, and in five years would be homeless also. I could not save enough capital from my present fluctuating income to buy anything, and rents had gone up and up. I knew that neither my mother nor my sister could help me. Financially they were as strait-jacketed as I was, and equally ignorant about property. Mr Shanklady had hinted as much to Helen and me.

'Of course, Mrs Barber has a husband to advise her, but you two ladies are on your own. I was Caspar's friend as well as his solicitor, and I should be honoured if you both looked upon me in the same way, and felt free to consult me on any little problems which may arise.'

Well, he would certainly hear from me.

In the meantime, enough was enough for one long sad day. I propped the White Cat where I could see him when I woke up, and fell into the soundest sleep of the past fortnight.

I remember very little about that first raw year of mourning. I was in my late twenties anyway by that time, so the end of youth was in sight. But at one swoop my father had taken fly-away Leila with him, and left a person behind with whom I was not familiar. His death had the same effect on me as my baby's abortion. It robbed me of energy, took the fun out of living, switched me off sexually. The latter was a mercy, because soon afterwards Jeremy went abroad and I had not the vitality necessary to attract or sustain a new love-affair. And Cass was not only my first death but my first corpse. I dreamed of him dreadfully for months afterwards, sitting sock in hand, stopped in his final joke, as though the reaper could not be bothered to hear him out.

'Here! Half a minute, old man. I haven't finished telling Celia about the appalling Mrs Foreman . . . '

'Sorry, Mr – er— . Can't wait.'

Then the finality of his going stunned me. Never to see him again. Not even once a year or once a decade to catch up with all the news. Not even once in my remaining lifetime. Never, never, never again.

I had no belief in heaven to comfort and uphold me. Like my father and Magda, I was a cheerful pagan. We warmed our hands at the fire of life and then departed for good. But my mother, like the Cullens, believed devoutly in God, Christ and the Anglican Church. She had put Zoe and me through all the usual religious hoops: christening, Sunday School and regular church attendance. Zoe went along with all of it like a seraph, but I baulked at every step until we reached the age of confirmation, when I flatly refused to have any more to do with organised religion. I expect my mother and sister prayed for me, and probably still do.

It sounds pretentious to say that my God was art, but my attitude towards it was certainly that of a dedicated disciple. I was its faithful servant. I paid it homage, sacrificed myself to its pursuit, lived according to its dictates, and found myself occasionally in a state of grace. But this was such a personal blessing that it could not help me in my present grief. I could not come to terms with my father's death. To think that he had been completely and finally erased was unacceptable. To believe otherwise was impossible.

I envied Helen and Zoe their faith in eternal life, their prayers of intercession for his well-being, their sureness that his sins though as scarlet should become as white as snow. I could not talk to them about my trouble, did not tell them that I had many times slipped into churches, bowed my head before the high altar, knelt in beseechment, sat in unanswered emptiness, and come away.

Once, only once, persuaded by a friend, I attended a public séance.

Had Cass come through saying, 'I'm in a pretty dismal place at the moment, Lee, but I intend to give it a new look!' I should have been won over. But only the Marys and Harrys and the like were called by the Harrys and Marys from the other side, and their messages were bland and vacuous beyond belief. Inside me I said, 'Sorry Cass!' and left, feeling I had let us both down.

Belief came of its own volition and in its own time. I mention this because it meant much, and left behind it a thread that I shall pick up somewhere, someday. About nine months later, in high summer, at an hour and in a climate and country which had no connection with those of his death, I experienced a visitation between sleeping and waking.

Grief takes as much energy as love. I had caught one cold after another through the winter and lost weight. Helen, whose maternal instinct drew her even from her own unhappiness, persuaded our kindly Mr Shanklady to use his discretion and give me a hundred pounds from my emergency fund so that I could take a holiday abroad. And I was lying down one afternoon on a hard little bed in a hot little room in southern Spain, exhausted and utterly depressed, when my surroundings and perceptions changed.

It was a fine spring morning, and I was standing on the edge of a wood in Normandy watching a new house being built, a house such as they used to build centuries ago, and still do for a price and a perceptive purchaser. The frame, in Tudor fashion, was wooden: a handsome skeleton, about to be clad. And in its doorway stood a man, dressed as a forester. He was admiring his work, but in another moment or so became aware of myself as watcher, and turned round. His long plain heavy-chinned face looked young and solemn. Then he smiled at me, becoming extraordinarily attractive, and in that Fernandel grin I recognised my father. Neither of us spoke, nor needed to speak. He lifted one hand in greeting and gave me a nod.

The vision faded and I came back to my present time and place, reassured, renewed, a different woman. I had been given a message, from or about him. My father was at work, was rebuilding, and had returned to his mother's country. He wanted me to know that he was all right, that I needn't worry about him or grieve for him any longer, that I could walk on.

I lay there a little longer, as one lies in the last rays of the sun at the day's end, basking and remembering. When the final glow had ebbed I rose from my bed, ready to live again. My listless acceptance of whatever fate threw at me had vanished. I stood, arms akimbo, assessing my present circumstances.

I had booked and paid extra money for a room overlooking the sea, not a cupboard overlooking a blank wall. My lavatory, wash-basin and shower seemed to be connected to each other, and the supply of water was intermittent. A prevailing smell of disinfectant suggested problems of another sort, and I had seen something crawling on the wall that I could not name and did not like. In a healthy spurt of temper, I unpacked my Spanish handbook and looked up the pages on requests and complaints. I intended, whatever and whoever it cost, to change my surroundings, take a bath, put on my gladdest rags, and go out to find wonderful non-tourist food.

From that time onwards I began to heal.

Cass's death affected us in different ways. Helen lost her commonsense, and instead of selling Whitegates and buying something small and practical, she installed herself as spiritual steward of my father's house. Our Mr Shanklady was dismayed. He approached Zoe first, by telephone, but found her too loyal to admit that Mummy was making a mistake. He then invited me to join him at a wine-bar in Glasshouse Street, where he and my father had apparently shared and delighted in many a fine bottle.

I dug out one of the chic little suits Colin Macintosh had bought, as being more suitable for both person and occasion than my gipsy concoctions, and arrived looking presentable. Ever the gentleman, Mr Shanklady complimented me gravely on my appearance, thanked me for sparing time to see him, and with the aid of a splendid Margaux persuaded me to exert my influence.

'. . . because your lovely lady mother is being totally impractical in this matter. I assure you that she is living on very little money now, and before the end of the year will be quite penniless. But she will not listen to me . . .'

She did not listen to me either.

'Darling, I know you mean it for the best, but I must keep Whitegates on for as long as possible. It's all I have left of Daddy.'

I reported back to Mr Shanklady, for whom my respect and liking increased with each meeting, and he produced a bottle of Pouilly Fumé to console us.

The Cullens solved our problem. Now in their early eighties, they died within weeks of each other that same year, and left everything to Helen.

'Not a fortune, by any means,' said Mr Shanklady judiciously, as we drank together yet again, 'but quite enough to keep the dear lady in Whitegates. Of course, it would be wiser by far to sell up, buy a smaller house, and invest the money. But that your gracious mother will not do.'

My gracious mother, not only reimbursed but now reinforced in her convictions, continued to act as chatelaine to my father's first creation, though its purpose as a family home and an advertisement for his skills had died with him, and now that he had died she was isolated there.

Zoe was thirty that year. No longer a flower-crowned Titania, no longer a golden girl, but a woman of beauty in her prime. A thirtieth birthday is any woman's first warning

278

sign on the road to old age. Still young and attractive enough to be an ornament to life, and mature enough to appreciate it, she knows that from now on it will be downhill, downhill all the way.

I'm glad to say that Matthew summoned up enough grace to mark the occasion with a table for two in Soho, at Quo Vadis. Under the worldly wing of Trudy Olsen he had become quite knowledgeable about where to dine, whom to know and what to see, though he lacked the intuitive tastes of a true man about town. There was always something laborious and self-taught about Matthew's achievements. And in spite of the outward show both my mother and I felt that things were not going well with them. Zoe smiled less, was more guarded about herself and evasive about her husband.

When I got back from Spain I bought a couple of day-return tickets and took Helen to Coventry to see the newly consecrated cathedral, in which religion and art and craft had been most wonderfully wedded. And as we stood transfigured by John Piper's sunlit splinters of stained glass, my mother confided that the Barber marriage was going through a difficult phase.

'Another baby, perhaps, would bring them closer,' she murmured.

I felt that I spoke for my father, then, as well as myself.

'Another baby is the last thing Zoe should think of. It would tie her hand and foot for the next five years. If she's having trouble with Matthew she needs all the energy she's got. And if they reach breaking point then two children are easier to bring up than three.'

My judgement was sensible but harsh. Helen's gentle optimism rebuked me.

She said hurriedly, 'Oh, there's no question of that. Things are just a little difficult at the moment. It will pass. It will pass.'

But I could tell she was worried about Zoe, and grieved for her trouble.

I slipped an arm through hers, and said gently, 'Cass would have loved this cathedral. Let's light a candle for him, shall we?'

To make her smile again.

Mr Shanklady had turned to me as a last resort and found an ally. He and I kept in touch, and I began to see why Cass had been his friend. There was a cavalier lurking beneath that respectable city front, and a perfect gentil knight behind the cavalier. He took an immense amount of trouble and ttime without charging us for it. When a bill was inevitable it was also as small as he could make it. One of these enlightened days I am hoping to persuade him to let me pay for the bottle of wine we still share on three or four occasions a year, but as yet he is too much of a gentleman to allow it.

As I had taken responsibility for my father's death I now took responsibility for Helen and Zoe in his place. I telephoned them both regularly, kept a finger on the family pulse, made a point of visiting them or inviting them to visit me. And when our first sad anniversary came round I took them both out to see the first James Bond film, *Dr No*, because that is what Cass would have done.

They were both shaken and stirred. The undoubted attractions of Sean Connery, the pace and ingenuity and the fact that they had thoroughly enjoyed themselves could not be discounted. But what of the moral tone?

'It's pure male fantasy. Pure entertainment,' I told them. 'Not to be taken seriously. If I took it seriously I'd throw a brick at the screen!'

But still, they said. Still. Shouldn't one . . . ? Didn't one . . . ? Wasn't it . . . ?

I listened to them musing aloud, trying to match what they had seen to what they knew of life, and utterly failing. Occasionally I punctured their illusions, as my father would have done, and made them laugh.

The afternoon had been a success. This evening my mother would not feel the edge of her sorrow, imagining what my father might have thought and said about the film. This evening Zoe would probably wonder whether I met men like James Bond frequently. They were children in the world of sex, my mother and sister. They were also, for the moment, my children.

Linking their graceful arms, walking them to their train, I was smaller and less impressive than either. But I was taking care of them, was in charge of them, and they were content to let me be so.

22

1963

To avoid the trauma of the previous festival Helen and I decided to spend Christmas by ourselves at Whitegates, and invite Zoe and her family to drive over on the 31st, let the New Year in and return late the following day. Not too long, as Helen said considerately, and not too short. She meant we could all enjoy ourselves for that length of time without Matthew getting bored.

Christmas was slightly eerie but very pleasant. And though there were only two of us Helen had dressed the big tree and produced a full-scale festival with all trimmings. We opened our gifts together in the morning, and rang Zoe to exchange thanks and greetings. Ate a traditional lunch at one o'clock, and listened to the Queen's speech. Entertained Mr Shanklady and the aunts with cake and mince pies at tea-time. And in the evening made a pile of turkey sandwiches, and watched an old film on television.

For one hundred and fifty years there had not been a winter like it. The snow began soon after Boxing Day and would not stop. From the midst of six-foot drifts Zoe rang us in the midst of ours, to cancel the visit.

'. . . and she says that Matthew's worried about getting back to work,' Helen reported. 'He's supposed to be flying to Austria on the third and he can't even dig the car out of the garage.' She added, in a passion of anger which was most unlike her, 'But wouldn't you think he'd be more concerned about leaving Zoe and the children in that remote village, in conditions like this?'

Then she sat down quickly, clutched her stomach, gasped and went white.

'I shall be all right,' she said with difficulty. 'It's my indigestion.'

I stood by her, unsure what to do. After a while the spasm passed and she smiled up at me relieved, though still pale.

'Darling, would you get me some Milk of Magnesia in warm water?'

She drank it and waited, as if there might be another attack. But there was none and her colour returned.

'I can't eat what I used to,' she explained, 'and we really were a pair of piggies over Christmas.'

'Christmas was four days ago,' I said. 'Would you like me to call the doctor?'

'Certainly not. He would only tell me what I know already. I mustn't eat rich food – and of course, for once I did. And far too much of it! I'm nearly fifty-eight, darling. I can't expect my digestion to be as sound as it was.'

I registered the attack and her answer as being unsatisfactory, but as it didn't happen again I let it slide to the back of my mind.

By New Year's Eve no one could get anywhere, transport came to a halt and the sea froze. Snowbound in darkest Surrey, I rang the Garret, but my two tenants reported no major catastrophes so far. Cass had made sure that the pipes were lagged, the window-frames puttied and the loft insulated. And I had brought work with me, so the little holiday with my mother extended itself usefully and happily: she sewing or cooking and I drawing and painting. She had cultivated the gift of being present without interrupting, except for cups of coffee at the right time, which left me free to concentrate. For which I thanked her.

'No need to thank me, Lulu. It's lovely to have someone to look after again,' she said. 'Apart from missing Cass the saddest thing is that I'm no use to anyone. Oh, I help Zoe out and keep in touch with friends and family, but life seems purposeless, somehow. I can live *by* myself, but not *for* myself.'

I was concerned about leaving her in her elegant wilderness, but had no choice. As soon as we were dug out, and I could start the car, I went home.

For six weeks everyone in the country suffered extreme cold and the sun never shone. It was the hardest, greyest, grimmest winter I had known.

Matthew did get away of course, and Zoe had a shocking time at the Old Rectory and drew heavily on her emergency fund for repairs. We knew, by this time, that she and Matthew were at loggerheads over her possession of the house and he refused to spend a penny on it. Helen thought that Zoe should appease him for the sake of the marriage, but I applauded her decision and advised her to stick to her guns. This she showed every sign of doing, and I must say that her firmness surprised me, since she had always preferred to please people rather than stand her ground.

Simon was eight in July. I could honestly say that I did not love him more than I loved Caroline, but I had a special feeling for him because he was the same age my child would have been, and there was a sympathy between us. In many ways, particularly in appearance, he resembled his father, very dark and quiet and inward-looking. But being lucky enough to have Zoe as a mother he had developed differently. His shyness was hopeful and engaging, and with the least encouragement he unfolded beautifully. And though he was not one of life's entertainers he had a wonderful sense of fun and loved anyone who made him laugh. Whereas Caroline, who looked like Zoe and acted like me, was bold and beautiful and always standing in the limelight.

Since Matthew and I sedulously avoided each other I did not attend Simon's birthday party, but gave him a separate celebration in London on the following Saturday. This began and ended at the Garret, so that we could all have coffee or orange juice before we started out, and the children could be admired by Ruth and Beatrice and tidied up before they went home. In between we lunched at a restaurant which gave lollipops for clean plates, and went to a cinema matinée. Zoe brought them up to town on a morning train, handed them over to me, and then spent the day by herself, shopping and browsing.

The Profumo case had everybody by the eyes and ears at that time, and she particularly asked me not to let the children see a newsreel. So we waited in the foyer and ate more ice-cream until *Zulu* started. I sat between them, watching their faces as much as the film, monitoring their reactions in case I had made a mistake. Caroline, whom no amount of bloodshed could appal, sat mouth open and eyes wide. But Simon straightened up at the first Zulu battle-cry, and his face was both rapt and fearful as if he too wore a red coat and a white helmet, and must fight in the African sun for Victoria and England. I loved him so much then that I should have liked to put an arm round him, but knew he would be offended. So we fought all afternoon at Rorke's Drift until the Zulus hailed us as heroes and disappeared over the hill, and we received our Victoria Crosses, and came out into the London sun and talked all the way home.

Ruth had made a special tea for us in her flat, and a second birthday cake for Simon, and the children held the floor while we fed and watered and listened to them. Simon said he had decided to become a soldier, but changed his mind when he heard they no longer wore the same uniform. And Caroline said she was going to be a soldier anyway and marry Michael Caine. She was very cross when we all laughed, and lay on the floor. So Zoe said they were tired after the long day, and she thought it was time for them to wash their hands and faces and go home.

I helped Ruth to clear away afterwards, and then wound my way slowly upstairs to sort out my accounts and my schedule of work for the following week. The room was warm and peaceful in the last of the sun, but the place seemed very quiet and empty without them.

I had recently, and sadly, parted from a man. We had met in the barren time after Cass's death and, not surprisingly I suppose, he was considerably older than me and something of a father-figure. His name and appearance and personality do not matter. His significance lies in the fact that he was a signpost in my personal life, and made me understand something for the first time.

He, too, was suffering a loss. He had been married for many years when his wife died suddenly and left him anchorless. Like me, he was shocked, seeking consolation and an illusion of security.

We began as friends and ended as lovers, which astonished us both. Between us for almost a year, we created that unreal and wholly felicitous world of two people, and passed together through such stages of delight that I thought, as I had thought before and would probably think again, that at last here it was. I had found it. The two of us had something special between us.

He was no more my type than Mr Shanklady, and yet I liked him as he was, and we respected each other's differences. He was an old-fashioned person with old-fashioned good manners and an exalted opinion of women and womanhood. And in the early stages of our affair his consideration and tenderness were such that he even worried about my reputation. His efforts to conceal our true relationship from Ruth, who would no doubt have explained the situation away even if she had found us in bed together, verged on the hilarious.

She thought him, 'Such a gentleman, my dear Leila. And utterly devoted to you. Of course, there was no need to explain why he was leaving so late, when we met by chance in the hall the other evening. I believe I know a true knight when I meet one. You need fear no familiarity from him, my dear. A kiss on the hand, total respect, and – dare I say it? – a proposal if you play your cards right!'

Their chance meeting had been around midnight, but as our love and appetite grew he did not leave me until three and four in the morning. And when we had crept downstairs, exchanged one last long kiss, and I had closed the door silently upon him, he would disengage the handbrake of his car and push it laboriously away from the kerb down to the end of the street. Then, a safe distance away, so that no one would connect his departure with my house, he started the engine as quietly as possible and drove off. By this time I had scurried upstairs in order to watch the tail lights disappearing round the corner.

It was ridiculous, of course. My neighbours, if they cared a fig, knew all about my private life by this time, yet his loving courtesy moved me. And so we continued, never quarrelling, bearing each other's idiosyncrasies lightly, adding bliss to bliss. Until, in the early hours of one morning, he started up his car outside my front door.

I suppose he was tired and did not think, but to me it meant something much more important. It meant that he had grown used to me and the relationship, that he could relax now the first fine careless rapture was over, that the end had just begun.

A few months later he met a widow in his own age group, with a similar background and tastes, and as our relationship was somewhat attenuated by that time we agreed to part amicably. So that it became, after all, only another affair.

Looking out at the evening sun on the chimney pots, thinking of the joyful Saturday behind me and the empty Sunday ahead of me, I had to admit that my life, though tailor-made to my requirements, was not enough. Like Helen, I needed someone beside myself to live for. Purpose I had already. Work I had already. But a man who loved me most in all the world, and whom I loved as much, I had not. And I thought how perfect life would be if I could enter an equal partnership, prepared to give yet not to sacrifice, without forced commitment to the other's relations or friends, but caring and sharing, living, growing and letting be, side by side. There was a song that year called 'The Answer is Blowing in the Wind' but it was obviously not blowing in my direction because I remained unenlightened.

My mother had inherited her talent for music from her father's family, as reported many times by Magda.

'Lovely player David's Mam was! Played the piano lovely, she did!'

Encouraged by the Cullens, the talent might have grown in importance, but Helen chose to be a wife and mother and only performed at home for her own amusement and our entertainment. She was to be disappointed in her daughters for neither Zoe nor I showed promise as pianists, though we enjoyed listening to a wide range of music. My sister gave up piano lessons as soon as she felt that Helen would not mind, and of course I retired early in the fray without worrying in the least about my mother's feelings.

But the gift, as gifts most beautifully will, was hovering over one of the third generation. Our Caroline, a tomboy in all other matters, became another person over the keyboard, and Helen said she thought, she really did think, that Caro might be a musician in the making.

So for her granddaughter's sixth birthday in November Helen wrote out a cheque which would pay for a year's piano lessons. Just to see how she got on.

And for her personal birthday treat, a repeat of Simon's with a difference, I took both children to a Robert Mayer concert on the Saturday morning. After another blow-out lunch and lollipop, this left a space in the afternoon which we filled by visiting the Victoria and Albert Museum, where Helen said we could see a roomful of antique musical instruments if we asked specially. So we did ask specially, and were personally escorted to a locked room in a far corner of the building, which was unlocked very ceremoniously. And there they were: virginals, harpsichords, clavichords, spinets. Gilded, inlaid with ivory. And each of them a masterpiece of art and craft. Of course, the instruments must not be touched, but for me they were so exquisite that it was enough simply to marvel at them. I resolved to come back by myself and bring my sketching block with me.

But my niece tugged the sleeve of my coat and whispered, 'I'd love to know how they *sounded*, Lulu!'

And I knew then that Helen was right, and Caro was a musician.

Eating a second birthday tea in Ruth's flat at five o'clock, I said to Zoe, 'Children are an education in themselves, aren't they? I mean, I'd never have gone to that room by myself. Probably never have realised it existed. If it hadn't been for Caro.'

'Oh yes,' said Zoe, sounding proud and sagacious. 'They bring the outside world in with them. It was Simon who told me about those Beatles.'

'Yes!' said Simon scornfully. Animated for once. 'And Mummy said "What beetles?" as if they were *insects*!'

'The Beatles', I said, determined to score a point with my nephew, 'are absolutely with it – and I'll buy you a record of "I Want to Hold Your Hand".'

He jumped up and down, crying, 'Good old Lulu!'

But Zoe said nervously, 'Remember that Daddy doesn't like that sort of thing, Si. So you won't be able to play it when he's at home.'

For many an autumn after my father's death I hated to come home late, and hear the telephone begin to ring as I put the key in the latch. On that particular November evening I remember thinking, 'This is bad news. Bad news.' And so it was, though not as personal.

' Zoe's voice, aghast, said, 'Lulu, I simply had to 'phone you. Have you heard about President Kennedy? You haven't? He's been assassinated in Dallas. Can you believe it? A civilised country like America. Assassinated.'

It was bad, but not as bad as I had feared it might be. The worst thing was the reason she telephoned.

'I've been by myself all evening and it affected me much more deeply than I would have thought. I tried to contact you earlier but you were out, and I simply had to talk to someone.'

I said, 'Doesn't that bloody husband of yours ever come home?'

'Oh yes,' she said. 'But he was working late tonight.'

I stopped myself from saying, 'Not again?' and substituted, 'Is anything wrong, Zo?'

She said, 'I'm a little bit worried about Mummy. I do think we ought to get her to see a doctor. She's been suffering from indigestion for months, and she keeps on dosing herself with Milk of Magnesia and saying she's all right, but she isn't.'

I said, 'Suppose I go down for the weekend and ask the doctor to call in?'

'Yes, that would be best. I'd come if I could but I'm rather tied down here.'

Early in December Helen had an operation which took five and a half hours, followed by remedial treatment, which was pronounced successful.

'At least,' our family doctor told me, 'it's successful as far as it goes. But she should have come to me a year ago. Cancer isn't a disease you can ignore.'

There are other forms of cancer. That same month, returning from a visit to Helen, who was in a convalescent home nearby, I dropped in on Zoe. It was a Friday and her cleaning lady answered the door, saying that my sister was tidying the garden ready for winter. I walked through the house and saw her long before she saw me.

She was standing in the kitchen garden, wearing an old mackintosh, hair screwed up into a bun on the top of her head. One gumboot rested on her spade and she was staring straight ahead of her, immobilised. It had rained heavily earlier in the day and the trees still drooped and dripped. I thought it the saddest time of year and she the saddest person, for in her face and bearing I recognised a devastating feeling of unbelonging.

Zoe

23

1964

When I heard Matthew's key in the lock I hurried into the hall to intercept him before the children could. But they were watching *Dr Who* on the television and did not hear him: Caroline sitting cross-legged on the carpet, nonchalantly confronting the Daleks, and Simon standing behind the sofa which acted as his fortress, saying that they didn't frighten *him*.

Matthew and I faced each other on the threshold, he surprised, eyebrows raised. I put one finger on my lips, nodded towards the sitting room, and beckoned him to come into the dining room. And there, once the door was closed, I stated my unalterable decision.

'The results of Mummy's hospital tests have come through. It's cancer again, and this time it's inoperable. They can't do anything apart from keeping her comfortable. She's dying. I'm going to bring her here and look after her for as long as it takes.'

Then he became what I needed: an understanding, even an affectionate support. He made a tentative movement with one hand as if he might have touched my cheek or drawn me to him, but there was a physical barrier between us these days and he smoothed his chin instead, thinking. When he did answer I could tell that he was sorry for my news.

He said, 'Yes, of course she must come here. For as long as necessary.'

He said, 'You look all in. It must have been a nasty shock. Let's have a drink.'

And poured two generous gin and tonics.

He said, 'When shall we collect her?'

I said, 'I must persuade her first, and that might be difficult. But so long as we're agreed on a line of action that's all that matters for the moment.'

I was grateful for his acceptance. I had not known how I would cope with his disapproval as well as her mortal sickness. For she must come to me. On that point I was adamant. My mother and I stood at a crossroads together, and I could not let her travel on alone.

He said, 'I shan't be able to do much, but I'll try to make things as easy as I can for you.'

The situation between us, as husband and wife, had been tacitly accepted. I suspected that he had a mistress. I believe he knew that I suspected it. But neither of us was going to admit anything because that would mean an explosion we could not afford. So we were leading separate lives. And these days, to be quite truthful, my happiest hours were spent in Matthew's absence.

Now, when the telephone rang, and his voice, slightly self-conscious in apology, said, 'Terribly sorry, Zo, but I shall be late tonight. It's a question of the willing horse again! Don't cook dinner for me, and don't wait up!' I felt relief. The prospect of having supper on a tray in front of the television, watching all the programmes I liked and he did not, such as *Hancock's Half-Hour* or *Maigret*, was a bonus at the end of my working day. Recently a programme had begun called *That Was The Week That Was*, which was witty and informal and made me laugh. I caught myself hoping that he would be late that particular night, and feeling disappointed when he was not. But whatever day of the week it might be, the thought of an uncomplicated evening put a warmth into my voice which was not for him. I would hear myself thanking him for ringing up. And in return he made an effort to be kind at home.

So arguments and recriminations had ceased and for

some months now we had entered on a peaceable parallel relationship, travelling side by side, never meeting. We no longer made love but we slept in the same bed, night after night. We shared meals and talked of unimportant things and were companionable. We came to terms with our own cancer. We had achieved a sort of understanding and balance. At what cost to ourselves and our relationship I could not say, but I was too bruised from past encounters to want to revive them. If to be out of pain was to be dead then we had died. To such a pass had our marriage come.

Matthew said now, 'If there's anything I can do to help, please say so.'

I answered, looking into my empty glass, 'If you could manage to be at home more often. The children hardly see you. Mummy will think it odd that you're away so much. Of course, I know you're busy.'

He nodded abruptly, and then said, 'Let's have another drink.'

Over the second gin we discussed how much the children would be told, and decided to tell them a half-truth, that Granny was very ill and would be living with us until she got better. Time and gradual realisation would do the rest.

Matthew offered to drive over to Southfields and tell his parents personally as soon as we had eaten, and I was glad to be absolved of this duty. Beneath Marian's glutinous sympathy would lie a certain exultation, because my mother was going to die while she lived. Also, his absence meant that I could telephone Leila and talk freely, without watching the clock or fielding his comments afterwards.

Her fly-away voice came over the wires from London, and I could picture her sitting on her scarlet divan, smiling in anticipation of some great event. She was spilling over with life. Her tone had that vibrant quality which I had come to associate with a lover. It gave off an air of abundance, of abandon, of fecundity. I felt at these times that if I were to touch her I should suffer a mild electric shock. Life's party, it appeared, was still on. For the minutes before I shattered that illusion I was angry, and I envied her.

'Lulu, it's me. Zo.'

Her squeal of delight made me laugh.

'Zo! I was thinking of you. Zo, the most amazing thing has happened . . . '

It was typical that she should put out her news before I could give mine.

' . . . you've rung at exactly the right moment. I'm all dressed up and ready to go out. Silver shoes with stiletto heels. My feet will kill me tomorrow! A flower in my hair. And a wild, wild costume. It's a fancy-dress party, and I'm a dryad! Isn't that crazy? It'll probably go on all night. I shan't be back until dawn.'

My fatal news must wait a while. I asked an obvious question.

'Has Jeremy Purchase come home?'

She laughed, and I could imagine her shifting her body into a more comfortable sitting posture. She was as free as my children, freer, because they were constrained by our difficulties.

'Haven't heard from him for ages. This is a new man.'

I attempted lightness, though leaden in flesh and spirit.

'I thought I could tell the signs! So what's this new man of yours like?' I asked as cheerfully as I could.

She spoke all in a rush, like a girl of eighteen with her first boyfriend.

'What's he like? Oh, Zo, he's absolutely fantastic. Frightfully suave, with beautiful dark-brown eyes and an equally beautiful dark-brown voice, and he melts me.'

'And has he got a beautiful dark-brown complexion to match?' I asked tartly.

I was remembering the summer she had brought a West Indian rock musician called Zak Blueberry to our village fête. We must have disturbed him as much as he disturbed us, because he got high on something, and had to be removed bodily from the refreshment tent. Matthew had sworn that was the last time Leila would be invited to a public event.

296

Probably she remembered too, but passed the memory lightly by.

'You're being snipey, Zo. He's what the Americans call a White Caucasian. I always thought that meant Russian!'

'Is he young and/or single?'

'Well, no. He's some years older than me. And married. But I'm not poaching!' she cried, sensing disapproval on my part. 'He was quite frank with me. His marriage has been over for years. They prefer to live their own lives and stay amicably together. He didn't try to chat me up by dangling a possible divorce in front of me. And I told him I'd sooner be dead than wed. So it suits us both.'

'How very convenient for you.'

'We're not hurting anybody,' she said defensively.

'I should be hurt in his wife's place. Or does she play the same game?'

'He didn't discuss her. I wouldn't expect him to.'

'Well, I hope she cuckolds him good and proper!'

There was a slight pause, then Leila said wistfully, 'You used to be all sweetness and light, like Mummy. And, to be quite honest, I preferred it.'

I heard myself say sourly, 'Of course you preferred it. It was very nice for Daddy, too, when Mummy kept smiling and trying to understand him. But I sometimes wonder whether her good behaviour didn't give him *carte-blanche* to behave as badly as he wanted to, while she sat at home and coped with the situation. I can't help feeling that if Mummy had been a virago, and screamed and made scenes and tracked him down and given him and his Celia Pipers hell, they might not have thought it was quite so much fun to have an illicit affair.'

Who was I talking to? Leila or myself?

Leila said very firmly, 'My bloke's marriage isn't like Helen and Cass's marriage. I can assure you that this situation is well under control on all sides.'

I thought of my arid bed, and the man who had promised to love and cherish me and cling only unto me as long as we both should live. Ten years was not a lifetime.

297

Through that perverse sympathy between us which allowed her to home in on my thoughts without fully understanding them, she winged me in passing.

'You should take a lover yourself,' she said naughtily, 'if only to make Matthew sit up and beg!'

From the barren anger of my being I cried, 'Oh, don't be so stupid!' Then conscious that I had betrayed myself, I added lightly, 'Where would I fit a lover into my present schedule?'

Very sweetly and seductively she answered my anger, 'Sorry, Zo. Didn't mean you to take me seriously.'

But she had ruffled me by putting into words a longing and an envy which could not be assuaged. I heard myself protesting too much.

'Lovers are only the beginning of a relationship. Why stop there?'

I imagined her giving the ceiling a quizzical upward glance, smiling a long crooked smile. She would reach for a cigarette while I lectured her, and then remember too late that she had given up smoking because it had been connected with lung cancer.

Her tone teased me.

'Do go on, Zo. I love hearing you clutch the chains that bind you!'

I lost my temper then, crying, 'The trouble with you is that you confuse liberty with licence, and you're afraid of responsibility. But nothing is ever worthwhile unless you work at it and stay with it. Just picking men up and putting them down, as if they were bargains in a sale, won't get you anywhere. There's no point in it, no purpose to it, no future.'

I had hit some target because when she replied the smile had left her voice. But instead of attacking me or defending herself she turned the argument aside.

'Oh well, each to her own life. Shall I tell you why I was thinking about you when you rang? This costume of mine, though made out of cheesecloth with loving hands at home, is terribly Peaseblossom. I was remembering your wedding day. And Jeremy putting a stone down on your veil.'

Anger dissolved like a dark figure into mist. I returned to the present moment, feeling empty, lost and sorry. I reminded myself that my sister could commit herself as deeply, love as much and be equally worthwhile in other ways. *Village Fête* hung on the wall near the telephone. I had been looking at it without seeing it. Now the picture came into perfect focus.

My mother had said in wonder, 'The countless loving hours that Lulu must have spent, bringing it all to life. And then to give it to you. Just like that.'

I accepted the reproach. I remembered the reason for telephoning my sister, and would have liked to delay it.

But she said, 'Zo. We've got ourselves side-tracked. You can't have rung up in order to lecture me on my wicked ways. What did you really want to tell me?'

I said in a rush, 'Mummy has had the results of her check-up, and I'm afraid they're not good.'

Leila leaped ahead of me.

'The cancer's started up again, hasn't it?'

'Yes. All over, apparently. And quite inoperable.'

'How long?'

'They can't tell exactly. Weeks, perhaps. A month or two at most.'

She was with and for me in an instant.

'What can we do for her?'

'I shall nurse her here. Come and see her whenever you can, won't you?'

'Of course I shall. I'll do more than that. I'll help in any way you think best. Does Mummy know?'

'Yes. She said she was being given time to put her life in order. Oh, and she doesn't want Magda to know how serious it is. We're just to say that she's not very well.'

There was a long silence. Then Leila spoke sadly.

'I'm casting the flower out of my hair. It seems inappropriate. They must dance from dark to dawn without me.'

'Don't be silly!' I replied, in the same tone I would use with Caroline when she threatened a scene. 'We'll go into sackcloth and ashes when it's time and not before. Now have a wonderful party. It won't help anyone if you don't.'

She did not reply to this, did not say whether she would or would not stay at home. For a moment she was dedicated to Mummy.

'Let me know the day she's coming to you and I'll design a special card to welcome her, and send a bouquet by Interflora. Oh, Zo! I've just had an inspiration. Yellow roses. Do you remember the King's Ransoms she gave you when you came to dinner at Whitegates just after your honeymoon? You stood on the doorstep there, holding them against a dark-blue velvet coat? "Zoe's worth a thousand kings' ransoms," she said.'

'That would be lovely. She'll remember it too.'

Leila cried vehemently, 'Oh, Zo, why must she die such a horrible death? Why couldn't she have lived until she was too old to care, and then died in her sleep? Why couldn't she have gone out like a light, as Daddy did? Why do good people suffer?'

She asked me as if I could tell her, but I was putting the same questions to myself and finding no answers at all.

My mother and I came to terms with her illness by reversing roles. She became my dependant, my sick child. Often, I called her 'Nell' as my father had done. And the days followed, one upon the other, in like pattern.

Each morning, when I took her breakfast, she would be awake already, sitting up in bed very straight, arms hugging her knees, staring out of the window with the intensity of a photographer imprinting a picture on her mind. She had grown very thin since she came to me, her brown bonniness giving way to a pale worn beauty more indicative of the soul than of the flesh, and her expression was infinitely sad. She was loving that well which she must leave ere long. The calendar on the wall held the secret day, the clock on the side-table the secret hour, minute and second of her departure, as they held the departure of each of us, but hers was more imminent.

Had we been less close I should have made some small noise or movement to attract her attention, to give her time to conceal her mood from me, but we had nothing to hide from each other and so I came in with her tray as usual.

'Ready for breakfast, Nell?'

'Yes,' she said. And then, 'It feels like a good day today. Isn't that a bonus? Oh, and there's another postcard from Magda. Isn't that sweet of her? Darling, I can't seem to put my mind to writing letters, perhaps you or Leila would send her a line? And do tell her that there's absolutely no need to worry, won't you? Tell her I'm getting better every day.'

Then she began an elaborate ritual of tea-pouring and toast-buttering, to show what an appetite she had.

'Then shall I leave you to it, darling, and come back later?'

But her sense of fitness must be satisfied first.

'Has Matthew gone to work? Have the children gone to school? Good. Is this the morning that Mrs Yates comes? . . . '

And only when this little catechism was answered did she turn to her breakfast saying, 'I *am* looking forward to this!'

She spoke heartily, but I saw that her interest had already diminished. I knew that when I returned to pick up her tray she would have put it aside after an effort to please me. A beggar would have starved on the result, and I wondered how long she could sustain life like this, and how we were both going to bear the waiting as well as the end.

I had one consolation. Matthew was being consistently kind at this time. His late nights were few, and the evenings when he was home early he made a point of sitting with Helen and reading to her while I rested. He took the children out most weekends for nature-study walks, attempting to educate as well as to amuse them, in much the same way as his father had once tried to please and occupy him. I think that in Matthew's case the intent never caught fire and the relationship remained cold and dutiful. But Simon and Caroline, well loved and outgoing, thought it all great fun and were delighted with his unaccustomed attention.

For my mother's sake and mine, Matthew and Leila even managed to cope with each other. Previously they tried never to meet, but now she was coming whenever she could make the time, and occasionally at the weekends. It was a case of quarrel or compromise, and they chose the latter.

In our long quiet truce the atmosphere of the whole house lightened. My inner burden lightened too. I felt that Matthew and I would soon be able to face and diagnose the sickness in our marriage, and nurse it back to life. But this must wait until later. For the moment enough was enough. Let him be unfaithful to me if he must. I had a death to honour first.

Then as the weeks passed and he continued to keep reasonable hours, and be kind to me and more interested in the children, I began to wonder if our marriage was already on the mend. So my mother's last illness became a time to live as well as a time to die, poignant, hopeful, bountiful.

She diminished in slow stages over the next two months. When she first came to me she retired to bed early, slept late and rested in the afternoons. Growing gradually weaker, she kept to her bed most of the time. Finally she stayed there altogether, with occasional excursions, when she would creep downstairs unexpected and unaided, in a state of bewilderment. This could happen in the night as well as the day, when the bond between us would tug me awake. She was drawn always to the kitchen, that living heart of the household. Sometimes I would find her standing or sitting there in silent contemplation. At others, when I had taken longer to rouse, she would have fallen asleep at the kitchen table with her head on her arms.

As nursing encroached on my nights as well as my days it became hard work running up and down stairs, and Matthew suggested that we turn the dining room into a temporary bedroom for her, and that I slept in the study next door. But she turned stubbornly against this idea, protesting and explaining vehemently.

'Darling, if you move me downstairs I shall know I'm done for. As long as I can stay up here I'm still alive.'

I could not say that she would die in any case, and life would be easier for me if she were on the ground floor. So she stayed where she was. And I wondered how one part of her could acknowledge death while the other still nourished hope, and where the hope had come from when the doctors could give her none.

'From life itself,' said Leila. 'She might be prepared to give up, but life isn't. There's still a lot of life in her body and it won't let go.'

My sister was the most valuable visitor of all. She acted as court jester to Helen, something for which I had no gift. She made her laugh as my father had done, with wry dry comments, with outrageous cynicism. She brought the sad, bad, mad world into my mother's room, paraded it, mimicked it, made fun of it.

'Darling! You don't really *mean* that!' Helen would say, laughing even as she protested. 'Darling, that really is *most* unkind!'

Then Leila would grin, and I glimpsed my father in my sister's face: impish, rakish, knowing and unrepentant.

Although, unlike Leila, I believed that most people were good, I was astonished by the amount of loving kindness my mother's illness generated. As the disease progressed, so did offers of assistance, both official and unofficial. The district nurse came in every day to help me wash Helen and make her comfortable. A rota of neighbours lightened my other commitments. Shopping. The endless laundry. Taking the children to school. Sitting with her while I caught up on sleep or chores. Leaving a fruit pie or a cake or a loaf of home-made bread on the kitchen table. Bringing fresh flowers from their gardens, fresh eggs from their hens. They visited her always with a smile, keeping up Helen's own pretence that she was facing a challenge rather than submitting to fate. Their conversations varied but the theme was the same.

'Now I'd say you were looking brighter today, Mrs Gideon!'

'Oh yes. Much brighter today! I don't give in easily, you know.'

'That's right. It's all in the mind, they tell us. And

303

the mind is a wonderful thing. I had an aunt – that three doctors had given up – who lived to be eighty.'

'Really?'

'Oh yes. Outlived them all.'

'Did you hear that, Zoe? About Mrs Cresset's aunt?'

So she clung to life, and was drawn by death, growing lighter and weaker and wearier, until September came and her spirit drooped.

'If only it was summer,' she said pitifully. 'I know the sun would give me strength to fight this thing.'

'The sun's still shining, Nell.'

'But it hasn't the strength of the summer sun.'

Leila brought her a crystal and hung it in the window where it would catch the sun's rays and make rainbows on the wall, and Helen took comfort from this.

But now my helpers became my contenders.

'You must bring her downstairs, Zoe. You can't carry on like this.'

'Can't you engage a night nurse, so that you'd get your sleep?'

'We shall have you ill next, and then what will happen?'

'Surely they'd have her in hospital for a week while you rested?'

Then I realised that Helen had stopped being a person and become a case. There was no one to fight for her apart from me, and Leila when Leila was there.

Still I said, 'I'll manage. She wants to die at home in her own bedroom. And that's what I want for her. I'll manage.'

Any rest or sleep she had now was by grace of the daily pills and injections, and the doses increased. When I lifted her she felt no heavier than Simon.

Still she said, 'If I can get through the winter there's hope yet.'

The vicar came to see her. He was a devout and kindly man.

'Put your trust in our Lord Jesus Christ. His yoke is easy and His burden is light,' he said to her as he left.

Her shoulder bones poked through her nightdress. Her

mouth puckered against the pain. Her lost dark eyes strove to see a faint spray of rainbows on the wall. I could not speak for rage and tears.

Matthew had to go to Switzerland for a week in October. He told me why, in business terms. I registered only that he was leaving, that Helen could not last much longer, and that I could not go on by myself. I rang my sister. She left Ruth Babbage in charge of the Garret, wound up what work she could and brought the rest with her.

The children were glad to see her, joyful in a subdued way. We reorganised our helpers, and nursed Helen turn and turn about. Leila chose the night-watch. It was more convenient for me to have the day, and she preferred the solitude. She fixed up a reading lamp on a table, shaded to avoid disturbing Helen, tilted to illuminate her drawing-board. So she created her strange and lovely worlds on paper and kept vigil.

The night-watch is the strangest and most comforting. The closest we get to the next world without going there, because we sense it through the dying person. In those final days I needed little sleep. No more than a few hours. Awake at five in the morning, I tiptoed into Helen's room, sat by her side, held her hand. Leila would nod at me, aware of the patient but absorbed in her work. I watched my mother sleep, watched my sister bent over her drawing-board, at peace. And the house which had absorbed so much of life and death for so many generations, watched with us like another and serener presence.

By the middle of the week I was feeling ambivalent about Matthew's return. Leila and I had established an alliance and organised a nursing service which worked perfectly, and I was loath to break it up. But broken up it was to be, and not by my husband. On the Thursday Helen went though one of her sad, exhausting, restless phases. On the Friday, when neither Leila nor I had been out of our clothes for twenty-four hours, I called the doctor, who looked very grave and insisted that we needed professional help.

'I'm just as concerned about you as I am about your mother,' he said to me. 'We can't afford to have you cracking up. And your sister doesn't look much brighter. I'm not advising you, Zoe, I'm insisting.'

And from out of the blue he summoned a scoured and beaming private nurse, who arrived on the evening of the same day to take over.

By this time Leila and I were ready to drop, and drop we did. For the first time since we were small girls we slept together in one bed like a pair of commas. An end was coming. Adrift, we sought the security of our beginnings.

It was twenty past two in the morning when the nurse tugged at my sleeve and whispered that there was a change and she thought we should come. And instantly I was wide awake. We pulled on our dressing-gowns and went with her to share the final crossing.

She was in some outerland of consciousness, between this world and the next. And we became aware that we were not alone. The whole room was peopled with shades of the living and the dead and Helen was talking to them.

'Cass has stayed with me all day. He'll be so tired.

'There's Magda standing in the corner of the room, wearing a funny hat. I wish she'd sit down. Ask her to sit down. She's come such a long way to see me. You shouldn't have come so far at your age, Magda. I would have understood.

'I know that's you, Mummy. Why are you staying by the door? Come in and bring Daddy with you. He looks cold. If only it were summer. He'd have the strength to fight this.'

And sometimes she would say pitifully to some invisible accuser, 'I'm sorry, I'm sorry!' or 'I didn't mean it!'

But what had Mummy ever said or done to harm anybody? And who could have needed an apology from her?

So we continued to sit on either side of her bed and to watch with her, as her regiment of allies and inquisitors passed before us. Then she ceased to talk and explain, returning to the body which was causing her such discomfort. She gasped for air, muttering, frowning,

306

turning her head from side to side in constant negation, her hands wandering restlessly over the sheets, as if her whole being protested against extinction. I was unfamiliar with the process of dying, and the death of my father and grandparents had only meant serene faces glimpsed in coffins before the lids were screwed down for burial.

'You mustn't worry about her. She's in no pain. She's under sedation,' said the nurse confidently.

I wondered at her confidence. How did she know what was happening to Helen underneath the drug? The glint in Leila's eyes, the curl of her lips, confirmed that we were thinking in unison.

The nurse spoke to my mother with cheerful familiarity. 'Now what's all this fuss about?'

She restrained the seeking bird-boned hands and tucked them tightly, neatly, beneath the sheet.

'There, that's better, isn't it, Helen?'

To me she explained, 'I talk to them just as if they were with us. You never know what might get through.'

Leila's nostrils were ferocious, but she held her tongue.

'She seems to be almost choking,' I said, almost choking myself. 'Wouldn't it be better if she was propped up?'

'Oh no. It's better to remove the pillows. They go faster, that way. We wouldn't want to prolong things for her, would we?'

My mother's loss of dignity, her helplessness, flayed me.

Leila said suddenly in a tone of surprising authority, 'You can leave us with her. We'll call if we need you.'

The nurse said brightly, unoffended, 'Just as you please, dear. I'll have a little wash and a little rest and then make us all a nice cup of tea. She'll be a while yet.'

And nodded her head as if to record the fact, and rustled out.

Leila and I stared meaningfully at each other, and with one accord released our mother's hands and let them wander where they would. We found her pillows and lifted her, so easily, too easily, and rested her head and shoulders upon them. Then we sat down again and waited. She was quieter now, dozing uncomfortably, semi-conscious.

Leila said softly, 'I scribbled a note to Magda before I left the Garret, and told her the truth. I thought it was only fair to warn her. I said that Helen hadn't wanted to worry her, but things had taken a turn for the worse. I said that she wasn't to dream of coming up. And that I would send a telegram when there was any news, and go down and see her when it was all over.'

'I'm glad,' I said. 'I was dreading the thought of telling Magda.'

'It was a strange relationship, wasn't it?' said Leila. 'They never seemed to click. Of course, she wasn't a mother in that sense. Not like Helen.'

'No,' I said. 'Not like Helen.'

This would be my greatest loss so far. For as much as I had adored my erring father it was my mother I loved best of all. To me she was the most complete and satisfying person I had ever known or could imagine knowing. So I soothed her seeking hands and cried very quietly, so as not to disturb her further, until she opened her eyes and looked at me, full of trouble.

I wanted to beg her, 'Don't leave us, Mummy!'

And then I realised that I was asking too much of her, as all of us always had done. I was demanding an effort which was beyond her capabilities. Because of her nature she would be bound to respond, and because of her condition she would fail, and then regret failing and take the failure upon herself. My weakness could only make her passage harder. And what was asked of me, by whom or what I did not know, was to give her leave to go in peace.

She was distressed, murmuring, 'Zoe. Don't . . . don't . . . don't . . . '

Don't what? Don't drag me back? Don't let me go? Don't worry, I'll get better?

I said, 'Mummy. Don't bother about anything. Matthew and I are all right now.'

She let out one long soft sigh and looked at me gratefully. So it was my marriage that worried her.

I said, 'We've been through a long rough patch, but even the roughest patch doesn't last for ever. I stuck it

308

out and now we're together again. Everything will be all right.'

Helen nodded then, just once in confirmation, as if she saw some answer beyond me.

'Such – happiness,' she said, slowly, quite clearly, and smiled.

All doubts left me. It would be all right. My mother had said so.

She asked, 'Lulu?'

My sister bent her little white witch's face over hers and answered factually, drily, 'Here I am, Helen. Are you about to waste some valuable advice on me?'

'Oh, Lulu!' I breathed, in horror. 'You shouldn't say things like that!'

But our mother nodded and laughed the smallest ghost of a laugh, and said most lovingly, 'Yes – she – should.'

There was a long pause. She blinked as if to ward off sleep.

She said, 'Funny – little – thing.'

Her eyes closed. We looked and listened carefully, but she was asleep not dead. And after a while we laid our faces on the pillow next to hers, as we used to do when we were children, and closed our own eyes.

She had never made a fuss about anything. It was the scoured and beaming nurse, coming in with her tray of tea to moisten the vigil, who was the first to discover that our mother had taken leave of us.

24

Matthew arrived home on the same day that our mother died. He could be extraordinarily kind when he felt the need. Perhaps it was a need to show himself to be admirable, to be responsible, to be a man on whom women could lean. He had always admired Helen. To him, she was an ideal, a symbol of womanhood or (more likely) motherhood, whom he could worship. He had dealt with my father's funeral arrangements for her sake. Now he attended to those of her own.

At the same time he was surprisingly understanding about the way that Leila and I needed each other and nobody else. He took charge of Simon and Caroline that weekend, and when Mr Dowse, of Kirton and Dowse, arrived in the evening he was both sensible and thoughtful: stepping aside, as it were, so the undertaker should know that though he dealt with Matthew in practical matters he must deal with us in emotional ones.

My sister and I were closer together, having lost both parents, than we had ever been before. Their joint absence assailed us.

'Now what would you ladies like?' asked Mr Dowse.

He seemed to be the prototype of all undertakers, dressed in decent dark and sober clothes. He removed his black bowler hat and made a little bow. He thanked us for asking him to sit down. He carried a large black leather-covered album tooled in gold, which he set on his knees before he drew off his gloves. Even his smile was toned down to befit the occasion. He was ready to help and equally ready to efface himself. He was prepared to put forward suggestions if we had none of our own, without pressing any of them, and to accept any decision we might make. But first of all he was anxious to discover, as delicately as possible, what we could afford.

Leila and I, who have no gift for taking hints, remained dumb.

Matthew set the tone of the meeting by saying, 'Nothing but the best. Nothing but the best, of course.'

No doubt he bore in mind that my mother had left a valuable property and a modest income behind her, half of which would belong to me. And yet I felt it was for Helen, too.

Then he made a gesture to indicate that our wishes in this part of the proceedings were paramount and he was to be relegated to the background. This put Mr Dowse on his professional mettle. He brightened in a subdued way, turned to a section of the album which was evidently the most expensive, and brought Helen into the conversation as an invisible third party to whom he referred as 'Mother'. Not 'the deceased', not 'the late Mrs Gideon', not even 'your mother', but simply 'Mother'. He leaned confidentially towards us, smoothing his hands and the pages of his album, and said, 'About the arrangements – Mrs Barber, Miss Gideon – what sort of coffin would you like Mother to have?'

We looked helplessly towards Matthew, but he stood back and nodded his head encouragingly as if to say, 'This is your decision. Your mother. This is her coffin. You must choose.'

We looked at each other, my sister and I.

Then I said, 'Our mother preferred the simple and elegant to the showy.'

Immediately Mr Dowse flicked over a page or two and spread out the album to show us coffins both elegant and simple. We chose a very pale oak one with plain silver handles, of which both men also approved.

'We call that one Camelot,' Mr Dowse remarked, and I thought how apt and how funny that was, and did not know whether I wanted to laugh or cry most.

311

He was saying, 'Now, did Mother have any last wishes as to how she should be dressed? Or have either of you two ladies any specific requests?'

Again we were speechless. We were not in the habit of dressing a corpse. Mr Dowse came to our assistance.

'With the gentlemen it doesn't matter so much, unless they want to wear a uniform, but very often a lady will want to be buried in her wedding gown or a favourite evening dress . . .'

I could tell that he was willing us to give the answer he wanted, but none of us had any idea what that might be. We looked at each other, perplexed.

I said helplessly, 'As you have so much experience in these matters, Mr Dowse, perhaps it would be best if you advised us . . . ?'

Again his face was suffused with a professional light.

'Very thoughtful of you, Mrs Barber. And, if I may say so, very wise. We do like to harmonise the details. Now, I think you said that Mother preferred the elegant and simple? I have photographs of the gowns here. Nothing elaborate, but seemly and in keeping.'

We chose Helen a fine white pleated gown with long sleeves, little cuffs and a high collar, reminiscent of a medieval shift. Mr Dowse approved.

'Would you like Mother to hold a cross, or wear any particular jewellery? No? Very good.'

Then he and Matthew drew apart and went into a conference about prices and newspaper announcements and whether there should be only family wreaths, or general wreaths, or no wreaths, or contributions to some worthy place or charity of our choice.

From which Mr Dowse emerged triumphant, saying, 'Well, I think that should be to everyone's satisfaction. I daresay you ladies would like to see Mother when we have her ready for viewing?'

He was so desirous of his handiwork being admired that we agreed.

'And you, sir?' he asked Matthew.

At this point I think that Matthew had probably had

enough, but he did ask us whether we wanted him to escort us there. And we were so relieved to hear the hesitation and doubt in his voice that we both said no, thank you. No, we would be quite all right, we would go alone.

Because we wanted to go alone. Any other person would be an intrusion.

'Any other members of the family, or close friends?' Mr Dowse asked.

Leila said, 'No!' too firmly, too fiercely. 'She's not to be put on show for everyone!'

I knew she was feeling, as I did, that she could not bear the trite comments of the aunts, the sugary hypocrisy of Marian Barber.

Matthew gave her an unkind look. Leila stared miserably at her shoes. But Mr Dowse was used to dealing with grieving relatives, and covered her outburst tactfully.

'No, of course not, Miss Gideon. I was simply making a routine enquiry. Now as we're having the funeral on Wednesday would it be convenient to meet you outside the Chapel of Rest early on Tuesday evening? About six o'clock?'

And so the arrangements were made, and Mr Dowse was pleased with all of us, and Matthew was pleased with himself, but Leila and I could be pleased with nothing and no one because we were bereft.

When he had gone we said, almost in a chorus, that we had no intention of wearing black, but Matthew said surely we must make some mark of respect for the occasion. So on the Monday we drove into Tunbridge Wells and we chose two identical Chanel-type suits in grey, a colour which matched our cheerless spirits. Though the day was warm, and the sky was scudding white and baby blue, and the air smelled sweet, we found no comfort in it.

But when we met Mr Dowse at the appointed place, still dressed darkly and soberly as became his profession, we could tell that all was well with him. He chatted about the weather, which he described as 'clement', and said he had great hopes for the following morning. He had listened to the weather forecast. Had we listened to the weather forecast? He thought that it might be rather a nice day. Yes, rather a nice day.

He hurried ahead of us down the gravel path, unlocked the gothic door of the Chapel of Rest, and let us in. Upon the threshold he paused and delivered a brief homily.

'I'm truly sorry that Mr Barber couldn't see his way to joining you ladies. There's a surprising amount of consolation to be drawn from the sight of a beloved relative at rest, particularly when the illness has been protracted. And I must say', he added with relish, 'that Mother is looking very nice indeed. I think you'll be pleasantly surprised.'

I dropped behind to whisper to Leila fervently, 'Oh, I do hope to God they haven't rouged and painted her.'

'If they have,' she whispered back fiercely, 'we'll wash it off, whatever anybody thinks!'

The Chapel was a curious little place which at first sight put me in mind of a hospital ward, because there were curtained cubicles to the right and left of the narrow hallway. The curtains were made of some soft rich blue material whose colour was echoed in the furnishings and decoration. Beyond them half a dozen Windsor chairs sat in front of a small altar. Two tall blue vases holding bronze and white and yellow chrysanthemums stood sentinel against the far wall. The ceiling was scattered with small silver stars and a stiff crescent moon. Everything was beautifully clean and polished. The atmosphere was a cross between Sunday morning and a séance. The undertaker's voice dropped a hushed octave lower.

'We have a lady who comes in every day to do the flowers.'

We stayed for a minute, hands folded before us, in a suitably reverent silence. Then Mr Dowse laid a pallid hand on the blue curtain to the left of us and said, 'We shall find Mother in here.'

He drew aside the curtain and showed us the light oak coffin with plain silver handles, lying high and open on its trestle. He motioned us to approach.

They had painted her, but so skilfully that we hardly noticed. She had lost a lot of weight, which made her look younger, almost childlike. Her face was peaceful now

314

and of a most exquisite pallor, the lines of suffering had faded.

There she lay, looking like the Lady of Shalott at the end of her journey, with her eyes closed and her hands, her still beautiful hands, clasped lightly on her bosom, holding a single rose.

'A lovely lady,' said Mr Dowse, in appreciative hush.

We could not speak.

'And you do see', said Mr Dowse with professional pride, 'how very nicely we've got her up. A most beautiful job.'

'Yes,' we said. 'Very fitting.'

Leila said on a breath, 'Who thought of her holding a rose?'

'Ah, now there again I must point to the caring principle in our business. The lady who laid Mother out brought the rose from her own garden.'

'That was very fitting,' Leila whispered.

He pointed to Helen's wedding ring and asked if we wanted to keep it or have it buried with her. But I said, 'No, leave it with her. She's worn it for nearly forty years. It's her ring.' And Leila agreed.

Afterwards Matthew said it was a stupid decision, and someone would be sure to steal the ring before the coffin was nailed down. But he didn't know that, and I still feel we were right and that it was what Helen would have wanted.

Mr Dowse waited with us, very quiet and dark and possessed by a sense of holy ritual, until we decided we had seen enough. Then one by one we touched our mother's cold hands and kissed her cold cheeks, and stood back and let him draw the curtain upon her final perfection.

He said softly, 'I believe you ladies were somewhat surprised when I asked you if there was any particular item of clothing that Mother might like to wear, but it's more usual than you might imagine. In fact,' with a little lift of one black glove to his mouth, a little cough, 'we have another lady here who asked to be buried in her dressing-gown.'

And he nodded at the cubicle to our right.

Our interest in the common round of life revived.

'Would you – would you like to see the lady?' he asked tentatively.

Now why should Leila and I want to see any other corpse? But somehow it was a way out of the occasion, and we felt it was only proper to go visiting two lots of dead. So we said yes we should.

'We always respect every wish of the relatives and of the deceased,' he assured us, anxious that we should know he meant no disrespect. 'But I think you will agree that it was far better to leave Mother entirely in our hands.'

And he drew back the second curtain.

Now Helen had known the awe and nobility of death. Death to Helen, however cruel and savage, had been a kingly tournament, an occasion from which she emerged an honourable loser. But to her companion in silence death had been a nuisance, someone who interrupted her while she was washing up. His advent had been a very ordinary affair. He was an unwelcome but not a distinguished visitor. So might the milkman or paperman have caught her in her curlers, unprepared. She was evidently not accustomed to luxuries. A new dressing-gown would be a great event, probably bought before she went into hospital. So she had decided to take it with her.

She was a small woman, perhaps in her sixties, still with a fair amount of dark in her hair, still with not too many wrinkles, and she had a little, shrewd, resentful, pursed-up face. The hands clasped on her breast had been ruined by manual work. They were roughened and creased, and the undertaker's art had not been able to render them the creamy marble of Helen's fingers. But blossoming around her was this astonishing nylon dressing-gown, with crimson and sky-blue flowers and emerald leaves, which could never have suited her in life and was downright garish in death.

In fact she and her death were so ordinary that she relieved us, in a way, of our sorrow. Our spirits lifted. We turned to Mr Dowse and said that we saw exactly what he meant. Nevertheless, we added hastily, so as not

316

to hurt his professional feelings, they had made her look very nice. Very nice indeed.

'Oh yes indeed,' he said. 'And yet – no disrespect intended – you ladies do see, don't you, how much better it is to leave it all to us?'

And we, remembering Helen at rest in Camelot, nodded our heads.

As he drew the curtains on the brilliance of the lady in the dressing-gown Leila said to me under her breath, 'I shall start giggling in a minute. When can we go?'

I responded immediately, putting out a gloved hand to our undertaker.

'Mr Dowse, we should both like to thank you very much. It's been a great consolation. But do you mind if my sister and I go now. We're feeling a little . . . ?'

'Oh, quite!' he answered. 'I do understand.'

And he clasped our hands in his and gave his little bow and walked off in the opposite direction.

Then Leila and I scrambled pell-mell into my car, and sat next to each other and held each other, and laughed and laughed and laughed.

'I don't know why it's so funny,' I said, 'because it's very sad really.'

Then we went off again.

Leila said, 'And Magda ringing up this morning. Poor Magda. She'd changed a pound note into florins so that she could go on speaking for as long as she wanted to. And every time the pips went and she put another florin in the slot, the rest fell on to the flo-o-or . . . oh, it isn't funny. I don't know why we're laughing . . . '

And when we had finished laughing we cried. And I don't know which did us the more good.

25

1965

Helen's will was very simple. There were no bequests. Her estate was to be divided equally between Leila and me. Our Mr Shanklady, though he mourned my mother, was pleased for her daughters. He said he would be delighted to advise us about possible investments. He reminded us that we should now be in the position my father had wished: owners of our own property with a small private income. He recommended that we sort out what furniture we wished to keep and put Whitegates up for sale as soon as possible.

Matthew's single comment was cool and non-committal.

'You're becoming quite a lady of means, Zoe.'

I had thought about my new position, and though I intended to keep it I was prepared to stand my financial corner. So I answered with some confidence.

'Oh, you needn't worry, Mat. I shan't be squandering it on a mink coat! I need quite a bit to keep Queen Anne repaired, and I thought we might discuss a few conversions. Later on, some of the money will come in useful for the children's education. Private fees and things like that. But first of all I thought I could treat you and me to a super holiday abroad. Leila says she'll come down and look after the children for us. Shall we do that?'

He was reading the Sunday paper and he shook it impatiently.

'Oh, I don't know. I can't plan that far ahead.'

I thought. It's starting all over again. Nothing has changed.

My mother's influence prompted me to give him another chance.

'All right then, we'll think about that. But what would you like to do or have as a real treat? I'd like to buy you something.'

He said, yawning, 'I shouldn't bother. I've got everything I need, thanks.'

My father's influence prompted me to tackle him head on.

I said, 'I'm not prepared to put up with this any longer, Matthew. Instead of being so bloody rude and furtive, and treating me like a colony of lepers, why don't you come out with it and tell me what's wrong?'

There was a little pause. Then he put down his newspaper and smiled at me as he had done that first evening when he stayed out. The evening, I believed, when his affair had begun.

'Nothing's wrong,' he answered. 'I have nothing to complain about. The lodgings are excellent. The landlady is – usually – gracious.'

There followed such an appalling row as shook the pair of us, and only ended when the children ran in from the garden, and stopped short at the sound of our voices, looking pinched and lost. Matthew walked out and left me to deal with them, and did not come back.

It was the first time he had ever stayed out overnight, except when he was away on business. We breakfasted the following morning without him. That is, the children breakfasted without him, asking where Daddy was, and I drank cups of tea and said he had gone to work very early.

During a sleepless night I had decided what to do when he appeared again. I was going to insist that we sorted our differences out, either by ourselves or with the help of a marriage guidance counsellor. Or that we should separate for six months or a year while we sorted ourselves out and thought matters over. But I would not live as we had done.

319

It was time to plant out my seedlings. Mrs Yates came on a Monday, and I left her in the house and worked until lunch-time, waiting for a telephone call.

After lunch I rang the office. The secretary was surprised, and said she understood he was working at home. I asked if I could speak to Trudy, but she was taking a day off. I tried her home telephone number, but only an answering machine spoke to me, and I left no message. I rang Leila for advice and moral support, and she was out. Once, I rang the police station, but Matthew had always been so furious if I involved anyone else in our private lives that I put down the receiver as soon as the sergeant answered.

My husband had slipped into that no-man's land he visited from time to time.

I sat by the telephone for a long while, hands between my knees, head bent, and waited. Then I planted the rest of the seedlings. The telephone did not ring.

I was in a quandary about the evening meal. In order to be ready for any emergency, I bought chops when I collected Simon and Caro from school. I told them that Daddy would be home late, gave them milk and buns absent-mindedly, sent them out to play, and sat by the telephone again.

At six o'clock I began that rambling and long-winded chore known as putting the children to bed. I bathed them, fed them, read to them and settled them down for the night. While I was making coffee the telephone rang.

A voice, less metallic and more tentative than usual, said, 'Hi, Zoe. This is Trudy Olsen.'

In one long gasp I said, 'Oh Trudy! Thank heavens! Trudy, I tried to get you at home but there was no answer. Matthew went out yesterday evening and he hasn't come back, and no one seems to know where he is.'

Her tone had lost its edge. She sounded slightly unsure of me and herself.

She said, 'Mat's here with me, Zoe. At the business apartment.'

I did not grasp the situation at once.

'But why hasn't he 'phoned me? Is he in some sort of trouble?'

She said, 'Zoe, I am truly sorry to have to tell you this, but Mat doesn't want to come back to you. He's been here all night, and we've spent all day talking things over. I wanted him to tell you himself, but I guess he just couldn't bring himself to do it.'

The situation was unreal, and all I wanted was straight information.

I said, 'If he doesn't want to come back here where does he propose to go?'

She answered, in a tone I would use to explain some simple fact to one of my children, 'He wants to stay with me, Zoe.'

With Trudy Olsen, who was now approaching fifty? With Trudy Olsen, who had been blessed with a rich, complacent husband? I had imagined some golden girl, young and seductive in a short skirt, luring him to her bedsitter.

As I did not respond, she went on, 'He and I have been more than colleagues and friends. We've been lovers for quite a while now. He's tried hard to make it work with you, but it's no go. He wants to stay with me.'

My mechanical, logical self asked, 'What about Howard? What does Howard say about this?'

'Howard wants what he's always wanted. He wants me to be happy.'

My mouth and throat were so dry that I was afraid I should croak, but the words came out clearly.

'Does Matthew want a divorce?'

'Why, yes. I guess he does. I guess we both do. But that depends on you, Zoe. That's up to you.'

'Is Howard willing to divorce you?'

'He surely is, and we shall part good friends – like we've always been.'

This time my voice failed me. To be the last to know. To be such a fool. To mean so little that I was left without information until she decided that I had a part to play in the final scene.

She said, quite humanly for her, 'Zoe, this is a lousy situation and a lousy thing for you to face by yourself.

321

We need to talk it over between the three of us.' Her tone brisked up. 'How about right now? How about you rustling up one of those wonderful old English baby-sitters of yours, and I'll send a cab for you?'

She was organising the end of my married life as she had organised Matthew's career, with galling efficiency. Then she sensed that I would not be ordered about. Her tone became friendlier.

'Or maybe you'd rather that Mat and I came over to your place?'

The day and the house were closing in on me. I was trying to come to terms with the fact that they were giving me an ultimatum, whereas I had been about to give one to Matthew. To receive them as a couple, to acknowledge their relationship in my own home seemed intolerable, a final invasion of privacy.

'No,' I said, and my voice was strong and clear. 'No, I'll come to you.'

Evidently Trudy preferred to meet me on her own ground. She sounded relieved, friendly, intimate.

'Do that, Zoe. And ring me back when you've found somebody, honey. I'll give you the number.'

I wrote it down with a numb hand on the telephone pad. My finger pressure printed the numbers three layers deep.

But my tone was neutral as I said, 'I'll ring you back.'

Baby-sitters had never been a problem, apart from paying for them. Without difficulty I summoned the widowed Mrs Yates and booked her from eight until midnight. Cinderella hour. Then I was faced with a typical problem. My inheritance being promised, not realised, there was so little money in my purse that I must raid the children's money-boxes to pay her. Caroline had only sixpence to her name, but Simon's childish thrift saved me from the humiliation of asking Matthew to reimburse me.

I rang Trudy and told her I could come, and when, and for how long.

She said, 'That will be fine. Have you eaten?'

'No. And I don't think I could.'

322

'Then that makes three of us,' she replied, almost in comradely fashion. 'I'll send out for sandwiches and open a bottle of wine.'

She said, woman to woman, 'Look, Zoe, I don't want you to think this is easy on any of us. Mat's taken it very hard. He's truly sorry. He should have told you a coupla years back, but he was scared of hurting you, and then your momma got sick and died. So things kind of dragged on longer than they should have.'

I could make no reply that did not sound savage.

I said briefly, 'I'll be waiting for the taxi at eight o'clock.'

And put the receiver down.

Then I showered, dressed and made up carefully for the meeting.

But as the taxi left our village and rural Kent behind and entered the outskirts of the metropolis my mood softened. Gradually I became relaxed and detached. A sense of fatalism possessed me. I reflected that this was what I wanted, though not in the way I wanted it. Mrs Matthew Barber's marriage was over and Zoe Gideon would preside over the final rites. I had no intention of making any kind of fuss. I simply wanted it to be finished as quickly and painlessly as possible.

The address Trudy gave me was a building near the Albert Hall: a solid many-storeyed Victorian establishment of red brick and white facings, whose lobby was large and high-ceilinged, with a turkey carpet runner and palms in pots and huge oil-paintings in gold frames, like an old-fashioned family hotel.

The porter, dressed in a gold-braided burgundy uniform, put aside his *Evening Standard* and telephoned Trudy to announce my name and presence. Then he asked me to sit down, and informed me that Mr Barber would be coming to show me the way. Courteously, he did not pick up his paper, open at the day's races, but remarked upon the weather which was cool but pleasant for the time of year. I said I had come up from Kent, and had been planting out most of the day. He said his garden was a window-box. He was a true Londoner, born and bred

323

within the sound of Bow Bells, and had been porter here for nearly thirty years.

As we exchanged small talk I thought of all the lives that had been lived around him, the people he had seen come and go, the multitude of second-hand experiences which had been his. And I wondered if he guessed the nature of my errand.

These thoughts did not distress me. I stood at one remove from my scene, and observed, until he said, 'Ah, here's Mr Barber, madam!'

I wondered whether we should shake hands. Pale and polite, Matthew stopped a little way from me and set the tone and distance of the occasion.

'Hello, Zoe. Good of you to come. We're on the third floor.'

The lift rose smoothly, lightly, and we stood side by side like strangers, looking straight ahead, saying nothing, until it stopped.

'This way!' said Matthew.

I followed him into a small but luxurious flat which Trudy had furnished in green, white and gold. It was supposed to be reserved for business clients, but a couple could live here very comfortably. In their spare time I imagined that he and she had been doing just that.

We passed a minute kitchen, whose open door revealed that little was cooked here, only reheated or kept warm. In the living room a large and expensive flower arrangement dominated the space between two deep windows. An empire-style settee flanked by two Queen Anne grandfather armchairs sat round an electric fire which mimicked a grate full of glowing logs, complete with brass andirons. The clock on the wall was in the shape of a sun spreading golden rays. The pictures were expensively and ornately framed. At a mock-Regency sideboard, fitted up as a cocktail bar, stood Trudy ready to dispense her own form of hospitality.

I heard my father say, 'When I'm given a rich client with damnable taste, and they insist on having what they want, then I reckon that fifty per cent of my fee is for swallowing professional pride. They may hurt my sense of fitness but I make damned sure they never hurt my bank balance!'

Then I saw Trudy and myself reflected in the long mirror behind her cocktail bar, and realised that my clothes were not elegant and fashionable but neat and pretty. I looked what I was, an English country lady in her thirties, come up to town for the evening dressed in her best. Whereas Trudy looked the sophisticated cosmopolitan. Her creamy sheath dress was almost the twin of mine, but had not been made at home in the evenings from a Vogue pattern. We wore our hair in similar fashion, drawn up on to the crown, but hers was subtly tinted with silver-gold strands, surrounded by a hairpiece of soft flat curls, and it glittered. Her diamonds glittered too, round neck and wrist and in her ears. Whereas my only jewellery was a cultured pearl necklace (wedding present), a gold wristwatch (twenty-first birthday present) and a wedding ring (now obsolete).

I felt totally out of place, and saw as a revelation that Matthew did not. At the Old Rectory I had viewed his weekend attempts to look the country gentleman with affectionate understanding. Here he was quite at home, made over into her image, and I knew I had not understood him at all. His frequent glances at Trudy were both grateful and relieved. Like his father before him he was silently asking his dominant partner what she wanted of him, and preparing himself to give it.

She was more at ease than any of us, though she lacked her usual ebullience. She repeated Matthew's words.

'Hello, Zoe. It's good of you to come.' But added, 'Sit down and make yourself at home.' Then she nodded at him and said, 'Take Zoe's coat, honey, and open the champagne, will you?'

Obediently he took the coat. Skilfully, he popped the bottle open and poured and handed the glasses. He took charge of the canapés: minute triangles filled with smoked salmon, ribbons of Parma ham wrapped round melon balls, little bundles of raw beef holding anchovies or black olives, mussels rolled into leaves of spinach, savoury morsels of chicken and veal, miniature stuffed tomatoes and eggs, filled crayfish shells. I had lived through the day on coffee and snacks, and the sight and smell of these creations filled me with hunger.

But as I saw my husband, whose help at home had been minimal, playing the waiter at Trudy's command, I felt first fury and then contempt. I was angry, too, at my own naivety. For years I had lavished love and care and encouragement on Matthew, believing this would eventually make him content with himself as well as the world, when what he needed was to be told what to do. As my father would have said, kind words are all very well but a kick up the backside works wonders.

I let Matthew wait on me. I reckoned that if this was the sort of man Trudy wanted she could have him.

We had arranged ourselves in a triangle. I sat on one side, she sat opposite and Matthew sat in the middle. He said very little for the next hour or so. Trudy and I did most of the talking. And I thought how appropriate his position was, being divided between us in the past and now being divided up in the present.

Trudy began by saying 'Matthew and I' but brought his name into the conversation without consulting him or asking him to take part. I suppose that they had discussed the various points beforehand and she came out front to declare them. I expect that this was the way she ran her business. Perhaps unconsciously she regarded my marriage as a take-over bid. Her tone was factual, unemotional and very pleasant, and I am sure that she bore me no malice. In simple terms I had something she wanted and she intended to get it.

She said, 'Naturally, Matthew and I want what's best for all of us. Now I guess you will agree with me, Zoe, when I say that you have done about all you can for Matthew, and what you have done is really great. But people change, and I reckon that Matthew has changed, and right now he could have so much more if he came to me. And if you feel the same way as I do about loving people, well then you want what *they* want, however much it might cost in personal terms.'

326

I doubted if love had ever cost her anything. Like Matthew's notion of sharing it was a one-sided business. I was reminded of my mother-in-law with her constant emphasis on the importance of love and her inability to rouse it or convey it. I had long since ended dialogues on love with Marian Barber and I had no intention of beginning one with Trudy.

I said factually, 'I think it would be best if we could sort everything out right now. And I should like', looking at my wristwatch, 'to leave before eleven, because the baby-sitter must go home at midnight.'

Trudy switched tactics with admirable speed and smoothness.

'Surely, Zoe. That's exactly what I want.' A glance at the silent Matthew, sitting hands locked between his knees, dark head bent, amended this statement. 'What *we* want. So let's get down to business.'

I had thought it was business.

So we got down to business.

She said, 'Are you prepared to give Matthew a divorce? Of course, you can cite me for adultery, or whatever old-fashioned thing they call it, but we don't want any fuss or unpleasantness. The whole thing can be done very quietly and amicably and I hope *quickly* – though you English do so love to drag your goddam heels! – on both sides.'

'Yes,' I said. 'I'm prepared to give him a divorce on the grounds of adultery.'

'Okay.' She came to the second point on her invisible agenda. 'Now I understand that your dear old English Rectory is your property . . . ?'

This had been and was such a sore point that I glanced at Matthew, who kept his head well down. But Trudy was not perceptive.

' . . . so you won't be needing Matthew to pay any mortgage? No? Well, that's good. And you've inherited money of your own from your momma . . . ?'

This could have been a lonely situation, but I was not alone. My father was with me.

I heard him say, 'Get as much as you can out of that

327

female mountebank while you have the opportunity. At the moment she's prepared to be open-handed. Later on she'll start counting.'

He said, 'Start divorce proceedings tomorrow.'

He said, 'And get rid of that bastard for good.'

The champagne had relaxed me, made me feel pleasantly high. I finished my first glass and Matthew poured a second round for all of us. Then at a nod from Trudy he removed the empty bottle and set another one in the silver ice-bucket.

'Well, why not?' she said to me, jokingly, as if she and I were the best and oldest of friends. 'You don't have to drive home!'

She and Matthew exchanged a smile over this pleasantry, and he pressed her hand to show how much he appreciated her fun and generosity.

Trudy said, 'So it's a matter of having enough alimony to live on and bring up your children, isn't it?'

I said, 'Surely the court will decide how much that is?'

Trudy said, 'Oh, I can be more generous than the court.' And again she corrected herself, saying, '*We* can be more generous than that.'

He lifted his head and looked at her, and she came up with point three.

'Of course, Matthew will want free access to the children. He will need to know that he can see them any time.'

I could have laughed, but did not and would not. He had taken so little advantage of unlimited access that I failed to see why he should now insist on it. My fear was that, being swallowed whole by Trudy Olsen, he might lose sight of them altogether.

I answered, 'I'm anxious that Simon and Caroline should see their father as much as possible. I want them to know that he loves them, even if the marriage is over. I want him to keep in touch and I shall make it as easy as I can for us all.' Then I delivered my ultimatum. 'But I must be given sole custody.'

I saw a flicker of something – amazement? amusement? – light Trudy's face momentarily. She answered with a wide reassuring smile.

'Oh, but of course. There was no question of any other arrangement. No question at all.'

She probably thought what a fool I must be to consider it. She had no intention of being lumbered with Matthew's children, nor any children for that matter. Children did not figure in her life. Yet I had not been saying it to her, but to Matthew, my ex-husband, the solicitor, and he knew that. He acknowledged my custody with a single sullen nod.

'What I was thinking', Trudy continued, ignoring this private exchange, 'was that they could come up to London and spend a day with us. They're old enough to travel around by themselves aren't they?'

'Not quite,' I said drily, 'and certainly not in London. Simon is nine and Caroline is seven.'

She brushed this aside.

'Well, whatever. Matthew could pick them up or we could send a cab. Anyways, we'll take them out sight-seeing and send them safe home again.'

So he was not to be allowed real contact. She was setting up a different father-figure, a Trudy–Matthew parent. And when she grew tired, as she would, of amusing two very young people who had a unique claim to him, she might well diminish or even drop the contact altogether. That was not my problem but would be Matthew's. And theirs, of course, poor things. And theirs.

'Would that be okay by you, Zoe?' Trudy demanded.

'Perfectly,' I said. 'But I must have time to prepare them first. A week, perhaps, to explain the situation to them in a way they can accept.'

'Oh, surely, surely. There's no hurry. We're busy this month, anyways. Take all the time you want, Zoe. All the time you want.'

This, too, she meant. But Matthew looked up once or twice while she was speaking, and seemed uncertain of this cavalier attitude. They were, after all, his children. He loved them in his own fashion, and probably more than he realised. I added a rider for their sakes, and I suppose for his. It takes more than an evening's decision to wipe out a marriage.

'And I think it would be less of a shock if they saw their father by himself at first, so that he could establish this new relationship with them.'

She did not like this suggestion, though she had to agree to it.

In one of his very few remarks, Matthew said gruffly, 'What about the summer holidays?'

Trudy cut in then, saying, 'Oh, that would be wonderful. We could do so much for them. But not this summer, honey. We have a pretty hectic schedule right through to the fall.'

'Oh, I wasn't thinking of this summer,' he said lamely.

Deliberately overriding her, addressing him, I said, 'Whenever you want to take the children on holiday, Matthew, we can arrange it. Everything can be arranged.' I tried to reach him. 'They're going to be hurt, and we must make them as happy as possible with each of us.'

But he turned his face away, mute and morose, and did not respond. There was a heaviness between us which Trudy dispelled with another of her nods. Matthew de-corked the champagne and poured our third round. Discussion had whetted our appetites. We finished the canapés. I ate mine slowly, thoughtfully. They were delectable. By any standard of eye or taste buds, they were a work of art. I complimented her upon them.

'Oh, f'God's sake!' she cried, with a yelp of laughter. 'You sound as if I *made* them, Zoe. I *sent out* for them. I can't even boil a kettle!' She had the grace to add, 'But I'm glad you like them.'

I thought how lovely it would be to have that much money at one's disposal, and even lovelier to have the leisure and ingredients to concoct them. And I thought how much of my time and energy would be released now that Matthew was gone, and that I could take a Cordon Bleu course and perhaps make a living from producing good food, and creating a temporary haven for guests in beautiful surroundings.

Trudy said, winding up the meeting, 'Well, unless anyone has anything to add, I think that's about it.'

Any other business?

We shook our heads slowly.

She was slightly at a loss. Her fingers hovered uncertainly, as if they needed to stack papers or shake hands. The transaction had been completed.

Matthew's expression was largely incredulous. He had been given what he said he wanted. But did he really want it? I could tell he was not sure. And I knew then that this was Trudy's decision, not his. That he relied upon her, was fascinated by her, and needed her, I did not doubt. On the other hand, had she permitted it, he would have been more than willing to keep his marriage and family intact, and see-saw all his days between the two of us.

I saw Matthew then as a man who would always be in subjection to a woman. He had become a solicitor because his mother wanted that. He had married me because I loved him and my mother saw him as my husband. But possessing me, rather than being possessed, he was at a loss. Lacking my orders, he did not know how to treat me or in what direction he should go himself. It was Trudy who told him what he should do and be, so he turned to her for guidance. And in his ignorance he forced me, who would have been his willing help and comfort, down roads which were not of my choosing. He had, in fact, driven the pair of us out of our youthful Eden and we could never return.

As if he could read my thoughts, but in his own way, Matthew said quietly, reproachfully, 'You've no one to blame but yourself, Zoe. You let your father run our marriage, and when he was dead you let him drive a wedge between us with the ownership of the Old Rectory. That spelled finish for me.'

And that must have been the point at which he drifted steadily towards Trudy instead of struggling to reconcile himself with both of us. Yet, knowing his weakness and her proclivities, I doubted if the affair could have ended any other way than this.

Except, my father reminded me, that you would have lost half your property to no good purpose.

Trudy remarked amiably, drolly, 'F'God's sake, Mat, it's

331

no good crying over spilt milk. That's old history. And like Ford said, history is bunk.'

I looked at my watch. Ten forty-three. We all stood up together.

Trudy said, 'Well, Zoe, I guess the only thing left is to wish you the best of luck. I'm sure that a lovely English lady like you will soon find somebody else to make you happy.'

Then she turned her back on me and said, 'Mat, honey, call a cab will you? And fetch Zoe's coat.'

And he did.

In the little hallway of the flat he stooped and picked up a carrier bag, concealed beneath his overcoat.

'Presents for you and the kids,' he mumbled. And as I clutched it, dumb with surprise, 'I bought you an electric percolator.'

He put up his hand as I tried to say something.

'No, don't thank me,' he said, and hurried me into the lift.

When the gate was closed, he said, keeping his distance from me, looking straight ahead, 'Tell the kids as nicely as you can, won't you? I'll come over next weekend to see them and to collect my things if that's all right.'

I said, 'I'll do my best. And please will you do something for me? I should like you to tell your parents. And I'd be grateful if you prevented them from coming over without warning to cheer me up. Tell them, please, that they must never do that. They must always ring me first.'

I was suddenly joyful, realising that they could no longer lay claim to my time and attention.

He nodded and gave a deep sigh, envisaging the scene ahead of him.

We had reached the ground floor, and my car was waiting. The porter wished me good-night. Matthew helped me into my seat and hovered in the doorway. We stayed perfectly still for a moment, staring at each other in amazement, wondering what kind of farewell was suitable.

Then Matthew said abruptly, 'Sorry about all this, Zo.'

Involuntarily, I put out my hand. But he shook his head, turned brusquely on his heel and stalked away.

In the car on the way home, anaesthetised with shock and champagne, I went over and over the interview. I thought that on the whole I had acquitted myself quite well. I hadn't cried or reproached them or made a scene. I had been straightforward and businesslike, and had stated my case. I should have my children, and my house and a reasonable if not lavish income. I could bring them up the way I wanted to.

It was not until I tiptoed into our bedroom that I realised he was never coming back again.

Exultant, I took possession of our bed which was now my bed. I moved into its centre, spread out my arms and legs, touched the corners of the pillows with my fingers, the corners of the mattress with my toes, stretched my neck, settled my head, and smiled into the darkness.

I was bruised. I was stunned. I had been meanly cheated. I sensed that this was only the beginning of another long rough road, and I should be lonely. But I was free, and at that supreme moment the realisation of freedom transcended all my hurts and winged me away to sleep.

When I had taken the children to school the following morning I christened Matthew's electric percolator, not without a pang, and made myself a large pot of coffee to see me through the morning's telephone calls. The first person I rang was Leila. She was wonderful, sounding so like my father.

'Strike while the iron's hot, before that bastard can change his mind! A couple of days waking up with Boadicea will make a lot of difference. Ring me any time you like. If you want me to come down I'll be there. And Zoe, get in touch with our enchanting Mr Shanklady. He'll take Matthew for all he's got.'

'No,' I said, 'there's no need for that. Trudy's prepared to buy me off.'

Mr Shanklady was kind but businesslike.

'Oh dear!' he said. 'I'm sorry to hear this, Mrs Barber. Nevertheless, these things happen. And my firm will be delighted to act for you. We must make an appointment to discuss the matter. Mornings are better for you, are they not? Perhaps Wednesday of this week at ten o'clock?'

The week went very quickly. At some hopefully auspicious moment I told the children that Daddy would be living away most of the time, but was coming home to see them and take them out as often as he could. They accepted the news without quibble or qualm. I suppose it was merely an extension of what they knew already. But when he arrived that weekend to empty his side of the wardrobe, and they realised that he was not just going away but going away for good, their reaction was devastating.

He had brought them more presents: expensive, extravagant presents in which I detected the choice of Trudy. Children's gifts to her meant huge soft toys. A wild striped tiger. A silky panda. Exquisitely lifelike, beautifully made. Simon and Caroline felt that they were being treated like babies, but were too polite to say so. They accepted their bribes with bewildered thanks, and stood by holding them while their father packed. I could see them wondering how to keep him, wondering what they had done wrong. They went away to hunt up bribes of their own. Simon gave Matthew his best biro, and Caroline gave him one of her initialled handkerchiefs.

I think he knew his gifts were inappropriate, and before he went he arranged to take the children the following Saturday to Regent's Park Zoo where they could see the real animals. They were heartened by this, but still unsure. I had made a special tea, but he said he could not stay that long, and this worried them too.

Simon said, 'But there's chocolate layer cake!' as though that clinched the matter. When it did not he said, 'You *are* coming back, aren't you, Daddy?'

'Of course I am!' he said. 'I shall be here to pick you up next Saturday.'

They hugged and kissed him in a strangling fashion, still holding their soft toys. They thanked him again for them, as if once was no longer enough. They were still holding them when he left. And they asked me several times a day for the next week if Daddy was coming back. By the time Saturday and Matthew arrived I was a tight band of apprehension. But they did go, and returned home with more appropriate presents, and a slightly furtive but shining air, as if they had been initiated into a new game.

This was the first of many trips into London that year, and they grew very clever at the game, my children. They played upon Matthew's guilt and my insecurity, and when they eventually met Trudy they played her for all she was worth. I was sorry to see how soon they could be bought and how quickly they learned the new rules.

But time passes and takes with it the sense of immediacy, and softens the sense of loss. I expect that Trudy grew impatient. Anyway she told them that she and Matthew were going to marry as soon as he and I were divorced. Then they went away on a long business trip, and left me to tidy up after them.

Leila

26

1965–1966

It took Zoe a year to get her decree absolute, a difficult year for all of us. Mr Shanklady and I were twin pillars of support: he legally, me emotionally. For Zoe, bereft of her mother and her marriage, had lost her bearings.

I think that she and I both drank more that year, though neither of us became drunkards. But whereas drinking had been for enjoyment it now became a prop. I would reach for the whisky whenever she telephoned, and I know that she reached for the gin whenever there was a crisis. To show her that I knew and understood this temporary reliance I asked Mr Shanklady's wine-merchants to send her a case of half-bottles of good claret. With it I enclosed a note which read: 'This is to keep you off the cooking sherry. One glass recommended before bedtime to help you to sleep.'

Thereafter, she drank a glass obediently at eleven o'clock every evening.

Zoe was not the kind of woman who takes refuge in a nervous breakdown, or becomes apathetic and lets herself and everything else go. On the whole her suffering was borne privately and in silence, but relieved by volcanic bursts of panic which she directed at me. Conflicting doubts beset her at these times. With the prospect of freedom in sight she dreaded that Matthew or Trudy would change their minds, and she would be pressed to take him back again. But then her deep belief in the sanctity of marriage asked

339

her another question. Should she have given in so easily? Should she herself not approach Matthew and offer him yet another chance?

I dealt with these ravings briskly, factually and in steely humour. I coped with her minor crises over the telephone, and her major ones with a personal meeting either at my place or at hers. I attempted to channel her thoughts into more positive directions, such as the future. For she had babbled of turning the Old Rectory into a select guest-house, and talked of taking a Cordon Bleu course to polish and extend her present cuisine.

'Oh, but I couldn't do it *now*, Lulu! Suppose I started to alter the house and Matthew came back?'

'Tell him to sod off!'

'Suppose the children got measles and I couldn't leave them?'

'And suppose you broke both legs and had to do your cooking on crutches? Zo! If you live in fear you won't live at all. Now listen to me. Remember that super song we liked last year, "The Times They Are A-Changing"? Peter, Paul and Mary? Well, that's what you must sing to yourself when you're feeling blue. I'm into psycho-cybernetics at the moment. What's that? It's a technique for using subconscious power. I've got a marvellous American book I'll lend you . . .'

Then followed a half-hour pep talk disguised in general chat.

'Have you read those other two books I left with you? Germaine Greer and Betty Friedan. You didn't like the Germaine Greer? Too tough for you, I expect. What about *The Feminine Mystique*? You got on better with that, but both the authors sound so angry? Well, of course, they're angry. Women *should* be angry. Bloody angry. Those books should ring bloody loud bells with you . . .'

Ending with a sweetener in the form of an invitation.

'Look, why don't we both go to the Chelsea Flower Show?'

And sometimes I raged inwardly at the constant drain on my energy, at the interruptions to my work and my private life. In fact my love life came to a halt that year. Only true love can survive the partner's family crises. The inconstant lover, confronted by such desperate realities, fades away.

The decree nisi came first, in November, just before Caroline's eighth birthday. The simple ritual took no more than fifteen minutes. Everything seemed to be very black and white and highly moral. Our barrister was a rubicund man with a velvet voice, who assured Zoe beforehand that she had done the right thing. In the courtroom he asked for her freedom with the utmost confidence. The judge, after some browsing among his papers, sounded equally certain that Matthew was a villain and Zoe an angel. He looked kindly at my sad pale sister over his half-moon spectacles, and asked her if the children were happy with her.

'Oh yes, my lord,' said Zoe, with the utmost sincerity.

He nodded as if he had already known the answer, put the children into her custody, pushed Matthew into the outer darkness, gave her conditional freedom, and wished her well.

Zoe stepped down from the witness box looking shell-shocked. But Mr Shanklady was pleased with the way it had all gone, and took the two of us for a rollicking glass of amontillado. True to form, Matthew had jibbed at paying my sister more than he needed to because she had a modest income of her own. But our legal warrior, giving him this point, had jousted heartily on behalf of Simon and Caroline and ensured them a long and excellent education at their father's expense. Understandably, he was in a mood of quiet self-congratulation.

'We have done well. Very well. I feel that your excellent father would have been relieved and pleased, this day. But', he remarked, 'let us be thankful that your lovely lady mother is no longer with us! How she would have grieved.'

Then he shook hands with both of us, reminded me firmly that the lease of the Garret had little more than a year to go, and he would be expecting to hear from me soon, and returned to his office.

We watched his brisk pinstriped legs striding away, saw him lift his rolled umbrella to hail a taxi and raise his bowler hat to us before getting inside. And as we waved him

341

away down the Strand we both admitted that we adored Mr Shanklady to distraction. Then we found an excellent French restaurant and ate a delicious lunch and drank a bottle of Mouton-Cadet between us, and Zoe caught the early afternoon train home.

I said, before we parted, 'Remember that you're riding high today and tomorrow you'll probably feel down. But don't worry about that because from now on everything is going to get better. Just promise me that you won't fall in love and marry some other bastard before I have time to vet him. And always ring me if you're feeling blue.'

Zoe said impishly, 'Yes, Mummy and Daddy!'

Then kissed both my cheeks and squeezed my fingers, to show that she didn't mean it, and asked me to come down for Caroline's birthday the following weekend. Matthew was abroad, and she was giving Caro a big party to make up for not seeing her father.

My sister was not yet out of her personal dark wood, but she was more than halfway. The decree nisi was a signpost for the future. It made her accept that there was no turning back and therefore she must go on. The decree absolute, coming in the spring of 1966, marked the end of an era.

I drove down to the Old Rectory on a Friday afternoon at the end of March, to be met by an ecstatic Simon and Caroline, who ran out at the risk of being run over and pulled me out of the car.

Shouting, 'Mummy's going to knock the wall down! Come and look!'

And ran me through the hall and kitchen, dragging at my hands.

Crying, 'Faster, Lulu! Faster!' like two miniature Red Queens.

At the end of the kitchen garden stood my sister, looking competent and handsome in her old style. Her blue slacks and gingham shirt reminded me of Helen, who had always been happiest in her casual clothes. Hands on hips, Zoe was talking to her general workman, Mr Prout, who listened deferentially. She had chalked an archway on

342

the bricks and was describing it to him. Her hands mimed the result on air.

' . . . set with a wrought-iron gate. I have a drawing for it, copied from one of my father's books. It must be in perfect keeping with the house. I know that Charlie Croftman has retired now but I wondered whether he would make the gate for us as a special favour? Such a fine craftsman. I shall be growing a white-flowered creeper over the archway. But, really, the whole idea is to open the view so that we can look out across the meadows to the hills . . . '

Mentally, I released her from my custody and handed her back to life.

27

I celebrated my thirty-second birthday by taking out a
young designer who reminded me of Sep, the difference
being that Tim was heterosexual and dependent only on
himself. We were not lovers, but passing friends. I chose a
Greek restaurant in a cellar where you provided your own
wine, and Tim ate a great deal and smoked my cigarettes,
and played the jester to pay for his supper. He was just
starting out in life, as I had done a decade ago, and he
needed plenty of food and encouragement. So did Zak
Blueberry, now on the scrap-heap at twenty-nine. But Zak
had a drug problem these days, and was an Old Man of
the Sea to any friend who tried to help him. I had finished
carrying Zak.

In fact, my friends were changing as I changed. And my
way of life must change entirely. The years at the Garret
were coming to an end.

I knew that Cass would have plucked me out of my
home long before this and probably sold it for the price
of his original investment. At the time of his death, lacking
capital, I could do nothing. The windfall of Helen's legacy
made a move possible but coincided with Zoe's divorce, and
my sister's problems had taken precedence over mine. Now,
as Mr Shanklady put it, I could 'procrastinate no further!'.
Now, time pressing, I must leave pell-mell. And though I
was sorry, I was not unwilling. The Garret had served its
purpose. I did not need it any more. The problem being
that I didn't know what I wanted instead.

The city was becoming less personal. More and more

344

offices, fewer and fewer homes, occupied its heart. Boroughs once regarded as dull and remote were now considered to be full of possibilities and conveniently close. *Only half an hour from central London on the District Line.* And as the city sprawled further afield its house-prices doubled and tripled, and rates were now the size of former rents.

Within the magic circle my legacy would buy me nothing grander than a small flat on a twenty-five-year lease. The prospect of being homeless or living in Rachman-like squalor at the age of thirty-three was terrifying enough, but to be in that position at fifty-eight did not bear contemplation. And once again, as in Camden Town, I felt responsible for someone besides myself. Beatrice, the lady archivist, could move on and pay her way with ease, but Ruth Babbage could not, and would be retiring on a pension smaller than her present wages within the next few years. So I must find a roof large enough to shelter both of us, and continue to play the part of landlady and friend.

Sitting in the back garden at the Old Rectory, sipping home-made lemonade, watching the children play with the new puppy, and looking out through the finished archway on to the hills, Zoe and I discussed the matter.

'Of course, you can always come and live with us,' she said. 'I'll rent you the servants' attics. You can decorate and furnish them as you wish. You've got your own back staircase. And we promise not to disturb you ever, or come in unless specifically invited. How's that for an offer?'

I thanked her sincerely, but had no intention of becoming a sisterly satellite. Besides, Zoe would marry again. She was that sort of woman. Every middle-aged widower for miles round was offering to mow the lawns, teach Simon to play cricket, and courting Caroline with pink ice-cream, in order to scrape her acquaintance. A few of them were quite reasonable. Not particularly exciting or interesting, but decent men and good husband and stepfather material. If one of them made it with Zoe and the Old Rectory I doubted that an artistic sister in the attic would be welcome.

345

'What sort of place are you looking for?' asked Zoe.

I replied truthfully that I did not know.

'Why don't you look down here in any case? There are some lovely properties in Kent. And the bigger the cheaper, if you know what I mean. You could make a real investment. Some of these rambling old family places are ripe for conversion. Of course, it would mean time and hard work, Lulu. You'd have to take it seriously.'

Zoe took property seriously. An excellent businesswoman had been lurking unsuspected beneath Titania's crown of flowers. She had worked out a year's plan of campaign, which included an au pair girl called Brigitte to look after the children, and a three-month Certificate Course at the Cordon Bleu School at Marylebone Lane. From September she would advertise a weekend in the country for those weary of London, and feed them gourmet meals. And this was only the beginning. Working out her costs, taking carefully calculated risks, she reckoned she could expand. She talked of buying the field and fallen barn adjacent to the Old Rectory. Her workmen had been alerted to tell her in advance of any local property, in poor repair, which might come on the market. She, who had always emulated our mother, was now proving to be her father's daughter after all. Cass would have been proud of her.

'We're only forty minutes from London,' said Zoe blithely.

And yet, despite the fact that it would be lovely to be near them, I didn't feel that I could. I felt it would be borrowing. Like borrowing an idea. There was a whiff of the second-hand about it, and I was used to queening my patch, even if the patch was small and unimportant. No, I had to find my own house, in my own place, in my own time.

I prevaricated.

'Of course,' I said, 'I have Ruth to think about.'

'Oh yes. I'd forgotten. Of course there's Ruth,' said Zoe, and waited.

'And we oughtn't to be this far out of town because of the expenses with fares and things. You know how proud she is. I mean, I can keep Ruth's rent down but I can't pay her fares as well. Even if I could afford them she wouldn't let me!'

I sought the counsel of Mr Shanklady and a thoughtful St Emilion.

Mr Shanklady said, 'You should look for a house at the poorer end of a good district, in the not-yet-fashionable suburbs – and believe me, my dear Leila, the city is growing at such a pace that the East End will be fashionable before we are done! That sort of property would be within your price range. After all you could improve it, and a well-kept house always increases in value.'

I knew he was talking commonsense, but it was not sense I sought, it was inspiration.

'You should come to the West Country,' said Magda, drinking red wine.

She is old now, really old. She keeps very much to herself. With one excuse and another, I reckon that she hasn't been to London since Zoe's wedding.

'You should come to Cornwall,' she says. 'For that money you could buy a manor house! And look at the beauty of it all. Look at the beauty.'

'Oh yes,' I said, 'the beauty is undoubtedly there. But you see, Magda, I need something else. I need life to be milling round me. I need the parade.'

Though sometimes, nowadays, I felt that the parade had gone by.

'Ah,' said Magda, 'I never did, you see. I always wanted to contemplate. Mind you, those later illustrations of yours, the ones since the White Cat, are very inward looking. If you lived down here in the quiet, instead of being distracted with all that noise and bustle, you'd use your imagination and go deep-er.'

'Yes,' I said, 'but I get my ideas from having life thrown up at me. Like a handful of pebbles against a window. They rattle against the pane and catch my attention. I must be in the midst of life. I can't sit and look at the sea, as you do.'

347

'No,' said Magda. 'I suppose that's why you were never an artist in my sort of way.'

An old pain stirred. I had never aired my hopes to anyone once the painting master had pronounced judgement on me, but I was surprised that Magda had not guessed how much I envied her. Oh, she was not a great artist in society's sense, not of national or international stature, not avant-garde, not fashionable, but she had made a special place for herself in her own sphere. To have an eye for Magda Lewis seascapes was to be a humble connoisseur, to buy them was to be a modest collector of rarities. She was the real thing, the true breed, an artist who had said to hell with everything and painted what she wanted.

We sat by her window and the curtains fluttered out in the wind from the sea. And I felt that I was very old too, and had been there for a very long time.

Magda said, seemingly at random, 'Some women are wives, and some are mothers, and some do a bit of both – like Helen and Zoe – and the rare ones are mistresses. I was always a mistress.'

'I was a mistress,' I said dreamily.

'I should hope you still are,' said Magda caustically, 'at your age!'

'Now and then,' I said, 'when the wind blows the right man in my direction. Now and then I am.'

'But I was never a mother,' said Magda. 'Never a mother. Even though I still love Helen, and miss her, and sometimes cry for her.'

Then she drank up her wine defiantly.

The sense of emptiness, which had been growing within me for the past two years, turned to hunger then. I thought of my child who had been denied life.

'An artist can't afford to be a mother,' said Magda firmly.

The curtain rippled outwards in the wind from the sea, and I was so long in replying that she had forgotten her statement.

I said, thinking of my child, 'Why can't a woman be both?'

But she was tired by then, and hungry, and had talked enough philosophy. So I went out, and found a fish and

348

chip shop, and brought our supper back wrapped in the *Western Morning News*, all hot and reeking of vinegar. And we ate together, with our plates on our knees, still sitting in front of her window. The food tasted saltier in the wind from the harbour, saltier and better. Magda, revived, shook more vinegar over her battered cod.

'Magda,' I said. 'Are you sure all that vinegar is good for you?'

'No,' she said, 'I'm sure it's very bad for me. But I'm having it just the same!'

Everyone was looking for houses for me. I spent my weekends rushing around to see what they described as 'the very thing for Leila'. But the houses were never quite right. Or perhaps they were absolutely right for me as I had been, but not for me as I was now. I remember one poem of a house, a perfect little duck of a place in Wimbledon village near the Common, which was custom-built for a single lady absorbed in her work. But though that was my image it was not how I felt.

The advertisement enchanted me because it was so absurd, because it spoke to me in my own terms.

It read: 'Grotty old house too far from local station. Has character. Offers freehold residence to anyone with sufficient courage to rebuild, restore, redress, renew. Only optimists, visionaries, eccentrics and hikers need apply.'

'Now don't dash into the estate agent's office dressed like Meg Merrilees!' said Cass, in my head. 'Saying it sounds exactly what you want. Because they're looking for that sort of sucker. Play it cool and keep your cards hidden. Preferably with an ace up the sleeve.'

So I fished out one of Colin's little outfits and turned up the skirt, which was now far too long to be fashionable.

'An old lady has been living there alone for twenty years. In fact died there,' said the agent, playing with a paper knife.

He glanced across at me from time to time to gauge my reactions.

'I'm afraid she was rather odd and not particularly clean. Bit of a hermit. Quarrelled with family, friends and neighbours.'

He sighed through his nose.

'There's been some difficulty with the will – or lack of one.'

He sighed again.

'You'll find it in an awful state,' he said. 'In fact, several pieces of her furniture still there. The things that the family didn't want. That were not worth having.'

Ah, I thought, remembering early days at the Garret. But then I've always inherited things that other people didn't want. I've always come along second and accepted their leavings. I shall be quite used to that.

I said, 'I can't look at it before the weekend. I'm too busy. No, it's quite all right,' as he began to murmur something about Saturdays being difficult, 'I don't need anyone to come with me, thank you. I prefer to go alone.'

He had the last word.

'I should wear a dust-coat if I were you,' he said humorously.

I didn't tell anyone I was going. I hugged the knowledge to myself as though it were an unborn child. On the Saturday afternoon I drove across London, down into the suburbs, and up a hill behind the little black tube station. The road was long and steep, tree-lined, hushed and respectable.

Like its neighbours, the Poplars was a typical late-Victorian family edifice. Unlike them it was dirty and neglected. There was nothing elegant or distinctive about it. Nothing that would have caught my father's eye. And yet, the agent was right, it had character. The hedges had grown very tall and bushy, and once inside the small garden it was surprisingly quiet and private.

I was not an expert, but years of living with Cass and watching him work on Whitegates, then the Old Rectory and finally the Garret, had taught me first principles. I had brought a penknife with me to probe the wood, and a notebook to jot down facts. I wrote, 'Front gate needs new hinges and probably new posts.' I walked up the tiled path. 'Several tiles missing.' I examined the porch carefully. 'Wood badly weathered.' I opened the front door with difficulty, because it stuck. And such a smell of dust and damp and old drains hit my nostrils that I stood back for a moment.

This long winding road of houses must have been built for people with rather more money than the average white-collar worker at the turn of the century. They were detached, for one thing, and the builders had given them individual features, and set some back further than others to vary the monotony. On this side of the road they were happily placed. The sun came into the back rooms in the morning, and into the front rooms in the afternoon. So that one could presumably start the day with a cheerful breakfast, and end it with an early evening drink in the parlour.

And it was a big house, much bigger than the Garret. Here I could have three spacious flats instead of three cramped ones. But this time I was going to command the ground floor, with access to both gardens, and use the conservatory ('several panes missing') as my workshop.

I went from room to room, and every room was dark, with its curtains drawn close, unwashed, and rotting. I pulled them back to let the sun in, and regretted touching them. I pushed up the windows whose cords were not broken, to let in air. Wallpaper hung in strips like peeled bananas. Some of the walls must be replastered, and I took it for granted that the whole place would need rewiring, as well as scrubbing, probably fumigating, and certainly decorating, from top to bottom. This place would cost me a small fortune in time and money. Which, of course, was why the asking price was so reasonable.

'Not reasonable enough,' said Cass, unimpressed. 'Beat him down.'

In the front bedroom was an old mahogany wardrobe, absolutely sound, a huge thing with a hollow cornice deep enough to hide three suitcases, and inlaid doors, and mirrors inside the doors, and two deep drawers beneath the cupboard which would hold a pile of blankets.

The sun was in that corner of the room, throwing an elongated pattern of the bay window across the floor, and I stood there for a while, sensing the spirit of the place. Here children had been begotten and born, parents and grandparents had died, for more than half a century.

My father's words rebuked me.

'To hell with the atmosphere, Lee. Look for woodworm and dry-rot.'

I stuck my penknife in the boards, but they were sound, too. Shabby, filthy, dusty, but sound. Then I turned to the great wardrobe again, took out my handkerchief and rubbed an arc of dust from the front panel. Its recent owner's neglect could not negate decades of beeswax and elbow grease. The ruby gleam, revealed, was so beautiful that I could not imagine why anyone would leave such a majestic piece of furniture behind.

'Too big,' said Cass factually. 'Too big to take with them. Too high for modern bedrooms. Too broad. Old-fashioned without being vintage. A good solid chunk of Victoriana. Not valuable, but worthy.'

Up and down the stairs I went, inside and out, looking and looking and taking notes. Much of the furniture was fit for nothing but firewood, to be burned in the overgrown garden at the back, or in the double-ovened kitchen range which had once shone with blacklead. I suspected that it would be temperamental and eat a small fortune in fuel, but I could bring my gas cooker from the Garret. Open grates meant that chimneys must be swept. Damp stains made me ponder on the state of the roof and drain-pipes, and the pointing was none too good. Every task reminded me of two more.

The lower half of the kitchen had been painted lincoln-green and the upper half pea-green, a very long time ago. The windows were set quite high in the walls, and it was big enough to cook food for all the occupants of the house. The solitary bathroom, obviously for the use of the owners, was in a similar state of decoration, but in cocoa-brown lincrusta and cream paint. On a raised pedestal, as if it were beached, stood an ancient cast-iron boat of a bath with brass taps and ball-and-claw feet.

On the windowsill in the garden room I found a solitary survivor: a straggling scarlet geranium which had been kept alive by a leak in the roof. I raided the water-butt and gave it a good drink.

'Hang in there!' I said to the geranium. 'I'll be back.'

Not only could I imagine myself living here, it was as if I had lived here before, as if the house had waited for me to catch up with it in the sixties.

'You will pay a surveyor to look this morgue over first,' said Cass, as I put my notebook away and prepared to lock up. 'The agent will tell you that other people are interested. Take no notice of him. Nobody is bloody interested but you!'

Downstairs, tempted by the open parlour window, a bird had flown in and was perched on the shelf above the fireplace, cocking its head, preening its feathers. I did not move lest I frighten it. The sun was pouring into the parlour and we were very still together, the bird and I. In a moment or two it flew out again.

I drove across country to Kent in a dream. I had the brochure with me, the notes I had taken, and the evidence of my penknife. And when we had eaten and the children were in bed, and Brigitte had gone out with her boyfriend, I laid everything before my sister.

I said, 'Zoe, I know this is my house. But how much would it cost me?'

She had taken to wearing spectacles for reading, and she put them on. She was relaxed and confident nowadays. Her youthful beauty and ebullience had given way to a handsome serenity. She reminded me more and more of our mother. I was as tranquil in her presence as once I had been with Helen. After a while she made a face, and laughed.

'Oh, my goodness,' she said. 'Yes, it seems feasible, financially speaking. If you put the boat out it will be an excellent investment. But it's going to cost you far more to restore it than to buy it.'

'So should I buy it outright, or should I get a mortgage and leave myself as much money as possible for repairs?'

'A mortgage would be best,' she said. 'But you have three black marks against you. You're a woman. You're self-employed. And your income isn't stable. Still, our darling Mr Shanklady would vouch for you, no doubt.'

'And, Zoe, I'll have a steady income from two rents, as well as what I earn. And I shall get something for the Garret. And I've managed before.'

She took off her spectacles and poured us a gin and tonic each.

'The only thing I don't understand', she said, 'is that five years ago you were kicking up a stink because Jeremy Purchase wanted you both to live in a house at Blackheath. Now, all of a sudden, you choose a place which seems to embody all the qualities you were criticising.'

'Times change,' I said. 'And we change with them. I have received my future commandments on tablets of South London brick.

'Thou shalt not play thy trad jazz records full blast at three a.m.

'Thou shalt not offend thy neighbours by sunbathing in the nude on thy back lawn.

'Thou shalt not flaunt thy lovers, who should preferably be British and White.

'Thou shalt not have a house-warming party which ends up in a police station . . .

'I can't think of the other six for the moment, but no doubt I shall. And don't think I'm going to turn respectable, sister mine. That would be too much to hope for. Far too much.'

28

1967–1968

Time was at my back. My new home, in its desolation, made demands upon me which the Garret had never done. There, I had been able to work at my own rhythm, content to earn enough money to keep afloat. Profit represented fun: a party or a present. If I felt inclined, I could paint a forest on my bedroom ceiling which gave me intense delight and cost no more than my leisure hours. Now time meant money, and profits were earmarked before they were earned, for the Poplars must be made habitable.

So I looked for quicker and more lucrative work. Film work, television work, calendars, posters, greetings cards. I poured it out like a professional cornucopia. I went anywhere and slogged for anyone who would pay me well. This was pure craftsmanship, not art, since it sprang from necessity rather than the creative spirit. Unlike my illustrations, these efforts were no sooner done than forgotten. Sometimes I still find a relic of that period, on a postcard stand at a holiday resort or in the stationery department of a store, and recognise it with a sensation of dread: returned momentarily to the sweatshop in which I toiled for two long years, with the clock ticking away at my back and the house's maw swallowing the proceeds and yawning open again to ask for more.

Yet I did not lack the occasional cakes and ale.

London had sprawled in more ways than one. I was

welcomed here because I was different. The suburban mind was broadening. I became part of a community of insiders who made room for outsiders because they found them interesting.

'Mind you, you're on the right side of the railway line here,' I was told, rather complacently. 'They're all pose, poverty and piano on the other!'

I was not the only oddity, and I made friends with the others. A silver-headed old Quaker walked briskly up and down the hill each morning, to do the shopping for his wife. He was a retired schoolmaster with an interest in the paranormal. A gentle, scholarly man, quietly and soberly dressed apart from his rakish black French beret. I was wearing a scarlet highwayman's hat when we met in the butcher's, and our headgear engaged us in conversation.

A large gracious Polish countess, like a ship in full sail, took in stray cats, and looked after them far too well while she found them good homes. None of their new owners could match the countess's hospitality so the cats constantly returned.

In a corner house at the bottom of the hill lived a charming Viennese lady doctor and her husband. His health had failed in a concentration camp during the war and he was only fit for light work. So he manned the telephone and mediated between his wife and her patients, and she ran a one-woman practice from home. Ruth and I registered with her as soon as we settled in at the Poplars, feeling that our health would be in sympathetic hands.

Oddities apart, the majority of people in the road here were families of all ages, sorts, sizes and wealth: from the family in oil, who were only here while the wife had her fourth baby, to the earnest young couple who bravely stuck a CND poster in their front window and were always asking for signatures on petitions. Nowadays I no longer marched, but I still paid up and signed.

I was on speaking or nodding terms with the parents, but it was the children who interested me most. Zoe was too busy to see me at the weekend, so I only saw Simon and Caroline briefly when we met in mid-week, and I missed them.

I have always felt comfortable with children. They are not as clever as adults but far wiser. They can be wildly improbable, utterly infuriating, dotty, delightful, and deadly serious. Growing beans round wet blotting paper, and cress on cottonwool, and jars of tadpoles into frogs; pressing flowers and printing the names beneath them; collecting shells and pebbles. And despite the fact that they are frequently foiled by grown-ups, they still hope for cream cake and circuses and happy ever after.

Beginning with a couple of neighbouring children, who found a way into my garden through a hole in the hedge, I started a painting class on Sunday afternoons in the garden room. The class was free and fun and I did not mind about mess – God knows that at that time I lived in mess up to the eyebrows! – and I pinned the most interesting results on a big cork board on the wall.

Everything changes, and I change with it, or perhaps everything changes because I have changed. This time I paid time and thought and care and attention to the decorating, and struck a balance between the correctness of the house and the colour I needed. Ruth and I were comfortably settled, the top flat was being advertised, and the first roses were budding in the back garden when I reached my thirty-fourth year.

Living from day to day, and each day lived to the hilt, I had made no plans to celebrate, and this year the date fell on a Saturday when Zoe was busiest. So I took myself to the Player's Theatre (*Late Joys*), of which Cass made me a member many birthdays ago, to celebrate alone. The performance did not begin until nine o'clock, and I booked a table in the Supper Room, which was crowded with Londoners and visiting colonials. And while I was looking at the menu the waiter asked if I would mind sharing my table with this gentleman from overseas.

The gentleman is thinner, browner, seven years older, and still very much Jeremy Purchase.

357

He has recognised me a few moments before I see him and so has the advantage of me, but I still think that his opening remark is a prizewinner.

He holds out both hands and says, 'Happy birthday, Sparky!'

I don't think my reply is too bad.

'Talk about Late Joys!'

He is home on three months' leave and has bought himself a temporary membership ticket. I believe that his impulse, like mine, is to scrub out our present plans for the evening, go somewhere else, and talk and talk and talk. For he is evidently as delighted and overcome as I am. But on reflection we need, though we do not say so, this entertainment to mediate between us while we grow used to the idea of being together again.

It is a crazy and glorious way to renew ourselves, in the past glories of a Victorian Music Hall. And when the chairman asks if there are any members present from our overseas colonies, and Jeremy stands up, terribly embarrassed but smiling sturdily, I could cry.

'May I ask, sir, where are you from?'

'India, sir.'

'The Indian *Empire*, sir?'

Much laughter.

'Yes, sir, the Indian *Empire*!' Jeremy agrees with gusto, and sits down to a round of applause.

And looks quickly at me to see if I am pleased with him, and clasps my hand and holds it hard when he sees that I am. Naughty songs, saucy comedians, nostalgia and coloured lights. Afterwards we dance together and smile and say nothing, because there is nothing that need be said. Here we are, together again.

And here is Ruth, peering over the landing stair-rail at midnight, in her sensible dressing-gown and plastic curlers, ostensibly to check that I am not a burglar, actually to check on me. The last two years have been scrappy, love-wise. She has been waiting in hope rather than expectation, but tonight she hits an emotional jackpot. She gives a little shriek and throws up her hands. Her pocket-torch falls to the hall floor and sounds as if it has hurt, if not mortally wounded, itself.

Jeremy's face is upturned. Though his hair is thinner and receding at the temples the light still slides down on it, warm and brown and silky. His smile is white and sound. His green eyes crinkle at the corners.

'Oh, my goodness me. Oh, surely it can't be. Not Dr Purchase?' Ruth gibbers.

'Yes, it's me, Miss Babbage. Good to see you again.'

She remembers the curlers and shrinks back into the shadows, both hands over her head. But she cannot bear to be left out of our reunion and calls from the twilight zone, 'Can I make you both some cocoa, Leila?'

Jeremy and I look at each other and smile, for time has returned. We invite her to share a bottle of wine, and when she has wound a striped scarf round the curlers she creeps downstairs in pink felt carpet-slippers and gets tipsy on a single glass.

We are older in years, in experience, and in loneliness now, Jeremy Purchase and I. We have lost the confidence of privileged youth and no longer believe that life was made for us, nor that we can always shape it to suit us. We have learned to compromise and accept, and we have reached our meridian. The sun is at midday. From now on, the shadows will gradually lengthen and eventually evening will come. We are ready, in short, to admit that we are not immortal, to consolidate what we have, and to settle down.

He has been guided all round the house and shown no impatience as I tell a tale in every room. He has asked about my work, looked carefully at everything, and given an opinion. He still does not know anything about art but he knows what he likes, and his praise is sweet.

In return I encourage him to tell me about his daily life, his hopes and aims and beliefs. I form pictures of his existence. If there is a human being, a very human being indeed, who is close to becoming a saint, then Jeremy Purchase is that person. Who would have thought it, fifteen

359

years ago, when he weighed down Zoe's veil with a stone, and stood on his head to amuse her bridesmaids?

Someone once told me that when I was painting I wore the look of love. Jeremy has that look when he talks of his work. In his world clean pure water is a luxury and he is very careful with it here. I am ashamed to think of the gallons we squander daily. For the sake of a village which interests him, and in honour of the help given by him and those like him, I transform an old cocoa-tin into a collection-box, decorate it with a picture of the world's poor, and install it on the hall table. We are collecting to buy a well. I start the fund off with the value of my latest royalties on *Night-walks of the White Cat*. Ruth Babbage posts a five pound note, which she cannot afford, into the slit (I shall have to find some way of making this up to her). Visitors and friends are blackmailed into contributing.

For ourselves alone, our love-making is gentler and more personal. We no longer grab pleasure with both hands and gobble it gloriously up. We partake at leisure, we savour, we sip. And it is wonderful to be *we* again.

This time around I make no pretence to Ruth that Jeremy is living in the empty flat upstairs. Indeed, needing the rent it will earn, I let it the week after his arrival. So there is no question about where he stays. He stays with me. Ruth can assume, if she wishes, that he sleeps on the put-u-up sofa instead of my grand brass bedstead. But she drops no hints and I make no explanations. Perhaps we have all grown up?

His leave is running out and he must return, is anxious to return, already a little bored with so much leisure. Once again he faces me with a decision. And once again I question him, but this time gently and seriously, not shouting and slapping my toast marmalade-side down on the table-cloth.

'Jem. Why should it be me who gives up a way of life, and not you?'

This time he does not wave away my work as being frivolous and unimportant, but answers just as seriously.

'I can't leave these people to fend for themselves, that's why. But I want you as well, Sparky. I need you

360

as well. I'm not pushing marriage – though it would be the simplest solution – just so long as we're together. For God's sake, Sparky, surely we can work something out?'

Then I am on the rocks, because no one can ever offer me more than this, and I shall be lucky to find another man of his kind and quality. To love someone as I love Jeremy Purchase, and as he says he loves me, is a rare thing.

But my commonsense creates a picture of me in India, having given up my independence, work, family, friends and house, in order to live his life and play only one small part in it, that of being his woman. Realistically, I picture myself with nothing to do and nowhere to go, important to no one but him, nourished by nothing but the attention he can pay me in his spare time. And I know that frustration and resentment wears love away in the end, and then he will have lost me, and I shall have lost myself and everything I had and stood for.

So I cry very much when I tell him that we must continue to go our own ways, and he is very kind and understanding, and our parting is sad on both sides. At the airport, just before we part, I remind him how we are and what we are, and what we have been to each other in the past and could still be in the future.

'We may not be able to spend our lives together,' I say, 'but so long as we stay alive to each other and meet now and again, that's all I ask, Jem. All I ask.'

He turns and waves at the last possible moment. That is the moment at which I still picture him. Turning and waving. Then I run out of the hall and drive off, crying like a fool and being a danger to everyone on the road, all the way home. Because I cannot bear to watch him fly away.

29

I waited a full fortnight after I had missed the second period before visiting my doctor. She confirmed what I knew already. Her narrow black eyes glanced at me to see how I took the news, and glanced away again. She read my medical card and notes, which would tell her that I was healthy and unmarried.

'Quite a shock, I think?' she said quietly.

'Well, it certainly wasn't planned,' I replied, equally quietly.

'And you are how old, Miss Gideon?'

'Thirty-four.'

'Ah! You look so much younger. You are getting married soon?'

'No. I'm not getting married at all.'

She observed me closely, her frosty shiny head with its knob of a bun held a little to one side. She remained beautifully objective, collecting her facts.

'But the child's father will help you financially?'

'I hadn't thought about that. He doesn't know about the baby. Anyway he's abroad.'

I thought how he would feel. Trapped probably. I was not sure how I felt, in a state between panic and fearful joy.

'I don't want him to pay anything,' I said firmly.

'You have your own house, I know. You have money also?'

'I'm a professional illustrator. I have some savings. I can manage.'

She said, 'It will not be easy. Mothers who do not

have to earn a living find it hard work. And you are not young.'

I did not know how to answer this. She came to the crux of the matter.

'You want this child?'

'Yes,' I said. 'I do want it. At least, I certainly don't want to get rid of it.'

Now she was interested. She must have expected me to ask for an abortion. She took off her glasses and rubbed the high bridge of her nose.

'You are not only a single woman and self-supporting,' she reminded me, in a friendly fashion, 'you are also an elderly primipara.'

I suppressed my first squeak of amusement in weeks.

'I use the term "elderly" in this particular context, of course,' she said gravely. 'You are aware of possible risks to yourself and the child?'

'Yes. I've been reading it up. I'm probably going to have a tough labour and the baby might be a mongol. But I've had German measles,' I added, 'so there's no fear of a Rubella baby. And though I look small I'm really very strong and wiry.'

She shrugged. A little continental lift of the hands and shoulders.

'It is necessary to understand the situation fully, Miss Gideon.'

'I've thought it out, and I'm prepared to take the responsibility.'

She put on her glasses again and said, 'Good.'

She worked out the date of birth and booked me into the local hospital.

'You will, of course, have financial help from the State. You are entitled to a Maternity Grant of twenty-two pounds, to help you to buy things for yourself and the baby. And for six months you are paid Maternity Benefit, so that you can take time off both before and after the baby is born.'

'I'll sit up in bed and sketch,' I said, feeling slightly restored.

'It's not so easy as that. You must rest,' she said

363

firmly, 'and feed your baby. Details you will be given from your local Health and Insurance office. I think it is four pounds, ten shillings a week before the birth. It is more after. Perhaps six pounds. But ask them.'

I was thinking how cleverly the baby had chosen its time of conception. I should be at home with it throughout the summer. We could both go down to Cornwall and stay near Magda for a month or two.

'You have any questions to ask me?' she said amiably.

I came back to daily life.

'Just one. I'm not sick in the morning but I'm absolutely off my food. I'm living on orange juice at the moment, and the occasional glass of champagne. Will it harm the baby if I don't have more than a bit of bread and butter now and again?'

'No, this will pass in another month or so. One glass of champagne, very occasionally, if it settles the stomach, will not hurt. But you should not drink alcohol and you must not smoke. As for the food – the baby, you understand, looks after itself, even at the expense of you.' She permitted herself a little joke. 'It will eat your bread and butter and you will have nothing!'

I smiled, and she wrote out a prescription for something mild to help my nausea, and said that if I was worried about anything I was to consult her. She added that I should be sure to attend the ante-natal clinic once a month and follow their instructions to the letter.

'We must keep an eye on you both,' she said.

She smiled again, as she handed me the prescription, and the smile was an endorsement of my happiness.

'I'm very thrilled about this baby,' I told her, full of bliss.

'I can see that,' she said, and smiled again.

An afternoon in the middle of the week was the best time to visit Zoe. I rang her up to make sure, and brought half a bottle of champagne with me. She took me into the sitting room, where a coal-fire burned in a graceful grate. Outside shone a rare November sun, and a breeze was playing with the fallen leaves.

Though Zoe had been glorious in her youth, she seemed more at home in her late thirties. She sat up like a queen, full of confidence and splendour, and her mouth held the beginnings of a smile.

Ripeness is all, I thought. It really is.

'Are we celebrating anything in particular, or just life in general?' she asked, as I drew the cork and it soared up to her exquisite ceiling and bounced off a plaster leaf.

I said, sounding as perky as I could, 'You're going to be an aunt, Zo. Let's drink to that.'

She raised her glass and drank, saying, 'M-m-m. I love champagne!'

It took her several seconds to connect the fact with me.

Then she set her glass down quickly and said, 'Oh no, Lulu! Oh, my dear!'

'It happens to all of us,' I said stupidly.

Which it did not.

She was stunned. Trying to be helpful, trying to say the right thing. She sounded like Ruth in a crisis, all half-sentences.

'Darling, don't misunderstand me. But don't. I'm sure you must be tempted. But don't. Not another abortion . . . '

'Another?' I cried, alerted. 'I didn't know Helen had told you about that. She made *me* promise not to say anything to *you*, dammit . . . '

'Oh, she was so upset, the second time that Jeremy Purchase of yours came back, and she told me more than she meant to . . . '

'Well, of all the bloody things . . . ' I said, furious.

We were off track already.

She said recklessly, 'I know about Cass's death, too. How you covered it up. That was brave of you, Lulu . . . '

'Jesus Christ!' I said between my teeth. 'What a pack of jabberers and promise-breakers people are! While I keep my bloody mouth *shut*.'

She said apologetically, 'I thought I'd best mention that while we were having things out.'

I said savagely, 'Like bringing other offences into account before the criminal is finally sentenced?'

She glanced at me sideways and smiled then.

'Nonsense. You're not a criminal, Lulu. What I meant to say was that I know how you must feel. How difficult it will be to adjust to a totally different way of life. And that your work is important. But think of the baby and think of yourself, and don't risk another abortion, Lulu. Please.'

I wanted to laugh and cry at the same time. Part of my condition, I expected, as well as the occasion.

I said, sitting up ramrod-straight, making a declaration, 'I don't *intend* to have an abortion. I *want* to have the baby.'

'Oh, good,' she cried, relieved. 'Oh, that's good.'

She sipped more thoughtfully this time. The news was not entirely good. She realised that, too. Her face changed.

To save her the trouble of asking, I said, 'But I'm not going to marry the father, or anyone else. So forget that. I shall bring it up without a father.'

She was coming to terms with the idea of a forced wedding. No wedding at all stymied her.

'But the baby will have to have a father,' Zoe protested, distressed.

I was possessed by a mood of desperate frivolity. Or by champagne.

'I do realise that. But having played his part, the father has retired gracefully!'

I could tell by the set of her lips that she was about to put matters right.

'Lulu, you mustn't be haphazard about this. You mustn't let him get away with it. Fathers are very important.'

'Oh, I don't know,' I said unkindly. 'Si and Caro seem to have managed very well without Matthew.'

She opened her mouth to protest, read my expression, and said, half-annoyed, 'Why can't you be serious about anything?'

'I'm absolutely serious. My baby chose its father with great care.'

'Lulu! Do I know him? Have I met him? . . . '

'Is he British? Is he white?' I asked the queenly fireplace. 'Zo, would you object very deeply if I said the father was Zak Blueberry?'

366

She looked aghast, brought herself round with an effort, and answered coldly and resolutely, 'I thought you told me that that man was addicted to heroin?'

'He was, but they've cold-turkeyed him. Whatever that is.'

She tried to make the best of the situation, and I relished her expression.

'Oh. Well. At least he's not on drugs . . . '

Perplexed and sorry, she returned to the fray.

' . . . and I must admit,' trying to be fair, 'that West Indians are wonderful parents, and those little brown babies are absolutely adorable . . . '

In another moment she would ask me to bring Zak down for the weekend. I burst out laughing. She was simply priceless.

I said, 'The father is Jeremy Purchase.'

She stared at me and shook her head from side to side in disbelief.

'My jaw drops yet again,' said Zoe, after a long silence. 'I thought that affair was over years ago.'

'He came home on leave in June. We spent what you might call our Indian summer together. And now he's gone back.'

She said, 'Does he know?'

'No. And I have no intention of telling him.'

The autumn afternoon changed its mind and withdrew the sun from our faces. The breeze became a wind and harried the leaves.

Zoe said in quite a different tone, 'May I ask why not?'

'Because I turned down a final offer to get married and live in India, and I'm not going to refuse him that and then expect him to support me and his child. It was my carelessness, anyway, not his.'

Zoe's lips tightened. Her voice and face lost its sweetness. She looked at me now not in love but in anger.

'This is a baby you're producing, Leila, not a party costume. A totally dependent human being who is going to be needlessly deprived and hurt, because its mother doesn't believe in family life. It is your duty, and Jeremy's duty, to give that baby a home.'

'What, out in some primitive Indian village? In *that* climate?'

'Look, Leila,' she said, determined to make me see sense. 'Our parents, despite their personal problems, gave us a stable, happy, healthy childhood, which is the best gift any human being can have. That's why you and I survive as well as we do. A child needs a father as well as a mother. Even the best mother, on her own, is not enough . . . '

I said, 'Just look who's talking!'

She protested vehemently, face flushed.

'My marriage may have failed, but that doesn't mean that I think marriage itself is wrong. Despite its difficulties, I believe it to be the best way to bring up a family. It's just that it takes two people to make it work.'

She was sad then, looking down at her clasped hands, but she had not given up her crusade.

She said, 'Have you looked at it from the baby's point of view? Other children can be so cruel. So can parents. And it won't be a baby for long. You'll both have to face the flak of schooldays and social occasions, and far beyond that. The complications are endless. It's going to be a constant social embarrassment. Of course, Magda won't mind – except that she doesn't like babies anyway! – but think of the aunts. And Mr Shanklady. Every time you're introduced to people, or you fill up an official form you're laying yourself and the child open to prejudice.

'Besides that, there's the practical matter of bringing up a baby, which is very demanding. Twenty-four hours a day, every day of the year. And, to be quite honest, Lulu, although you're wonderful at entertaining children, would you have patience for the daily round and common task?'

She was in full swing by now.

'Then there's your work. You need to earn enough now to support two people. And children are a very expensive commodity and become more so as they grow older. And your work, as you have always made clear, demands most of your time and the minimum of interruptions. But you're not going to be able to tell a teething infant that you have to meet a deadline by the afternoon post. You can't expect it to sleep through the night or never to catch measles.'

I drank more champagne but it could not lift my spirits. I was weary and queasy and had expended a colossal amount of nervous energy already. Yet I tried to answer, saying something about having the baby with me in a carricot while I worked.

'For the first few months you could,' said Zoe relentlessly. 'And then what would you do with it? Stick the poor thing in a playpen, where it would spend all day trying to attract your attention? And what after that, when the child is crawling, walking, running round, and getting itself into mischief?'

I had thought about this, and produced my solution.

'I'll have a Brigitte to look after it in the daytime,' I said.

'Brigitte isn't exactly a paragon,' Zoe replied crisply.

'I don't need a paragon,' I answered, with some asperity. 'I'm not a paragon myself – as you've been busy pointing out!'

She ignored my annoyance. Her tone indicated that she knew all about babies and was always right.

'It may be difficult to get a girl at all, in your position. The agencies are pretty stringent. You're supposed to be responsible for the girl's moral welfare.'

From the depths of my beleaguered self I said wearily, 'Zoe, all I need is a little help and understanding, and I'll manage fine.'

She spoke more considerately then.

'I don't mean to be unkind, Lulu, but you must look at this situation from every point of view. Not just your own. Your baby will be half-Jeremy. It may look like him, inherit his particular talents, have the same interests. You're not just producing another version of yourself.'

I said steadfastly, 'All right, then. I've done it once and I can do it again. We'll march with the CND, watch football matches, save up our pennies for another Indian well, and spend our Sundays in the Science Museum. I respect Jeremy's beliefs, even if I can't give up my life to them. And I don't expect or want the baby to be a copy of me. I'm an individual, not an egotist.'

369

She sighed, but must continue to lecture.

She said, without an atom of belief in my judgement, 'Can you honestly tell me that you've thought this situation through?'

I divided the last of the champagne scrupulously between us while I pondered my reply.

I decided that I was not going to stay to tea and see the children, or to supper and have a long cosy sisterly chat by the fire. When our glasses were empty I was going straight back home, and it would be a while before I came here again.

I said, 'I have thought it through, Zo. And I came to a different, and if I may say so, a more honest conclusion. I think it's wrong to trap a man with a child, and if marriage with Jeremy Purchase wasn't going to work when we were single it certainly won't work with a baby.'

She began to say that a baby often binds a couple together, but I would not let her finish. I had had enough adages for one afternoon.

'That's crap,' I said. 'Sheer and utter crap.'

I could tell by her expression that she was at a total loss. She lifted her hands and let them fall into her lap. In her deepest sister-self I knew she feared for me because I had left the safety of the domestic trenches and entered unknown and uncharted territory, and she could not shield me from danger.

The enemy were all about: respectable wives and mothers who would consider me irresponsible and immoral; men who would regard me as easy prey, and my choice of single parenthood as a slight on their sex; and the mortar bombs of social code which at any moment could explode at my feet and send me flying rag-doll into the air. Had I been widowed, divorced or deserted, a brave little woman in a sad plight, society would have extended help and sympathy. To choose of my own free will to bring up a child without a father was asking for trouble.

She said, slightly chilly but still trying, 'Promise me one thing at least, Lulu. Write and tell Jeremy about the baby. Even if you don't want him to marry you or finance you

370

he should know. Fathers have rights as well as mothers. Truly.'

I conceded one point.

'All right. I'll do that. Because it's his child and he has a right to know. But I shall ask nothing else of him.'

Then I delivered my sermon, which was far briefer than hers, but just as telling.

'You seem to believe that I live as I do in order to shock people. I thought you understood that I live as I am, by my own principles. And I let live. Which you do not. And the only difference between you and me, Zoe, is that you happen to think like the majority, which makes life a lot easier for you. But it doesn't necessarily mean that you're right.'

I had, in our childhood, screamed at her and even once or twice hit her. In our adolescence I had defied her and quarrelled with her, and we had disagreed in our maturity. But I had never spoken to Zoe in that fashion or in that tone before.

I could tell she was hurt, by the manner in which she accepted my early departure and stood watching me as I drove away, arms folded over her chest as if I had dealt her a heavy blow. But she was not wounded half to death, and I was.

30

Ruth has arrived home a little earlier than usual and is standing in the hall, sorting out the afternoon mail, when I come in.

She says coyly, holding up an airmail envelope, like a delicate morsel for an eager dog, 'This one seems to be from Dr Purchase!'

I am too used up for fun and small talk. I merely thank her, and carry Jeremy's letter away into the privacy of my front parlour. It is that time in the late afternoon when the London light is at its most evocative, a bland and dusky gold.

Here I pour myself a double whisky and, in deference to my condition, add a long squirt of soda water.

'Don't worry. I shan't be making a habit of this,' I assure the baby, 'but today is one of the worst in my whole life. And who's to know? You could be another chip off the grandfatherly block. Cass used to say that whisky was nature's medicine!'

Out of habit I sit on the carpet, cross-legged, to read.

After a rambling introduction, Jeremy has written, ' . . . you're abso-blooming-lutely right, of course, Sparky. It isn't enough just to love somebody. You must have common interests in order to share a daily life. And you're wedded to your work, and I'm wedded to mine, and never the twain shall meet. I've given it a hell of a lot of thought since I left England, because if there was anybody I'd have chosen to share my life with it would have been you, you independent little cuss. Still, that wasn't to be.

372

'I'm wandering on, talking to you on paper, without getting to the point.

'There's another doctor here, in her early thirties, who has faced the same problems as you and come to the same conclusion. She'd more or less written off the idea of marriage, and I wasn't looking for anybody either. We were just good friends and working partners when I came to England. But knowing that you and I were never going to make it seems to have set something off between Livvy and me since I got back. I'm not saying that I've fallen madly in love with her but I like her a lot, and she's attractive and intelligent and kind. You'd like her too, if you knew her.'

The tears I had withheld all afternoon now rolled down my face.

'No, I bloody wouldn't!' I said, loudly, fiercely, and took a swig of whisky.

'Above all, we've got just about everything in common. Except that she isn't crazy like you. I shall miss your craziness, Sparky. So she and I have decided to get married, and having given my word to one woman I shan't be fooling around with another. Once wed I shall stay wed.

'I know this is bound to be something of a blow to you, Sparks, because we've been part of each other for years. I don't flatter myself into thinking it will break your heart – and I shouldn't want it to, either! – but I hope you'll miss me a little bit, for old times' sake.

'So wish me well, Sparky, as I wish you. And thanks for everything. I'm not trying to downgrade us by saying it was fun, I mean that as the highest compliment I can pay, because I'm one of the many who enjoy fun but can't conjure it up. You're a magical sort of person, Sparks, and I hope that life gives you back as much as you put into it.

'Love and God bless and take care of yourself. I mean all those things. Jem.'

Ruth Babbage says tremulously from the doorway, 'You looked so ill when you came in, Leila. And spoke so shortly. Quite unlike your usual self. And when I was on my way upstairs I heard you say something and start crying. And

I couldn't leave you in trouble. Forgive me for intruding, dear.'

I push the crumpled ball of a letter towards her across the carpet and curl into a ball of grief, rocking to and fro on my haunches, weeping into my lap.

After a while I hear her say, 'Oh, I'm so sorry, my dear. So sorry. I always felt he was the right one.'

She touches my shoulder timidly. 'Let me do something for you. Let me help.'

I realise I must look demented, and sit up slowly, trying to hold my sobs, trying to dry my eyes. But sobs do shake me and tears continue to spill over.

I take another swig of whisky, and say as cheerfully as I can, 'It's been a bloody awful day and I'm pregnant, too.'

And brace myself for the silence that falls upon us, soft and thick as a mantle of snow. I am too beaten to look at her.

I say stiffly, face averted, 'I know this will shock and embarrass you, Ruth, and I quite understand if you want to give me notice. The baby is Jeremy's, of course, but I have no intention of going back on our original decision not to marry. I'm not even going to tell him about the pregnancy now.'

I think it as well to state all my intentions.

'Nor shall I pretend, for the sake of social appearances, that the father and I were engaged and he walked out on me or died abroad, or any such face-saving dodge as that. I shall say that I am bringing up this child without a father.'

I start to cry again, which rather spoils the effect, but manage to finish on a bold note.

'And those who don't approve of us must leave us!'

Gently, her hand removes the empty glass from mine.

She says very kindly, 'You shouldn't be drinking spirits in your condition, Leila. Let me make you a nice cup of tea.'

I attempt to disguise a sob as a light laugh.

'Can't drink tea. Or coffee. Only fresh orange juice. Oh, and the occasional glass of champagne. But I had that today with Zoe.'

374

Sensibly Ruth replies, 'Then it will have to be fresh orange juice. Now do get up off that draughty floor, dear, and come and lie down on the sofa.'

I say, crying and gulping wildly, as she helps me to my feet, 'I've had such a set-to with Zoe, and I was counting on her. She made me feel as though I ought to be dragged through the streets and whipped at the cart's tail. She made me feel like Toad when Badger lectured him, and he rolled over on his face, with his legs in the air, and was shaken by sobs of contrition.'

I remember that I must now fight for both of us. I hold my head high.

'Not', I add, with a hiccup, 'that I'm contrite in the least. I am not in the least contrite.'

'Put your feet up, dear, and take long deep breaths. I'll be back in a minute.'

The sobs are less frequent, becoming long snuffling sighs. My rainstorm is over. I lie watching the light on the wall of the villa opposite, and drift.

Ruth returns with an exquisite concoction of orange juice, ice and apple mint in a frosted glass, and sits on the end of the sofa while I sip and sigh.

Smoothing her decent grey skirt over her decent middle-aged knees she delivers a little speech.

'You have done so much for me, Leila, over the years, that I shall count it a privilege to be of use to you now. And I am not shocked in the least. I am not . . .'

Here she covers her mouth and gives a little cough of self-satisfaction.

'. . . I am not even surprised. After all, you and he loved each other, and I am first and foremost – I hope – a woman of the world.'

She is suddenly radiant, ridiculous and astonishing female that she is, crying, 'And with such unusual parents what a wonderful baby it will be!'

The early evening light is turning us both into showers of gold. In smiling silence we welcome the child, knowing it to be a person of importance.

Still I must say hardily, 'The baby will be illegitimate,

Ruth, and I've no doubt, in a respectable district like this, that people are going to whisper in shops and look at me sideways, and ask you how I am, and how you feel about it. And pretend to be concerned, when they don't care at all but are only curious and hoping for the worst possible news.'

She nods and is thoughtful for a few moments.

Then she says, 'Yes, of course there are closed and narrow minds, but we shall know who our real friends are. I can think of many of our neighbours who won't allow it to make any difference to their friendship.'

I have let the top-floor flat to two male students. She recruits them as members of this present crusade.

'Tom and Dennis, for instance, won't mind in the least. They're very modern young men. A good thing to have a male influence in the house, too, Leila. So that the baby has a balanced outlook . . . '

She punches two cushions to softness and puts one at my back and the other behind my head. I lean against them and let her words and the light slide over me.

I am thinking that in a strange way things might have turned out for the best. Life is perhaps wiser than I, giving me a second chance, allowing me to retrace steps along the baby road, making good that which had been spoiled fifteen years before. Now that my mind is made up, and my news broken to those it will most affect, I am daring to savour the vigil and hoping for a fine outcome.

Ruth is talking about Zoe now.

' . . . always admired her, of course, and been grateful for her friendship. A lovely woman, so like your dear mother. But, despite her domestic difficulties, your sister is one of life's favourites and she expects it to smile on her. She has no conception what it feels like to come last in the line, to be given the toy that was left over . . . '

Playing Peaseblossom to Titania. Painting up the furniture no one else wants.

' . . . had two sisters myself, and I was the youngest and plainest. They both married and moved away, too busy with their own concerns to worry about me.

376

Though this does not apply to you and Zoe, who are very close . . . '

My child will not wear her children's hand-me-downs. And this time, when I buy a special baby shawl, I shall keep it.

' . . . but I find you a far more interesting person than your sister. And Jeremy – Dr Purchase – puts my feelings into words when he talks about the fun. Bless me, I have had the most amazing time in the last ten years, just living in the same house with you – though trying not to intrude, of course – because one never knows what will happen next. Such excitement! And then – such talent . . . '

A glorious portrait of myself is emerging. Not Lulu the social outcast, but Leila Gideon of the highwayman's hat. Illustrator extraordinary. Magical person.

' . . . and it is very ungenerous of Zoe to suggest that you would not make a good mother. You may not be conventional but I would have described you as a very caring person, and children are unconventional by nature . . . '

Nevertheless, I must buy a copy of Benjamin Spock's baby book tomorrow, read it from cover to cover, learn and inwardly digest.

' . . . and concerned only with the moment. And the ability to live in and for the present, and to take joy in life, is your talent also . . . '

The parlour is full of sun. I open my eyes and smile at her. Renewed in spirit, bathed in loving kindness, I need no more than a long sound sleep before picking up the latest challenge.

' . . . suggest you have an early night. I'll bring you a light meal on a tray. We must keep your strength up. Things will look brighter in the morning.'

My eyes are closing in anticipation of these delights when the telephone rings, and forces them open.

I say drowsily, resignedly, 'That will be Zoe.'

Saying she's sorry and she didn't mean it, and can't think what came over her, and what can she do, and she'll sew all its little clothes for me, and would I like the picture screen, and Brigitte has a cousin who loves babies and wants to live in London for a couple of years . . .

'Would you mind answering it for me, please, Ruth? I haven't the energy for another scene, however pleasant.'

Ruth draws herself up and asks, 'What would you like me to say to her, dear?'

'Tell her that I'm very tired now but I'll ring her tomorrow, and not to worry, everything will be all right. And give her my love . . . '

'I shall also tell her', says Ruth, very dignified, picking up the receiver, 'that I stand your friend in this matter. As she should do.'

Which loyalty I attempt to acknowledge with an outstretched hand.

But the hand is falling away, as I am falling away, into sleep. And in that sleep another form, another love, another life awaits. Enough has been seen and said and done. Time now for a new departure.

From a great distance I hear my unexpected ally say in her most secretarial voice, brisk, friendly and detached, 'Hello? Oh, hello, Zoe. This is Ruth. I'm afraid that Leila isn't available at the moment. No. She came in very distressed, I'm sorry to say. Yes, very distressed indeed . . . '

31

Love, marriage, birth and death are of such fundamental importance that humanity instinctively reveres them. And lovers, bride and groom, mother and child, the dead, take on the symbolic divinity of icons. Consequently, pregnancy is generally regarded as a blessed condition, and I am enjoying its privileges.

My family and close friends fuss over me. Most of my neighbours show their continuing goodwill. Others, even though they disapprove of me, are careful not to upset my sensibilities. They do not cut me exactly, but nod coolly and pass by on the other side of the street, and I have lost a few of my young art pupils. But no one has tarred and feathered me, pushed abusive notes into the letter-box, or asked me not to darken their doors again.

The rest of the world pays homage to my swollen belly. I never have to stand in the tube, queue in shops, or carry heavy baskets. Buses wait for me. Cars halt so that I can cross the road in safety and in my own time. From the moment I hove in view total strangers jump to attention, lickety-split, with a big smile and a 'How are you today?' For once in my life I am an object of universal care and concern. For once I am apparently behaving as nature intended.

It is a godlike position to be in. I wonder how I shall bear to rejoin the mortals when the child and I are separate?

There have been hurdles to take, of course. I endeavoured to make my farewell to Jeremy both graceful and generous, saying I did understand, and wishing him and his future wife good luck, long life and happiness. I posted part of myself with that final letter, and though I am great with his child I still feel empty when I think of him.

My various employers have taken my condition in their stride and have been utterly charming. They all made special note of the fact that I would not be able to work during the summer months. Yet today, absent-mindedly, two of them have sent manuscripts for me to read and hopefully illustrate. Tomorrow I must telephone and explain my position all over again. And I do not intend even to glance at the manuscripts, though one of them is by Bill Musgrove, and he and I are a natural working partnership. For this is child-time.

Child-time.

Zoe has come full circle, of course, and telephones daily with some new offer or suggestion. She wants me to bring the baby to the Old Rectory when the hospital turns me out, and convalesce in luxury. But this is her busy season, and I don't want us to impose on her.

Us. I shall be us, then.

Also, I think that I would rather make mistakes by myself at home, with only the sympathetic and equally inexperienced Ruth standing by. But we shall see. And in August the infant and I are off to Cornwall for a month. I have rented a cottage near Magda, and then she can enjoy us without being burdened. For she is very old indeed now, over eighty, but still stubbornly independent and still painting.

Everything that any child could possibly need, from Zoe's old Dunkerley pram, which has been revamped, to a superfluity of matinée jackets, is ready and waiting. I am ready and waiting.

So my time is my own for the next few weeks. And when I have had my afternoon nap, and made myself a mug of tea, I sit blissfully at the parlour window and watch the world go by. The hedge provides a certain amount of privacy. The gateway is my picture frame. It is a Friday, one of those late-May afternoons when all the trees have come into leaf, the air smells of spice and the birds sing

380

of summer. Four o'clock. Distaff time. Our road, which has been quiet all day, becomes pleasantly noisy. Schoolchildren patter past in sandals, wearing straw hats and blazers, girls chatting, boys shouting. Mothers take the hill more slowly, pushing their babies, burdened with groceries. The baker's van stops and starts, calling from house to house, certain of a welcome.

My hands, peacefully folded above the baby mound, unclasp and reach for the sketching block which is never far from my side.

And, at the moment that I put pencil to paper, a ramshackle Edwardian perambulator glides along the top of my hedge. Relic of a more gracious age, its rusty springs are still capable of a gracious sway. In proportion to its size the wheels are large and airy. A shattered black hood, drawn to full stretch, has phantom grey streaks where the folds have been. Upon its battered black coachwork gleam princely flourishes of faded gold.

Mouth open, I watch it glide mysteriously as far as the gate, at which point it reveals itself as being on top of a load of pans and mattresses, pulled by a patient pony, led by a man in a flat checked cap. And as horse and man and cart move into view he gives his street cry. 'Ra-a-ag and Bo-o-one.'

I can no longer jump to my feet but I do a fair imitation of moving quickly, and rap smartly on the window, calling, 'Wait a minute! I'm coming!'

The rag-and-bone man is an old acquaintance of mine, though we have not done business together for a while. With the courtesy due to my condition he bawls through his cupped hands, 'Take your time, darlin'. Take your time.'

As I arrive on the pavement, blown but triumphant, he grins sideways at me, rolls a cigarette between creased brown fingers, licks the edge of the paper, and says, 'Lookin' for a nice pram, darlin'?'

And has his mild joke ruined by my answer.

'Yes, I am. How much?'

He puffs hard at his skinny cigarette, eyes like cracks,

trying to assess the situation. Am I stony-broke and desperate?. Gone mad? Having a bit of fun?

He sees that I am serious and begins a professional spiel on the aristocratic connections and matchless quality of the perambulator, without mentioning a price. But I am wise in street bargaining and cut him short.

Saying briskly, 'I'll give you ten bob – and that's five more than it's worth.'

Outraged, he cries, 'Ten bob? It's worf every penny of ten pound!' And adds quickly, 'But I'll let you 'ave it for a fiver, darlin', seein' as it's you.'

Knowing I shall refuse this, he does not wait for an answer but launches into another spiel, 'Only needs a bit o' polish, and a new 'ood.'

'I'll give you a pound, and that's my last offer. Do the wheels work?'

'Only need a drop of oil on 'em. Say three pound ten!'

'They're jammed solid with rust, aren't they? Lift it down and show me!'

'Two pound ten, then.'

'What? With the inside all mould and spiders!'

We settle on thirty shillings if he will carry it bodily round to the back garden.

Chivalrously he pulls a rag from a sack on his cart, to clean off the worst grime.

'No, don't touch it!' I cry. 'I'm going to paint a picture of it as it is.'

'Wish I'd 'a known!' he grumbles and sighs, as he hauls my Edwardian acquisition round the side of the house, through the lattice-door and down to the far end of the garden.

His plaint continues as I follow him. Seasoned jousters, we charge each other with lances of accusation and contempt.

'That's what 'appens when you try to do someone a good turn. Fought it was for the baby, I did. Felt sorry for you, I did . . .'

'Oh, rubbish,' I say cheerfully. 'What about that chest of drawers you had from me, and only gave me a jam-jar with a goldfish in it. And the bloody goldfish died anyway, the following week . . . '

'Full o' wood-worm, that chest o' drawers. Infected a whole lot o' stuff . . . '

He puts the perambulator down on top of the garden dump, as being an appropriate place. His cigarette is a wet brown stub, which he drops onto the lawn and treads in emphatically. When he has pocketed my money he rolls another. Meanwhile I walk backwards, distancing myself from the perambulator, peering through the frame of my forefingers and thumbs.

'Set o' loonies, you artists,' he remarks amiably. 'Paintin' a bleedin' ol' pram! Well, I seen it all now. Yes, now I seen everyfink, I 'ave.'

'Don't go, please!' I say firmly. 'I can't move this thing round myself, and I want it in exactly the right position.'

'Bloody 'ell!' he remarks to the heavens. 'And you already done me down to thirty bob? 'Ave an 'eart, lady!'

But the lady has no heart, and he is a good-natured man.

My chief friend and fusspot finds me still sketching in the garden in the early evening, just as, she says, the dew is falling. And the dew, apparently, is a very treacherous article, to be avoided at all costs by pregnant women.

'I don't see why,' I remark obstinately. 'I've got a cardigan on.'

'Your hands', says Ruth, touching them, 'are stone cold. No, Leila, really. I do beg you to come in out of the evening dew.'

Actually, I am rather cold, now I come to think of it, and hungry too.

'Let me run you a warm bath,' says Ruth.

A hot one, she has told me, is also injurious for some reason.

'Let me cook you a nice lamb chop. Two chops. We must feed you up.'

I remove myself from the world of the perambulator and study her. A small, grey, kind, tired, worried lady who needs more care than I do at the moment. For she is weary of the day's work while I am in a state of exasperated exaltation.

'Ruth,' I say, 'you have no idea how bloody difficult it is to get the essential nature of that pram . . . '

'Indeed?' she says, glancing over her shoulder at the relic with genteel reproach. 'It isn't staying there permanently, is it, dear? It looks rather peculiar, even in a neglected part of the garden . . . '

'I've been sketching the damn thing for hours, from different angles and distances. I've tried pen, pencil, charcoal. It still looks nothing more than a knackered old pram . . . '

'Which is exactly how I should have described it myself – well, not exactly . . . '

'I don't know what I want of it, you see. Don't know what it's all about . . . '

'And think how distressed your dear mother would have been', says Ruth, 'to find you out sketching. In your condition. In the early evening dew . . . '

We return to the house, a curious couple, each talking of different things.

The idea of the perambulator becomes as demanding as the baby. I lead a double life in these last weeks of pregnancy, nourishing the child in my body and the picture in my mind: a servant to them both. They have me playing Figaro to the pair of them. Waiting my turn at the ante-natal clinic, I sketch various compositions. Painting in the back garden, I set a timer to remind me to eat lunch.

Those who love me and watch over me are distressed by my preoccupation.

'You should be *resting*, dear,' says Ruth, 'and thinking of *beautiful* things.'

Glaring at the perambulator, whose condition is steadily deteriorating.

'Art is a form of meditation,' I reply, 'and beauty is in the eye of the beholder.'

'But it's so *sad*!' cries Zoe, looking askance at my subject. 'It reminds me of my poor Dunkerley rusting away in the shed, at the Clapham flat. And anyway, Lulu, you should be concentrating on the baby, like a nice placid little moo-cow.'

'You could say that I'm constantly chewing this cud!' I answer smartly.

Long grass grows up between the wheels. The hood is spattered with birds' offerings. But rain has recently washed the coachwork, and the faded flourishes gleam dull gold. The perambulator may be down, but it is definitely not out.

'Now if it was a handsome-looking baby carriage in a nice park,' says Ruth, arbiter of public taste, 'with a pretty baby in it, and a lovely young mother sitting on the grass, and perhaps a faithful dog . . . '

I can tell that she feels she has solved my problem.

'Brake Baldwin painted a picture rather like that, around 1910,' I say. 'Called *Nanny in Kensington Gardens*. This pram will be the same vintage.'

I know that she is trying to help, so I conquer my natural impatience and find an illustration of the painting. She likes it a lot, and makes further suggestions.

'Well dear, the subject may have been done before, but I've never *heard* of Brake Baldwin. And 1910 was a long time ago. People forget. Why don't you paint something charming like this?'

'Because I don't want to be charming. And I don't want people in it, either.'

Ruth wears an expression which suggests I am being unnecessarily difficult.

'What is a picture without people?' she says reproachfully.

As June burgeons, so do I. My body is heavy, clumsy, restless, longing to throw off its burden. My mind, preoc-cupied with its own creation, is just as anxious for relief. But it is not yet time. I try the pram in oils, in gouache, in pastel and in water-colour. Nothing works. I wake between half-past four and five o'clock in the morning, crawl out of bed on all fours, wrap myself in a warm red robe for Ruth's sake, and steal out to see the effect of first light on the garden dump. Alone in the early world, I sit on a wicker chair in the dew and contemplate the perambulator: its present state, past glories and its uncertain future. Until, one morning, I cease to fret around the subject and enter into it.

I become the perambulator. Once fertile, now barren. Once elegant and necessary, now battered, useless and at the mercy of time, rag-and-bone men and dotty artists who are obsessed with me and do not know why. If they leave me here long enough I shall be quite grown over. Hidden in the long grass, sheltered by the laburnum tree, I shall become a natural breeding-ground for nature. Insects, moulds and fungi will find a home with me. If the briar springs its barbed-wire fence across I should be safe enough for a nest. A hedge-sparrow hops on to my handle, head on one side. He is assessing my possibilities with the eye of a potential owner–occupier. Next spring I may be in business.

That was some days ago. The sparrow has long since flown, but not before my pencil captured him. I have been working intensively, reminded at intervals by my body that I must eat and drink and rest and sleep. As I give birth to this, the other birth is overdue. I pray that the baby will hold on just a little longer, and that I can finish one creation before I begin the other. The picture is so much part of me that I find no difficulty in making it manifest, but the technique I am using is infinitely demanding, detailed and meticulous. I am working in drybrush.

I paint the undertone in broad wet washes. Then, dipping a smaller brush into colour, with finger and thumb spread out the bristles and squeeze the moisture from them, so that the hairs are dry enough to provide texture as well as pigment. Brushful by painstaking brushful, layer upon patient layer, objects at last develop and take their final form. Long coarse blades of grass. The wood-grain in the fence behind, whose planks are warped with age. The stinging growth of nettles, and the wild and humble friends of waste land: rosebay willow herbs, yellow coltsfoot, and cow parsley. A band of wet grey English summer sky. And the perambulator itself, riding high on the garden dump, with the sparrow perched enquiringly upon its handle.

'What is a picture without people in it?' Ruth had said reproachfully.

But people were presumed here, even in their absence. The picture suggested generations of people, and a host of stories. The melody was visible. The theme was elegaic. The subject was personal experience.

'All experience is valuable,' my mother had said to us.

Steadfast even in her final days.

And added quietly, for herself alone, 'Perhaps that's why it's so expensive.'

At the bottom right-hand corner of the picture I paint in fine black strokes. 'Leila Gideon. June 1969.'

THE PEABODY LIBRARY   387

Columbia City, Indiana

THE PEABODY LIBRARY
Columbia City, Indiana

DISCARD